DIVINITY FALLING

Divinity Falling

NOUR ZIKRA

Lightbringer Publishing

To my three guardian angels in heaven:

Aunt Houda, Uncle Nabil, and Great-Aunt Georgette.

Chapter ONE

ADRIEL

Flames tore through the feathers of my large white wings. The crimson blaze spread farther and farther up, scorching through my muscles and bones, which I thrust back and forth in an effort to keep me in the air. A wail erupted from my throat as I plummeted to the ground. I could feel nothing but the flesh on my back tightening, burning red. The feathers slowly turned to ash, leaving nothing where my wings had fluttered just moments ago.

"Father," I shouted. "I'm sorry!"

He leaned down, silent, and placed a firm hand on my blistering shoulder. The flames danced harmlessly around his fingers. His eyes were watery, yet he showed no anger. He was as calm as ever.

"What will happen? Are you sending me to the fire?"

Instead of responding, he turned his back to me and walked away. Bright rays shone around him, growing stronger as they engulfed his body until he disappeared without a trace. Blinded for the first time by the beautiful light, I shut my eyes. Within seconds, something strange began happening behind my eyelids. Small beads of liquid pushed out, trickling past the ridges of my cheeks. They tickled my skin. When I finally opened my eyes, I found myself in total darkness. The ground had disappeared. In its place, a black hole inhaled me into its depths.

I crashed onto alien ground, my exposed knees scraping against the gravel and mud. Red oozed out of my skin, sending thousands of twinges through my body. My voice rushed out in a seemingly endless scream that shook my Adam's apple. For a moment, I didn't move as I watched the blood—*my blood?*—soak into the soil and rocks. Then a rush of cold wind stirred me, forcing me fully into consciousness.

My wings had burned out of existence, leaving my raw, burnt back uncovered and icy. What would I do without my wings? *How will I fly?* More importantly, where was I, and why wasn't the rest of me burning?

I fought past the mind-numbing pain and straightened. Acres of land with colossal sassafras trees stood in salute. Behind me lay a narrow, paved road with a faint, flickering streetlight. I moved in its direction.

Finding no crosswalk in sight, I walked by the forest's edge and hoped to find some sort of guidance. The road was empty, but it curved toward a deserted gas station with a broken, tilted sign that read *"Towhee Petroleum."* This had to be

Earth, because it sure wasn't Hell. That was, unless Father had placed me in infinite captivity, doomed to walk in pain forever.

The silence of the night made it hard to tell whether people were tucked inside their homes or nonexistent, and as I moved farther down the road, my fears doubled. Convenience stores and little shopping outlets lined up behind the gas station, all displaying *"Sorry, We're Closed"* signs. The small parking lot leading out onto the road was more rubble than concrete, and cigarette butts and dead tree leaves littered the area. It smelled odd, almost acidic.

"God," I said, looking up at the cloudless sky with all its blinking stars. "What do I do?"

Just when I thought my question would go unanswered, something tiny lit up in my peripheral vision. It flew past my arm, its light fading for a moment before glimmering again. I smiled and reached to catch the firefly. It drifted away before I caught it, moving toward the road. An instant later, bright lights gleamed in the distance, growing more powerful with each second. As the lights neared, I could clearly hear a whirring engine. A red car sped down the isolated road, racing by the vacant stores and buildings.

I ran to the center of the street and began waving my arms high in the air. It took the driver a second to register my presence. The car shifted to the side, grinding against gravel before stopping in the mud on the side of the road, five feet from where I stood.

My chest heaved and the sound of my new, beating heart drummed in my ears. I moved my hand to block the car's high beams that illuminated the entire area and stepped closer until I stood by the driver's window, where I saw a young woman in her early twenties sitting with a white-knuckled grip on the wheel. Her wide eyes stared back at me, a tear dripping down one cheek.

I raised my hands, palms facing her. "Hey, don't be scared. Please . . . I'm just lost."

She looked back at the road and bit her lip. A heartbeat later, she hit the gas pedal with her foot.

"No, no," I yelled. "Please."

The car inched forward before slowing down, the tires spinning in the soft mud. She hit the pedal harder, but the car was stuck.

My heart pounded as I moved closer to her side again. "I'm really hurt. I just need some help, okay?"

The woman turned to face me. Her big eyes studied me, moving down my body and pausing just below the shroud that covered my hips to mid-thighs. I followed her gaze to my bleeding knees.

"I'm just hurt," I repeated. "Just a little, okay? Don't be scared of me."

The woman nodded, put the car in park, took off her seat belt, and opened the door. The rusty hinges creaked, sounding like they might break and come right off. She took slow, measured movements until she stood with the door between the two of us.

My eyes met hers, and I realized for the first time that I was intruding upon her life in that precise moment when she clearly wanted to be alone on this lonely road. The white around her irises had a faint red to it, the same red the tip of her nose and apples of her cheeks displayed. Avoiding my gaze, she blinked and composed her face. Then she really looked at me.

"What happened to you?" Rosy Cheeks nodded toward my bleeding knees.

I looked down at my body. *What must this young woman think of me?* I was half-naked, bleeding, and muddy, and she couldn't even see my burnt back yet. Telling her the truth was not an option. "It's a long story."

Her hard, uneasy stare told me she didn't buy my excuse. "How can I help you if I don't know what happened? You could be a bad guy."

"I'm not."

"Sorry, but I can't help you."

She leaned down to get back inside her car, leaving her hand on the door's frame. I reached out and gripped her hand, just strong enough to keep her from leaving. She whirled around and tried to pull her hand free, but my hold tightened.

"I can't tell you what happened. But I can show you my back." I freed her hand and turned around, letting her have a full view of my raw, blistered flesh.

She let out a small gasp and, a second later, had her hand on my upper arm, tugging for me to face her. When I turned, she was looking down at the ground.

"I'll take you to the hospital or something." She shut her eyes. "Just please don't show me that again."

"I won't."

She glanced at her car and sighed. The tires had sunk in the mud. It was my fault, really. She'd had to brake and swerve to avoid hitting me.

"Let me push the car." I didn't exactly know my new strength, especially with the pain I felt, but I needed her help, and there was no way out of here without me helping to fix the situation.

"Okay." She sat inside the car and started the engine.

"Please don't drive away, okay?"

She didn't answer.

I trudged to the back of her car and placed my hands on the bumper. Tree tar and decomposed bugs made the surface bumpy under my skin. The small effort of pushing felt like weights were pulling at my arms, tearing my shoulders from their ligaments. The palms of my hands were suddenly clammy.

"Are you pushing?" Rosy Cheeks shouted.

I was trying, I wanted to say, but my head started to spin and I couldn't force the words out. Sweat trickled from the roots of my jaw-length hair down the nape of my neck just as a vile, sour taste hit me. My mouth opened, releasing what must have been vomit. In that moment, I knew with absolute certainty that I had truly become human; God's punishment for what I'd done.

The engine stopped again. Rosy Cheeks rushed over and stood a few feet away, keeping her distance. She avoided looking directly at me, probably because my slouched, disfigured back was in perfect view.

"Are you all right?"

"No, but I'm going to push this car if it kills me." I straightened and put my hands back on the dirty bumper. "So, come on, put the car in drive."

She pulled her hair back and shook her head. "You could really die." But she went to the car anyway and started the engine.

I pushed as hard as I could with this new, weak body, my muscles pulsating and my heart furiously pumping blood. The car didn't budge. With each forceful, useless shove, my vision dimmed. In my angel form, I could have simply flapped my wings at this car and it would've toppled over like a tiny fly blown in the wind.

"Hey, the car's not moving," she said over the droning engine.

The edges of my vision went completely black. "No," I muttered. "It has to."

In the dimness around me, a small dot of light rested on my hand. The car slipped forward, moving away from my sweat-slicked fingers. The dot of light flickered, and my sight came back. The car, which had been a foot away from me, had now rolled onto the paved road. I looked down at the back of my hand and saw the firefly resting there.

Rosy Cheeks came to stand by me. "How'd you do that?" Her eyes were wide again as they searched me, trailing across my shoulders and arms, wanting to know the secret of my strength.

"I don't know."

She wrapped her arms around herself and moved to her car. "Let's just go."

A few moments later, we were on our way. I sat in the passenger seat, slouched forward so my burned skin wouldn't rub against the fabric.

She glanced in my direction before turning her attention back to the road. "You should buckle up."

"Buckle up?" I looked around and saw the seat belt most humans use to guard themselves while in a car. "Oh, I get it." I reached for the belt with my sore arm and groaned. It took a second to "buckle up."

Rosy Cheeks watched me with quick glances, her brows scrunched and her lips in a tight line. Every time her head turned toward me, her wavy brown hair slid over her shoulder. "Seriously, what happened to you?"

I gave her a weak smile. "You wouldn't believe me."

She sucked on her bottom lip for a moment before looking at me again. "Try me."

I couldn't help smiling at her reflection in the passenger window. "You're relentless."

Her eyes shifted back to the road. "I have a right to know. I rescued you, didn't I? You'd still be out there if I didn't happen to drive by. You could at least tell me why you're wearing that Jesus diaper thing." Her mouth dropped open for a split second. "Are you in a cult?"

I sighed and tried to change the subject. "My name is Adriel."

This didn't distract her. She looked at me out of the corner of her eye, one eyebrow quirked.

"What's your name?" I asked.

She took a left turn into a big parking lot and drove until we were in front of a large building with a giant sign that read *"Latrobe Hospital."*

"This is it," she said.

I glanced at her for directions, but when she didn't give any, I opened the door. "Thank you for helping me."

"Sure."

I stepped out and ever so slowly bent down to talk to her one last time. "You never told me your name."

She smirked, her eyes dancing with glee for the first time that night. "You never told me what happened."

Just like that, she leaned across the passenger seat, closed the door by pulling at the handle, and drove off.

I watched her taillights disappear, leaving no trace.

Chapter Two

ADELAIDE

My worst fear was being just another tragedy on the news, and tonight proved to me just how easy it was for that scenario to become real. I could imagine headlines reading "22-Year-Old Female Found Dead in Pennsylvania Wilderness." Lucky for me, Adriel—if that was his real name—had left me in one piece.

Still, even after I'd dropped him off, I could almost feel his presence in my car. It felt like the scent of his scalded skin had clung onto my polyester seats and wrapped itself all over me, disregarding my personal space. I cringed. Finding him alone on the road like in a scene straight out of a horror movie had alerted my senses, and his never-ending persistence to learn my name had set warning bells ringing in my head. But maybe I was just too tired to judge him correctly after the week I'd had. All I knew was that having him in my car, even for a short duration, had made my stomach knot.

Ten minutes after dropping him off at the hospital, I stopped by the nearest gas station to fill up Lucy, my 1991 red Oldsmobile. It had creaking doors and peeling paint, but I loved the trusty machine. The car was nowhere near empty, but I needed some fresh air. I stood in the chilly night, breath escaping my mouth in a fog, and waited on the nozzle to feed the gas tank to the brim while I checked my phone.

Throughout the drive from Pittsburgh to Latrobe, my cell phone had received several text messages, some from my boss and coworkers asking why I hadn't shown up to the office earlier today. The remaining messages had come from Lizzy, my best friend and roommate. I'd already read most of these messages and had chosen not to respond.

"Addy, where the heck are you?" Lizzy's first text had read. "I'm at Euphoria." Attached with the message was a photo of Lizzy and a few mutual friends at our favorite club. With a margarita in one hand and the phone in the other, Lizzy had somehow managed to get the selfie to include three friends standing behind her, all flashing their pearly whites at the phone screen.

The person standing closest to Lizzy in the picture was our next-door neighbor, Nate. He had his arm draped over Lizzy's shoulders and his cheek pressed against hers, though they weren't officially a couple yet. His smile reminded me of another person, which sent my heart hammering in my chest. With a knot in my throat, I pushed back the tears.

After fifteen minutes of me not responding to her first text, she sent another. "Everything okay? Please text me back. I'm worried."

She had sent a couple more while I was with Adriel, but my hands were too shaky at the time to check the phone. Leaning against the car now, I considered whether I should tell her what was going on. That was when my phone started ringing and flashing Lizzy's name. My thumb hovered over the answer button. Three rings later, I rejected the call.

"Addy, I know you're there. Why aren't you answering?" Lizzy texted a few seconds later.

Staring at the starry sky, I searched for the right response and came up with: "I'm fine. I'll tell you when I'm ready. Staying at Reed's dorm tonight."

"Addy," she wrote back, "you know you can tell me anything, right?"

I couldn't blame Lizzy for worrying. We never kept anything from each other. Ever since the day we'd met four years ago during our freshman year at Mountain Peak College, we knew we'd be best friends. We had bonded over my poster of Lucille Ball crossing her eyes behind crazy glasses. But still, I ignored her message now and sent a quick text to Melissa, my boss, letting her know I had a family emergency. It was a lie I could live with. I apologized for not telling her sooner, hoping that my good record at work would get her to be lenient for a few days as I glued myself back together.

The gas nozzle released its hold on the tank and the machine printed a receipt. I shut the fuel door and went on my way.

I sped down the almost-empty streets, slowing only when I thought I saw a white car with light bars on top. Being pulled over by a cop was the last thing I needed tonight. Although, I wouldn't be surprised if my week went downhill again.

Devin. I could picture the blonde from his Facebook photos. At every second of my day, images of them bombarded my brain. All I saw was blond hair covering Devin's face as they kissed while she straddled him, blond hair floating over his bed, blond hair moving over his chest when she trailed kisses down his body. I didn't know how to get the nightmare out of my brain, how to tuck it away and pretend that it didn't exist.

That was the secret Lizzy and the rest of my friends didn't know. For the past week, I'd faked a happy face in front of them only to go to my room later and cry myself to sleep. How could I tell them that Devin, who had been with me for two years, broke up with me out of the blue? How could I tell them I suspected he cheated on me?

My brother was the only one I really cared to be with and talk to about this. He wouldn't push me with questions.

I raced through the short ten-minute drive to Saint Vincent College, my brother's school. Faint light illuminated the road. I passed by acres of cornfields, the corn leaves pale and short with the fall season, then turned right onto Beatty County Road. Eastern white pine trees stood guard on either side of the street.

Inescapable in its grandness, Saint Vincent Basilica loomed in the distance. Even when the road curved, the basilica remained the center of attention, as if the tranquil trees were guiding any passersby toward the house of worship.

Within a few minutes, I had Lucy parked under a shaded area next to Saint Benedict Hall and was walking over to the building's entrance with my duffle bag in hand. I texted Reed to come downstairs and open the door for me, since I couldn't enter without a student ID.

When he emerged from the main doors, he flashed his old childish grin that made the corners of his eyes crinkle. Even though he was my baby brother by three years, he threw his arms around me and lifted me into the air as if I were the younger one. He was wearing his favorite navy-blue sweatshirt, the same one he'd had since high school; it smelled like fresh, clean laundry.

Reed was my half brother. We shared the same mother. Unfortunately, we had no idea who either of our fathers were. Though we did know we were both the products of one-night stands.

After putting me down, Reed touched his ID to the sensor by the door and pulled me into the building, taking my bag from me. "You only visit when you need something. But it's okay, I forgive you." The big smile remained on his face. "I've really missed you."

I smiled back and pulled him in for another hug while we waited for the elevator to reach the lobby. "I've missed you too."

In just a few minutes, we had reached the third floor and turned the corner down the hall from the elevator. We entered Pod F, where Reed's dorm room was located. He peeked in, scoping the place, before gesturing for me to follow. A moldy smell hit me as we walked into the heated common area.

Within the pod were eight dorms, four on the right wall and another four on the left, all parallel to one another. In the middle of the pod was a shared living space with a dull brown sofa, wooden chairs, a wooden table, a big-screen TV mounted to the wall, an Xbox, and a stereo. There were two community bathrooms, one by the entrance and one on the far end of the pod right behind the living space.

One guy slumped on the sofa with headphones in his ears, his eyes closed. I could hear a low beat coming from his direction. We walked past without him noticing.

The TV was on, but no one was watching. The news anchor of the local Latrobe channel spoke as graphic images of a wreckage played. I slowed down to listen.

"This morning in Syria, fighter jets bombed the University of Aleppo. At least eighty-two people, most of them faculty and students, are dead, and many more are injured."

What's new? I shook my head.

Reed's room was the last one on the right. While he was unlocking his door, the bathroom door flew open and a tall guy with sandy blond hair and light freckles stepped out and paused to study me. He had a young face. His eyes narrowed, then he cocked his head and smirked. "Aren't you that girl Reed snuck in last semester?"

Reed rolled his eyes. "Shut it, Sam. This is my sister." He got the door open and yanked me in. Though before he closed the door again, he stuck his head out and, grinning, said, "Come near her and I'll tell everyone how you've already wet your bed seven times in the year we've known each other."

I caught a glimpse of Sam blushing as Reed slammed the door.

"Woah, that poor guy," I said. "I guess I taught you well."

Reed sank onto his bed and frowned, dropping my duffle bag beside him. He kept his eyes fixed on the Avenged Sevenfold poster taped to the wall across from him above the second bed in the room and said, "Addy, you won't tell Erica I sneak girls in, right?"

Erica, our mother, was someone I hadn't spoken to in a long time. "Nah, I won't tell her."

A Swiss Army knife lay on the bed beside him. He moved it out of my way so I could sit next to him.

"Nice knife," I said, but he didn't seem to hear me.

I slumped down on the mattress and looked at the poster he was so intent on scrutinizing. The image illustrated a gravestone with a skull carving on it. A pair of hands tunneled out from the ground beneath the stone.

"Hey." I nudged him with my shoulder. "First off, it's not like Erica has a right to judge us; she's done worse things. In fact, both of our very existences are the results of her bad choices." I lay back on the bed and stared at the white popcorn ceiling. "Second off, I have been avoiding that woman for months. So, your secret is safe."

He threaded a hand through his hair. "No, that's not what I meant." He stood up and paced the room. The legs of his baggy cotton pajama pants flapped against each other. "Remember in eighth grade when I had my first date, and Erica got so happy she started saying shit like how I'm obviously the fun child, just like her?"

"Yeah, I think I remember that."

"Well, I don't want her to ever say that again. I'm not like her. If she finds out, she'll probably send me boxes of condoms or want to go clubbing with me."

Too much information, I wanted to shout.

On my thirteenth birthday, I told a few of my friends to wait for me while I went to ask Erica where the candles were. It was the only birthday party I'd ever had at home. It was also the first birthday party that Erica had ever allowed. I reached her bedroom door and knocked. After a moment of silence, I yanked the door open and found her in her bed making

15

unusual noises. Clothes were scattered all over the bed and floor. Her back faced me, and I saw her legs wrapped around the hips of a naked man. She yelled at me to leave.

I sat up, cringing at pretty much everything Reed had said and reminded me of. "Reed . . ." I put my hand up to stop him from talking. "I said I won't tell her. Now please stop sharing info about your sex life."

A small, innocent smile pulled at the corners of his mouth. "Sorry." He slumped against the bed again and looked at me with his hazel eyes, a feature we didn't share. "How are you feeling?"

I tried to give the most genuine smile I could fake. "I've been better, but, you know, life goes on." My throat tightened as I pushed back tears.

I reached for my duffle bag and rummaged through the contents, searching for my pajamas. I had come here in a hurry, stuffing the first items from my closet I'd laid eyes on into the bag.

"You sure you're okay? We can talk about what happened."

Half of what I'd packed now lay in a pile on the floor, and the rest just looked like a blur in the black hole that was my bag. I tried to calm myself because, after all, I did pack my pajamas. I was sure of it. They had to be somewhere in there.

"Yeah, I'm okay," I said.

I picked through the shirts and pants on the floor again, making sure the pajamas hadn't slipped through somehow without me noticing. I could tell Reed was watching me, still trying to figure out if I was all right. I flipped my duffle bag upside down and dumped everything on the floor. And there, right on top of my mountain of clothes, lay my flannel pajamas.

I exhaled and sat up, knowing full well some tears had crept out.

"It's been a long day." I avoided Reed's worried eyes. "I'm just going to bed, but we'll talk about everything tomorrow."

"Okay." Reed grabbed my hand and squeezed. When he let go, he stood and walked out of the room.

After changing into my pajamas and using the bathroom, I turned the light off and tucked myself into the second bed in the room. Light coming through the window behind me exposed four ants pacing across the windowsill. I watched them for a second, wondering why they weren't asleep like their friends. Maybe, like me, they weren't pleased with the mold in the building.

Cell phone in hand, I scrolled through Devin's recent pictures on Instagram. Him and that blonde out at a club. That blonde sitting in his lap. That blonde with her hand on his chest.

Tears poured down my cheeks. They dripped onto the pillow, dampening my ear and matting my hair. A sob lingered in the back of my throat; I pushed my face into the pillow and let it out. Devin and I were supposed to be together. We were in love—or at least one of us was. Had I been delusional to think everything was going well?

Stop! I shut my phone off and threw it onto the corner of the bed. No more. No more looking at Devin's new girlfriend.

I closed my eyes and let the tears shower me.

†

Light kisses trailed across my cheeks to the edge of my lips just as a hand brushed my hair out of my face.

"Hey," a quiet, masculine voice said, firing warm breath against my ear.

My hand stroked the soft cotton of the bedsheets underneath me. When I opened my eyes, blue eyes stared back at me.

"Hi," I said, smiling at the handsome face of my boyfriend. "What are you doing here?"

Devin's lips brushed mine. When he withdrew, he had a dimpled smile on his face. "Why wouldn't I be here?" He sat at the edge of my bed inside my apartment, as if nothing had changed in the past week.

"Because . . ." I sat up and put my arm around his neck. His silky, short strands tickled my skin. Unable to help it, I pulled him closer. "You're with that other girl. The . . . the blonde."

He smirked and leaned down to give my forehead a gentle kiss. "You're dreaming, silly."

Moisture trickled down my cheeks, but instead of continuing past my chin, it glided over my ears. I peeled the bed covers off me and put my feet down on the tiled floor. My hand moved to my face, but I didn't feel any wetness on my cheeks.

Devin grabbed my thigh, squeezing through the fabric of my pajamas. He no longer smiled. He just looked at me like a statue forever in deep, silent thought. The ocean in his eyes danced in waves, flickering left and right in front of my own dark ones.

I pushed his hand away. "So, this isn't real?"

He smiled again. "It's as real as you want it to be."

Shaking my head, I stood up and put distance between us. "Then I want you to get out of my dream. I don't want to see you."

Confusion swept his face. "Why?" He moved toward me, but when I inched away, he stopped. With a sad look in his eyes and a small nod of the head, his body began to vaporize, his limbs turning into steam and puffing out of existence. "If that's what you want." His voice trailed after him. Then, just like that, he was gone.

I felt a tear dribble from my eye, but when I tried to touch it, my fingers came up dry again.

The queen-size bed called out to me once more, its sheets as welcoming as a hug. I threw myself onto it facedown and waited for sleep that never came. In the silence, the sound of banging on the door made my heart leap. Turning, I saw not my bedroom door, but a wooden gate that rose high and mighty all the way to the ceiling. In the place of the normal doorknob was a handle in the shape of a slithering snake, its tongue splitting off and pointing in separate directions.

That gate. I knew that gate. I'd seen it in my dreams for as long as I could remember. Always a closed door with a giant shadow emanating from the crack at the bottom, just like one was now. From the way the shadow altered in shape, becoming small then big again, it was obvious that whatever was casting it was in constant motion.

The unknown creature on the other side of the gate knocked for a second time. The walls of my room shook. Taking a deep breath, I decided it was time to see what was back there.

I took wary steps toward the giant door, my arm reaching for the ice-cold metal of the slithering snake and pulling the handle down. The gate thrust open, shoving me to the floor with great force.

I fell on my back and sat there, stock-still, for a moment. Through the strands of hair that covered my eyes, I saw smoke surging toward me. When I lifted my head up, bright yellow-and-red flames bolted at me.

Around me, the walls shook, the floor vibrated, and picture frames fell from the wall and off my corner desk. Even the wooden gate rattled against its hinges, almost as if the inanimate object was having a seizure. I pressed my hands to the tiled floor, feeling the tremor deep in the earth. The taste of burning charcoal and meat infiltrated my mouth amidst the smell of smoke.

The shaking jolted me awake. I found myself in Reed's dorm. I could feel tears on my face, so I wiped them off with the back of my hand. The curtains of the window behind me were parted to the side, just as I'd left them before I went to bed. Through it, the campus's lights shone in, illuminating bits of the room. I let my eyes adjust to the dimness.

And then I heard it.

A crash outside Reed's dorm brought me to my feet. I ran to the door, shoving it open and making my way to the center of the common area.

When I got past the bathroom, I noticed the cracked TV screen. Right on the carpet beside the TV lay a game controller, as if someone had thrown it around like a Frisbee. My first thought was that someone got too aggravated by his video game and took his anger out on the screen.

But then I noticed the shirtless burly man in the corner of the room. He wasn't anyone I recognized, though I didn't really know enough people at this school to recognize many. He wrestled with someone on the carpet at an angle that blocked the other guy from view.

"Get off me!" the helpless guy lying on his back screamed.

It was Reed. He made the sound he'd once made when he was nine and had bounced off his bed and landed on the floor, his leg sloped in an awkward direction. Instinct kicked in. I threw myself on the shirtless man, grabbing his shoulders and pulling him away from my brother.

Reed crawled backward and yelled, "Addy, get back!"

"What's going on?" I wrapped my arms tightly around the man's torso, keeping his arms by his side. "Who is this guy?"

"Addy . . ." There was warning in Reed's tone. His eyes grew wide a second before the shirtless man moved his head back, slamming it against my skull.

"Ow!" I let go.

The man, not waiting for me to get back up, jumped to his feet and went straight for Reed. With him so close and facing away from me, I noticed that his bare back was scarred, much like Adriel's. The skin wrinkled around his shoulder blades, looking like two crescents that faced opposite each other.

My heart raced faster, pulsating in my ears. My legs felt like water. I muttered with a quavering voice, "What are you doing?"

The man grabbed Reed in what looked like an embrace, and then they both vanished from the room, reminding me of how Devin had disappeared in my dream.

"Reed!" I shouted, running over to the spot where they had both been struggling just a second ago. I patted the carpet as if they had shrunk and hid in the dusty, old material and my patting would make them come out.

While I crouched on the floor without any obvious answers, it occurred to me that it had to be a magician's trick. How else could they have become invisible?

Behind me, a door opened and someone stepped out into the living area. I looked over my shoulder and saw Sam. His hand shielded his eyes from the bright light in the room.

21

"I'm trying to sleep, guys," he said. "Why are you screaming?"

I got up and ran past him into Reed's room. I took off my pajamas and pulled jeans and a random shirt on. To top off my mismatched outfit, I wore a hoodie to protect myself from the October cold, though I had never been the type to mind the chilly air.

On top of Reed's bed, the Swiss Army knife caught my attention. I tucked it into my back pocket. I grabbed my duffle bag, stuffing everything back inside it before I looked for Reed's Saint Vincent ID and keys. They were hanging on a pin by the door. I yanked them off and dashed outside.

Back in my car, I threw the duffle bag on the seat beside me and started the engine. I needed to find Adriel. He and my brother's kidnapper both had the same back wounds. I couldn't help but think they were somehow related. What were the odds of seeing two men with the same horrible burns and scars in one night? Not to mention that Adriel never told me what had happened to him. He never actually denied being in a cult, either.

Driving to the hospital didn't take long. I parked in the guest parking lot and sprinted inside the big brown building. At the reception desk, a middle-aged lady in a green scrub suit sat typing on her computer. She must have been blind as a bat, because she wore glasses so thick they looked like they were bulletproof. As soon as I reached her, she looked up.

"Hello," she said, a kind smile on her face.

I didn't have time to greet her, so I just dove right in to the matter at hand. "I want to check up on a man I dropped off a few hours ago. He had back burns and said his name was Adriel. Is he still here?"

She blinked a couple of times, her eyes huge behind the glass lenses. She kind of had the face of the big bad wolf from "Little Red Riding Hood," only sweeter and more grandmotherly.

"Do you know his last name?" she asked.

"No, but I dropped him off around ten." My eyes darted around the hospital. The place was surprisingly quiet, with only two people walking down the hall. As the lady typed more details into the computer, I tried to think of other ways to describe Adriel. "Um, he had some sort of white cloth wrapped around his bottom, if that helps."

She typed something into the system and bobbed her head. "We do have a John Doe. Looks like we were unable to gather any information about him. Maybe that's him? He was taken to the emergency room at 10:05." She pointed down the hall to my right. "Follow the red 'Emergency' signs all the way down. Then ask the front-desk nurses to let you into Room 340. It looks like he's in there right now, recovering."

"Thanks." I speedwalked toward the emergency room. Following the lady's instructions, I passed by rooms with sleeping strangers and beeping heart monitors and found the room Adriel was in without talking to any nurses.

Instead of knocking on the door, I strolled right in. There was a sage polyester curtain around the bed, so I couldn't see him at first. I yanked the curtain to the side, walked through, and pulled it back in place so that no one would notice me murdering Adriel. If that was what it took to get my brother back, I would do it. No question about it.

Adriel lay there on his side with some sort of ointment covering his back. His eyes were closed, and he kept groaning. To my surprise, his burns had become less severe than they were hours ago, unless I had imagined the bloodred, melting flesh in the dim light of the road.

"Hey." I squatted so that I was at eye level with him.

His right arm hung off the side of the bed. When he didn't open his eyes, I elbowed it and repeated my greeting.

A grunt escaped his lips. A moment later, his eyes fluttered and opened halfway. "Rosy Cheeks," he murmured. Behind his half-closed lids, his dark-brown irises regarded me.

"I can't believe I drove you in my car," I hissed. "Where the hell is my brother?"

His lids drooped more as his eyes rolled back into his head. He was no longer paying attention. I elbowed his arm again. When he came to, he said, "Hmm?"

"My brother! Where is he and what are you doing to him?"

"What are you talking about?" But his speech slurred, which made it sound more like "Wa ah you talkin' 'bout?" Luckily, I understood the language of the drunk, which his language resembled right now.

"Dude!" I grabbed his head in both my hands and hoisted it up, forcing him to look at me. In the process, my fingers tangled with the smooth strands of his brown, jaw-length hair. "I know you're in a cult. Now tell me where my brother was taken."

Silence filled the room. He gazed at me through tired eyes, but I didn't care. He deserved the wounds and the pain. He deserved to rot in the hell he was spit out of tonight.

"Tell me where my brother is," I repeated.

He blinked. "I don't have anything to do with it, but I think I know."

I removed one hand from his head, turned it into a fist, and punched him directly across the jaw. I was aiming for his eye, but my hand-eye coordination was off. With a wail, his head collapsed on the pillow and his sticky back pressed against the bed.

"Tell me everything or I'll kill you."

I hoped I had his full attention, because I really didn't feel like becoming a murderer tonight.

Chapter Three

REED

The earth spun, shifting all around me, swallowing me whole and spitting me back out. My body shrunk and expanded in mere nanoseconds. Addy's scream echoed after me, but I was gone.

"What are you doing?" I yelled as the freak of a man with the thick scars and creases on his back carried me away. I kicked wildly, my foot meeting his leg.

My physical strength must not have been up to par, because he kept moving. He threw a punch into my stomach, blowing the air out of me. "Shut up!"

We moved through a cavelike area, his filthy arms tight around me. The bastard lifted me off the ground with every step he took. The farther we traveled inside the dark cavern, the more claustrophobic I felt. A rush of hot air hit me, reminding me of the pervasive, sweltering atmosphere from the brick pizza oven at my first high school job.

Sweat trickled down my chest, soaked my pants, and dampened my socks. My hair clung to the nape of my neck, and mucus dripped from my nose to my lips, tasting like salted oysters.

Something crunched beneath my feet. Narrowing my eyes at the shadowy land, I saw small creatures stir. Roaches? Maggots? I couldn't tell.

At some point, the nauseating warmth of the place must have suffocated me. I blacked out. I came to when the shithead, good-for-nothing scumbag threw me to the ground a while later. I didn't know how much time had passed.

Groaning, I tried to get up on my feet, but exhaustion hit me.

"My lord, I brought you the blood child," the sleazeball said.

Ten feet away from me, sitting on a throne made of what looked like bones and human skulls, a man stared at me. He wore a suit of armor that matched the pitch-black of his eyes. His black hair fell over the side of his face, reaching just above his shoulders. In his lap lay a tranquil, bright-yellow viper. He gently stroked the back of its head with the tips of his fingers.

"My child." Looking at me, he stood up, tossing the snake to the ground. It slithered around the throne, its tongue hissing in and out.

I pushed myself up to sit on my knees.

The dark-eyed man now stood just a few steps away and had a grin on his face. He dropped to his knees right in front of me and touched his hand to my cheek. His skin scalded mine where he touched. I groaned.

"No," he muttered, the grin washing from his face. He seemed heartbroken. With a frown, he jumped to his feet and grabbed the scumbag who had dragged me here by the throat. "This isn't my blood child." He squeezed the man's neck. "Who did you bring me?"

The man with the scarred back whimpered. "He . . . he was there when I felt it. I felt it around him, my . . . my lord."

Still holding on to his throat, the dark-eyed man lifted the scumbag into the air. "This. Isn't. My. Child." He spat each word. "You've wasted my time." He brought his other hand up and snapped the scumbag's neck. A loud crack echoed through the cave.

Just like he was throwing out trash, he tossed the man to the ground.

My eyes became the size of baseballs. I crawled blindly away from this monster. The dark-eyed man shouted for someone to take me and ordered another hideous person to get him his real blood child.

"Bring my child tonight, or you will end up like Marcius."

I struggled to my feet and tried to run, but I didn't get far. Another half-naked man restrained me. He hauled me out into an adjacent chamber with a big prison cell in the dead center of the room.

"What a joke! It's obvious you're not Lucifer's child," the new man said as he threw me into the cell.

I landed on top of slimy insects, some of which started crawling on me.

"See you never, kid." The man turned, giving me a perfect view of his scarred back, and walked out of the room, slamming the wooden door behind him.

The blood drained from my face. Did he just say Lucifer? *These people are crazy. What kind of fucked-up gang is this?* That man had killed his own . . . what? Who was the scumbag? His friend, his henchman? He was dead now, just like I would be soon. I felt sure of that.

Addy had no way of finding me. I was screwed.

Chapter Four

ADRIEL

Rosy Cheeks came back for me with a scowl on her face. She shoved my arm to the side, the action making the blisters on my shoulder sting again.

Her piercing, dark eyes were narrowed and cold. "Hey," she said, her voice full of rage.

Between the slits of my eyes, I stared at her, examining the hard soldier façade she put on. It reminded me of the way she'd looked into my eyes hours ago. Her expression had been full of sorrow, but she'd blinked all the tears away, collected herself, and let her face harden. Though deep down, the angel in me could still sense she was in deep emotional pain.

My throat was dry, but I managed to force two words from my lips. "Rosy Cheeks."

Without any warning, she spat her next words at me. "I can't believe I drove you in my car." She bit her bottom lip with her teeth and peeled a piece of dry skin off. A tiny drop of blood crept out, but she continued eyeing me with a hard stare, as if she didn't even notice what she had done to herself. "Where the hell is my brother?"

Brother? I didn't know anything about Rosy Cheeks' brother. I didn't even know her real name.

Too tired to think straight, I closed my eyes for a second. A tiny speck of light flickered in the darkness, reminding me of the firefly from earlier. This time, though, the light started growing bigger and bigger. Behind my lids, I saw nothing but a warm, radiating sun.

An image flashed before me. I saw a young man—maybe eighteen or nineteen years old—getting dragged through what looked like a damp cave. His eyes were big and amber, yet something about him reminded me of Rosy Cheeks. His facial bone structure was sharp like hers. He had large pit stains, and around the collar of his T-shirt, a giant puddle of sweat slowly trickled down his body. He was struggling against someone, someone with a scarred, ugly back . . . just like mine.

When I opened my eyes again, Rosy Cheeks was yelling at me. She continued questioning me about her brother. No matter what I said, she didn't seem to believe me.

"Dude!" She grabbed my head in both her hands, her fingers gripping my skull, and lifted my face off the pillow. "I know you're in a cult. Now tell me where my brother was taken."

That was when I saw it. Her features . . . the young man's features. Although strange, I knew I'd just had a vision of Rosy Cheeks' brother.

"Tell me where my brother is!"

I swallowed some saliva to hydrate my throat and said, "I don't have anything to do with it, but I think I know."

She landed a painful punch across my jaw, sending me falling against the bed on my blistered back.

"Tell me everything or I'll kill you."

Something about her rigid tone told me she wasn't kidding. It took me a moment to realize how doomed I was. Rosy Cheeks needed me to tell her what I knew about her brother, and my life depended on her believing and trusting me. After all, she'd made it perfectly clear that she wasn't afraid to hurt me.

But how would I tell her that her brother was kidnapped by a fallen angel? A demon, to be exact. In what world would she believe me if I told her I was a fallen angel too?

Taking a deep breath, I said, "It's a long story, and I'd feel safer telling you somewhere not here."

One of her eyebrows lifted. She stood up, moving away from me. "You want to go somewhere, just the two of us?"

"No, no. I just can't tell you with so many ears nearby and people checking in."

She crossed her arms. "Fine, but we're going wherever I choose." She came closer again, placed one hand underneath my left shoulder and the other on the side of my stomach, and shifted me to my side again. "Can you stand?"

"I can try." Feet on the ground, I pushed myself into a standing position and grunted. The burns on my back felt as if they were peeling off.

"Are you walking out like that?" She pointed at my naked chest and the shroud around my bottom.

When I shrugged, she told me to wait and hurried out of the room. She came back a moment later with a maroon sweatshirt, jeans, and socks.

"Here, put the pants and sweatshirt on." She handed everything over and turned away. "It'll hide the burns and that disgusting ointment on your back."

Even though my skin screamed in agony, I lifted my arms up and tried to pull the sweatshirt over my head. I must have made a loud noise, because she whirled around and came over to help. She yanked the sweatshirt down, helped me put on the pants and socks, put my arm over her shoulders, and started walking out with me dragging myself beside her.

I could feel the ointment soaking through the shirt, which felt sticky and moist. Still, by some miracle, the ointment had made the pain less severe in the past few hours I'd had it on. I let out a breath of relief.

"Where did you get the clothes?" I asked as we reached the hospital's main door.

She glanced at me and shrugged. "I stole them."

Rosy Cheeks slipped me out of the hospital. No one even batted an eyelash. In the car, she took my hand and ripped the patient wristband off my wrist before driving off.

Shivering, I wrapped my arms around myself and groaned when the burns stung. I tried not to press my back too hard against the seat, but with Rosy Cheeks' sudden shifts and turns, I couldn't always avoid the contact.

"Where are we going?"

She didn't answer.

We rode in silence for the next fifteen minutes or so. When she finally stopped the car at a diner with a sign out front that said *"Creed's,"* she said, "Come on." She helped me stand up again, but I felt much better, more balanced, this time.

A sign that read *"Open 24/7"* lay against the diner's door. I could see a couple of people sitting at the bar eating and drinking before we'd even stepped in. A few sported light scarves around their necks. I didn't blame them. Breath escaped my mouth like steam, and I shuddered.

Upon entering, a strange aroma struck me. I'd never smelled anything like it and couldn't figure out what it was. I kept sniffing the air, the warm, sweet scent filling my lungs.

Rosy Cheeks chose a private booth in the back of the diner, presumably so no one could hear us talk.

She sat across from me with her arms crossed. "Tell me everything you know, but be careful. If you try anything, and I mean *anything*, the people here won't let you get away with it."

Her words were thick with irony. I thought back to the beginning of mankind, to that time long ago when I became a guardian. Now, I was sitting in a diner getting accused of being the opposite of what I had always been.

"I won't hurt you."

She leaned forward, her hair flowing past her shoulders. Her dark-brown eyes searched mine for answers. "Where is Reed?"

I placed my hands on the table and hoped she would believe my next words. "Let me start from the beginning. I'm not human. At least, I wasn't a few hours ago."

"Excuse me?"

"Just bear with me. Please." I inched my body forward and spoke in a whisper, not wanting the waiters to hear.

Rosy Cheeks, who had tensed, moved away just a sliver.

"The burns on my back aren't from a cult ritual. There's no cult involved here. Whoever took your brother, he's not someone you want to deal with."

One of the waiters came over with a pot in hand and placed a mug in front of both of us. "Hello, my dears. Coffee?"

Rosy Cheeks gave a single nod of the head. "Please."

The waitress poured her a hot, dark liquid from the pot and shot me a glance. "And for you?"

I looked between her and Rosy Cheeks, unable to decide. Was it normal to accept coffee? I didn't exactly have money to pay. Although, the steam blowing from Rosy Cheeks' mug tempted me with its enticing, rich smell.

Rosy Cheeks spoke for me. "He'll have a glass of water. He's recovering."

The waitress smiled and walked away. That left me without any coffee to try.

Rosy Cheeks gestured with her hand for me to continue. "You were saying?"

"You don't want to deal with the creature that took your brother."

"And why not?"

"Because . . ." I tapped my fingers against the table, stalling for more time to gather my thoughts and decide what I would say. I resolved to go with the truth. "Because that thing is a fallen angel."

35

Chapter Five

ADELAIDE

"He's a what?" I'd had it with Adriel. He was clearly crazy.
"Are you out of your mind? Did you think you could speak
nonsense and I'd be stupid enough to believe you?"

Fallen angel, he'd said. He had to be batshit crazy!

Reed's Swiss Army knife dug into my posterior. I was
practically sitting on the metal object. Pretending to adjust the
bottom hem of my shirt, I reached for the knife in my back
pocket and hid it in my fist. With my other hand, I reached to
take the coffee mug and sipped the warm drink, my eyes never
leaving Adriel. I had to stay cautious and watch his every
move.

Adriel kept his gaze steady, never once flinching. "I'm telling the truth."

"Yeah, and pigs can fly."

He drew in a long breath. "Look, I'm a fallen—"

The waitress came back, cutting Adriel off mid-sentence. She set a large glass of water in front of him and placed a straw on the table. "Here you go, hun. Would you like anything else?"

The burgundy apron she wore reeked of bacon and eggs far more than the diner did. She was looking at both of us, so I told her we were good for now.

As soon as she left, Adriel leaned in again. "I'm a fallen angel." His voice was so low, I probably wouldn't have heard him if I hadn't been bending over the table, sipping my coffee.

My hold on the knife tightened. "What the hell are you talking about? Are you trying to keep me from finding my brother? Is that what they told you to do? To stall?"

"Again, I'm not in a cult."

"Then where is my brother?"

Adriel looked down at his hands, took a deep breath, and looked back at me. "He's in hell."

I jumped to my feet. "That's it!"

All the people in the diner turned in their seats, curious. Nothing this loud ever happened here at night.

My patience reaching its limit, I said, "I'm calling the cops."

I threw eight bucks on the table to cover the cost of the coffee and the tip and marched out. The diner's door jingled when I jerked it open, and I ran to my car.

"Hey," Adriel called out behind me.

I unlocked Lucy and was about to jump in when his hand gripped my arm.

"Hey." He spun me around and was towering over me, all six feet and whatever inches of him. "I promise I'm telling you the truth."

The knife remained in my hand, but it was secured shut and useless there in between the two of us. Adriel's eyes shifted to it a smidge of a second before coming back to my face. To my surprise, his grip on my arm loosened just enough for me to be able to tug myself away and run.

But I stayed there, feeling stupid for doing so but unable to help it.

"Look at the burns on my back. They're not from a cult. They're . . ." He looked up at the star-filled sky. "They're from my wings burning."

Somehow, someway, I needed to get away from him. "Let go of me." I tried to breathe evenly; he needed to see I wasn't afraid of him. "Let go."

His hand dropped to his side and he took a step back. "I'm sorry."

At first, I couldn't move. My legs trembled. I was afraid he would see the fear in my eyes. Drawing in a breath, I placed one foot inside the car. He wasn't stopping me. I would call the cops when I got back to Reed's dorm. I had the entire plan figured out.

I only managed to place one foot—just one foot—inside the car, because in that instant, something knocked Adriel down to the ground.

"What—" Adriel started to say, then his back hit the pavement and he shrieked in pain. On top of him was another half-naked man with a scarred back.

I could've—should've—jumped in the car and raced off. Still, if Adriel was being attacked, then he wasn't responsible for Reed and was at least partially telling the truth. And that meant this man with the scars knew where my brother was.

I moved toward the man. "You piece of scum," I yelled and kicked his head.

The man tumbled to his side, giving me a chance to reach a hand to Adriel and help him up.

Adriel stood between the two of us, blocking my view. But when the man rose to his feet, I noticed what was wrong with him. Aside from his disfigured back, his eyes were solid black—not a drop of white in them. He was staring at me.

Adriel shoved him away.

Righting himself, the man spit on the ground. "You're pathetic." He glared at Adriel as if he were a cockroach carrying brown egg sacs.

"What do you want with her?" Adriel asked.

"That's none of your business." The man punched Adriel in the stomach and laughed, watching him drop to his knees.

I leaned over to help Adriel up, but the man grabbed me by the shoulders with callused hands.

I protested and kicked back in vain.

"Don't scream. No one will hear you." Before me, the man's black eyes wavered, turning brown for a nanosecond. "Shh."

Something shifted around me. The Swiss Army knife fell from my hand, and I didn't have time to reach for it. My body contracted. For a moment, I was smaller than a single atom. The world looked like billions of freckles coming together to form shapes.

I wanted to throw up.

The man snickered, the sound coming from deep within his chest. "Fascinating, isn't it?"

I felt my body return to its normal size; it was a heavy sensation, one that made the weight of my pumping heart almost overwhelming.

"Come on." The man pulled me through a cavern.

As soon as we entered, my body started pouring sweat. It felt like we'd stepped into a vast sauna. We passed by a hole in the cave wall. There were stairs leading down from it, though I couldn't tell where they led to. The man dragged me away before I could get a better look. Still, the smell of barbecued meat wafted out of the hole, making me salivate. I wondered if that was a kitchen.

"Are we in a restaurant?"

"Shh."

Something boomed from the hole. Concentrating, I heard a loud, unnerving scream.

At last, the man led me into a huge chamber. The heat was less severe here, though not gone. The damp air clung onto my skin, suffocating me.

"My lord," the man holding me said, "I brought you the true blood child."

Blood child. Was this a sick joke, some sort of prank Reed put on for his amusement?

Opposite from us, a man with shoulder-length black hair sat on a corpse throne. Like my kidnapper, his eyes were also solid jet-black. Craniums and bones stuck out from his high seat. A viper, yellow as a lemon, curled around his leg and rested its head on his thigh. I swallowed. If this was a prank, it was an elaborate one.

While he studied me, crazy, irrational thoughts popped into my head. I wasn't good enough. Emptiness and a feeling of being alone dug into my chest. I'd failed Reed. My own mother hated me. *I* hated me. No wonder Devin had left.

40

Tears threatened, but I blinked them away at the last second.

"Saleos," the man said to my kidnapper while glancing at me with a grin. "Are you sure this is my blood child?"

"I can sense her noble blood, my lord. You are without a doubt the father. Marcius assumed too quickly earlier."

The man raised an eyebrow and continued to beam. "So, you are my daughter." He said it matter-of-factly, like he truly believed I was related to him.

Perhaps I was this creepy man's daughter. After all, Erica had never mentioned a name. She had never even described what my dad looked like. My father could have been anyone. I had no clue, and this man with the scary eyes was just as likely to be related to me as anyone else. But I really hoped this man wasn't the one. I would rather be the daughter of a butcher than the daughter of a creepy man sitting on a chair of skulls.

Somehow, I got the courage to speak, even though every nerve in my body told me to run and hide. "I can't be your daughter. I've never seen you in my life."

The man chuckled. "Is that not how it is most of the time? Kids growing up not knowing who their parents are? Like stray animals, they are brought into the world. Useless beings." He placed his hand on his chin. "But you are far from useless."

"You don't know anything about me."

"But I do. I could sense you all the way here." He gestured around himself.

The half-naked man named Saleos still held on to me. I tried to wriggle free, but it was no use.

"Saleos, let her go," my potential father ordered. "She will not run."

"Yes, my lord."

41

Saleos stepped away, leaving me alone in the center of the room with both the crazy father wannabe and his probably poisonous snake eyeing me. I did a quick scan around the room, but Reed wasn't there. There were only three others aside from us, plus lots of insectlike creatures crawling all over the rocky walls.

The black-eyed man rested his arms on the skeletal armrests of his throne. "I do know you, my child. You see, you have my blood coursing through you. That means we have many things in common."

"If you know me," I said, wiping sweat from my lip, "then tell me: What was the first word I ever spoke? Hell, do you even know my name?"

He chuckled. "You are saucy."

"And you're not my father."

"Actually, I am, even if I do not know your name. Besides, I can prove it."

He stood up, the viper sliding off his leg and slithering away. He strode over to where I stood, snapped his finger at one of his lackeys, and told him to bring a cup.

My hands shook as my ears drummed with the rush of blood. I had to find Reed, but I needed to stay calm first. I wouldn't be able to get him out if I was scared.

If Reed was even here.

Facing me now, the man with the eerie eyes loomed just a foot away, not caring much for boundaries and personal space. Other than the complete blackness in his eyes, he was a good-looking man with a sculpted, oval face, thick, arched brows, thick lashes, and slender cheekbones. I didn't want to admit it, but he did kind of look like me.

While I studied him discreetly, he made no such attempt. His eyes ate me up the way some hungry men look at women at bars, their gazes lingering in places they shouldn't. He looked like he was deciding when to leap after a prey. He moved around me and touched my hair. I spun around. Without shame, he licked his lips and let a grin manifest.

This sexual predator was not my father.

His lackey handed him a wooden chalice engraved with a snake coiling around its circumference. The man clutched the chalice in both hands and smiled at me like we were old friends.

"In a minute, you are going to discover the truth," the black-haired man said, his breath stinking of dill pickles and raw fish.

He tilted the cup my way, showing me it contained water. At first, I thought he was offering me a drink. It didn't help that I was thirsty from walking through the smoldering cavern. When he produced a needle from who knows where and pierced the tip of his thumb with it, I knew that wasn't the case. A droplet of blood oozed out. He let it fall into the chalice.

"This is for you." He offered me the drink.

I held my hands close to my chest, not wanting to take the disgusting blood-water chalice. "What do you expect me to do with that?"

To my horror, he grabbed my left hand and wrapped it around the cup. "Drink it."

His touch gave my hand a strong electric shock, one that surged through my arm and struck the vein in my neck. I pulled away, almost dumping half the cup's contents to the ground.

"Now, now." His black eyes stared into mine. "This will show you what you have been missing all your life. I swear to God this will not turn you into a mule. Just take one sip, and the truth will be yours. Do you not want to know who you are? I promise it will be sweet."

"And if I don't?"

"If you don't . . . well, let us just say your brother will make a few fashion statements with his flesh." He grinned, baring yellow, rotten teeth.

He does have Reed!

At that moment, I wanted to throw the cup in his face and make a run for it. And I was about to, but I remembered the other men in the room and how strong Saleos was; they were all probably just as strong. I didn't have a fighting chance.

"Drink," he ordered, nudging the cup toward my lips.

I placed the chalice close to my mouth and said, "I'll drink this if I get to see my brother." Bargaining was my only option.

He nudged the cup toward me again. "You will see him after."

With my heart pounding, I let the water graze my tongue, hoping with all my being that no trace of this lunatic's blood went into my mouth. I looked into his dark eyes and forced myself to swallow the tiny sip. Bitterness and acidity washed over my tongue, stinging every nerve there. I thrust the cup back into his hand, almost punching him in the gut with the effort.

"Good girl . . ."

His words echoed all around me. I fell on the hard, stony ground, and everything around me began turning black.

"What did you do?"

No one answered.

My hands felt around, searching for another body, a wall, anything. For a second, I was sure the man had blinded me, but when a bright, hot flame appeared before me, I knew that wasn't the case. A harsh, deep scream sounded from behind the fire. I started crawling backward, wanting none of it. I was ten feet away when the flame expanded, rushing in all directions. Another scream rang out, vibrating the earth beneath me. I squinted my eyes and looked through the blaze, searching for whoever or whatever was there. That was when I saw them. The huge white wings enclosed within the flames.

The wings flapped around, attempting to extinguish the fire. Little by little, they were turning to ash. Wind carried some feathers away. One of the feathers flew into my hand. Its edges had turned charcoal black. I stood up and rushed to the other side of the wings. I wanted to see what was there.

I came upon the dark-eyed captor who claimed he was my father. He didn't seem to notice me as he shrieked in pain. The wings were attached to his back, and everything was burning.

"Hey," I said. "What is this? What's going on?"

He continued to scream, ignoring me altogether. His eyes never even met mine.

"Hey. Can you see me?"

To my right, a luminous, dazzling light flooded the night sky. A gentle, sweet voice emanated from within. "Lucifer," it spoke. "You have made your choice. You are hereby banished."

Lucifer?

Lucifer, my black-eyed captor, covered his eyes and squinted at this new light. A snarl ripped out of his throat. "You will pay for this, Father!"

The light and the fire died in unison, leaving me in darkness again. I stood still, afraid of what would pop out next.

Distant sounds of footsteps against wet ground echoed toward me, followed by whispers. The darkness turned to brown, and shadows darted left and right.

"Tell me," a man with a charming voice spoke. He was just a dim figure in my peripheral vision now, but I could tell he was smiling by his lighthearted tone. "Do you live in the area?"

A young woman giggled. "Do you?"

The woman's long brown locks waved in the air. Suddenly, her profile came into perfect view. Soft features, big brown eyes, a slim body. She looked familiar. Maybe I knew her back in college? She wore a black, strapless top and tight leather pants and had a choker around her neck from which a diamond pendant of the letter E hung. She looked like she was on her way to a nightclub.

"I'm from around," the man said as he, too, came into view. Once more, I observed that he was my captor, who also happened to be Lucifer, a fact I tried and failed to wrap my mind around. He had his long, black hair and the same slender cheekbones. However, his eyes weren't black; they were dark brown, like mine. He put his hand on the woman's shoulder and leaned in, murmuring something in her ear.

She froze for a second, her eyes staring off into the distance. "Yes," she answered.

He put his arm over her shoulder and turned her almost in my direction. I gasped. That woman. I was looking at the spitting image of my mother, only from years ago, when she was about my age. The E-shaped pendant on her necklace stood for her name, for Erica.

"Erica!" I wanted to warn her, even though I couldn't stand the sight of her half the time. "Erica, don't go with him."

It was like she couldn't see or hear me. I was a ghost.

"Erica." Tears poured down my face. "Erica, he's the devil. Maybe literally. Don't go . . . don't go with him."

They walked off into the night with him resting his hand on her hip.

"He's the devil!"

As they disappeared, I felt the blood in my body heat up in my veins, leaving red trails all over my pale skin. I screamed, but the blood was boiling, burning, blistering inside me.

"What are you doing to me?" I shouted at the nothingness around me.

Inside my head, a vision arose. I saw Lucifer's naked body entangled with my mother's. I wanted to puke, but I felt heavy all of a sudden, like the earth had begun pulling me down harder than the rest of humanity.

My blood cooled down to its normal temperature. I stood there panting. Within me, I felt power, strength. My blood was dark and thick, like molten lava. I didn't know what that meant, though the idea that I was born out of something evil scared me.

My eyes closed for a moment as I tried to figure out how I would get out of this mess. When I opened my eyes again, I was back in the cavern. Lucifer stood in front of me, baring his nasty teeth in a grin.

His yellow viper had made its way between us and coiled itself around both my leg and his. I kicked it away and moved out of its grip.

"You're Lucifer." I stared straight into his black eyes.

"And you are my daughter."

I shook my head. "You drugged me. You made me see what you wanted me to see." I could feel the darkness in my blood, but still. That didn't prove anything.

Still smiling, he said, "You could take my blood for testing, at which point you will see the truth. However, you do not have time on your hands, child. Besides, I am the greatest thing to happen to you. I could give you anything you desire. Do you not want all your wishes granted?"

He was right. Even if I was still just a human, there was something stronger, more depraved inside me. That alone put suspicion in my head. Despite how much I didn't want to believe him, I sensed he wasn't lying. Still, I ignored his comment about fulfilling my desires and didn't move my eyes from his.

"May I know your name?" he asked.

"Adelaide."

"Adelaide. Now that is a noble name."

I crossed my arms. "You said I could see my brother if I drank from the cup. Now, where is he?"

He waved over one of his men. Turning my head, I saw a hideous man dragging a pale Reed in. He was struggling, trying to free himself. When he saw me, he surrendered and let the man bring him over.

"Addy," Reed muttered. Beads of sweat dripped from his brows to his lips.

My Reed, my baby brother. He had always been my child in a sense; I couldn't remember how many nights when we were kids that Erica would leave us alone and he'd beg me to sleep beside him so the boogeyman wouldn't get him. Seeing him like this tore my heart out of my chest.

I dashed forward, pushed the man away, and wrapped my arms around Reed. "You're safe now. I promise."

Lucifer gave a bitter laugh. "Do not make promises you cannot keep."

"What are you talking about? You said I'd get my brother back if I drank."

Lucifer moved to his skeleton throne and sat there. "That was not at all what I said. I told you that you would see your brother. I never said I would give him back."

My hold tightened around Reed's weak body. His head fell against his shoulder, and he closed his eyes.

"What are you saying?" I glared at Lucifer. "What was that crap about granting my wishes, then?"

Lucifer tapped his nails against the bones of his seat. A hollow clanking sound resounded. "I want you to do some things first."

"What kind of things?"

He smiled. "Being the devil, as you probably figured out, means I can manipulate people." He grabbed his viper off his leg and stared into its eyes like he was mesmerized. "I can compel them—at least the weak ones. They just want to please someone, and I am always there for that."

"What does that have to do with me?"

"Well, you *are* my daughter. If I am right—and I know I am right because I can sense it in our shared blood—you also have the power of compulsion."

Reed opened his eyes and brought his face closer to mine. "Addy," he whispered. "Don't do what he says."

"It's okay, Reed." I stroked his cheek and cleared the sweat from his eyes. "I will get you out."

"No, she will not," Lucifer said. "Anyway, as I was saying before I was rudely interrupted, you, Adelaide, can compel people just like I can. But I need you for much more than that. You see, you are not just a manipulator; you are a manipulator with feminine appeal, and I need you to entice people to join me, to devote themselves to me. Together, we can rule the universe."

I snorted and let my lips stretch into a smile for the first time in this awful place. "And why the hell would I do that?"

"Because." Lucifer pointed at one of his men. "I have the power to kill your brother."

Saleos came forth and jerked Reed out of my arms. I pulled back, and it became a tugging war.

"Don't let them take me," Reed begged, his eyes like bronze, round marbles.

"Let him go," I demanded, but Saleos didn't stop.

Reed fell back into Saleos's hold and got hauled into the corner of the chamber.

Turning to Lucifer with a fire unlike anything I had ever felt, I stormed over to his throne and wrapped my slim, long fingers around his throat, earning a bizarre smile from him.

"I have always wanted a fighter," he said. "I am a father just like my father, but unlike him, I have the most beautiful ruby there ever was."

I spit in his face. "I will not manipulate people for your gain, you sadistic piece of shit!"

He put his hand over mine and, with no effort, freed his neck from my clutch. "I'm stronger than you, my child."

He waved at Saleos, and when I looked back, I saw the grotesque man holding a blade against Reed's middle finger.

My heart sank.

"Now, you do what I ask." Lucifer wiggled his fingers at me. "Or your brother loses his fingers and toes. Which will it be?"

Chapter Six

Adriel

It was all but a second. After the demon knocked me down, he grabbed Rosy Cheeks and disappeared. In that second, I wasn't sure if she would ever come back.

I was still on the ground when she emerged from a portal shaped like her body. She crashed on top of me, her head falling onto my chest, and drenched my sweatshirt with her sweat.

She lay there motionless, her arms resting on my sides.

"Hey," I said, gently lifting her face up.

Wet strands covered her eyes. I reached out and tucked them behind her small, double-pierced ears. Her eyes were closed, curtained by thick, long lashes, and her forehead burned. I held her close and sat up, ignoring the pain in my back and letting her head rest against my arm.

"Rosy Cheeks." I put my ear over her chest and waited to hear the *thump thump* of her heart. I had never done that before, never heard the sound of a living heart. When I felt the heartbeat, I exhaled. "You're okay. Thank God you're okay."

She coughed, her eyes blinking open. She sat in my lap as her eyes adjusted to the dimness of the parking lot.

"They have Reed," she whispered.

When she set her eyes on mine, they reflected my image in their dark depths. I watched her, unable to blink.

"You were right about the demons," she said.

The longer she stared at me, the more I felt the air get sucked out of my lungs.

"You were right."

I stood and helped her to her feet. Her eyes never left mine, and I couldn't for the life of me look away. It was like she was controlling me.

"How long were you there?" I asked.

"In hell?"

She dropped her gaze to the ground and let go of my hands. In doing so, she also released me from her hold. I felt my chest pump at its normal speed again.

"A little under an hour. Why?"

"You weren't gone long here." I looked inside the big windows of Creed's, at the faces we had seen a moment ago. "You were in hell for just a second."

Her eyes grew wide. "How is that possible?"

None of heaven's messengers ever paid attention to time, because time was just a human construct. When you're immortal you don't care to hold on to every fleeting tick of your heart. Hell worked the same. Rosy Cheeks had just experienced that without realizing it.

"Time doesn't really exist in hell. You could have been there for many years and still come back to this moment."

Her head sprang up, displaying wide, petrified eyes. "So, Reed could be there for years? He could come out a seventy-year-old man?"

"Not exactly. Heaven and hell have special characteristics since they're not on the same plane as Earth. The aging process is halted completely over there. You may still breathe, and your blood may still flow, but your lungs and heart won't decay or age whatsoever. Reed could be there for years through his perception of hell's nonexistent time, but only a month for us. Either way, he will come out at the exact same age as when he was taken in."

She turned her back to me and ran both her hands through her long locks. When she spun back around to face me, her eyes were bloodshot and sparkly, like a red moon's reflection in a lake.

"We have to get him out."

"We will."

Moving closer, she fixed her eyes on me again and pulled at the cords that bound my soul and body together. "You don't understand, Adriel." She was just a foot away now, her head barely reaching my shoulders. "I'm Lucifer's daughter."

My breath caught in my throat. I wanted to say, "You can't be his daughter. You're just a human," but the words wouldn't come out. Her spellbinding eyes transfixed mine, weakening any control I had over my new human body.

"He wants me," she said, "because I'm capable of creating an army for him. He wants me to get people to write his initial on their bodies using their blood; he said that's how I recruit them, how I sell their souls to him."

Those eyes. Those big almond-shaped brown eyes. Lucifer had them too. Still, people looked like other people all the time. And fallen angels were not exempt from lookalikes in the human world.

She pulled away. "Come on. I want to get out of here." Her Swiss Army knife lay on the ground. She reached for it, tucked it in her back pocket, and got into her car.

I followed her and got into the passenger seat. The right words still hadn't popped into my mind, so I sat there regarding her, wondering what kind of life she had lived with the blood of my enemy coursing through her.

Ten minutes into the drive, I started wondering where we were headed. Rosy Cheeks drove fast, moving between lanes and cutting off slower cars like she had no time to spare.

"My name's Addy," she said when we pulled up to a red light. She glanced at me, but this time, she didn't hold me hostage under whatever power she had discovered in hell. "Short for Adelaide."

I continued to examine her face, her obvious likeness to Lucifer. When I didn't say anything, she took it as her cue to talk more.

"I didn't know who my father was until tonight." Her grip on the wheel tightened. She took off, hurrying down the street and dodging a light just as it changed to red, her car roaring. "And now I have the devil's blood in me, my brother is in hell, and I'm supposed to gather soldiers for the devil's army. Oh, and if I don't, Reed dies."

"I won't let him get hurt." The words rushed out of my mouth on instinct. I had always protected my humans—or at least, I had tried to do what I thought was right—and even though I wasn't an angel anymore, I felt the same impulse with her.

"You're a fallen angel too, aren't you?" Addy was stating the fact more than looking for an answer. "God burned your wings."

My wings. They were so strong. Now they were gone forever. Yet, I was still better off than other fallen angels. I looked at the pale, blue-purple veins in my hands. They were new. No angel—winged or fallen—had ever had blue veins. Black maybe, for the demons, but never blue. "I'm fallen, but I don't think I'm like the rest of the demons."

"So, what are you?"

Somehow, I had made it to Earth and descended into a human body, whereas my long-fallen brothers had gone straight to the furnace of hell to rule and torture all the strayed humans. "I guess I'm human now."

She was silent after that for a while. She rested her head back against the headrest and said, "I don't feel so good."

I had been watching her for a while, but it wasn't until then that I realized her sweaty face had paled. Every couple of seconds, when the streetlights flashed in her face, it was apparent that the rosiness in her cheeks had faded away.

I leaned toward her in panic and asked, "Do you want to go to the hospital?"

She said no and kept on driving for a minute, though she did slow the vehicle down. When we neared a gas station, she put her signal light on and pulled into the parking lot.

"I'm just nauseous." She stopped the engine and wiped moisture from her forehead with the sleeve of her sweatshirt. "I'm going inside to wash my face and get some water. Come with me?"

I followed behind her. She staggered right and left, looking like she would topple over any second. When I tried to steady her, she shrugged one shoulder and moved away.

"I'm fine." She pushed the gas station's shop door open and skidded in, barely lifting her feet off the ground. "Give me a minute. I won't be long."

In the back of the store was a sign that read *"Restrooms"* in big bold letters. Addy moved in that direction, disappearing behind the women's door.

A few minutes went by and she still hadn't come out, so I knocked on the door. "Are you okay in there?"

She came out without any sweat on her face, and some color had returned to her cheeks.

"I'm better," she said.

I kept an eye on her as she made her way to one of the refrigerators to grab a drink. She chose two iced honey lemon teas and walked to the register.

In line, she looked at me with heavy eyes. "You know what I don't understand?" she said, her voice the only sound in the store. "Why would Lucifer do this now?"

The place was mostly empty, except for the person before us in line and the owner of the store. Still, I couldn't help but whisper back, "What do you mean?"

Addy imitated my soft tone when she saw me glance at the two men within earshot. "I mean, he had all the time in the world—literally since the beginning of time—to procreate and use his child for whatever he is trying to do. Like, he wants war, right? Why didn't he just get his army a long time ago? And don't get me started on the war. What war is he even planning?"

We moved up to first in line, and she placed her drinks on the counter.

"That will be four thirty-five," the owner said.

She paid him, and we walked out.

"Here." She handed me one of the bottles. "You didn't drink anything since we left the hospital. You're going to need that."

Condensation ran down the bottle, feeling cool against my hand. Within the container, the brown liquid sloshed around like mini ocean waves. Suddenly, my throat felt dry. An image flashed in my head of my burning wings. The heat—my throat felt that heat, and the sensation of the heat dying out, leaving everything ashen.

Addy studied me in between sips. "Drink some. You'll feel better."

I opened the bottle and brought the rim to my lips. I looked at her for approval. When she nodded, I let the tea ever so slowly pour into my mouth. The word "heavenly" popped into my mind. Never had I known the power the coolness of a drink had to soothe and wash ashy sensations away; but then again, I had never had any ashy sensations until this night.

Sighing, I licked the lingering taste of tea from my lips. Since I'd never tasted anything before, I didn't know how to identify each flavor.

"Tastes good, right?" She grabbed her keys from her pocket and fumbled with them until she found the right one. "The honey and lemon are good for getting the sugar level up."

So, this is what sweetness tastes like. I took another gulp before we got back into her car.

Back on the road, she returned to her talkative behavior. "You still haven't answered my questions."

Once more, she was racing through the streets like a wildcat charging after its prey. I just couldn't figure out what her prey was.

"Where are we going, exactly?" I asked.

Down the horizon, a hint of blue highlighted the early hours of the morning. Soon, the sun would follow, flashing its bright rays across the world for my new human eyes to witness.

Addy set her sleep-deprived eyes on me. "We're going to my apartment. Unless . . ." She looked back at the road with creases between her eyebrows. "You know, unless there's somewhere else you want me to drop you off?"

I didn't even have to think hard to realize that I had nowhere to go. Thus, I told her, no, I would go with her. "Besides, I promised I'd help your brother, and I'm not breaking that promise."

The frown dissipated from her face. "Good. You can start helping him by answering my questions about my father."

Addy drove down the highway alongside other cars without shifting through lanes like she had earlier. Her heavy eyes were glued to the road, making me wonder if she was listening to anything that came out of my mouth.

"You probably already know that Lucifer wasn't always bad." I looked at her as I spoke, waiting for any reaction her face might unveil. "He was actually God's favorite angel, his right hand."

Above us, the dark heavens transformed into a light blue with a smidge of yellow along the skyline, but instead of watching the transformation, I took the whole picture in. I saw the colors of the waking sun glow against my skin, warming me as if I had my wings wrapped around me. Beside me, Addy's dark-brown eyes glimmered in the soft light. The rays even revealed reddish strands in her hair.

"He was God's most loved son." I tipped my head to see her face better, hoping to read her thoughts through body language, but she had a dead expression on. "And hypothetically, you could say he was like a spoiled first child."

We drove by a few stores before a green sign that read *"376 West Pittsburgh"* emerged on the right, and Addy sped up, hurrying to take the exit.

"But Lucifer didn't like that God made all the decisions. He wanted to have free will, and things spiraled from there."

Addy glanced at me. "I know this. A quick google search will tell you all that." She took the far-left lane and pressed down harder on the gas pedal. Her car's engine rumbled, slowing down for a split second before taking off faster than before. "Tell me something I don't know. Why is he doing this *now?*"

She was right, of course. Most humans knew the basic facts; Lucifer had made sure of that. He wanted to have more power, more control over heavenly decisions, and God refused. An angel was an angel, and God was God. But Lucifer couldn't stand that.

Still, this young woman that sat beside me wasn't just an ordinary human who happened to know the basics. Addy was Lucifer's daughter. She had been living a normal life, as far as I could tell, up until last night. How could I tell her that she was a pawn? That her whole existence was orchestrated?

"You might not like what I have to say."

"I don't care. I need to know everything if I'm going to have any control over the situation."

Another exit emerged, taking us to Grant Street. Addy slowed down at this point. We drove by old churches and tall buildings with raised flags at their entrances. The streets were small, and everything else was huge.

My eyes drifted upward, searching for the point where the buildings touched that bright, warm sun. "Wow."

"What?" Addy watched me in between glances at the road.

"Nothing." I continued looking around while I told her what I knew. "Lucifer didn't just start this war now. We've been—" A knot tightened in my throat, and I pushed back tears. I couldn't call myself an angel anymore. "The angels have been fighting Lucifer since his fall. That's how long he's been planning a war. But he has always failed."

Addy stopped at a red light and regarded me. "And that's why he needs me?"

"Yes."

"And he made me for that reason?"

"Yes."

Her chest swelled and deflated several times in the span of five seconds. She turned to the road and stared at the light until it flashed green, and she took off, her face losing all expression again.

"You're probably not the only child he has," I said. "Chances are, he made many in the hope they'll do his bidding here on Earth."

She sneered. "And what good would that do? He wants to fight God, right? What is he going to gain from people? People are weak."

I thought of her, how she had punched me in the face a couple of hours ago. For a small person, she was not weak. I smiled. "Don't underestimate humans. They can surprise you. And to answer your question, Lucifer doesn't want a few people. If I know him at all, I can tell you that he's planning on making a huge army whose souls are his. And with that, he can take down God's angels."

"So, he wants to take God's place?"

"No. He can't do that, even if he destroys all the angels. God is immortal and strong. Lucifer's true goal is to gain a large following so he can be worshipped like our Father. He would never admit it, but he desperately wants God's admiration. He looks up to him, but he wants his approval for all the wrong reasons, and he's rebelling in a catastrophic way."

Addy fell quiet. She turned down a narrow street and drove for a few minutes before turning at the light.

I had no idea if we were close to our destination, but I was tired of sitting with my back inclined forward. It didn't hurt so much anymore. There was a small twinge in my shoulders, though it wasn't anything that would kill me.

As if she had read my mind, Addy asked, "How's your back?"

I shifted in my seat, trying to get more comfortable and lose the stiffness in my lower back. "Better, I think."

"Good." She directed her piercing gaze at me. "I have another question for you."

I felt a tug on my insides and found myself swimming in the depths of a brown river, getting pulled down, drowning. "Go ahead," I said, unable to look anywhere but into her almond eyes.

Addy looked away, leaving me to blink the daze off.

"Why did you fall from heaven?"

Chapter Seven

ADELAIDE

Adriel didn't answer my question right away. He closed his eyes and remained still for a few seconds.

"I did something bad," he said at last. He looked out the window and avoided all eye contact. It was kind of funny, since he *had* been staring at me the entire ride.

"I figured that." Those burns on his back were clear in my mind, raw and red like pomegranate. However, they didn't tell me much. "What could be so bad that your wings got burned, but not bad enough to make you go to hell?"

He clenched his jaw so tightly that I could see his muscles flexing through his cheek.

We were ten minutes away from the apartment. I slowed down in the hopes of learning more about him before arriving at our destination. Just as I was about to say something to end the awkward silence, I heard knuckles cracking and looked to find his left hand fisted and pressing down against his leg.

"I was a guardian angel," he said, "to a single mom whose son had locked-in syndrome, which basically left him paralyzed and unable to talk."

I tried picturing Adriel in his angel form with his wings. If he looked anything like Lucifer before he fell in the vision forced upon me after drinking from the chalice, Adriel's wings would've been huge and white. Maybe he even used those wings to fight off demons when he was doing his guardian duty.

From the corner of his eye, Adriel glimpsed at me. When our eyes met, he drew back, turning to the window again.

"The kid was fourteen, but he was getting worse. My charge . . . his mom, Jenna, was depressed watching him in that state. It was like watching him trapped in a dead body. So, when she . . ."

He choked on his words and fell silent for a moment, leaving me to wonder if guardian angels felt the same emotions their humans felt.

"So, when she decided it would be best to end his life, I didn't guide her against it. I let it happen."

I pulled into Sunny Meadows Private Residences, where Lizzy and I lived. I had just a few minutes to get information out of him before we went upstairs. I thought of the questions I needed to ask and said, "How do angels guide people? Can they show themselves?"

He seemed surprised by the detailed question, but he answered anyway. "No, we communicate on a subconscious level. People call it their 'gut instinct,' but it's just the guardians guiding them."

I parked the car in front of my apartment building and shuffled in my seat to study him.

Hours ago, I had wanted nothing to do with him, and now he was the closest tie I had to Reed. Was it cruel of me to ask him tough questions? Probably. But those questions were the only way I could learn enough about heaven and hell.

"And God kicked you out because you let the lady kill her son?"

"Yes."

"Why didn't he send you to hell?"

Adriel took off his seat belt and finally looked at me. "I don't know. I've been trying to figure that out myself."

†

With my duffle bag in hand, I led Adriel up the stairs to the third floor. He seemed stronger than earlier, walking with his back straight even though it rubbed against that maroon sweatshirt I'd stolen from the hospital.

It was seven thirty in the morning, which meant that Lizzy was up and getting ready to head to the modeling studio where she worked. At the door, I gave Adriel a final once-over. He looked normal enough, or at least as normal as a person wearing socks without shoes in public could look.

"Okay, here we go." I pushed the door open and moved past the pumpkin Lizzy had set near the entrance. Though Lizzy knew Halloween wasn't for three more weeks, she couldn't resist.

Inside, Lizzy stood by the kitchen counter, spreading almond butter on a slice of whole wheat bread, her morning ritual. In front of her, she had a bowl of thinly sliced bananas. Her eyes lit up when she saw me a second before her brows raised in question at the unfamiliar man standing by the door.

"Hi." She gawked at Adriel with her head tilted to the side the way she always did when she saw an attractive man.

I threw my bag on the floor. "Hey. I decided to come home early."

"And . . ." She pointed at Adriel standing beside me. She wasn't smiling anymore. In that second, I had a feeling I knew what she was going to say. "That's not Devin."

No, he wasn't Devin. Pushing back the lump in my throat, I swallowed, took a deep breath, and said the first lie I could come up with. "This is my cousin, Adriel."

Lizzy's face brightened. She dropped the bread and spreading knife onto her plate and rushed toward us with her wedge shoes thumping against the wooden floor. "Addy's never mentioned you." She stuck her hand out at Adriel. "I'm Lizzy."

Adriel hesitated for a second before realizing that she wanted him to shake her hand.

"Nice to meet you," he said.

"You too." When she dropped his hand, she grabbed mine and pulled me toward her room down the hall. "Will you excuse us a second, Adriel? I just need to talk to Addy really quick."

Over my shoulder, I saw Adriel give a single nod. His eyes followed me all the way into the other room until Lizzy shut the door behind us.

"So," Lizzy started. She sat on her spacious turquoise bed and patted the spot beside her. "That makes you the second Addy in the family."

I sat down and raised an eyebrow at her. "What do you mean?"

"Addy is short for Adelaide, but Addy could also be short for Adriel."

"Yeah, I guess so."

A peppermint scent washed the room, coming from the diffuser on Lizzy's nightstand. On the chair by her closet was a baby-blue men's button-down shirt. It looked like it belonged to Nate, our neighbor.

"That's awesome! There are two Addy Shaws around." The corners of her mouth quirked up. She pulled her blonde strands in a high ponytail. "He's cute. Is he dating anyone?"

A snicker escaped my lips when I thought of the fallen angel having a romantic relationship with Lizzy. Adriel, who seemed to struggle with a simple handshake, and my bubbly best friend. It was just too ridiculous.

Lizzy didn't seem to think so. She let her hair fall and crossed her arms. "What's so funny?" A frown took over her face. "You don't want me to date your cousin?"

"Shh." I put a hand over her mouth. "He could hear us if you talk louder." When I felt safe she wouldn't make a fuss, I released her.

She kept her arms crossed. "Why did you laugh?"

"I'm sorry. He's just . . ." An angel? Someone I didn't know before last night? "He's just a crazy cousin. A big clown."

"A clown?"

"Yup. He's a clown. He puts on that big red nose and plays with balloons. He's a big hit at birthday parties, though."

She rose from the bed. "Really? But he looks so elegant."

Clearly, she hadn't noticed his socks. Or my sweaty clothes.

I shrugged and pointed at the shirt on the chair. "Isn't that Nate's?"

It was her turn to giggle. "Shut up! It's nothing, okay?"

"Whatever you say, chief."

After giving me a meaningful look that said, "Don't speak of this again," Lizzy opened the door and headed into the living room. I followed her.

Adriel was studying the oil painting of a woman sitting with her bare back to the artist that Lizzy and I had placed above the couch. When he realized we'd come out, he looked away, flustered. He glanced between the two of us, seeming unsure of what to do.

Lizzy smiled at him, grabbed her purse off one of the kitchen counter stools, took her breakfast, and headed for the main door. "I'm off. See you both later."

Once she closed the door, I took a deep breath and ushered Adriel to the bathroom. He tailed after me down the small hallway. I opened the door to my room, which was perpendicular to Lizzy's room, and led him past my bed and desk, where all my folders, sketches, and work projects lay. When I opened the bathroom door, I let him go in first.

"So, I figured you don't know how to use any of these things." I pointed at the toilet, sink, and shower in the sliding glass enclosure. "But you probably should, or you're going to end up in some embarrassing situations."

He placed a hand against the wall and smirked. "I may not have used a bathroom before, but I do have an idea about it."

I wasn't sure why, but I felt my face turn into a bright tomato. How ridiculous! Trying to help a man who had been a guardian angel; he should have been telling me what to do, not the other way around. I took a step back and laughed at myself for being an idiot. Surely he knew a thing or two about the importance of relieving the bladder.

"Thank you for the gesture, though." He covered his stomach with his hand. "Besides, you're right. I think I do need to use the bathroom."

"Oh." I took a few more steps back. "Okay. There's soap right there, and if you want to use the shower, there's shampoo. You can find a clean towel in the cabinet right there." I pointed above the toilet. "I'll go find you some new clothes to wear and I'll leave them right outside the door."

The bathroom door clicked shut. I dashed for the closet, searching the floor for any of Devin's shirts that I threw down there in my crazy state after the breakup. I found several and clutched them tightly, struggling to keep the tears away. They smelled of Devin and his spicy aftershave.

"Damn it," I muttered and threw them back on the floor.

The past week had ruined those shirts for me. Devin's new girlfriend probably had a bunch of them in her room. I was the ex, the reject.

I picked one of the shirts at random, trying to pretend it didn't belong to Devin, and tossed it at the bathroom door. It slid down and lay there like a lumpy ball. Once it hit the floor, I didn't look at it. I hurried to Lizzy's room and yanked her closet open. Somewhere in there had to be some men's pants, most likely belonging to Nate.

Staying as calm as possible, I delved into the jungle that was her closet. Dresses, shirts, and skirts of all lengths—both fancy and casual—clustered together without room to breathe. Occasionally, I couldn't figure out where one item ended and another began. Just as I was about to give up, I found a pair of men's jeans smooshed against one of Lizzy's casual shirts in the corner of the closet. I snatched it from its hiding place and went back to my room, where I dumped it over Devin's shirt.

With that done, I hurried out of the room with my keys in hand. In the living room, I threw the main door open, scampered out, and proceeded to slam the door shut without stopping to lock it. I ran downstairs, taking a moment to breathe only when I got back in my car.

And I was off.

I drove aimlessly at first. Reed kept creeping into my mind. I pictured him with bloody fingers and a sweaty face, so pale he looked like he'd die if he stayed in the heat long. My baby brother. My best friend before anyone else. My buddy in crime. What would I do if I lost him? And to Lucifer, of all people?

Tears trickled down my face. I blinked them back. No. I wouldn't lose control over the situation. I would get him out even if I had to sell my own soul to the devil. Which I may have already done.

My car stopped. I found myself in front of another apartment building, one surrounded by large oak trees. I stepped out and stood, frozen, for a few minutes. When I got the courage to make a move, I marched upstairs.

On the second floor, I knocked on the first door. No one answered. I knocked harder and harder and harder, my knocks turning to bangs. After what seemed like forever, someone unlatched the chain on the other side and opened the door. I pulled my hand away, feeling an ache in my now-red knuckles.

Devin stared at me, obviously confused. He didn't smile, and the dimples I'd come to love stayed hidden.

"Addy?" His eyes traveled from my head down, probably wondering why I was dripping sweat. "What happened?"

Not waiting for an invitation, I pushed past him. My shoulder brushed against his side, and I felt a chill go down my spine. I planted my feet in the center of the living room and crossed my arms, waiting for the right words to come out of my mouth.

He stood in front of me with his hands in his pockets, wearing sweatpants and an old, wrinkly white T-shirt I used to love because of how soft its cottony fabric felt whenever I wrapped my arms around him.

I shoved the memory out of my head and opened my mouth to speak. "Did you cheat on me?"

His eyebrows lifted and he sneered. "What?"

"You heard me."

Silence fell. I could hear a car pull up outside, its tires turning into a parking space and crunching against the gravel.

Devin chuckled and ran a hand through his hair. "Come on . . . I've moved on. You should too."

It had barely been a week since he'd broken up with me without a reason. Moving on seemed ridiculous. What I wanted was for him to admit his infidelity. Maybe then I could try to put him behind me.

"Devin," I said, and took a step closer. I fixed my eyes on him as I spoke. "Did you ever love me?"

As if I had enchanted him, Devin kept his eyes on mine and didn't blink or move away. "Of course I loved you."

I took two more steps and stood just a few inches from him. "Did you cheat on me?"

His lips parted like he was about to answer, but no words came out. I pushed myself against him, resting my hands on his chest, all while keeping my eyes locked on his.

"Devin, I need to know. Did you cheat on me?"

"I . . . didn't."

Against my thigh, I felt his cell phone vibrate. My eyes still on his, I dug my hand into his pocket and pulled out the phone.

"What are you doing?" His tone was hard, though he didn't try to pull away or take the phone from me.

With the phone's lock screen still on, I glanced at the text and sighed. It was just a message from work. I put the phone back in his pocket and looked at him. "Devin, I want the truth."

He blinked a few times before freezing again. "Addy, I didn't want to hurt you." He moved his head closer to mine. "I'm so sorry."

"What are you sorry for?" I needed to hear it. I needed to hear the words.

"I slept with someone else when we were together."

"When did it happen?"

Devin blinked like the spell had broken. But he didn't move away. "I'm so sorry, Addy." He looked at me with wet eyes. "It was two months ago, and it's been eating at me."

I dropped my hands from his chest and moved away. "How could you?" He had made me feel like I was the one who messed up. I'd felt guilty thinking that it was me who screwed things up, who made him fall out of love. But it wasn't my fault; it was his.

"You deserve better." He grabbed my hands and pulled me against him. "I'm sorry, Addy." He rested his forehead against mine. "I'm sorry."

I felt moisture on my cheeks. It took me a moment to realize that it was his tears, not mine.

"Don't say sorry. That word doesn't mean anything anymore coming from you." I pushed him away and unsheathed Reed's Swiss Army knife from my back pocket.

"Addy . . ."

Ignoring him, I drew the reamer out from the knife. It was small and sharp and looked like the offspring of a small knife and a big needle.

"Addy, please. I need you to forgive me."

I didn't want to look at him. I reached for his hand and flipped it, palm up. The hand that held the knife trembled, but I let the pointy end of the reamer make contact with his wrist. Without thinking too much about it, I cut the letter L into his skin.

"Ow!" He jumped back and clutched his bleeding wrist with his other hand. "What did you do?"

My eyes watched the blood ooze out. The "L" imprint looked a lot like blotchy red ink on paper.

Devin's eyes met mine, though he wasn't the same as a moment ago. His pupils were dilated and dark. "Addy, why?"

"Oh my God." The knife fell from my hand and landed on the carpet. I stood there for a second, watching the blue in his eyes get distorted. My legs trembled, but I managed to reach down, grab the knife, and run out of the apartment, leaving Devin with Lucifer's initial on his arm.

Back in my car, I threw the knife into the glove compartment and raced out of the neighborhood. My head throbbed, and my heart drummed in my ears.

This can't be happening! This can't be happening! What have I done? The words repeated in my head like an endless recording. *What have I done?* His eyes, his blue eyes, the pupils expanding, turning the oceans into black pits—that was all I saw.

I reached for my phone on the dashboard and dialed my mother's number, something I hadn't done in months. She picked up on the third ring.

"Well, if it isn't my daughter," Erica said. Noise of people talking and laughing erupted in the background. "What made you call?"

Chitchat was the last thing I wanted to do. "Who's my dad? Tell me everything you remember about him."

She hesitated on the other end of the line and whispered, "Hey, this isn't a good time. I'm at the nail salon."

"No. I don't have time for your excuses. I need to know, and I need to know now."

"There's not much to tell. I didn't know him."

"Try to remember."

She sighed. "He was tall and had your eyes. He never told me his name. I just don't know. I was with another guy at the time, but we did a blood test, so we know you're not his daughter."

I reached Sunny Meadows and parked in my usual spot. "Anything else you remember?"

She thought for a moment and said, "He was charming. That's all I can tell you."

"Great. Thanks."

"Hey, Addy?"

She sounded like she was smiling, and that made me cringe. She was probably prepping herself for a wild date.

"Yes?" I said.

"I miss you."

The words made my stomach churn. I knew deep down they were lies. I still remembered how she had come home drunk one night after Grandma Di, her mom, died. She'd lashed out at Reed and me, calling us names and telling us she should have given us up for adoption. Those words back then had been the truth. She had meant them.

"Addy?"

73

Not wanting to go down that road, I hung up. As soon as I did, I remembered Devin. I had just done . . . something to him, and I didn't know if there was a way to take it back.

Chapter Eight

ADRIEL

Water trickled down my body, warm and tender. It washed the dried blood off my back and knees, making me feel almost like myself again. Almost.

Minutes seemed to go by. I didn't move. I stood underneath the showerhead, relishing in my Father's masterwork on Earth. Humans had it good . . . really good.

When I got out of the shower, I stepped in front of the mirror and studied myself. I had never seen my face; never needed to. I'd had my wings, and they were more than enough to satisfy me. However, as I stood looking at my reflection, I felt like any other human with a fragile body.

I shifted so that my back faced the mirror and looked over my shoulder at the burns. Hours ago, my skin was raw, but now red, bulging scars had replaced the blisters. I ran my fingers over some of the scars and felt a sting. They were obviously still healing, but they weren't as bad as they should've been.

Outside Addy's bathroom door, a pair of jeans and a crumpled T-shirt waited for me on the floor. After wrapping my shroud around my bottom, I put on the clothes and inspected myself in the mirror once more.

The first five-o'clock shadow I'd ever had screamed of my mortality. Along with the blue veins and the beating heart, I was a walking, talking man with numbered days. How many days exactly? I didn't know.

My reflection was still eyeing me when my vision blackened. From within the darkness, a single firefly appeared, its light blinking on and off as it hovered inches from my nose.

"Hey," I said. "Who are you?"

The firefly froze in place, its big black eyes watching me. I waved my hand around, trying to touch it, but I felt nothing where the tiny creature should have been.

"You're not a firefly, are you?"

The insect flapped its wings again and flew away. I tried to follow it and crashed into the bathroom sink.

"Wait, where are you going?"

The firefly had left.

Everything stayed black for a few seconds, though my senses were more aware of everything around me. Out of nowhere, Addy came into view. She wasn't in the room with me; I could tell from the shadowy edges of my vision. She wore the same clothes she had earlier, but she was in someone else's living room. Dozens of dirty plates and old takeout boxes sat on the coffee table behind her. Her eyes were wet and red.

"Did you cheat on me?" she asked someone.

I concentrated on the direction she was looking at. My view shifted to the left, stopping when a man with a slightly crooked nose came into view.

The man laughed. Addy didn't think he was funny. After arguing with him for a moment, she pressed her body against his.

"Devin, I need to know," she said. "Did you cheat on me?"

Devin's still eyes mirrored Addy's angry face for a long time before he finally gave her the answer she seemed to want. Still, even that answer made her angry.

"Addy, please. I need you to forgive me," he said.

The pupils of his blue eyes started dilating. Addy didn't notice, because she was digging one of the tools in her knife into his wrist. When she finished and his skin had a bloody *L* on it, she looked up.

That was when she noticed his eyes turning pitch-black.

"Oh my God."

†

I sprinted out of the bathroom when my eyesight returned and rushed from room to room, only to find Addy gone, like my vision had revealed. I felt in my gut that it was too late; Addy had begun Lucifer's mission.

My fear was proven right when I flung the main apartment door open and found Addy with her keys in hand and tears running down her face.

77

Her eyes met mine and she opened her mouth in a sob. "I screwed up." She wiped her eyes with the sleeve of her sweatshirt, but more tears fell.

Her hands were shaking. I grabbed one of them and pulled her inside the apartment. She didn't struggle. When we got into the kitchen, she staggered against the counter and cried.

"I messed up so bad."

Wanting to get to the bottom of her actions, I straightened her up and turned her to face me. "You just sold his soul. Why did you do that?"

She was staring at the floor. Upon my words, she looked up, eyes wide. "How do you know what happened?"

I realized I hadn't told her about my visions, how I'd seen her brother in hell and now her and that man named Devin.

"I've been having visions since I became human." I shrugged like this wasn't a big deal and leaned against the counter. "That's not what's important right now, though. Why did you cut Lucifer's initial on that man?"

Addy paced the room, stopping just once to grab a water bottle from the fridge. "That's what I was asked to do. I help create Lucifer's army by marking people with Lucifer's initial using their blood, and Reed goes free. Otherwise, he dies. What else can you expect me to do?" She took a gulp of water and set the bottle down on the counter. "My brother is more important than all those souls combined."

I watched her for a minute without saying a word.

"What?" She threw her hands into the air and raised her tone. "I'm sorry, but that's the truth. My brother matters to me!"

"It's not the only way to get Reed back. You didn't have to sell that guy's soul."

She stopped pacing and looked me dead in the eyes. "That *guy?*" Her nose wrinkled. "That guy deserves what he got."

"Then why are you so nervous?" I moved away from the counter and stood tall in front of her. "If you truly believe that you did the right thing, why are you acting guilty?"

She flinched. "Because." She flapped her sweatshirt collar against her chest to draw air in and cool herself off. "Because I wish I didn't have to be the one to hand him what he deserves."

"You mean you don't want to act like God."

"No, I don't."

"Then don't help Lucifer. He might be your father, but that doesn't mean you have to help him. We'll get Reed out another way."

"He is *not* my father," she hissed. "I might have his genetics, but I'd burn in hell before I make him my dad." She took off her sweatshirt, revealing a red tank top underneath. "And how do you propose we get Reed out?" She threw the sweatshirt on the kitchen stool.

With her glowering up at me, I couldn't think of an answer. "We'll think of something."

"Yeah? Well, that's not good enough."

She took off for her room and left me pondering everything on my own. Was she right to go along with Lucifer's plan?

Just like her, I'd messed up big time. I let a woman kill her son thinking I was doing the right thing. Where had that gotten me?

Addy didn't know any better. She wanted her brother back. And it just so happened that she was willing to do whatever it took, no matter the cost. I knew that much from her actions today.

Chapter Nine

ADELAIDE

Locking myself in my room was the easiest thing I did that day. Away from Adriel, Lucifer, Devin, and Erica, I felt like I was back in my old life for just a split second.

I threw myself across the bed and lay there, facedown on top of the white cover, muffling the moans that kept coming out of my throat. It was bad enough that Adriel saw me at my lowest point. I shuddered. The idea of him hearing me cry was worse.

Devin kept coming back to me. His eyes. His begging. His confusion.

The monster he became.

Two weeks ago, I had woken up beside him, felt his cold nose against my bare neck, kissed his lips, and had a good conversation about our plans that weekend. Now I'd lost him forever. Never again would I hold him and smile. No more would hearing his name bring me happiness.

My throat felt like it was being sliced in half and chopped into pieces to be thrown in a salad bowl for demented monkeys to feast on, and the harder I tried to push back the tears, the more the pain increased.

Adriel was out there in the living room doing God knew what, but it wasn't my responsibility to babysit him. Besides, everything started happening the minute he showed up. Though he was technically blameless in all this, I just didn't care.

No, I didn't care.

At some point while crying, my body surrendered to sleep.

✝

The wooden gate with the slithering snake for a handle stood big and menacing in my dream again. This time, however, it stood ajar.

Standing a foot away, I looked into the dim entrance with narrowed eyes. "Hello?"

No one answered.

I reached an arm into the darkness and instantly felt heat travel from my fingers all the way to my armpit, which started sweating. If this wasn't the entrance to hell, then nothing made sense. I swallowed and inched forward into the tunnel.

Fire blazed on either side of me, close enough that I felt its force but also far enough that it didn't scorch me like a human getting barbecued. I took one slow step at a time and avoided turning my head—not even half an inch—out of worry that my hair would burn. When I finally reached the end of the tunnel of fire and stood in an empty cavelike chamber, I was panting and dying for the chilly wind of October.

In the middle of the floor, not too far from me, a crack suddenly split off in many directions. The fissures grew bigger, tearing the ground and opening the earth up. A scream echoed in the room. It took me a second to realize it had come out of me.

I started to run, but when the entirety of the ground got sucked into the abyss, I got dragged down with it.

†

I pushed myself off the bed, feeling sick to my stomach, and stood in total darkness. It was night outside. I glanced at the alarm clock on my nightstand and saw 7:00 p.m. flashing, which meant I'd slept almost the entire day.

Sweat drenched my chest and tank top. I wanted nothing more than to feel the cold air outside. I lifted the glass of the window next to me and let the icy chill inside. The rush of wind cooled me down, helped me breathe again.

I left the window open and went into the bathroom. I hadn't showered since yesterday morning. I couldn't take the sticky, stinking sweat permeating me and my clothes. I took off my tank top and jeans, mentally promising to burn them later, and hopped in the shower.

After using half of Pennsylvania's water, I left the bathroom and searched my closet for just the right thing to wear. When I found it, I slipped on the skintight, one-shoulder black dress and adjusted the lace hem. I brushed the knots out of my wet hair and applied eyeliner and mascara to my eyes.

Just as I finished, someone knocked on the door.

"Yes?"

"It's me," Lizzy said and came into the room. "Woah, look at you." She eyed my dress with a smile. "Is it date night?"

She still thought I was with Devin. Eventually, she would notice he wasn't coming around. There was no need for me to talk about it. "No, Devin's not coming along."

Her eyebrow arched up. "Then where are you heading?"

"Euphoria."

I grabbed my red clutch bag from the closet, stuffed my keys and wallet into it, and headed out of the room. Lizzy followed.

"I was thinking of going there myself," she said. "Will your cousin be going?"

"Cousin?"

"Adriel." She tilted her head toward the sleeping figure on the living room couch.

Oh. I stared at him for a moment, wondering whether he was comfortable on his stomach with his legs extending far beyond the armrest.

"I don't think so," I said. "He is recovering from a terrible back burn."

To show her that I was right, I marched in my stilettos to where Adriel lay and lifted the shirt up, uncovering the flesh on Adriel's back. To my surprise, the burns had almost healed. In their place were red scars, ones that should've taken many more weeks to form.

"He looks fine to me." Lizzy stepped closer to him. "Man, is he a heavy sleeper or what?"

I shrugged. "Must be the medication."

"Well, now he can come along to the club."

"Maybe."

My stomach growled, reminding me that I hadn't eaten in a day. Lizzy shadowed me all the way to the kitchen and stared at the leftovers inside the fridge with me. Homemade hummus dip, vegetarian lasagna, soy milk, and a bowl full of kale salad. I didn't want any of those things; they were Lizzy's. I grabbed the one thing that appealed to me: the days-old spring roll container. I took one spring roll out and chomped it down. Lizzy stood in silence with her hands on the counter, waiting for me to finish.

"Lizzy, you're being weird."

She crossed her arms. "That's only because you are." She looked at Adriel on the couch and back at me. "I'm not blind. I saw how sweaty you both were this morning."

I cringed. I grabbed a water bottle from the fridge and stared at its label for a long time. "So?"

"You've never mentioned a cousin named Adriel before."

"So, I've never mentioned him. That's not a reason to go all Sherlock on me."

Lizzy tapped her clean and perfectly filed nails against the counter. "Addy, I've met your family. It pretty much consists of your brother. You yourself said you've never met any of your relatives and don't even know who your dad is. I know when something's off."

I twisted the cap off the bottle and took a swig. When I set the bottle down, I was ready to take off. I started to head toward the door, but her words stopped me in place.

"Adelaide Shaw, where were you last night and why are you avoiding Devin?"

My head fell back. Unable to evade the questions anymore, I let out a groan. "He won't be coming back. Okay?" I stared at the empty white wall above the door and tightened my hold on my clutch bag, making it wrinkle under my fingers. "He cheated."

Lizzy didn't say anything and didn't move. I took that as my cue to leave.

Chapter Ten

ADRIEL

My wings felt heavy as they kept me in the air, flapping slowly just above the bed. Below me, Jenna, the human I protected, sat by her sleeping son's side. She stroked his face and hummed a slow melody.

Matt had closed his eyes just a moment before. Jenna placed his arms over his stomach and chest, likely trying to give him the most comfort he could get. He couldn't move on his own. It was up to her to help with that.

I could sense the sadness stewing inside her. Her son would never have a life, never make friends, never go to college. She would have to tuck his arms this way and that for the rest of his days. She would have to bathe him like a newborn.

Tears fell down Jenna's cheeks and made their way to her chin, where they fell, one by one, over Matt.

The worst part was that she knew Matt hated being dependent on her. Every time she fed him, his eyes danced back and forth, begging her to make things different.

On the days she took him to the park in his special wheelchair, he watched the kids leaping from monkey bar to monkey bar with all the freedom in the world. Their limbs worked just fine, while he had to sit there with his head stuck in the same exact position and stare out like a ghost trapped inside a corpse.

Jenna knew all those things. She knew how badly her son hurt. For the past five out of fifteen years of his life, she had known. And I, being her guardian angel, knew that what she wanted to do, though wrong, was the only way to make things right.

So that night, I let her do it. I let her release him from his pain.

†

Someone kept shaking me. "Adriel? Dude, wake up."

I remembered Addy and the punch she'd landed across my face at the hospital. Was she back for more punches?

"Rosy Cheeks?" I opened my eyelids just a crack.

Inches away, Addy's yellow-haired friend Lizzy crouched and gawked at me. A strong-smelling perfume wafted off her skin. It wasn't bad, just too sweet. She wore a shimmering gold top that came an inch short of her belly button, an unzipped leather jacket, and tight leather pants to match. She smiled when she saw I was awake.

"You were mumbling in your sleep." She rested a slim hand on my bicep. "I think you were having a nightmare."

I sat up, forcing her to drop her hand to her side, and glanced around the room. "Where's Addy?"

Lizzy stood and grabbed a wallet off the living room table. "We're going to find her."

"We?"

"You and me, silly." She placed a pair of black sneakers in front of me and waited for me to put them on. When I finished, she started walking toward the door, her heels clacking. "By the way, I know you're not her cousin."

Jumping to my feet, I hurried after her. "She told you?"

"Kind of."

Lizzy locked the apartment and almost ran down the stairs. I tried keeping up but was out of breath after the first floor. My legs had never needed to work this much.

"Hurry up," Lizzy shouted from the bottom stair.

When I finally got to the parking lot, she was fiddling with her keys.

I ran a hand through my hair. "Sorry."

She spun around and headed to her car, not waiting for me to catch my breath. She was a lot like Addy, impatient and slowing down for no one.

We were on the road stuck at a red light when she looked at me and asked, "Did you sleep with Addy?"

"Uh . . ." I crossed my arms over my chest and fidgeted in my seat. "No."

"You sure?"

"We don't have those kinds of feelings."

Lizzy put her finger on the tip of her nose and giggled. "You make it sound like having 'those kinds of feelings' is crazy talk."

After fidgeting some more in my seat for the remainder of the ride, she pulled over at a club with a sign out front that read *"Euphoria"* and ushered me to the doors where a tall, buff man with a scarab tattoo peering out of his V-neck let us in after a flirtatious exchange with Lizzy. All she had to do was coil a straight strand around her finger and smile at him.

"That's how it's done!" she screamed over the music and flashed her white teeth at me.

"That's how what is done?"

"We got in for free."

Lizzy stepped to the bar and looked around the crowded room. A guy came toward her with drinks in hand, and she smiled at him.

"Right on time," he yelled over the blaring music and handed her a drink.

Lizzy nudged me and said, "Adriel, this is Nate, our neighbor." Her eyes swayed back to Nate, glimmering with a secret.

Nate leaned in and planted a kiss on her cheek before reaching his hand out to shake mine. "Hey."

"Nice to meet you," I said, "but I have to go find Addy."

I didn't wait around. I dove into the crowd of dancing bodies. The music pulsed within me, making my heart leap like it was going to fall right out of my chest. I pushed through people, looking from face to face to make sure they weren't the woman I was searching for.

When I got to the other side, I was ready to give up. Addy clearly wasn't at the club.

And that was when I saw her, across the room near the DJ booth, wearing a tight-fitting black dress. Her arms were wrapped around a man's neck, and she brushed her body against his as they moved to the beat of the wild song. For a fleeting moment, my eyes were hypnotized, moving over every inch of her, gliding over her legs and trespassing on other territories. I swallowed. *Angels don't think this way.* I blinked out of the daze.

After putting her hand on the back of the man's head, Addy pulled him down toward her and said something in his ear. The man didn't blink, but he seemed to like whatever she said because he grinned at her and gave her his hand, palm up.

"Stop!" I yelled.

No one heard me over the deafening music.

I shoved myself into the crowd again, pushing through to the other side. Some people gave me dirty looks, while others refused to move out of the way. By the time I reached Addy, the man's arm had blood dripping from it.

"What have you done?" I shouted from behind her.

She spun around to face me. At first, her eyes were wide, but then they softened and looked a bit sad.

"Just doing my job."

"This isn't your job, though."

She placed her arms on my chest and looked at me. "I have to bring Reed back, and that's what I'm doing." She gave me a small shove and stomped past me.

The man she was dancing with laughed. I stepped up to him and studied his pupils, hoping by some miracle the *L* cut wouldn't work on him.

"What are you looking at, man?" he hollered.

His eyes had glazed over, taking on a charcoal color.

Not wanting to start a fight with a demon without my wings, I raised my palms in front of me and backed away. "My apologies!" I stepped around people to search for Addy and saw her exiting the club. I ran after her.

She had reached her car in the parking lot when I made it to the door.

"Addy, wait!"

She stopped and crossed her arms.

A few people to my left lingered against the side of the building with cigarettes in hand. When a gust of wind came by, the acrid smell of clinging smoke hit me. My nose wrinkled in disgust, and I moved away from the group.

Addy's big eyes looked up at mine when I made it to her car. Her face was still, emotionless.

"What you did in there," I said, "that was really stupid. You turned another man."

"I did what I had to do. Like I already said, Reed comes first." She opened her car door and looked at me. "Are you coming or what?"

I hesitated for a second. When Addy stepped inside, I moved to the passenger side and hopped in, unsure of what was going on, why she was letting me go with her.

"Addy, what makes you think you had to do that?"

She started the engine and pulled out of the lot like a leopard in a wild-deer chase. I braced myself for another speedy ride.

"You seem to forget that Lucifer had a demand, and if I don't do what he wants, he'll kill my brother."

"But how do you know that he will keep his word? Just because you're helping him doesn't guarantee he won't hurt Reed."

A long, ceaseless honk jolted me in my seat. The car came to an abrupt, screeching stop behind a white pickup truck. I looked at Addy, who still had her hand on the horn.

"Idiot," she said, cutting in front of the truck.

"Addy." I needed her to understand, to get her to think for a moment. "You can't trust Luci—"

"I don't have a choice." Her tone was rigid.

"You do."

She pursed her lips. We drove in silence all the way back to her apartment.

Chapter Eleven

ADELAIDE

I woke up the next morning with my temples throbbing. Six people. I'd sold six people's souls to the devil yesterday. The repercussions had to be big. Like ending-up-eternally-in-hell big.

No matter. It had to be done.

From the other room, I heard giggles and laughter. Because the house tended to be quiet early in the mornings, the noise struck me as odd. I changed out of my pajamas and into casual clothes and left the bedroom.

In the kitchen, Lizzy stood slicing bananas and strawberries while a pan with pancake batter heated on top of the stove.

The aroma of freshly brewed coffee encircled the entire room, awakening my senses and my desire for a sweet sip. Directly in front of Lizzy, Adriel, who was still in yesterday's clothes, sat on one of the counter stools with a grin on his face. He was in the middle of sharing some sort of wisdom with her. Pausing at the end of the hallway, I watched him and wondered what an ex-angel had to tell a human fashionista.

"It's just a beautiful sight to see," he said. "Shades of green, bright pink, and the orange-yellows, all coming together and mixing and dancing."

Lizzy nibbled on a big piece of strawberry and set the rest of the fruit she had sliced in front of Adriel. "So, you lived in Alaska for a while?"

"Visited for a few years. It was a long time ago."

"Wow. I'll be sure to put the northern lights on my bucket list."

Adriel grabbed a piece of strawberry and a piece of banana and stuffed both into his mouth at once. He closed his eyes for a second before swallowing. "That's so delicious!"

I stepped forward into the kitchen. "Good morning."

Both turned to greet me, though Adriel's eyes seemed to do more than that.

Wanting to avoid his gaze, I set my sights on the coffee maker filled with warm, dark liquid. The pot called out to me. I made a dash for it, passing by Adriel and dodging his stare. When I reached the coffee, he spoke.

"Addy, could we talk?"

"About what?"

When Lizzy and I first moved to this apartment not long ago, we had made sure to always keep two mugs by the coffee maker. One—mine—looked like a cow with a tail for a handle, and the other—Lizzy's—looked like an insomniac owl with its eyes wide open. I grabbed my mug and poured myself some of the divine drink.

Adriel stood. "Can we talk in private?" He grabbed another piece of strawberry and started moving toward the hallway.

Though I doubted Lizzy knew anything, I still looked to her for answers. She shrugged like she knew what I was thinking.

Sighing, I put the coffee down and followed Adriel. He stood in front of my bedroom chewing the remnants of the fruit but didn't say a word until I opened the door and let him in. Using my heel, I shut the door after us for privacy. The minute it clicked against the wall, Adriel spoke.

"We need to talk about what happened at the club." His tone was rough, which kicked my defenses into gear. He paced around the room, pausing to look at my scattered work papers on the desk, most of which were of furniture and wall paint selections. "For your safety, and the safety of the rest of the world, you can't do anything Lucifer asks you to do anymore."

Of course, I knew Adriel was right. Back when I was a few years old, Erica used to drop baby Reed and me at her mother's house so that she could go out at night with her random boyfriends. During those frequent sleepovers, Grandma Di would teach me about Jesus and warn me to never let the devil tempt me. She was a devout Christian. I never took her too seriously as a kid. And Erica had obviously never taken her seriously, either, because she defied her every wish. Grandma Di died when I was just six, so her teachings had faded quickly. However, I knew now that she'd been right about the devil. He was real, and he was tempting—no, forcing—me to his side by using Reed.

And while I knew all of this to be true, I didn't want to admit that Adriel was right. With my hand perched on my hip,

I looked him square in the eyes. "Who are you to tell me what I should and shouldn't do? You're just a fallen angel."

Taking a deep breath, Adriel moved closer to me, close enough that I couldn't help but glance at the tight muscles of his chest that projected through the cotton shirt I'd given him.

"Listen." His voice was gentler now, and his eyes begged mine to get on the same page. "I might be a disgrace, but I still have my perception, and I can tell something is off. Lucifer is planning something big, something none of us ever expected."

He kept looking at me long after he finished talking, and since I had no idea how to respond, I stood there awkwardly looking back at him. One of us had to break the spell.

I lost the staring contest when I looked down.

"Addy?" He tilted his head down to look at me. "Do you understand what I'm saying?"

A quick nod did the job. He stepped away, satisfied. Still, while I did understand him, I didn't intend on following his empty guidance.

†

Secrets could kill, but only if discovered. That was my motto for the night as I slipped on a miniskirt and a black crop top with long bell sleeves and tiptoed out of my room, stopping just short of the living room.

The room was silent and dark, the only light coming from a salt-crystal lamp by the couch. Peeking past the wall of the hallway, I tried to see if anyone was in the kitchen. When I found no one, I rushed out of the apartment and locked the door behind me.

I chose Club Euphoria again. When I arrived, I examined myself one more time in the car's visor mirror. Drunk strangers on the dance floor would probably never notice, but anyone with clarity of mind would be able to see the worried crease between my brows. Still looking in the mirror, I practiced a seductive smile with teeth, and when I found one that didn't look forced, I stepped out. I tapped Lucy gently on the roof for some good luck, leaving a sweat mark on the paint from my clammy palm.

"Crap," I mumbled under my breath and wiped my hand against the fabric of my skirt.

At the door, Lukas, the bouncer, was checking people's IDs and deciding who to let in. He was like the god of the nightclub, rating people's worth based on age and appearance. The last time I had to stand in his long entrance line was the night I turned twenty-one. Strutting toward him now, I watched him turn his head and scan me from the head down, lingering on my bare stomach.

"Adelaide Shaw," Lukas said, giving me a grin. "Two nights in a row?"

The music blasted all the way to the door, shaking the earth and my heart.

I smiled back and touched Lukas lightly on the chest, my fingers sweeping over his scarab tattoo. "Are you sick of me?"

"Never." He drew the rope away from the door, giving me ample room to walk inside the club.

"Thanks, Lukas."

With a wink, he watched me go in.

Skimming over the crowded dance floor, I examined all the potential people in the room. A tan man wearing a gray vest stood in the corner of the bar shouting something into a brunette's ear. She gave him a sideways look and rolled her eyes. He didn't seem to notice, or at least, he didn't seem to care. On the dance floor, a drunk woman in her thirties was trying to pull the pants off the man next to her. Even though he was laughing, he kept breaking away.

So many. So many people whose absence might not make a difference for others.

After calculating which person to go for first, I decided on the unrelenting man at the bar who still harassed the brunette, even though she had shrugged him off multiple times. Besides, the dancing drunk woman would never have worked out. I didn't know how I would even begin to seduce her.

I snaked my way to the bar, eyes on my target. The man in the vest looked up, noticing me noticing him. I moved past him and the woman and glanced over my shoulder. Leaving the brunette alone, he was on my heels in seconds.

On the dance floor, I spun around, eyes fixed on him. He moved in, his hands reaching out to rest on my hips. The rhythm carried me, swaying me. Vest guy closed the distance between us, obviously excited to have finally succeeded in getting a female to look at him. To my bad luck, he smelled of curry and garlic.

I flashed him the smile I'd practiced and pulled his head closer, speaking in his ear. "Can you do something for me?"

Pulling back, his beady eyes gleamed with a need for approval. "Anything," he said.

His big lips parted like he was about to kiss me. I shook my head, stopping him.

I took his hand in mine and flipped it like I had with the six others, Devin included. Vest guy kept his mouth shut and waited, his other hand gripping my waist. I pulled out the reamer from Reed's Swiss Army knife, which had been tucked in my bra this whole time, and traced an *L* on his wrist. In the dimness of the club and its flashing lights, no one noticed anything. When blood began spilling out, I told vest guy to clutch the wound with his hand and leave it to dry up.

He blinked once, seeming to be in a trance as he stared at me. Then the white around his irises shifted to black, a sign that his soul was no longer his. One down. I quickly moved away, leaving him by himself on the deafening dance floor.

Once more, I walked around the room. Men and women, bodies on bodies. The bartenders, a man and a woman, busied themselves serving drinks. Around them, the people at the bar seemed to be getting along.

Glancing at the other side of the room, I found a man standing alone eyeing the crowd with a drink in hand. I headed his way. With all the people on the dance floor, I couldn't see him clearly, just the outline of him and his jaw-length brown hair. Still, he seemed like the perfect sacrifice, all by his lonesome.

Ten feet away from the man, I froze. His eyes found mine. He set his drink down on a table beside him. *Adriel.* He watched me with a mixture of anger and worry on his face. Like a regular human, he wore jeans and a white shirt with the top buttons unbuttoned, baring skin and collarbones at the base of a long, taut neck. My breath caught in my chest.

I turned to go, not waiting for him to interrogate me. Like last night, he had ruined my plans by being in the wrong place at the wrong time.

"Addy." He was behind me at the door in seconds, his hand spinning me around by the elbow.

I collided with him, no space between us. His firm hands wrapped around my waistline to steady me, his eyes on mine. Neither of us spoke. For a moment, I thought I saw his eyes drop to my lips. But it happened too fast, and when he opened his mouth to speak, I told myself that I'd imagined it. Not that I knew for sure, but I assumed angels didn't think that way, not even fallen ones. I felt crazy even thinking that him holding me like that might mean anything.

"You said you understood," he said.

"I never agreed to anything, though." I pulled away and kept walking, knowing he would trail behind me. Just a few rows down, my car waited. I hurried in its direction.

"What you're doing is dangerous, Addy. Are you aware of that?"

"What matters is bringing Reed back."

"You're being irrational here."

I spun around and pointed a finger at him. "No. That would be you. Doing nothing is irrational."

He closed his eyes. "I can't help you if you refuse to be helped."

"Then tell me, Mr. Bigshot." My finger was still gunned at him. When he came closer, it almost touched his chest. "What is your big plan?"

Adriel didn't get the chance to speak. Before he even opened his mouth, soft feathery wings twice my size encircled me, and I screamed.

"Melodramatic, are we?" a voice said.

The wings moved away, letting light back into my vision. Beside me stood an angel with a man's face, but I didn't see a hint of facial hair anywhere. Long, thick locks of brown hair covered the angel's head, reaching all the way down past his shoulders.

"Hello, Adelaide," he said, bowing with his wings outstretched on either side of him. "My name is Madadel. I am Reed's guardian."

At the mention of my brother's name, I jumped forward. "You're Reed's angel?"

"Yes."

I looked at Adriel, who had started pacing around the parking lot, seeming confused.

"Adriel?" I called out, but he ignored me.

"He cannot see or hear you." Madadel lifted his hands into the air and let them hover over something that flickered.

Upon a closer look, I noticed the translucent shield around the two of us, like a tent made of thin saran wrap that was so clear, it was almost as if it wasn't even there. I tried to poke it, but the shield moved with my finger, growing wider.

Madadel smiled. "Nice trick, huh?"

Taking my hand away from the shield, I glared at the angel.

"Why are you frowning, beautiful Adelaide?"

"You let my brother get kidnapped by a demon."

Madadel's wings ruffled in the breeze. "I did no such thing. I was not allowed to interfere."

Raising an eyebrow, I reminded him that he was interfering now by standing here in front of a human.

"No such thing," he repeated. "You have the devil's blood in you. You are not fully human."

"But I am a human, nonetheless."

"Still, you know of angels and demons. Besides, that is not what I meant at all. I simply could not go after Reed once he was taken to hell."

Adriel stood near us but had no clue we were there. He looked right through the shield, searching for me.

"Do you know him?" I asked Madadel.

Madadel smiled. "Of course! Adriel was my brother."

"Good." I reached out, making the shield stretch, and wound my hand around Adriel's. He jolted and looked down at his hand. I pulled him in. His worried eyes softened when he saw us.

"It's you," he said, looking at Madadel.

"It is me."

Music blared from the club. Under the rhythm, the shield pulsated the way water speakers leap up and down to a tune. I placed my hand against the thin wall of the shield and felt the beat pass through my arm and drift off across my body.

"Addy," Adriel said. "What's going on?"

I glanced between him and the angel, whom I scowled at. "He's Reed's guardian angel. He let him get taken to hell."

Adriel stared at Madadel's wings with awe, looking as if he might grab the soft feathers and run his fingers through them. He caught himself and shifted his gaze back to the angel, his fingers twitching at his side. "Madadel, what exactly are you doing here?"

"I came to warn Adelaide about her actions." Madadel wrapped his wings around himself and looked at me. "She is aiding Lucifer in raising an army, which makes it our job—the angels' job to stop her."

My hands fisted, and I advanced on him. "You let my brother get taken to hell, you piece of—"

"Addy." Adriel cut me off with a hard stare of disapproval before focusing on Madadel again. "She is right. An innocent boy is imprisoned in hell. We need to get him out."

It was Madadel's turn to frown. He glanced between the two of us. "I am afraid *you* cannot do anything. We, the angels, are doing everything in our power to figure out a way to get Reed back into this world." His wings extended, flapping like he was about to take off. "Take my word, I will not stop until Reed, my charge, is safe. But you, Adelaide, have to stay put."

"What about me?" Adriel moved closer to the angel. He looked into Madadel's eyes with fear in his own. In that moment, he seemed like a little child, unsure of himself in so many ways. "Why was I sent here?"

Madadel placed his hand on Adriel's shoulder and smiled. "Brother, you were given a second chance. Take it and do better."

"But why?"

"God has a plan for you."

Madadel pulled back and took off into the air. As he did, his shield collapsed around us, turning him invisible and bringing us out of hiding. I glanced around the nightclub's parking lot. Either no one had noticed us appear out of nowhere or they just didn't care enough to make a fuss about the crazy spectacle they had just seen.

Adriel and I exchanged looks, not knowing what to do next.

†

After stirring in bed for hours thinking about what Madadel had said, I turned the lamp on, got up, and walked around the room with bare feet, feeling the cold tiled floor underneath me.

"Stay put," the angel had said. I should have told him to stick it where the sun don't shine. He was Reed's angel and hadn't done a thing when the demon came and kidnapped him. It had been *me* fighting to pull my brother back, to keep him safe. Where had he been? Just watching from the sidelines like it was all a game?

I was not allowed to interfere. Such bullshit.

Work projects lay on my desk. I studied what I had so far. Photos of furniture and home décor along with my own creative sketches of interior designs—full of artistic details right down to custom wall shelves and unique ceiling lampshades—were piled up next to a folder filled with interior shots of the house I was in charge of remodeling and designing with my team. It had been days since I'd touched the project, days since I'd even thought about it. I had to do it at some point if I wanted to keep my job, but for the life of me, I just could not think straight.

She is aiding Lucifer in raising an army. He'd made it sound like I wanted to help Lucifer destroy the world, like I'd volunteered to be his evildoer.

My throat felt dry. I left the room and tiptoed to the kitchen. Adriel lay on the couch, surprisingly on his back, in nothing but pajama bottoms, possibly Nate's. The room was dim except for the salt-crystal lamp, which no one had bothered to turn off. The light illuminated Adriel's face with an orange-red glow and gave me a clear view of his thick, long lashes resting against the lines of his cheeks. And just down yonder, a strong chest led a trail to hard abs and perfect lust handles, which dipped at the edge of his pants. I watched him for a second like a teenager gawking at a picture of a hot actor before scurrying to the fridge and grabbing a water bottle.

When I turned back toward the living room, Adriel was sitting up and watching me.

"Hey," he said.

"Hi."

"Can't sleep, either?"

I shook my head. We both didn't move for a moment, just looked at one another. He ran a hand through his hair, the muscles in his chest contracting, and swept a few strands behind his ear.

"Are you comfortable on the couch?" I said at last.

He shrugged. "It's not too bad."

I glanced toward my room and dug my fingers into the soft plastic of the bottle, making a crinkling sound. A span of approximately twenty feet separated Adriel from my room. All I had to do was say the words, and he'd be in there.

As I opened my mouth, I told myself I would probably regret the decision later. "Come on," I told him, already moving in the direction of my room. "We can share a bed."

If he felt hesitation, he didn't show it. Jumping to his feet, he hurried after me.

In my room, I lay on my side nearest to the window, which a full moon shone through, while Adriel sat on the edge of the bed and stared around the room. He rested his elbows on his thighs, giving me a clear view of his arched back and the long set of notches in his spine. Around his shoulder blades, the scars had almost vanished.

"I don't want to make you uncomfortable." Turning halfway, his eyes darted toward me. "The bed isn't that big. I don't want to take too much space."

Reaching out, I placed the tips of my fingers over his rough scars and felt the tautness of his skin. His eyes closed. A breath escaped his mouth.

"Your scars are practically gone."

He opened his eyes and slid under the covers beside me, turning on his side so that he faced me. The moonlight struck his face. Between us, a third, small person could have fit while barely touching either of us.

From a very short distance away, Adriel's eyes rested on mine. "Is this okay?" he asked.

I nodded.

"Do you . . ." His dark irises were on my face, searching for something. "Do you want to talk about what happened tonight?"

I shrugged. "That angel had no right. He let my brother get hurt."

"That's not what I'm talking about."

I remembered Adriel standing in the back of the club, watchful. He had reacted to my presence so fast, like he'd been anticipating me all along. Like he was waiting.

"How did you even get there all by yourself?" I placed my right hand underneath the pillow and my left between the two of us, near my torso. "You were there before me, weren't you?"

He didn't deny it. "I had your friend drop me off. I knew you would come, and I needed to stop you."

"But you didn't. I turned one guy."

The muscle in his jaw clenched. "By the time I saw you, it was too late. I'm sorry."

I smiled. "You're sorry? I'm making your life a living hell, and *you're* sorry?"

"It's my job to protect." The corner of his mouth pulled into a smirk. "I've been failing a lot at that."

After he had shut his eyes and fallen asleep, his chest rising and falling with the covers draped across him, I wondered if Lizzy was in the adjacent room, or if she had stayed at Nate's tonight. I wondered what Devin was doing that second, whether he was in his apartment or out with Lucifer's demons. I wondered if Reed was all right.

I wondered if the man beside me was actually a man, one with human emotions and desires. I wondered if things would work out.

And then I fell asleep.

Chapter Twelve

ADRIEL

The light of early dawn washed the room with a creamy hue and revealed natural reddish strands in Addy's dark-brown hair; they stuck out like individual red roses in a field of leaves. Addy lay on her back with her face tilted in my direction, fast asleep, her full lips parted.

How could a human look so beautiful, so angelic, and yet have the devil's blood? Lying on the plush mattress with the soft cotton bedsheets, I wanted to lean in and stroke her hair, maybe even coil a strand around my finger. Never before had I been this physically close to a human. A yearning bigger than anything else made me want to feel the texture of her soft curls, move my fingers down their long lengths, brush the skin of her shoulder, and glide my thumb across her hand, in the curve of her palm where the skin looked the softest.

I wanted to *feel* her in all her humanness.

I drew myself away from her and sat up, my heart pounding against my chest, my hands clammy.

Stop. Madadel had said Father was giving me a second chance, that I needed to do better. Why he had chosen me, of all the fallen angels, to be human, to have a beating heart and a new beginning, I didn't know. But if I had to do better, that meant I needed to stop acting out of line. Stop feeling.

My mistake with Jenna, my human charge, was that I'd let my emotions cloud my judgment when it came to deciding how her son lived his life. Falling for those foolish emotions again with Addy would ruin everything and probably cement my place in hell. That was what Madadel had meant.

Ignoring my beating heart and all the weird sensations that came with my human body, I left the bed and found the T-shirt Addy had given me the first day. It lay on the floor by her closet like an unwanted, forgotten friend. I threw the shirt over my naked chest and strode to the door, winding my hand around the knob.

Before I'd even left the room, shadows wrapped around my vision. I stumbled against the door, my hands stabilizing me, and stood still, waiting for whatever came next. The firefly returned, its body twinkling on and off like a flickering Christmas light, and just watched me.

"What is it now?" I asked. "What do you want me to do?"

The firefly's light died out, vanishing from my sight for the second time in the past few days. I let my forehead bang once against the door.

"Adriel?" a soft, feminine voice called out from behind me. I moved my head in that direction but couldn't see anything but darkness. "What's going on?"

"Addy," I said, "just wait."

"Are you all right?"

I didn't answer her. From the darkness came shapes, twisting and turning like a kaleidoscope until an entire world emerged before me. Addy came into view. She was inside a cave holding on to a young man who couldn't keep his legs from bending and whose body slouched against her. I concentrated on the young man she clung to, finding an alive, pale Reed. He'd changed since the first vision I'd had of him. He hadn't lost weight or anything—that was impossible in hell—but he looked worn down, like he had been neglected and left by himself without water in the center of a desert for days or weeks.

My vision shifted. I noticed a third person in the room standing near Addy and Reed. When I zoomed in on him, I almost laughed. Although I couldn't hear the conversation, I watched myself talk to Addy.

"Adriel?" Addy spoke again from the real world. "You're scaring me."

The vision began to break, and I placed my hand in front of my face to block the shining rays coming from Addy's bedroom window. In just a few seconds, the real world was visible again.

"What's going on?" Addy sat on her knees at the end of the bed, the waves of her hair falling over her shoulders and back in a big, tousled mess. The bed cover had been pushed back with her and was twisted around her legs.

An idea struck me as I looked at her and thought of the vision, of Reed in her arms. We were clearly all in hell, which

109

meant that we had somehow gone through and managed to get Reed.

"Hey," I said, moving toward her. "We're going to get Reed out. You hear me?"

She stared up at me, the red in her cheeks bright from sleep. "How?"

"I had a vision of us in hell. You and me. And your brother was there."

Leaping off the bed, she rushed to me and clenched her fingers around the shirt I wore, just above the hem. "Tell me everything."

†

Addy paced the room as I told her what I saw. When I finished relaying everything down to the smallest detail, she bit down on her bottom lip and looked out the window.

"If I saw us there," I said, sitting with my back against the bed's upholstered headboard, "that means we discover a way to go there, and soon. All my other visions came true almost right after I saw them in my head."

Droplets of water dripped from the foggy window, indicating the cold weather outside. Still, the room radiated with light from the sunrays coming in. Weird combination, I thought. Hot and cold. I watched Addy's inexpressive face and considered the human blood traveling through her veins, mingling with her demonic blood.

She drew the window open, letting cold air in, and moved toward the bed. "Are you sure we were in hell?"

I reminded her how we were with Reed in a cave, just like the one he was dragged into in the first place.

She was silent for a moment. When she looked up, an idea twinkled in her eyes. "I think I know how we can get there." She sat on the edge of the bed and tugged on a feather poking out of her pillow. "You're a fallen angel, right? Can't you go there like the rest of them?"

"I'm sorry, but I'm human now. The other fallen angels don't exactly have blue veins or stubble." I scratched at the shadow of hair across my jaw. "You've seen them with their permanently scarred backs. They're not human; they're demons. I'm the odd one. I can't open the gateway."

"Is that the thing I went through?"

I told her yes, and thought of the moment she had come back through the portal, how she had fallen on top of me. It had only been two days ago, but it felt like weeks had passed with all that had happened in that short time.

Once the feather—no more than the size of her little finger—came free from the pillow, Addy twiddled it between her thumb and index finger. "We can ask Madadel if he could get us in there."

"No. Angels can't go through the gateway unless a demon lets them."

Addy held the small feather in both her hands and tore it apart, yanking the soft barbules from the quill. I looked away, the soft hair at the nape of my neck standing up. My visions hadn't deceived me yet, so I knew for a fact we would make it to hell. Addy was looking at me when I glanced at the fallen, torn feather sprinkled on top of the bedsheets.

In a sense, Addy was fallen too. However, rather than choosing her own path, she was fallen by design, born with demonic blood she didn't ask for. Was she the key to getting into hell?

"Addy, what if you could get us in? You have Lucifer's blood."

She shrugged. "How would I even do that?"

"I don't know, but there has to be a way. And between the two of us, you're the only one with some demonic blood."

A gust of wind shot through the open window, causing the parted curtains to soar in our direction. I felt small prickles descend my arms. The sensation made me shiver.

Addy didn't seem to care about the cold. Her pupils dilated. With a smile stretching the corners of her lips, she dropped back against the pillow and lay there breathing the fresh, icy air. No words came out of her for a while. I watched her with both awe and fear brimming inside me. Then she said something I didn't expect.

"I don't feel cold anymore. Not completely. Not since I went to hell." She stared at the white ceiling and traced the sheets underneath her with her hands by her side. "It feels really hot all the time now." She looked at me. A shimmer flashed in her big eyes and she stifled a sob. "Am I . . . am I evil?"

With the fire that had been in her eyes a moment ago gone, her shrunken pupils searched my face for an answer, good or bad. For the first time in the past two days, I saw her for what she was: a small, delicate human. I was a lot like her now that I had lost my wings and my angelic strength.

I reached over and lightly nudged her hand with the tips of my fingers. "Hey, you're not evil. Evil people don't worry that they're evil. You're the same person you've always been."

"How do you know?"

"I just know."

She closed her eyes. "Maybe. Maybe not. If it's all right, I think I want to be alone for a little while."

I moved my hand away and stood up, feeling a tightness in my chest. If she was the key to entering hell, we'd discover it soon enough.

Chapter Thirteen

ADELAIDE

Adriel had called it the gateway. I thought about that for a while, envisioning the massive wooden gate from my dreams. Was that the entrance to hell? Had I had the answer this whole time?

When Saleos, Lucifer's minion, had taken me to hell, the portal looked nothing like the gate in my dreams. It was simply a hole through space that encompassed our bodies and swallowed us with it. Perhaps my gate was a different entrance, like a side or back door.

Wind brushed my loose curls against my face. I closed my eyes and told myself to fall asleep, even though it was still early morning. I needed to get to that gate. I needed to test my theory, or we might never find our way to Reed like Adriel had promised we would.

It took a long time before my mind quieted. I opened my eyes, finding everything hazy. Picture frames, which were supposed to be hanging around the room, had fallen on the floor like someone had come in and struck them from the wall. Broken glass lay scattered everywhere. I got up, put my slippers on, and moved toward the door, crushing glass with each step.

I stopped. The gate appeared in place of my door, open like the last time I saw it in my dream.

Is this the gateway to hell? Or am I dreaming even now?

Red flames led me through the entryway. I took steady steps like before, my heart thumping at the knowledge that once I made it inside the chamber, there would be no ground to stand on. Sweat marks grew all over my shirt, making the fabric stick to my skin.

To my surprise, when I made it through, the ground that had collapsed and pulled me down with it the last time was actually there. Unbroken. Not a single crevice in it. Taking a deep breath, I stepped into the center of the room and looked around. If I was in hell, there had to be a way to find Reed.

"Hello?" I called out.

"Hello, hello, hell-o-o-o," my voice echoed back in response.

Adriel's vision showed us both in hell, and yet here I was, all alone, trying to find my way in. Was he wrong? Did he just assume that he would be with me when that was not the case?

In the back of the chamber, I noticed something shift, like a body running and hiding in the shadows. Near that area was a column that grew among the cave's icicle-shaped formations hanging from the ceiling. The column was vast toward the top but thinned out at the bottom, like a giant needle meeting the ground. If I squinted enough, I thought I saw bare feet peeking out from behind the column.

I moved one step at a time, my slippers barely scraping against the ground. When I made it a few feet away from the column, the person jumped out. Or at least, I thought it was a person; then I saw the wings. And the face. I screamed and jumped back, nearly falling on my behind.

Adriel stood before me, his eyes looking right through me like I wasn't even there. His white wings flew open, revealing a solid, lean chest.

"What now?" Adriel said.

The question wasn't targeted at me. When I looked behind me, I realized whom he was talking to.

"Now you learn how to kill several demons with a few strokes," Lucifer said. He stood parallel to Adriel with great white wings of his own. His eyes were brown like mine, not black and empty.

Out of nowhere, demons emerged, seeming to crawl from the cave's shadows. They were clearly not fallen angels. They looked like a human and crocodile half-breed with long talons, sharp teeth, and thick green scales where skin should've been. Two of the demons rushed at Adriel, moving past me like I was invisible. A horrible whiff hit me, smelling a lot like decaying meat. Another demon, standing on two feet, reached with its claws to slice Adriel's flesh while the other two grabbed each of his legs and went in for a bite.

"No," I shouted, storming in to stop them. When I tried to grab the tallest demon, my hands went right through its torso.

I stumbled forward, my entire body passing inside the demon like it was composed of air. The demon's talons swung. I watched with horror as he slashed Adriel's throat and blood oozed out. Adriel cried out in pain and flung his wings out, tossing the demon quite a distance. The other two demons still had their sharp fangs sunk into his legs. He kicked them off, hurling them away after their ugly friend.

"You are doing it all wrong." Lucifer sprinted toward the three demons hissing on the ground and used his wings to fly in the air. He kicked two of the demons back. The third demon reached out with its talons, but Lucifer grabbed its head and broke its neck. Bones cracked, and the demon slumped to the ground, its head hanging at a bizarre angle. He chased the other demons down and did the same quick motions, killing them before I even had time to blink. He wiped his hands together, dusting off any dirt. "That, my friend, is how you do it."

Adriel clutched at his bleeding throat, his chest rising and falling violently. He frowned in the direction of the dead demons. "So, the trick is to grab them before they grab you. Is that it?"

Lucifer grinned. "You are a quick learner." He marched to Adriel's side and drew Adriel's hand away from his neck. "Let me have a look."

Adriel let him. He dropped his hand, tucked his wings behind him, and let Lucifer touch the wound.

"You are getting stronger." Lucifer trailed a finger through the blood dripping from Adriel's neck. "But there is much to learn."

Adriel's eyes gleamed, and he smiled. "Will you teach me everything?"

"Yes, my friend. I will teach you, and then you will help me with something." Lucifer's grin bore white, spotless teeth that glinted in the dimness of the cave.

"I will do anything you ask. Just name it."

"Very well. First, let us make a better warrior out of you, and then we can continue."

My heart pumped in my ears, blocking out any other noise. I had shared my bed with that man. I retreated from the two angels and moved toward the entrance, where the hallway was lit by flames. What had I just seen? I couldn't tell if hell made people hallucinate or if this was some sort of vision from the past. If it was the latter, what did that make Adriel? Was he Lucifer's friend? Was he collaborating with him behind my back?

This time around, I ran back the way I had come without thinking about the fire blazing on either side of me. The heat assaulted my body, but Lucifer was behind me, and I didn't want to stay in the same room as him. A couple of burns were worth me escaping.

When I reached the end, the gate was shut. From this side, there was no handle to pull on, no way to exit. I banged on the door, which reminded me of the sounds I'd heard just a few nights ago at Reed's dorm moments before he was taken. Had it been a monster lurking behind the gate that night, or was it just me trying to get out? Perhaps the dream I'd had was a vision of this moment, of me stuck in hell.

The gate loomed over me, mocking me for being on the wrong side.

"Help," I shouted, but I didn't know who would hear me. I had walked here in a dream where no one could follow.

I kicked at the gate, hoping it would snap out of the wall. No such luck, though, and I found myself sagging to the ground with my toes curled in pain.

"Oh, God, no." I placed my forehead against the wooden surface of the gate and closed my eyes. Right behind that door was my room, just out of reach.

A loud explosion made my ears ring. I was thrown high into the air and came crashing down a few seconds later on top of a smooth, cold surface. Dust and embers rained down on me. Standing up, I squinted and realized I was back in my room. And yet, it still felt hazy, like a dream. Broken picture frames lay everywhere.

"This is when you wake up, Addy," I said to myself.

I moved to look out the open window. However, when I touched the glass, my room shifted around me like the static on a TV screen when it loses signal. The gray spasm kept going until my room merged with another location that looked a lot like the cavern I had just come out of. My room clashed with the cave's columns, my bed and other furniture disappearing every few spasms. Adriel—this time without any wings—walked in through the broken gate, which also happened to be where my normal bedroom door was.

"Addy, what's going on?" He took long strides toward me, his eyebrows furrowed with worry.

The room was in chaos. Still, Adriel had somehow managed to stay without becoming part of the static.

I flinched back and collided with the window when he closed in on me. "No, don't touch me!"

He reached his hands out and steadied me. His fingers felt cold around my arms. "Don't worry. You're just going through the gateway."

Blinking a few times, I realized what he was saying.

"You figured it out, Addy. You got us into hell."

Shaking my head, I tried to push him away. "Let go, or God help me, I'll kill you in this dream."

119

Adriel's grasp tightened. His eyes clouded over, a deep crease appearing between his brows. "Addy? What dream . . . ?"

"Don't say my name." I shoved one last time, but he pressed his body against mine, and then I couldn't move.

The room shook. I felt my body contract like a piece of clay being balled up in a person's fist. Adriel grunted something and wrapped his arms around me. I couldn't fight him anymore, not with my ears ringing and the world growing so vast as I shrunk into a freckle before bursting up back into my normal form. His hands were on my hips when we emerged in hell's damp cavern. He stared at me for a few seconds. I pulled away from him, my palms raised, keeping space between us.

"Did I do something?" he asked.

I opened my mouth to answer when a shrieking scream erupted from behind me. Adriel's eyes grew wide. I swiveled around and saw nearly a dozen demons creeping on all fours toward us.

"Run!" he yelled, taking my hand and pulling me after him.

I yanked my hand free but ran with him. The demons screeched and hissed, their noise shaking the caves. Looking back, I saw their claws digging into the ground as they sprinted after us. Adriel and I moved through tunnels, and I wondered if he knew his way around. He'd been close to Lucifer all along; he'd lied to me. I hurried my steps and ran past him, ignoring him when he called my name.

At the end of the path, a forked tunnel came into view. Both sides were pitch-black with no sign of life. Taking a deep breath, I ran into the right tunnel, hoping there weren't any slumbering demons there. Adriel stomped behind me. My hands moved in front of my body in search of monsters and walls I might come crashing against. I could feel cuts gathering on my fingers and arms as I scratched against things in the darkness.

"Addy." Adriel's voice came from not too far away. I felt his hand brush against my back. "We need to find an exit."

In that instant, my hands hit a wall. I stopped, my hands pressed against solid metal. Adriel followed, his body colliding with my back. The demons squealed behind us, sounding closer and closer with each ticking second.

Adriel's hands felt the wall and occasionally touched my own. "It's a door. Help me push."

I put my weight against the metal door and shoved as hard as I could, with Adriel doing the same beside me. The demons hissed in the tunnel. They were getting close and sounded like starved hyenas on the prowl for an easy kill.

In front of me, the door budged. I shoved harder. Adriel grunted, pushing with all his might. The door finally pulled loose from the tunnel wall. Light swarmed in from the other side. We both jumped through just as the demons came leaping after us. Adriel hurried to close the door, but a demon dove inside, his pointy teeth bared at us.

With the door shut, Adriel and I faced the demon alone. The hideous, reeking monster surveyed the two of us, almost like it was deciding whom to eat first. When it started moving toward me, Adriel pushed me back and jumped in front of the demon.

The unsightly beast growled at Adriel, its crimson gums drawing back and revealing the actual size of its teeth. It stood tall like a human and moved on its hind legs. With only two feet separating them, the demon grabbed Adriel with its claws and opened its mouth wide. Adriel let out a cry. When the toothy monster tried to take a bite, Adriel grabbed it by its scaly neck and cracked its skull.

Or at least, he tried.

An angry snarl resounded from the base of the demon's throat. It shook its head out of Adriel's grasp and moved to jab its talons into his chest. Adriel looked pale.

"Stop!" I screamed.

The demon's vertically slit pupils zeroed in on me. Its claw hovered near Adriel's flesh.

"I'm Lucifer's daughter," I said. "You will obey me."

Adriel exhaled when the demon pulled away. For a second, all seemed under control, then the demon crawled over to me with snot dripping out of its nose. It moved around my feet, sniffing at me in between hisses. I closed my eyes and stood still, waiting for the end to come.

"Addy," Adriel said after what felt like a long time. "Addy, we're good."

I opened my eyes to find the demon no longer near either of us. Instead, it crouched in the corner of the small chamber, chewing on the claws of its hind leg, sharpening them. Adriel grinned at me.

Waving my hand at the bizarre demon, I said, "Hey, can you take me to see my brother?"

The demon stared at me while licking its jagged claws with its long tongue.

"Reed," I said. "He's human. Yay tall." I raised my hand a foot above my head. "Has hazel eyes, which is a color close to light brown, just so we're clear."

A growl escaped the demon's throat, and then it was on all fours again. It bobbed its head up and down like it understood what I was saying and started moving toward the door we had just come through. Adriel and I followed, pulling the door open and walking down the empty tunnel. The other demons must have gotten tired of waiting and left.

While the demon moved ahead of us, Adriel reached out and took my hand. He leaned close and whispered, "Is this a good idea? Following a demon?" His warm lips nearly grazed my ear.

A rush of warmth passed up my spine, a sensation I'd only ever felt with Devin back when we were happy. I looked at my hand in Adriel's. I wanted so badly to hold on tight to the feeling, but I had seen the vision of Lucifer teaching Adriel how to kill demons, and I didn't know what to make of it. Was it real? Were they close? I drew my hand away and fisted it by my side.

Adriel frowned, but he didn't ask any more questions.

"Here." He poked my hand with a small metal object.

When I looked down, I saw it was Reed's Swiss Army knife.

"When I saw the gateway opening, I grabbed it from your bedside table. I thought you might want it."

Nodding, I took it from him. "Thanks." I tucked the knife into one of the front pockets of my pajama shorts, thankful that they even came with pockets, and continued marching after the monster.

Maybe I would give Reed his knife back and buy one for myself once he was safe. I was so close to finding my brother. In no time, he'd be back home.

All would be right again.

Chapter Fourteen

ADRIEL

We faced another door after walking through tunnel after tunnel. As we walked, Addy's eyes darted around, scanning the ceilings and shadows as we passed by. Whenever the demon paused, she'd wince like it was going to turn around and attack; when it continued, she'd take a deep breath and follow. Now, it seemed like we had reached our end point. The demon bowed low and sniffed at the edges of the door.

"Is Reed behind here?" Addy asked, her voice low.

The demon snorted, spewing rancid snot on the ground. Both Addy and I moved away. The fiend began digging at the foot of the door, its talons pushing grainy rocks and stones out of the way.

"Okay." Addy pushed forward, touching the door while keeping her distance from the beast. "We'll open the door if you'll just step back," she told the monster.

When the demon crawled a few feet away from us, I thought about telling Addy she was a demon whisperer, but then thought better of it. Encouraging her to be like Lucifer was not a good idea.

Avoiding the snot on the ground, I helped Addy get the door open. It didn't take too much effort, nothing like before. When we pulled it ajar, Addy rushed into the room without trying to be discreet. If a demon was hiding inside, she didn't seem to care.

"Addy, wait." I reached an arm out to stop her, but she was already gone.

I went after her and saw her standing motionless not far from the door. A large prison cell wrapped around half of the room.

"Addy?"

Her eyes stared straight ahead. Following her gaze, I realized why she had frozen.

Reed lay on the ground inside the cell, his eyes shut and his face pale, just as I'd seen in my vision.

"Oh my God," Addy whispered under her breath, loud enough for me to hear. She ran toward the cell and dropped to the ground not far from her brother. Her hands wrapped around the cell bars. I couldn't see her face from where I stood, though I didn't need to see her to know she was scared. Addy reached her arm between two bars, barely brushing the tips of her fingers against her brother's cheek.

"Don't worry," I said. "We'll get him out."

I looked around the chamber for a way to unlock the prison cell and found a big metal key hanging from a nail on the wall right beside a door that looked similar to the one we'd just walked through.

"Here's a key." I took it down and hurried to the cell. I inserted the key into the hole and twisted it, turning the tumblers inside the lock. The cell door swung open silently.

Addy jumped to her feet and pushed past me to go inside. "Hey, it's going to be okay." With shaky arms, she bent down and held Reed up against her. "I'm here now."

Not knowing what to do, I stood, completely silent, and waited for Reed to come to.

She wiped the sweat from his face with her palm. "Please wake up, Reed."

"Here." I crouched beside her and took Reed from her. "Check his pulse."

Without hesitating, she placed her index and middle fingers against his neck. A moment later, she exhaled. "He has a steady pulse. Why isn't he waking up?"

"He's been through a lot."

"Yeah, and it's all my fault." She stood up and helped me pull him into a standing position. "Can we take him through the gateway like this?"

"Yes."

I put one of his arms over my shoulder, and Addy did the same with his other arm. Together, we managed to get him out of the cell.

A few feet away from the door we'd come in, we stopped. The demon blocked our path. It stood on its hind legs and growled.

"Seriously?" Addy said. "I thought we already befriended you."

The beast's gums pulled back, revealing its strikingly sharp teeth. Behind it, more demons appeared. One by one, they closed off the exit. We both took a step back.

My voice low, I said, "Move slowly toward the other door. We just need time for you to open the gateway."

Reed's head lolled to the side, facing me. His eyelids lifted, and he registered me through the slits. "No," he muttered. "Leave me alone."

Addy's voice wavered when she spoke. "It's okay, Reed." She took another step back. "We're getting you out of here."

"Ade." Panting, Reed looked at his sister. "They're demons."

"I know."

"No. This one," he whispered and bobbed his head once in my direction. "Is a demon too."

As soon as Addy's eyes met mine, she looked away. She put her forehead against her brother's and whispered back, "He's not a demon. You have to trust me."

The demons facing us cried out, their lungs filling with an obnoxious sound so shrill my ears felt like they were going to pop and go deaf. Reed closed his eyes, his nose and forehead scrunching in a silent scream. Addy was the only one who didn't react. She backed away from the beasts, pulling us with her.

Once we had inched our way back, I pulled the door open. "This way." I guided Addy and Reed out of the room.

Demon after demon dashed after us. Their claws swept left and right, trying to tear our organs out.

"We just have to—" I jumped back and dodged some talons. "We just have to hurry up and open the gateway. Can you do it, Addy?"

Addy screamed and retreated, forcing us to move with her.

"I don't know!" She kicked at the demons.

I glanced in her direction and saw blood seeping through her pajama top over her stomach.

"Come on. You can do this," I said.

"How? I don't know what I'm doing."

Still ducking away from each demon's strike, I lowered my right hand from Reed's back and placed it over Addy's hand, where she held her brother. At first, she didn't seem to notice my touch. After a few seconds, she looked my way, just for a moment, her eyes the color of the night during a full moon, shiny and dark all at once. My heart expanded just then, air passing throughout my body and swirling into my lungs, making me lightheaded.

"You can do this," I repeated, hoping my words would make a difference.

We moved down another tunnel. The demons kept coming, taking a step each time we did, staying close to us.

Addy was quiet as she, for the most part, evaded the hits coming her way. When demons scratched her, she pushed Reed back and tried to shield him with her body. I could feel cuts across my body too. Although they stung, they weren't as bad as the burns my back had endured a few nights ago.

When we neared the end of the tunnel, the world around us flickered. Addy's room blended with the cave and the demons for a second before dying out. Breathing in and out, Addy tried again and again to keep the gateway in place. All her attempts failed.

We hit a dead end just as a dozen or more demons closed in on us with their killer teeth and claws. Next to me, Reed's knees gave out. Just as his eyes closed, Reed's head slumped over his sister's shoulder. His weight suddenly felt heavier.

"Come on, Addy. Get us out of here!"

"I'm trying!"

Some of the demons up front opened their mouth and retracted their gums, ready to devour us whole. Saliva dripped from their pointy teeth like we were some delicious feast to be had.

I tightened my hold on Addy's hand and closed my eyes, not wanting to see our end.

However, the end didn't come. Neither did pain nor screams nor the silence of my heart.

My eyelids flew upward. The demons were still there, but they weren't trying to eat us anymore. They kneeled on the ground with their heads bowed. In the center of the circle they formed stood the one being I wanted to strangle until his black, rotten eyes popped out of his narcissistic head.

Lucifer's lips pulled up at either corner of his mouth, but his eyes didn't smile. "Well, well. If it is not my old friend, Adriel, here with my child. I see you have lost your wings. Should I welcome you to my kingdom?"

Chapter Fifteen

ADELAIDE

Lucifer's voice rang in my ears, breaking through my concentration. The gateway closed before I could even blink, leaving us facing the devil.

Lucifer flashed his teeth at me and said, "You thought you could slip past me and reunite with your frail half brother? How did that turn out for you?" He directed his attention to Reed. Black, hollow eyes scrutinized my brother for far too long. "I had higher hopes for you, Adelaide, but then you went and did this." Shaking his head at Reed, he took a step forward. "I will give you another chance. Leave your brother here, return home, and do what I asked of you. You will be rewarded. I will give you a house of your own, money fit for kings, and anything else you can imagine. Perhaps you could have your own private island with servants at your beck and call. Does that not sound delicious?"

I felt a lump grow in my throat and clung tighter to Reed. Lucifer could hurt me, he could keep me as his prisoner, but not my brother; I needed to save him.

"What will it be, Adelaide?"

My silence spoke for me.

Adriel's thumb pressed harder against my hand where it rested on Reed's back. Through my peripheral vision, I could tell he wasn't looking at me. He was looking at Lucifer straight on with a hard, defiant look in his eyes, his jaw tense.

Ignoring Adriel and Reed, Lucifer kept his attention on me. "The demons sensed you, Adelaide. Every inch of this goddamned hell sensed you. You have my blood. You were foolish to think that no one would know who you are here."

"Don't talk to her like that." A thick vein in Adriel's forehead protruded, looking like it might snap in half.

"I will speak to my child the way I want, fallen angel."

Adriel clutched my hand tighter. "Addy, open the gateway."

"The gateway?" Lucifer let out a chuckle; it echoed throughout the cave, piercing my ears like a shrill audio frequency only I could hear. No one else seemed bothered by the sound. "You do realize that anyone with demonic blood can open the gate to Earth and jump through, even I? Which means that no matter where you go, I can follow. Do you really think you can hide from me?"

Reed's head still slumped forward in total unconsciousness. The things he had gone through, the isolation, the shock, the fear; would they leave him scarred?

"You took my brother and used him to threaten me," I said. "You've never been my father. I'm just a pawn in your stupid, evil game. I did what I had to do to save him, but that's it. Your game ends here. I won't help you anymore, and you can't force me. If you kill him, you might as well kill me."

"Oh, child. You have no idea how helpful you have been the past four days. The few people you turned have turned others, and they have turned others, and then others more. A sizable army has already formed thanks to you. And frankly, my daughter, I do not need you any longer."

He stepped forward, a frown eating half of his forehead. I moved back an inch and felt the bumpy wall against my back. We were at a dead end. No way back, only forward—toward the devil.

All around Lucifer, crouching low, the demons hissed at us as if given a silent command.

I needed to distract them, so I kept talking. "Then why use me at all? You have people doing your work. Why me?"

Adriel's hand squeezed mine harder, but I didn't know what he was trying to tell me. Was he scared? I was scared. For a moment, I thought I felt his pulse ticking against my hand, surging through my skin, and sending a signal to my brain, like a warning.

Lucifer walked closer. Only a few feet separated us, and he kept shortening the distance. Reed's Swiss Army knife weighed heavily in my pocket, cold and powerful.

"I will not give you the satisfaction of knowing your purpose," Lucifer said. "I got what I needed out of you."

Another step. I held my breath and pinched the knife between my fingers without pulling it out from its hiding place. Reed stirred beside me, but his head stayed low.

Inches between us now, Lucifer's black eyes stared at me. He didn't smile. He didn't move. He just looked at me with those two black holes of his.

"I'm your daughter." My voice was low, but I knew he heard me.

Lucifer placed his hands on either side of my face and pressed hard. His skin burned. Adriel's hand gripped mine tighter than before. My eyes watering, I struggled to free my head and discovered I couldn't, and there was no way to avoid the heat beating against my ears and cheeks.

Opening his mouth to speak and letting a sour smell drift into my face, Lucifer said, "Yes, you are my daughter. Which is why I will not kill you. No, your suffering will be far worse than death."

I sensed Adriel stiffen, his hand like a rock over mine. Remembering the Swiss Army knife in my pocket, I surreptitiously took it out and flicked it open with my thumb. Lucifer looked at me with no emotion on his face. The more I stared back, the more I thought I saw black ink leaking from his black eyes.

My knife was in my hand one second, and the next it was half buried in Lucifer's chest. I looked away from his face and studied the wound I'd created right where his cold, empty heart should be.

He staggered back, removed his hands from my face, and looked down at the knife in his body. For a second, his lip quivered like he was going to cry.

Then, a high-pitched laugh exploded from deep within his throat. It went on for ages, and all the blood drained from my face.

"Did you really think I could be killed that easily?" He gripped the knife and pulled it out. "I am the devil, child of mine. Do you think I did not make certain long ago to create a weapon so powerful that no one would know what it is or how to use it against me? I protect myself with that weapon, and I have made certain that you will not interfere."

The Swiss Army knife fell to the ground. Black blood marked every inch of it. And yet, Lucifer hadn't even flinched.

Shutting my eyes, I tried to summon the gateway once more. I felt the atmosphere shift around me, turning from hot to cold. Through closed lids, I pictured my room and the three of us standing in it. When I opened my eyes again, we were on the other side, standing in my room. All three of us.

†

We laid Reed down on my bed, removing all his warm, damp clothes, except for his underwear. He was burning hot, so I ran to the bathroom, grabbed a bunch of towels, soaked them in running water from the sink, and ran back and placed them all over Reed's body. Adriel grabbed a bottle of water from the fridge and poured a small amount into Reed's mouth, just enough to help him satiate his thirst but not enough that he would choke while unconscious.

The apartment was empty, which was good because I didn't know how I would have explained everything to Lizzy.

Wiping some of the sweat from Reed's face, I said, "Is he going to be all right?"

"Let's hope so." Adriel pointed at the blood on my shirt. "What about you? Are you all right?"

I lifted my shirt up a little to uncover the wound underneath. A red cut, not too deep, had left half of my stomach bloodstained.

Adriel grabbed one of the wet towels, crouched down, and cleaned around the cut, his other hand resting against my hip to steady me. "Does it hurt?"

I winced. "Not too much."

He glanced up at me, his irises dark and troubled and mesmerizing. "Are you sure?"

"Yes, don't worry. It'll heal."

Lucifer's eyes, the way he'd stared at me as the knife went through him, were still in the back of my mind.

"He said he had a weapon. What did he mean by 'I have made certain that you will not interfere'?"

Adriel shrugged.

I placed my palm against my brother's forehead to check his temperature. He was burning up. I couldn't tell what that meant for his long-term health.

Reed opened his eyes halfway and muttered a jumble of words. It took me a moment to understand him. He was asking me what had happened and wondering where we were. Leaving his mouth hanging open, he revealed a swollen, dry tongue.

"Hi, Reed." I took the bottle of water Adriel had used and, lifting Reed's head up a little, poured some of the liquid into my brother's mouth. "You're safe now. We got you out."

In between gulps, Reed said, "That was the devil."

"I know."

"You do?"

"Yeah. I was there the night they took you. Don't you remember?"

His blank expression answered my question.

"How long were you in hell? Can you remember?"

"It felt like weeks. Why didn't you get me out sooner?"

"Oh, Reed." I set the bottle of water down and met Adriel's eyes. I wasn't sure what to do next. Adriel didn't seem to know either. "I have something to tell you. Just please don't freak out, okay?" I said to Reed. "The night they took you, they came and took me too. I saw you there, you know, in hell. I . . . I guess you can't remember because you were out of it."

"Why'd they take us?"

"Well, Lucifer took you to threaten me."

"Why?"

"Because." I swallowed. "I'm his daughter."

Reed's eyes grew wide. "Is this a joke?"

"No, I swear. I'm telling you the truth. He kidnapped you to get me to cooperate with him. I've never met him in my life, Reed, and then you were gone, and he made me drink something, and I saw everything. I know it sounds crazy, but it's true; he's my father."

"That can't be true. You're human. You're my sister."

"Yes, I'm human, and I'm your sister. But I also have his blood."

"Are you half demon?"

Was I? Looking down at my pajama top, I eyed the red stains. Lucifer's blood was black, while mine was clearly not. "No, I don't think so."

Behind me, something crashed to the floor. The noise sent me jumping away from the bed and spinning in one quick motion. Picture frames went flying to the ground not far from my feet. I raised my fisted hands to form a shield in front of me, ready to punch whatever monster had appeared.

"Whoa, it is just me," Madadel said. He looked out of place standing between me and my only desk, like an eagle in a canary's tiny cage. Tucking his wings by his side, he moved closer and stared down at my brother.

"No!" Reed shrieked and shut his eyes. "Leave me alone!"

I stroked my hand against Reed's cheek. "It's all right. That's just Madadel. He's your guardian angel."

Reed looked up, his panting slowing down.

Madadel's long locks fell over his face. Through the curtain of hair, he smiled at my brother. "I did not mean to frighten you, Reed. I am here to protect you."

I crossed my arms. "You mean the way you protected Reed the first time?"

"I am sorry, Adelaide, but I could not interfere. I fought the demon off as much as I could while he was invisible to the human eye. However, once he became visible to humans, I could not do anything."

"Why not? That's a stupid rule if you ask me."

"That is just the way it is."

"He's right, Addy." Adriel stood to the side, almost as if he were purposely keeping distance between the angel and himself. "Angels are not allowed to interfere directly with hell. To be fair, this is the first time Lucifer has taken a human to hell without permission."

Rolling my eyes, I said, "Do people usually volunteer to go to hell?"

Madadel tromped around the room, picking up the picture frames he had knocked to the ground. He scrutinized each photo—some of Lizzy and me, others of Reed and me, and one with Devin—before setting them back on my desk. "A few have, actually."

Adriel touched my shoulder to grab my attention. "Since the beginning of mankind, we have fought demons who taunted humans. They usually try to mess with people's heads, either physically hurting them or getting them to hurt themselves. The demons do awful things to make the humans think they are seeing things that aren't there. When people claim they're seeing demons, they get laughed at." He frowned and looked away. "Demons love demeaning people this way. Angels fight them, though. Without showing themselves, the angels fight back to protect their humans. This is the first time that a demon has grabbed a human and taken off for hell, where angels can't go on their own."

"Because he thought Reed was Lucifer's kid, right?" I pressed my hand against the cut on my stomach. Somehow, the wound had already sealed. "That was why he went after him, wasn't it?"

"Yes, until Lucifer learned otherwise and ordered another demon to get you."

"I'm so sorry, Reed."

Reed tried to sit up but drooped back against the mattress. "Can I have more water?"

The bottle was nearly empty. I helped Reed gulp down the rest and brought him a few more bottles. Once he felt satisfied, we decided to let him rest.

Before leaving the room, I gazed down at my brother one more time. He looked so young, like the little kid who always used to make his way to my bed at night and tuck himself in before I even got there. I could still see him smiling at me from between the sheets and saying, "You'll scare the boogeyman away, right?" Reed was exactly the same now, smiling up at me, his hazel eyes half-shut, looking to me to keep the monsters away.

"Hey," I said. "We're just going to be in the other room. Try to rest, okay?"

Reed nodded.

"I'll keep the door open. If you need me, just call my name."

I kissed him on the forehead, grabbed my cell phone from my nightstand, and walked out. I took a moment to look at my phone. The time on the screen read 9:14 a.m. It had been 8:50 a.m. right before I'd fallen asleep and woken up in the dreamlike state, which meant that Adriel and I had gone to hell and come back to the exact same moment we'd left.

There was also a text message from Lizzy on my phone from last night that I hadn't noticed until now. Lizzy wrote that she was next door with Nate. Her message ended with a winking face emoji. I sent her a text back telling her good morning. It was good luck she hadn't been home earlier when everything went down.

In the common area, Madadel and Adriel stood many feet apart. Adriel hovered by the kitchen counter, his back to the angel, while Madadel gazed toward the one big window at the end of the room. When I walked in, they turned to me, relief on their faces.

Looking at Madadel, I said, "Once Reed wakes up and is feeling better, I want you to take him somewhere safe and hide him."

Madadel flashed a set of flawless white teeth. "I cannot personally take anyone anywhere, sweet Adelaide. However, if he wants to go somewhere, I will follow and protect him."

I had a feeling the angel was talking about protection against immoral choices. Frowning, I rephrased my sentence. "What I'm asking is to keep him from demons. Use your angel shield or something."

"I can do that."

"Good. I'm counting on you this time. Don't let Reed down."

Madadel bowed low, though he kept his eyes on me. "I will not. You have my word." When he straightened up, he moved to the couch and made himself comfortable in the center. His wings took up the rest of the couch, leaving no room for anyone else to sit.

I excused myself and walked out of the apartment, needing some fresh air after the busy morning we'd had. Sitting down on the top step of the stairs, I closed my eyes and let the fall wind swoop around me, cooling me down. For a while, the world calmed, and I listened to the rustling of leaves and chirping of birds.

I was lost in the moment, tranquil, until I felt something cottony come into contact with my bare skin.

My eyes shot open.

Adriel sat beside me on the step, the pajama bottoms he wore touching me. He looked toward me, his expression somewhat sad.

"Why were you afraid of me earlier?" he said. "You know, when the gateway opened."

I took a deep breath. Was it wise to tell him the truth? I wanted to lie, yet I knew it would bother me if I did. Deep down, I would always doubt him if I didn't face him now. "I saw a vision of you and Lucifer," I responded, "but I think it was a vision of the past, because you both still had your wings. You seemed to know each other really well."

He sighed. "Yes, we were close." He crossed his arms but didn't look away. "But that was thousands of years ago."

"Before he fell?"

"Yes. He wanted me to join his mission to take over God's kingdom. I was the first angel he told."

"But you didn't do as he wanted?"

"No. He wanted to create a secret legion to assassinate his fellow archangels. I couldn't stand for that, so I told on him. That was how he fell."

An old memory came to mind of Erica and Grandma arguing over God's existence. When Grandma Di preached about God's all-knowing power, Erica would say that if he were truly powerful, he wouldn't let bad things happen around the world. I didn't agree with Erica on most things, but she'd had a point there.

"God is omniscient, right?" I said. "He had to have known what Lucifer would do. Why didn't he stop him?"

"Because Father likes to let things play out the way they are supposed to."

Lucifer could have killed Reed. I shut my eyes again and tried to concentrate on the sounds of nature and nothing else. But I just couldn't. Reed could have died because of Lucifer, who was a creation of God. How could I accept that?

Adriel's fingers were suddenly against my face, pulling my head toward him. I opened my eyes and froze. He stared at me with a wild look in his eyes. He tucked a few strands of hair behind my ear and trailed his fingers down my jaw to my chin, sending shivers down my spine. His thumb—and eyes—moved to my bottom lip, tracing its curve ever so gently. I felt my face heat up. For a second, I hoped he would lean in and do more.

He pulled away, slipping his hands inside the pockets of his pajama pants. Erratic breaths escaped my lips. I stared down at my knees, not wanting to show him I'd felt something.

Changing the subject, I said, "Lucifer was God's favorite child. So how could God stand knowing what he knew and not stop Lucifer?"

From the corner of my eye, I saw Adriel smile.

"Because God is not human. He is objective and fair."

"Thousands of years later, and Lucifer is still out to take God's place. What good is being objective if it's going to get people hurt?"

From behind us, someone coughed. We both looked over our shoulders. Madadel stood in front of the apartment door, shooting Adriel a disappointed glare. I wondered how long he'd been standing there watching us.

"If I may interrupt," he said. "Lucifer is just a tool our Father uses to test humanity. The real question you should ask is: What will people choose—good or evil?"

I stared at the angel for a long time. Even Adriel didn't know what to say.

Finally, Madadel pointed in the direction of the apartment. "I believe Reed is hungry. His stomach keeps grumbling in his sleep."

That was my cue to go inside.

†

Lizzy had come back that evening, but not really. The second she walked through the door, I knew she was on a romantic high. Grinning like she had a secret she was desperate to share, she waltzed her way into the living room, moved past Adriel like he wasn't there, and rushed toward me. I sat on the couch watching an *I Love Lucy* episode on TV to keep my sanity in check when her arms suddenly wrapped around me.

Less than two hours ago I had dropped Reed and Madadel off at Saint Vincent College and come back, despite being reluctant to do so. Reed slept nearly the entire day, only waking up to eat and shower. In the evening, he asked me to take him back to school. Although I protested, nothing would change his mind. He needed to get back to normal life, he'd said.

While my brother was able to move on so fast, I just couldn't. With Lizzy hugging me like nothing had changed, because to her nothing had, I felt the urge to cry. Four days ago, I was just as ignorant. Though I had been sad over Devin breaking up with me, I hadn't been worried about my brother getting hurt or the consequences of selling people's souls to the devil.

"Addy, I think I'm in love," Lizzy said, still embracing me. "I seriously think I'm in love."

I patted her on the back and rolled my eyes while she couldn't see me, remembering that she'd asked me about Adriel's relationship status just a few days ago. "I'm so happy for you, Liz. Nate's a nice guy."

I was a bad, bad friend.

She thanked me and sauntered to her bedroom, where she stayed the entire time Adriel and I sat in the living room.

Later that night, Adriel and I shared my bed again, keeping to our respective sides. I wasn't sure when I fell asleep, but at some point, a scream and something crashing outside my bedroom door woke me up. I lay on my side, facing Adriel, who was no longer on his side of the bed. His forehead practically touched my own, and his hand had intertwined with mine, leaving me to question which one of us had done that and whether we had both wanted to.

Freeing my hand, I left the bed and tiptoed to the door, my ears working hard to pick out noises. I cranked the door handle and pulled it at a snail's pace until I could peer through the opening into the dark corridor. Nothing was there. I glanced over my shoulder. From the moonlight coming through the window, I could see that Adriel was still, his thick lashes lying against his cheeks. I wanted to get back to bed and cuddle against him.

"What the fuck are you?" Lizzy screamed from the kitchen.

I pushed the door open all the way and ran out. Even in the darkness, movement was noticeable in the living room. I slowed down and began inching my way forward. There was a faint light on in the kitchen. It took me a moment to realize the fridge was open.

"Lizzy?"

"Addy," she murmured from somewhere on my right.

My eyes moved to the floor. Lizzy crouched at the corner of the counter, clasping the legs of one of the kitchen stools and holding the stool out in front of her. She stared straight ahead. I followed her gaze. Two men with scarred backs fought an angel with red, long curls and the face of a young woman. A thick shroud covered the angel's private parts.

Lizzy dropped the stool and crawled toward me. "We have to get out of here."

One of the demons held down the angel's wings while the other wrapped his hands around her neck and squeezed. The angel fought back, pushing the demons away with a shove of her wings. They crashed on top of our living room table, breaking it, then got back up. One of them punched the angel in the stomach. She didn't make a sound, though I thought I saw pain flash across her face.

Lizzy grabbed onto my leg. "Addy, we have to get out."

Ignoring her, I grabbed an empty vase off the counter and threw it at the nearest demon. It struck his back and fell, shattering on impact with the floor. The demon didn't seem bothered by what I'd done.

The angel glanced at me and shouted, "Get out of here!"

Was she Lizzy's angel?

"Addy, leave!" she said again as she took hold of one of the demons and twisted his neck back, killing him before I could blink.

I grabbed Lizzy's hand and helped her to her feet. We moved to the front door.

And stopped.

Another demon grinned at us, a sword in his hand, blocking our path.

Lizzy and I retreated, and the demon followed. The angel threw her body in front of us and kicked the demon away.

"Come on," I said, running back to Lizzy's room.

Lizzy and I shut the door behind us. I pulled her with me into her closet to hide. At least there we were covered by hanging clothes.

Lizzy's hand found mine in the dark. "What were those things?"

"Don't say anything."

We stayed quiet and listened to the noises outside, neither of us able to tell who was winning.

Chapter Sixteen

ADRIEL

Sometime during the night, I awoke for just a moment. Addy had been rolling around in her sleep, muttering random words about her brother and that guy named Devin, who I suspected had been her boyfriend based on the angry look that flashed across her face whenever his name came up.

I touched her arm. "Addy, wake up. You're having a nightmare."

She opened her eyes and looked at me. A tear fell down her cheek; she wiped it against the pillow and shifted her body closer to me. I moved my hand to her face and wiped off the remnants of the tear.

"You're safe," I said.

Her hand took hold of mine, and our fingers intertwined.

That was the last memory I had of that night before waking up again hours later to find Addy gone and the spot beside me cold.

In the darkness of the apartment, I stepped toward the kitchen. People's voices were audible from the hallway. I stopped before the corner and peeked over at the living room. In the kitchen, the fridge door had been left open, shining dim light into the area.

On the opposite side of the apartment, a demon's body slumped across the living room table while two other demons fought off Simiael, a guardian angel I knew well. In the midst of the struggle, Simiael noticed me and flashed me a warning glance.

With an upward bob of her head, she indicated the corridor behind me. "Get them out of here!"

I ran back, stopping at Addy's doorway. "Addy?"

No one responded, so I continued to Lizzy's room.

"Addy? Lizzy?"

The blinds were down over the window, leaving the room pitch-black. I stole inside, rushed around the bed, and felt around with my hands. No one was in the room. I glanced at the window, considering whether they could have gone out that way. A second later, I realized it would be impossible to jump from a three-story building without getting hurt.

They had to still be in the apartment, and if they weren't in the living room, they had to be here. I got down on all fours and checked under the bed. Nothing.

I'd almost walked out of the room when I remembered the closet. I darted to the door and jerked it open. From behind the shelter of hanging clothes, two people gasped.

"It's me. It's Adriel."

"Shit." The voice sounded like Addy's.

Hands grabbed me, hugging me.

"Oh my God," Lizzy murmured near my ear in between sobs.

I grabbed Addy's hand and pulled her out of the closet. "Come on. We have to get out of here."

Addy leaned back, almost like she was afraid to take another step from the closet. "But they're out there."

"It's all right. Simiael can distract them long enough for us to leave."

"Simiael?"

"Your guardian angel, Addy."

"Oh."

Addy moved forward, pushing past us as if the knowledge that her guardian was out there had fueled her. She bolted into the living room, not waiting for us to follow, and stood watching the angel.

"Simiael." She exchanged a look with her guardian before glancing back at us. "I have to help her."

"Addy, no," Simiael said. "Leave, now!"

Simiael battled the demons, one with a sword in his hand and the other holding her wings down. The demon thrust the sword at her. In defense, she grabbed the sharp side of the weapon with two hands and pushed it away from her body, slicing her palms open. Blood trickled from her hands to the floor.

"No!" Addy sprang at the demon, ready to snatch his sword, but he seemed to sense her coming and spun around.

Lunging forward, I grabbed Addy's wrist and yanked her back in time, the weapon missing her by an inch. The steel sword slashed through nothing but air. The demon growled and returned to fighting Simiael.

I wound my arm around Addy's waist and pulled her away from the scene, taking Lizzy with us. On the kitchen counter, I saw a set of keys. My centuries as a guardian angel had come down to this, and quick thinking was a must. Without pausing, I snatched the keys, hoping they were to the apartment and one of the girls' cars.

"No, no!" Addy cried, trying to go back for the angel.

I opened the door, letting in a blast of wind, and got Lizzy out. Addy, on the other hand, kept resisting.

"Addy, we can't stay. She can't hold them for too long."

"Then let's kill them."

My ears picked up a faint gasp. I looked behind me and saw the demon driving his sword through Simiael's throat. It was too late. The angel's eyes met mine as she fell to her knees on the floor. Blood spilled from her neck, and when she coughed, the blood came out of her mouth too. She collapsed facedown.

Eyes full of tears, Addy screamed and struggled against me. She begged me to let her go. She wanted to run back inside, though I wasn't sure if it was to help the angel or harm the demons.

We didn't have time to spare. The demons moved in our direction. I knew that if we kept standing there, we would meet the same fate as Simiael.

"Addy, stop," I shouted at her. "She's gone."

I dragged her outside the apartment and slammed the door shut before the demons could reach us. Addy glared at me, but when I started tugging her down the stairs, she stopped fighting. While her hand felt warm, the cold wind chilled my bones and sent goosebumps up my arms.

Lizzy made it to the parking lot first. I couldn't blame her for wanting to get out of there fast. She stood waiting for us.

When we reached her, she looked between the two of us. "Now what?" She covered her neck with her hand like she was remembering the sight of the sword impaling the angel.

I dangled the keys in front of the two of them. "Whose keys are those?"

Addy grabbed them from me. "They're mine."

"Can you drive?"

She nodded, tears still streaming down her face. She wiped the moisture away and hurried to her car with both of us following behind.

In the distance, I could hear the demons dashing down the stairs. A look over my shoulder showed me they were close to reaching the sidewalk.

We jumped in the car, me in the passenger seat, and took off right as they caught up.

†

Addy parked the car in front of a gas station and turned off the engine. The tears had dried on her face, but her hands wouldn't stop trembling. She crossed her arms and looked straight ahead. For a while, we were silent, except for the sound of Lizzy sniffling every few seconds.

When Addy finally spoke, there was no emotion in her voice. "What do we do now? We're out here, but they can still track us."

In a hushed tone, Lizzy said, "What's happening? I don't understand anything."

Addy ignored her friend. "We're totally screwed."

"We could keep driving," I said.

"No, we can't." Addy glanced out the window, checking behind the car. "They'll find us like they already did, and they'll kill us like Simiael."

Simiael had been one of my many sisters. I felt bad about her death, but the thought of something happening to Addy made my heart pound so hard that it pulsated in my ears.

I studied Addy's face, the way her eyebrows furrowed and the way she bit her bottom lip and peeled a piece of skin off with her teeth without twitching from pain. I wanted to bite that bottom lip too, find out what her mouth tasted like.

Blood rushed between my legs. I looked down at my pants, horrified.

Don't think about her mouth, don't think at all. I repeated the mantra in my head.

"We're all dead," Addy said.

Her harsh words brought me back to my senses.

"I won't let them get to you," I told her.

Seeming not to hear me, she checked the rearview mirror. "Lucifer warned me. He said I had no place to hide. I didn't listen."

"Hey." I touched her arm, and she jolted from her seat. I looked her straight in the eyes, avoiding any other body part. "I won't let him get to you."

"How?" Her eyes held mine, twisting and turning my soul. "Can't you see he already got to me?" She didn't bat an eyelid, keeping me frozen under her spell.

"Addy . . ." I swallowed. "You're doing it again."

"Doing what?"

"You're messing with my head. Please, stop looking at me."

She dropped her gaze. "Sorry."

151

In the back, Lizzy took off her seat belt and moved toward us. "Will someone please explain what is going on? They almost killed us and you guys won't tell me why."

Like her friend, Addy took off her seat belt and spun around in her seat. "Really, Lizzy? We're in danger here and need to figure out what to do, and you want to know what the fuck is going on?"

Lizzy sniffed. "Yes."

"Fine."

Starting from the night she found me, Addy told Lizzy everything, rushing over the part about how, at this very instant, an army of humans worked for Lucifer because of what she did. At the mention of the two nights at the club when she turned several people into demons, her eyes dropped and she tapped her foot against the car floor. "I had to compel them," she said. "I needed to save Reed."

After that, Lizzy slumped back in her seat and didn't say another word.

†

We decided to call on Lizzy's guardian angel for protection; it would be the easiest way to shield ourselves. Besides, with Addy's angel gone, we had no other option.

It was four in the morning, which I still considered night. The three of us felt drained and needed to sleep. Out loud, I asked the guardian to help us—all of us. We waited on the angel to show himself—or herself—but no one came.

Lizzy chewed on her long fingernails, her head resting against the side of Addy's seat. "What if I don't have a guardian angel?"

"You definitely do," I said. "Every human does."

Addy sighed. "I don't. Not anymore."

"You'll get another. Maybe not right away, but you'll get one."

"But what do we do now? We're sitting ducks."

"Hey, what is this?" Lizzy pointed at something inside the car, not far from her face. "Do you see that?"

A translucent film wrapped around the three of us, spreading in all directions, covering the car. In the dark, seeing it was difficult, but if I concentrated, I could just barely spot the sliver of a light-blue tint surrounding us.

"The angel's shield," Addy said. "He's here."

Lizzy smiled. "Really? My angel is here?"

"Yup. It only took him a decade."

After that, the night was easier to bear. We slept in the car, Addy and I with our seats reclined all the way back and Lizzy lying in the fetal position. They weren't the most comfortable sleeping arrangements, but we surrendered to the night quickly.

Chapter Seventeen

ADELAIDE

A hand shook me from the darkness of sleep. I opened my eyes, saw a woman's face staring at me, and recoiled.

"Don't be afraid," the woman said. "It's me."

I had to blink a few times to recognize her. Up close, she looked young, not so much a woman but rather a girl in her late teens. Red curls flowed down her shoulders, creating a huge contrast to her impeccable white wings. She smiled, though all I could focus on were the beautiful brown freckles on her cheeks.

"Simiael," I said.

"Hello, my sweet Addy."

Wanting to make sure she was real, I reached to touch her face and felt silky skin.

"Are you really here?"

She ran her fingers through my hair, something Grandma Di used to do. "It is only a dream, but I am truly with you."

I grabbed hold of her hand. "They killed you. I saw you die."

Her smile was soft, understanding. "A spirit never dies, Addy. They destroyed my body. Even so, I will be reborn into another."

"As an angel?"

"Yes."

She looked to my right. "He has a strong soul, even if he doesn't know it yet."

I had been looking at her and nothing else, afraid if I aimed my attention elsewhere, she would disappear. But her words made me curious. I looked around, finding myself in my cherished car, Lucy. Next to me, Adriel slept with his head against the door, and Lizzy rested in the back.

Simiael had been sitting on top of the dashboard, her legs extended forward between the two front seats. Although she should have been confined in the small area, the car seemed much bigger with her in it. Even her wings had room to move.

"This is a dream?" It looked too real to be a dream, and yet it didn't really make sense.

"It is an angelic dream." She coiled a strand of my hair around her finger before letting it go and moving on to another strand. "I will have to leave soon, though."

"Where will you go?"

"I will be floating around heaven until I can be reborn."

I squeezed her hand. "Will you be my angel again?"

"I don't know. I don't control these things."

I wanted to tell her I was sorry for the things I'd done, for doing what Lucifer wanted despite her trying to protect me from behind the scenes. Though before I could say any of that, her image began to fade. It started with her wings, then her body, then her hand on my head. The last things to vanish were her smile and her gentle voice.

"Goodbye, my Addy," she said. With that, she was gone.

Darkness took over my dream for a while, but I didn't exactly feel like I was in a dream. Instead, I felt as if I were in a black room with my senses heightened. I could hear air leaving and entering people's bodies.

Reaching to my right, I felt around in the dark until I found Adriel's arm. Heat emanated from his skin, too hot to touch. I let go.

"Adriel, what's going on?"

Adriel didn't answer. Though someone else did.

"How did you get here?" an unfamiliar, hoarse voice said. I couldn't tell if it was male or female. "Are you lost?"

I crossed my arms over my chest and looked around, trying to pick up any movements.

The voice snickered. "Can't see, dollface? Let me help you with that."

Hot, wrinkled fingers clasped my wrist. I moved back in my seat, but the person or thing kept holding on.

"Who are you? What do you want?" I said.

Two small balls of light floated in the air no more than a foot from my face. They hung parallel to each other and flared with intense heat.

My free hand went up to my face, shielding my eyes from the glare. "What *are* you?"

The thing let go of my hand. "I was once just like you."

With my hand half in front of my eyes, I saw the figure more clearly. The balls of light illuminated a nose, lips, a neck, and a human shape. The thing's lack of clothes revealed a skinless body covered in nothing but skeletal muscle tissue and veins.

"What's wrong, pretty one?" The disfigured thing trailed its red, veiny fingers over my arm. "Never seen something like me before?"

Goosebumps descended my arms. I stared back at the lights, realizing they weren't lights at all. They were eyes burning with fire.

Pulling my hand away, I grabbed the metal part of my seat belt, ready to smash it against the demon's face.

"I guess I shouldn't be surprised." The demon thing flashed its yellow teeth at me. "You wouldn't know your own power if it stared you in the face."

I went to strike the demon with the seat belt's end, but the monster disappeared right before the metal could hit its raw, skeletal head.

I jumped from my seat, waking up. The sun was rising in the distance, coloring the sky a shade of yellow. Adriel had been asleep. When I started moving around, he jolted awake.

"What happened?" he said, reaching to touch my arm. He whipped his head back, checking on Lizzy. "What's going on?"

Had it all been a dream? Staring at Adriel, I tried to figure out what I'd just seen. Simiael had felt real, and so did the demon. So real, in fact, that I couldn't tell the difference between them and people in the waking world.

Adriel leaned toward me, his eyes full of worry. He tucked one side of his hair behind his ear. "Are you all right?"

I rested my head against the backrest and thought back to the beginning of the dream. "I saw Simiael in my sleep. I think she was real."

He grinned, something he hadn't done before. His whole face brightened. "She probably was."

"She said she will be reborn again."

"Very few angels die, but those that do get reborn."

"I didn't have time to ask her about that. She was gone too fast. How can she be reborn? I thought angels were already spirits, and spirits can't die."

"You're right. Simiael isn't dead, but her body no longer works. You should think of an angel's body as armor. It is what they use to protect the world."

Glancing around the car, I could still see the transparent shield. Lizzy's guardian angel must have been working hard all night to keep us out of sight. So, how did the demon find me?

"I also saw a demon," I said. "In my dream, after Simiael left."

"What kind of demon?"

"It looked skinless and veiny. I'm not sure what it was."

A frown took over his face. "I've never seen a demon like that before. There are three types of demons. You've seen two of them so far: fallen angels and the hounds of hell. People who die and go to hell—or are turned into demons while alive, I suppose—are the third type. None of those look anything like what you just described."

I shrugged. "I guess it was just a dream."

He smiled but didn't say anything else.

†

We sat in a nearby coffee shop called Mike's Coffee Hour at a table in the corner of the room, away from the big window. The aroma of coffee and cinnamon stuffed the air. Muted news played on the TV mounted on the wall across from us. Other than the barista behind the counter, we were the only ones in the shop.

"Where do we go after this?" Lizzy said as she finished eating an entire ham-and-cheese croissant sandwich she'd only started chomping down on less than two minutes ago. She wiped her hands clean on a napkin before sipping her warm pumpkin spice latte.

I looked down at the table in search of my phone and remembered that I'd left it back home along with my wallet. A groan escaped my throat. "We have to go back to the apartment. We don't have a choice."

"Yes, we do." Lizzy's eyes were wide as she shook her head back and forth. "Nothing says we have to go back there."

Indicating our night clothes, I reminded her that we couldn't stay the way we were. "Besides, we don't have our phones or money on us."

Lizzy's eyebrows raised in confusion. "How did you buy us food then?"

Adriel had been silent this whole time, nibbling on an egg, bacon, and cheese sandwich. At Lizzy's inquiry, he glanced up, his eyes meeting mine. A silent message passed between us. Although it appeared to pain him, he put the remains of his sandwich down and wiped his hands clean. Several crumbs landed on the table. It took him a moment to stop eyeing his food.

"Addy?" Lizzy stared at me, the cup of coffee barely touching her lips.

Looking down at the table, I said, "I kind of had to compel the barista."

"What?" Lizzy pushed her cup away and eyed the barista. "Weren't you just telling me last night about all the people you had to compel? You said marking them with the devil's initial when they're emotionally vulnerable automatically relinquishes their souls. Addy, this is so wrong. Did you mark this guy? Please tell me you didn't."

"I know it's wrong, and I didn't mark him!" I sprang from the table. "Do you think I like any of this? I'm very aware of how screwed up everything is. But what choice do we have? What choice do *I* have?"

Adriel bent forward and grabbed my hand. His touch felt cold, nice. The line of his jaw was tense, though. "We always have a choice."

"And what is that in this case?"

"You didn't have to get this food."

"Fine. You guys can starve for all I care." I pulled my hand away and started walking out, leaving my own half-eaten cream-cheese bagel and full cup of coffee.

As I neared the door, an image on the TV caught my attention. I stopped to check it out. Noticing my interest, the barista turned the volume up. The news showed a small church, only a few blocks from my apartment, on fire.

"This is the third arson case targeting religious establishments in the last twenty-four hours right here in Pittsburgh," the anchorwoman said. "The fire department was at a mosque earlier this morning putting out a fire that had spread into the acres of land behind the structure."

The news pulled a clip of firefighters spraying down a burning mosque with water followed by another clip of the fire occurring at the local church now. Flames exploded through the windows, and the exterior white walls of the holy institution were quickly enveloped with fire and ash.

"It appears that some firefighters have just entered St. Peter Catholic Church. It is unknown as of yet whether people are inside. In the mosque fire earlier today, the gardener of the establishment was on site and claims the fire was started by a white male in his early twenties. The gardener was stabbed twice outside the mosque right before the fire took place. He was taken to the hospital and, according to the doctors, will fully recover."

"What the hell?" I said in a hushed voice.

My head hurt. I put my sweaty fingers on my temples and attempted to massage the ache away. I had a feeling in my gut that these crimes were related to me, to the people I'd turned into monsters.

And what about Devin? What if he was the one behind the fires?

I pushed through the door, eager to get away from being confronted with the reality that everything was my fault. I stood in the cold wind, my hands on my bare knees, breathing in and out. Moisture traveled down my cheeks. Beneath me, the ground shook—or maybe it didn't, maybe I imagined it. But it felt like it shook. I would rather fall headfirst on the concrete and die from head trauma than be conscious in a world that was disintegrating because of me.

A single bell chime rang as the coffee shop's door opened. Footsteps sounded behind me. Before Adriel spoke, I knew it was him, because as always, he was the perfect angel, the hero of this corrupt thing called existence. I wished he would stop acting so righteous. For someone who fell from heaven, he sure as hell made me feel bad for my actions.

"Addy." He stood in front of me, his hands reaching for my shoulders and straightening me up. "You don't know if any of it is because of Lucifer."

Biting my lower lip, I tried to keep calm. "It's because of me."

"You don't know that."

"Except I do."

More tears fell. I tried to push back the hatred I felt for myself, to not show him the tears, but I couldn't control any of it.

"I sold Devin's soul, then I sold a bunch of other people's souls. Based on what? My biased judgment of who they were in a single moment?" My hand went up to my hair, pulling it out of the way. I walked away from Adriel, pacing the sidewalk in front of the shop. "You can't just say this isn't on me, because we both know that's a lie. I messed up big."

A scream sounded through the parking lot. Adriel rushed toward me, but I didn't understand why. His arms pulled me in. He held me against his chest, one of his hands supporting the back of my head.

Another scream rang through my ears. This time the sound seemed muffled.

"We will fix everything," Adriel said. "Please calm down."

With my head pressed against his chest, I craned my neck up to look at him. Why was he holding me and telling me to calm down? What had I done?

"It's all going to be fine, Addy."

I saw my reflection through his brown eyes just then: the tears streaming down my face, my gaping and trembling mouth, my disheveled hair. I realized I was the one who had screamed.

Hiding my head in the crook of his neck, I let one last cry out. He held me still, saying nothing, his arms wrapped around me. When the tears dried and I felt strong again, I pulled away a little, just enough to look at him.

He placed his icy hand on the side of my face, his eyes dancing back and forth between mine. "Whatever is happening, I promise we will fix it together."

"How?"

He shrugged. "I don't know yet, but we will."

"I hope so."

With no space between us, blood rushed to my cheeks. I couldn't escape the hardness of his chest or the smell of the coffee he had just sipped. Adriel smiled, glancing at my lips, then back up. I was suddenly aware of his left hand on my lower back and his right one on my face.

"Rosy cheeks," he whispered.

"What?"

His dark eyes stopped moving, and that wild look I saw in him yesterday returned. He bent his head forward, his lips crashing into mine. His hand shifted to cradle the back of my head, holding me in place.

I closed my eyes, feeling nothing but his soft lips, the pressure of his thumb on the side of my neck, and the icy air around us.

With a sigh, I let him have me. His tongue slipped in, tasting of caramel and dark coffee, my favorite. Wind burst around us, leaving his nose cold where it brushed against my skin. I pressed my hands against the taut muscles of his chest and felt his heart beat violently alongside mine.

Tightening his grip on my waist, he pulled me even closer. Every inch of him pressed against me, and I couldn't help feeling his bulge nudging my leg. An electric charge fired down my spine.

Wanting so much more, I let my tongue meet his halfway. A primal moan roared in his throat, and with it came a stream of warmth into my mouth. My legs became limp. And when I thought he couldn't turn me on any more than he already had, he sucked on my lower lip, his teeth grazing my skin just as he pulled away.

"I'm sorry," he said, breathing like he was out of air.

"I . . . It's okay."

He let me go and stepped back. "That was out of place."

I put my hand on my lips, feeling the intoxicating sting of his teeth as if they were still there.

"I just shouldn't." He ran a hand through his jaw-length hair and closed his eyes. "I'm sorry. That was really out of line."

I swallowed, feeling a sharp pain in my throat. "It's okay."

"I shouldn't have done that. I'm supposed to do better."

Turning away from him, I tried to compose myself. My heart pounded, and I wished it would stop entirely. He didn't want me; he didn't want me because he could do better. I couldn't even blame him. Who would want the daughter of the devil? Taking a deep breath, I told myself I felt nothing for him. Because I didn't. I didn't. *I didn't.* And because he didn't want me in the same way.

I whirled back around, my face dead of any emotion. "It's okay. Let's just forget about this."

He took a step toward me, sadness in his eyes. "Addy—"

"Let's get going," I said, cutting him off. Before he could say anything else, I walked inside the coffee shop.

Lizzy sat in her chair, looking at her polished, clear-painted fingernails. She was obviously pretending she hadn't witnessed an entire show outside the window.

"Come on, let's get out of here," I said.

She frowned. "Are we really going back to the apartment?"

"We don't have a choice."

"Yes, we do."

I grabbed my warm cup of coffee and leftover food from the table, taking a big bite of the bagel as I headed out. A rich, creamy goodness clung to my tongue, though I was sad to get rid of the caramel taste of Adriel's mouth.

Lizzy trotted behind me, leaving her coffee at the table. "You're still going to eat that? You didn't pay for it."

"When the world is back to normal, I'll come back here and dump a fifty-dollar bill on that barista's counter. Does that sound good to you, Mom?"

She crossed her arms and walked out without holding the door open for me. "I don't like your attitude right now." She hurried to the parking lot.

Adriel waited by Lucy. When I avoided eye contact with him, he took the backseat, letting Lizzy sit in the front. He didn't say anything in the car, but I occasionally saw him looking at me through the rearview mirror.

†

At Sunny Meadows Private Residences, I parked Lucy as close to our building as possible in case we had to run out again like we did last night. Adriel and I got out of the car, but Lizzy didn't budge. She kept her arms crossed and looked into the distance, reminding me of six-year-old Reed when he threw tantrums.

I watched her through the windshield. "Liz, are you coming?"

She shrugged and looked away. "I don't feel right about this. I already told you." She rolled her window down a smidge.

Upstairs seemed quiet. I glanced up at my bedroom window on the third floor, but it wasn't like I was going to see much inside from where I stood.

"Come on, Lizzy. You don't even have to come in with us. You can stay with Nate."

At the mention of her boyfriend's name, she took off her seat belt and hurried out of the car. "Is it safe there? What if something happened to him?"

"We won't know until we go upstairs."

Lizzy mumbled something and marched toward the building.

On our floor, the three of us stood in front of the apartment, staring inside. The door had been left open all night. The stool Lizzy had used as a shield against the demons had been tipped over at some point—I couldn't remember when—and lay on the floor. In the background, I spotted a segment of Simiael's left wing, now smeared with her blood. Even the pumpkin Lizzy had left outside was smashed to pieces, leaving orange guts all over the floor.

Lizzy shuddered and rushed toward Nate's door. After a few knocks, he opened the door, sleep still in his eyes.

"What's going on?" he said.

Nate's short hair stood up in opposite directions, divided into three messy, triangular shapes above his head. When he saw us standing behind Lizzy, he raked his fingers through the bird-nest hairdo.

Lizzy wrapped her arms around his neck and rested her head against his chest.

"Hey, everything okay?" he asked her.

Lizzy met my glare and gave me a subtle nod. When she looked up at Nate, she had a smile plastered across her face, though it didn't reflect in her eyes. "Yeah, we just had a robbery while we were out getting breakfast, but we're fine."

"Oh, shit." Nate let go of Lizzy and moved toward our apartment.

My heart thumped in my chest. For a second, I pictured Nate finding Simiael's body. I imagined his eyes turning red, his forehead creasing, and him running out of the room to call for help. I saw him having an angry conversation with the police, leading to our misguided arrest.

Thinking quickly, Adriel grabbed the door handle to our apartment and closed the door halfway. "You don't want to see the mess, friend."

Nate bobbed his head. "No worries, man. Did you call the cops?"

"Yes." Adriel's eyes flickered my way. "They already came and left."

"Good, good."

Lizzy strutted over to Nate and pulled him toward his apartment. "Baby, let's leave these two to sort things out."

"Yeah, sure."

"Hey, Nate," I said. "Can Lizzy stay with you for a few days, actually? I don't feel comfortable staying in the apartment right now, and I don't think she should either."

A smile stretched across his face in answer, and the two of them disappeared inside his home. Once more, it was just Adriel and me.

Feeling the slimy pumpkin gut underneath my feet, I moved inside and stepped around broken glass and rocks from the salt-crystal lamp strewn on the floor. Behind the kitchen stool, Simiael lay with her wings outstretched, the way we'd left her. Or almost the way we'd left her. Someone had engraved a message into the flesh just above her wings. The jagged cuts read, *"You will regret leaving."* I knew the message was for me.

Crouching down beside Simiael, I stroked her red curls and looked at her blood-speckled face. She was beautiful, despite being dead and pale. Her eyes remained open, and it felt like she was staring inside my soul. They were green with a black halo around the irises. As I closed them, I wondered what she was up to at that moment, whether she had been given another angelic body already.

"We should bury her or something."

Adriel squatted beside me. "Her body should disappear from this world in a few hours. If she hadn't been visible to the human eye when she died, no one would be able to notice her right now."

"So, her body will just vanish into thin air?"

"Pretty much."

I left Simiael on the floor and moved past the chaos in the living room, pretending I wasn't sad over the rustic coffee table the demons had broken that Lizzy and I had bought over a year ago.

When I made it to my room, I became even more upset. As if my picture frames hadn't endured enough over the past few days, they were piled on top of my desk and smashed in the center so that their glass had cracked into pieces. My work papers and folders covered the floor around my bed, and I couldn't tell which project files belonged together. They'd even destroyed my sketches, ripping the paper pads into unrecognizable shreds. If I hadn't already lost my job from neglecting to send any work in since last Thursday, I would probably lose it now.

Adriel came to stand behind me at the door. His feet crunched on the ground. For what felt like a long time, we both stared at my ruined bed. The white comforter had been sliced vertically in half, without a doubt by that demon who had killed Simiael with his sword. Parts of the mattress had been torn too, revealing cotton and fine straw.

"Why would they do this? They didn't gain anything from destroying my apartment."

"They're demons. They don't need a reason."

I strode around the room in search of my phone, to no avail. It wasn't on my nightstand where I usually left it. It wasn't under my pillows or the bed, either.

"Did they take my phone? Can they even use it in hell?" A hoarse laugh escaped my throat. "This is ridiculous!"

What I really wanted to do was rip the demons' throats in half.

Adriel moved to the bathroom. A moment later, he walked out with the garbage can in his hand. "Is this your phone?"

He tilted the can in my direction. Inside, my phone sat in a pile of old toothpaste tubes, used floss, and fallen strands of hair. The screen was cracked, just like my picture frames. Groaning, I reached in and took it out.

"Can you still use it?"

"No. But I can do this." I removed the slot on the upper left corner of my phone and took out my SIM card. "Now I

169

have my identity back." I smiled at him before remembering his rejection less than half an hour ago.

Opening my desk drawer, I searched for my old phone. In the back, I found it. I inserted the SIM card into it and turned it on. Surprisingly, it still had some juice.

"They clearly aren't that bright," I said.

I grabbed the phone's charger from the drawer, retrieved my wallet from my purse, and packed a couple of outfits and toiletries for Adriel and me for the next couple of days. I put together anything I found of Devin's and told Adriel to search Lizzy's room for Nate's clothes and add them to the duffle bag.

He crossed his arms, much like Lizzy had earlier that morning. "Isn't that stealing?"

"Nate is my friend, and he's Lizzy's boyfriend, so I think he'll understand. Besides, she had his stuff for like a month. I don't think he'll notice them gone now."

"Fine, but I'm returning everything to him when we come back."

I bit my bottom lip. "If we come back."

He started out the door, heading toward Lizzy's room. "We will," he called as he went.

Chapter Eighteen

ADRIEL

Jenna's face came to my mind as I sifted through Lizzy's closet. A few hours ago, Simiael had died, but the last death I'd witnessed before that had been Jenna's son, Matt. Nearly moments before I'd become a human, Jenna had kissed Matt on the forehead and covered his face with a pillow. I had watched from above, thinking it was the best choice, the only way to end Matt's misery and Jenna's pain.

Who knew I'd lose Jenna and Simiael, two beings I knew well, in such a short time? Now Jenna was out there, probably being prosecuted for doing what she'd thought was right for her son.

Down the hall, I could hear an unfamiliar voice talking, though I couldn't pick out the words. I dropped everything in my hands and rushed to Addy's room. She wasn't there. I ran to the living room, where the sound was coming from. Addy stood in front of the TV with the remote control in her hand. She had changed out of her pajamas and was now in jeans and a plain white T-shirt. She kept distance between herself and Simiael, as though she feared getting blood on her shoes.

"Look at the news," she said without looking at me. "They're saying crime rates have increased in the past two days in Pennsylvania."

I moved to stand next to her to better see the TV. Unable to help it, I stared at her profile. She pressed her rosy lips together as she concentrated on the news. She was unaware of me, of the hungry way I watched her, craved her, even. Only a little while ago, she had been in my arms. I wanted to reach out again and hold her against me. Body against body. Mouth on mouth. Hands in her hair, hers on my chest.

"This is crazy," she said, bringing me out of my reverie. She was still talking about the news.

Putting some distance between us, I looked at the TV screen.

The newswoman spoke about the three fires that had occurred earlier today and mentioned multiple battery cases in the past forty-eight hours. Two people were nearly beaten to death and five others were killed from severe knife wounds. "Police have not been able to track down the persons involved," she said. "However, they are working on finding out who is responsible for these crimes. We will keep you updated as we learn more."

Addy put her hand on top of her head and pulled her hair back. "Is this because I took Reed? Because I'll do it again if I have to. But is that why this is happening?"

"Evil will happen no matter what we do. It's just how Lucifer and his demons are."

"It's never been this bad, though. This world has always had corruption. We've always had wars, murders, people hating people, but evil never grew this fast. Two days, and all of this?" She waved the remote at the TV screen. "What will it be next? Killing babies? Feeding poison to the poor?"

It was scary how far her imagination jumped.

She left the TV on and headed back down the hall into her room. I followed behind her.

"Sure, it's bad, but Lucifer and his demons are not indestructible, Addy."

She grabbed her duffle bag from the foot of the door before moving to Lizzy's room.

"But I couldn't even hurt Lucifer," she said. "You were there. You saw what happened."

"That doesn't mean he can't be hurt."

She shoved every item of clothing I found of Nate's inside the duffle bag. When she finished putting everything away, she handed me the bag to carry.

Heavy with grief, her eyes met mine. "You were his friend before he fell from heaven. You probably know him better than anyone. Do you know anything about his secret weapon?"

I thought back to yesterday morning, to the way the color had drained out of Addy's face when she saw Lucifer pull the knife out of his chest and drop it to the ground. Daughter against father, and he was merciless.

"Adriel, come on, you have to know something," she begged, her hand reaching for my arm before she changed her mind at the last second and dropped it to her side.

"If he has a weapon, he must have created it after he fell. I have no idea what he was talking about."

"But what could be so powerful? What is he protecting himself with?"

"I really don't know."

Frowning, she walked back to her room. She disappeared inside her bathroom for a moment, and when she came out, she had her hair pulled back into a ponytail. I stared at the contours of her face, at the perfect symmetry of her cheeks and nose and eyes, at her small, double-pierced ears. She took my breath away, but I couldn't think like that. I'd caused enough damage already.

"Are you going to stay in your pajamas?" She stared back at me. I realized in that instant that I was standing in the dead center of her bedroom door, blocking the exit.

I went into the bathroom, changed clothes quickly, and met her in the kitchen.

Like a warrior ready for battle, she snatched a couple of knives from one of the drawers and strode out with her back straight and her head held high.

"Let's get out of here," she said.

Taking a deep breath, I glanced at Simiael's body one last time before closing the door behind us. The angel would be okay, though it could be a while before I saw her again. I hurried down the stairs, Addy's duffle bag in my hand.

†

Not far from the apartment complex, Addy stopped the car in front of a convenience store. Without saying a word, she hopped out, taking her keys and wallet with her.

I opened the car door. "Addy, where are you going?"

She didn't look back. I left the duffle bag in the car and headed after her. If anything happened in my absence, not only would I be unable to do anything, but I would also regret not protecting Addy.

Inside the store, Addy marched through the aisles, never stopping to check out the products she walked past.

I walked behind her, my attention being pulled this way and that. Some aisles smelled like roses and lilies, and before I could ask where the scents were coming from, I noticed candles and air fresheners. As I followed Addy, I surveyed the bright-yellow signs taped to specific rows to indicate sales and buy-one-get-one-free deals.

"What are you looking for?" I inquired.

Addy stopped walking, and I nearly crashed into her while looking at a variety of bags containing white undershirts on the row to my right.

She grabbed two bags from the opposite row and tossed them at me. I caught them just before they fell to the floor.

"I'm looking for these." She walked off in a hurry, her face red.

It took me two seconds to study the bags and realize what they were. I smiled. Men's boxer shorts flustered Addy, and she was getting them for me.

I continued after her, passing aisle after aisle until I found her in the back of the store standing in front of the tools and supplies section. She was looking at a couple of different multitool pocket knives similar to the one she'd used on Lucifer.

I took one for analysis and pulled out all the attachments. "You do realize that you can't kill him with this, right?"

"Just because I can't kill Lucifer with it doesn't mean I can't use it to protect myself."

She examined one of the red, bigger pocket knives by grazing the sharp edges of each tool against her fingers. I waited for blood to seep out, but she was gentle with the knife, not letting its tools cut her.

"His demons are apparently all over the place, and we just lost Simiael. Plus, Lizzy's guardian is with her. This," she said, raising the knife in my direction, "is the best we can do."

Taking the bags of men's boxer shorts from my hand, she moved to the front of the store to make the purchase.

†

Back in the car, I could tell Addy had no idea what to do next. She made a few quick calls to Lizzy and Reed to make sure they were still safe. Once she hung up, she sat looking at the parking lot around us for a while, not saying anything.

A middle-aged couple moved past the car on their way to the convenience store. Addy shrank in her seat, her eyes fixated on the man and woman.

"They're just people," I said.

"For now."

Addy started the car and began driving. In a few minutes, we were on the highway, traveling away from her apartment.

I closed my eyes and let the morning sun shower me, like it had on my first day as a human. Even now, the warmth continued to amaze me.

With my lids still shut, I asked Addy, "What's the plan?"

When she didn't say anything, I looked at her.

"Addy?"

She shrugged. "I guess I just want to be as close to Reed as possible in case they come back for us."

"Are we going to stay with him?"

"No. But somewhere nearby."

The highway was full of dawdling cars. Addy explained that everyone was heading to work at that time, which was why they were driving so slowly. We sat in traffic, moving what seemed like mere inches every couple of seconds. Addy checked her phone multiple times and fidgeted in her seat. She checked her rearview mirror often, her eyes scanning the road behind us.

It took us more than forty minutes to exit the highway. Addy stepped on the gas like she always did, speeding as if something was chasing us, which I couldn't exactly dispute. She seemed to know the area well. For the first time, I realized I knew nothing about her. Had she lived here all her life? What was her childhood like without a dad? Did she ever have a father figure growing up?

Moving through back roads, she managed to avoid traffic lights and the sluggish flow of cars.

"We're almost there," she said.

I didn't know where "there" was, but my eyes surrendered to sleep before I could ask.

In the darkness, the firefly returned. Its light beamed brighter than before. For no reason other than my imagination going wild, I thought the little creature looked happy.

"Hey." I put my hand out, palm up.

The firefly came and rested in the center of my palm, its eyes fixed on me.

"You keep disappearing before I get the chance to talk to you."

The firefly's light wavered for a split second, then lit up again.

"Are you here to show me something?"

The little creature flew off my hand. It hovered close to my face, its small wings flapping gently.

"What is it?"

The firefly tapped its leg against my nose, then took flight in the other direction.

"Wait! Please come back." My voice sounded far away. "I have some questions."

With the firefly gone, darkness came back.

"Hello?" My voice, a mere whisper, sounded as if it came from another room. I called out at the top of my lungs, but that didn't make a difference.

My body shifted in this black hole. I had no sense of direction, no way to differentiate up from down. As if my old wings were carrying me, I rose up. I floated for a long time, and when I fell back down, I landed softly.

Sense of the space around me came back, although I was still in the dark. The surface underneath me extended past my arms and legs and felt like cotton. It reminded me of Addy's bed. Instinctively, I reached out, searching for her.

"Adriel?" Her voice reverberated like a sweet chorus of angels.

Something stirred above me, trapping me in place by the hips. A hand rested flat on my chest. Moving my hands around, I felt legs on either side of me. I held on, trailing my fingers up, up, up until I found a set of hips.

She came down, her lips meeting mine, her hair everywhere. I groaned, pulling her closer and gripping her waist. I lost myself in her, feeling nothing but her touch and smelling only her. She was a succulent rose in the dark.

When she pulled away, I opened my eyes. Her face hovered above mine. Bright lights shone behind her.

I reached for her face and asked, "Are you an angel?" It was a stupid question, one that I knew the answer to. But she was just so beautiful, so pure, so light, I felt certain in that moment she was an angel. With my hand tangled in her hair and her dark-brown eyes staring into my soul, pulling me inside her, inside her being, I just knew.

I shouldn't have been feeling what I felt. It was wrong, I knew that. But I didn't care just then. Not when she looked down at me with her full lips parted. Not when her cheeks blushed the rosy shade I loved. If wanting her meant descending into hell, I would want her just the same.

Yellow light glittered in the distance, like rain made of gold. It drizzled behind Addy, seeming to pour on her. She smiled.

I held her tightly. "What's going on?"

The light engulfed her. Her body lifted off mine, turning weightless.

"No, don't go!" I brought her hands to my face. "Don't go . . ."

Her smile faded with the rest of her.

I lay alone on the featureless mattress now. I dropped my head back, missing her. The yellow light kept growing where Addy had been. It surged through the space around me, blinding me.

From the golden glow emerged a pair of wings, gold like the sun.

"Michael," I said. My hands reached out to touch the shimmering yellow feathers, which belonged only to one angel. They were both soft and strong at the same time.

Though they felt smooth against my skin, their roots were hard. Nothing but his own strength could yank them out.

I sat up, expecting the archangel to make an appearance any second.

As expected, he burst into existence from the golden light. I thought he would be in his armor, but his chest was bare. And yet, he had strapped his famous sword onto his unbreakable belt. He stretched his golden wings back, flexing the muscles in his chest and shoulders.

His eyes glimmered with happiness as his glistening feathers and blond hair ruffled in the air. He smiled and said my name in greeting.

"What are you doing here?" I asked.

He placed his hand on my shoulder and squeezed. "I'm here to protect you."

I whined from the pressure of his hand. I shut my eyes, feeling moisture threatening to trickle down. "What . . . what are you doing?"

He didn't respond. I still felt the tightness of his grip on my shoulder, but from the darkness behind my lids came an image.

"Do you see?" Michael said, his hand steady on me.

I groaned. There was a fire. It grew from afar until it reached me. On the other side of the fire, a person was running.

Michael's hand squeezed harder. "Listen to the voice."

"There is no voice." I couldn't hear anything. I could only see.

"Pay attention."

The blaze cloaked the air. Everywhere I looked, there was a thick red film, and I saw dark smoke around the edges of the fire. Michael's fingers dug into my shoulder, reminding me he was still there.

I looked through the red haze, my vision's lens shifting forward. It zoomed in, showing me a clearer view of the person I saw running earlier. The figure stood behind the fire, an arm covering his or her mouth.

"Listen to the voice, Adriel," Michael repeated. "This is important."

I could only hear my heart pounding in my chest. Was that what he wanted me to notice? That I was human?

"You are not listening, Adriel."

"Listening to what? Michael, I don't know what you're talking about."

"Shh. Just listen."

Taking a deep breath through the pain, I tried to listen past the hammering of my heart. I was about to say I didn't hear anything again when the sound of wind gusted past me. The figure behind the fire looked like he or she was coughing. Hunched over, the person's eyes stared through the red, foggy cloud of smoke. For a split second, the eyes glanced right through me. Dark brown, wild, and angry. I recognized those eyes.

"Addy?" I muttered.

"Yes." Michael's grasp on my shoulder never faltered, but his voice stayed gentle. "Pay attention to her. Pay attention to what is around her."

He sounded like a loving grown-up speaking to a child. It reminded me of the way Jenna had spoken to her son throughout the years before he passed away.

I looked at Addy through the fire, though I doubted she could see me. It was just a vision, after all. I wasn't really there.

She moved out of sight.

"Where is she? Where did she go?"

"She is just behind that door. She is outside a house."

My eyes narrowed. Right where Addy had been standing was a window, and to the right, where she'd disappeared, was the door Michael was talking about.

A distant shout came through the fire, the first real sound I'd heard. I tried concentrating on just that sound until I heard a clear voice.

"Erica!" Addy yelled.

Over and over, her words kept coming. First like a whisper, then growing into shaky screams. Suddenly, I could hear nothing else.

"Erica, where are you?"

The door opened. Addy appeared before me. Flames whipped in her direction, escaping out onto the street. She ducked, avoiding the fire. Another figure appeared behind her. A man. He pulled her away. She clutched at his hands around her stomach, almost like she was trying to pull them from her body.

"That is you," Michael said.

"What's the meaning of this? Why are you showing it to me?"

Addy continued to shout as I dragged her away from the scene. All the visions I'd seen in the past few days had come true. Was this vision about to take place too?

My vision's lens drew back, zooming out and away from Addy and me. I thought of Reed. We were driving toward his college. If his dorm was on fire and he got hurt—or worse— Addy would be destroyed.

"No," I said. "She'll be heartbroken. You have to save him."

"This is Adelaide's mother's house," Michael said. "You are still not paying attention."

"To what? What is there other than Addy and the fire?"

"Listen to the fire."

"What?"

Michael's fingers seemed to tear through my flesh. I screamed, but he hushed me.

"Adriel, this is important. I need you to truly pay attention."

Tears poured down my cheeks. I felt them stream past my chin, slide across my neck over the hollow point of my throat, and run down my chest, soaking the cotton shirt I wore.

"I can't!" I cried out. "I can't."

"Yes, you can."

I took another deep breath and did what he asked me to do. I listened to the fire.

It thrashed through the room like fire tends to do, consuming everything like a hungry beast in battle. I knew that couldn't be it. No way was that what he wanted me to hear. So, I listened harder, even though my shoulder was in itself on fire.

"Ade," the flames seemed to murmur. "Ade."

"I hear her name," I said. "Or one form of her name, I think."

"Keep listening."

"Ade . . ."

The fire started screeching in my ears, loud, high-pitched, earsplitting. I opened my eyes, exiting the vision.

Michael's hand eased off my shoulder, and he let out a harsh breath. "You let go too soon."

I fell onto the mattress, my hand holding the swelling spot where Michael's fingers had dug in. Tears kept spilling from my eyes. They drenched the bed, leaving me feeling like a child, out of control. My body trembled, and I gripped the edge of the mattress with my other hand, trying to get a hold of myself again.

Michael placed his hand on my back. "Tell Adelaide to drive to her mother's house."

Gazing up at him through the wet blur, I saw him smile. I had so many questions, but I couldn't bring myself to open my mouth. I knew if I did, I would probably scream.

He lifted his hand away from me, placed it over his heart, and said, "Your journey has just begun."

The burning pain in my shoulder began to dissolve—Michael's doing.

Michael's smile remained as his golden wings extended behind him, ready to soar. The yellow, glittering light came back into view, and he was gone.

In a few seconds, I was breathing evenly, my heart back to its normal rhythm. Lying on the mattress, I imagined myself as a firecracker dwindling in cold water.

Chapter Nineteen

ADELAIDE

Adriel winced in his seat. His eyes had been shut for some time, but he kept panting and groaning. I parked the car in front of a motel just a few minutes from Saint Vincent College and waited for Adriel to wake up. His hands fisted. Every vein in his body seemed tense. It was the tears, though, that broke me. *What is he dreaming about?*

"Adriel?" I shook his shoulder gently. "You okay?"

His fingers uncurled. He reached out and clenched my forearm with both of his hands.

"Adriel?"

Like iron claws, his grip was tight, too tight. Blue veins swelled in his wrists. I fought to free my hand, but he was strong even in this sleeping state.

"Adriel, please!"

The color had drained from my hand. If he kept squeezing, I had a feeling my tiny wrist would break.

His eyes shot open and he stared ahead like he didn't know where he was. For a few seconds, he just blinked. When he looked at me, tears dripping down his cheeks, his chest expanded and he let out a sigh.

"Addy . . ." Looking down, he noticed his grip on my hand and released it. "I'm so sorry."

"What happened?"

Wiping the tears off his face, he rested his head back against the headrest. "I had a vision, but it wasn't like anything I've seen before."

"What do you mean?"

He rubbed his left shoulder and winced, his hair falling across his face.

"I saw Michael." He looked at me through red, wet eyes.

In my head, I went through a list of faces I knew. I thought of my coworkers, who I hadn't seen since last Thursday, just before my entire life turned upside down. I even thought of people I'd seen at Euphoria, like Lukas and some of the bartenders. When I couldn't match a face with the name, I said, "Who's Michael?"

"The archangel."

"What?"

"I saw the archangel Michael in the vision. Actually, I saw him in my dream, and he showed me a vision." Removing his muscular hand from his shoulder, he brought it to my face.

"You were there too." His fingers entwined in my hair, right behind my ear.

His skin was warm against mine, but the good kind of warm. He didn't feel like the burning heat coming from deep within me. Without thinking, I leaned into his touch, my eyes closing for a sliver of a second. He responded by pulling my face toward his. When I was mere inches from him, he stopped.

It would have been a lie if I said I didn't want him to kiss me again. Still, when I remembered how he'd treated me just a few hours ago after kissing me, I resolved not to let it happen a second time.

Maybe it was exhaustion, but his eyes drooped in the outer corners, making him look somewhat sad. He let out a breath, one that traveled in a straight line and touched my mouth.

Shaking my head, I pulled away. "What was the vision?"

As if I had shaken him from a deep slumber, he sat straight in his seat, his eyes wide.

"Addy, you have to drive. You have to drive right now."

"What? Where?"

His hands reached for the steering wheel. "Turn the engine on. Go. Go."

I did what he said and sped out of the motel's parking lot. He tugged at his seat belt, mumbled something under his breath, and pulled his hair back behind one ear.

"Hurry."

Once I hit the main road, I slowed down to the posted speed limit since the streets were still busy from the morning rush hour.

"Adriel, where am I going?"

"You need to drive to your mother's house."

My foot almost slammed on the brakes. If it weren't for traffic and the possibility of causing a car crash, I would have stopped the car in its place.

"What do you mean, drive to my mother's? Are you crazy?"

"No, I am not crazy. She is in danger." Adriel tapped his foot against the floor of the car. "Michael wanted me to warn you. Her house is on fire."

"But I don't talk to Erica."

"That's not going to change the fact that she's about to burn alive."

He had a point. No matter how much I despised Erica, I had to save her. Maybe that was the difference between her and me. Despite her not wanting to keep me as a child, I would move mountains to make sure she was okay, even if she wasn't in my life.

"Okay," I said. "We're driving to my mother's."

After a few minutes of studying me in silence, Adriel set his eyes back on the road. "Why do you not want to see your mother?"

It was a simple question with a complicated answer.

I chose to respond with a question. "Why would anyone want to see that woman?"

All those times she'd left Reed and me alone in the house without a babysitter and gone out with her men didn't even come close to the full reason why I couldn't stand the sight of her. It wasn't that she'd told us she wished she gave us up for adoption. And it definitely wasn't when I'd walked in on her having sex during my thirteenth birthday party.

"Let's see," I said, my hands gripping the steering wheel like my personal stress toy. "The woman has no moral fiber in her. She is a terrible parent—no, calling her a parent implies that she parented, which she did not."

I gritted my teeth together. When I felt a twinge in my jaw, I switched to biting my lower lip.

"Hey." Adriel placed his hand on my knee. "You don't have to tell me if you don't want to."

"I know, but if I don't tell you, you'll think I'm a bad daughter. You'll assume the worst."

"I won't."

He moved his hand back to his side, sat back in his seat, and waited. I took a deep breath and thought about telling him everything. After all, he had been a guardian angel. Wouldn't he understand?

When I began talking about Erica and my childhood, I felt calmer. "Erica left me to parent Reed almost as soon as he was born. If that wasn't bad enough, she basically kicked me out of the house the day I hit eighteen. I had been working at a photography studio since I was fifteen, so I took the money I'd saved up and got myself through college. It wasn't easy, but I managed. I even helped Reed go to school."

"To Saint Vincent College?"

"Yes."

Adriel smiled. "Vincent is a very quiet man."

"You know the saint?"

"I've met him in the holy kingdom."

"You mean heaven?"

"That's the one."

I continued telling him about Erica and all the things wrong with her. For one, Erica had never gotten along with her mom, my grandmother, who'd raised me the first few years of my life. For two, she just sucked.

"You know, she refused to buy me decent clothes when I hit puberty because she was worried I would compete with her." I sneered. "What kind of mother thinks like that?"

"That just means she suffered an internal loss," Adriel said. "Something was hurting her, and she didn't know how else to handle it."

We were two minutes away from reaching Erica's house. I did not feel ready to see her, but I drove on, knowing the full weight of her safety lay on my shoulders.

"But what could hurt her so much that she'd leave her own kids to fend for themselves? What would make her do that to us?"

"People have different ways of dealing with things."

"That doesn't justify what she did."

A thin, cheerless smile appeared on his face. "I never said it did."

For the last few minutes of the drive, I thought about having to face Erica. It had been years of silence on my part. Did she look older now? Maybe wrinkles had taken over her face since I'd last seen her. Or maybe she'd gotten plastic surgery to sustain her youth, even though she was just forty-three years old. The truth was, I hoped she'd shriveled up like the witch in *Snow White*. I wanted her to look as ugly as her rotten soul.

Adriel was looking out the window. I glanced at him and said, "Did you see Erica in the vision?"

"No. Just the burning house and you."

We entered my childhood neighborhood, passing by houses decorated with fake spiderwebs and carved pumpkins. The Edisons' house, just ten houses down from Erica's, had been repainted in taupe stucco. When I lived here, their house had looked like a giant mustard container.

I took a deep breath and drove down the road. The Rivera and Patel kids were playing in their connected backyards, tossing a basketball back and forth between the four of them. For protection against the cold, some of them wore hoodies and beanies. They were teenagers now; the last time I saw them, they were still in elementary school.

Smoke wafted into the air as I neared Erica's. From the outside, everything seemed the same. Quiet beige home with a brown roof, lonely in the corner of the neighborhood. It was undecorated. Years of neglect had made the lawn brown and dead. The house looked normal, really. Exactly how I remembered it.

"We're here." I indicated the disheveled house to our right.

I parked on the side of the road and stepped out, Adriel following me. Smoke drifted out of the chimney. *That* was not normal. My mother never used the fireplace. Besides, she was never around to bring wood and set up the fire.

I put my hand on my head and ran my fingers through my tied hair. "The house is on fire, isn't it?"

Adriel glanced at me and then back at the house. "I think so."

My feet moved by themselves, dragging me forward against my will. Condensation ran down the big front window. Behind it, everything was foggy. I wiped the glass and looked through.

Red. The house was blazing red on the inside, yet the outside looked normal, as if nothing was happening. *What the hell?* I thought. *How is this even possible?*

Who had done this? Was it an accident or a deliberate attack?

"Addy!" A warning tone vibrated in Adriel's voice as he followed after me. "You need to call for help."

The fire had already devoured the curtains and nearby furniture. It swarmed the room, wrapping around the hallway and disappearing farther inside.

"There's no time to call 911. I have to get her out." I called for Erica, hoping she wouldn't be in the house. "Erica! Erica, where are you?"

I rushed to the front door and tried the handle. The door swung open, heat and smoke escaping. The heat burned, and I fell down on all fours before it could scald me.

"Addy!"

Adriel's hands wrapped around my waist. He hauled me away from the door.

"No, no!" I yelled. "We have to get her out!"

My fingers burrowed in between his in a failed attempt to detach his flesh from me. He told me to stop, said it was too dangerous, but I just couldn't help it. Erica was in there. No matter how much I hated her, she was still inside, and she needed help.

A few neighborhood kids ran into the yard. Adriel yelled for them to call for help.

Salty tears trickled to my lips. "I have to help her," I said in a trembling voice. "What if she's inside?"

Adriel breathed warm air into my ear as he pulled me into him, my back pressing against his chest. "You can't help her if you're dead."

His words washed over me, and I surrendered. I stood limply in his arms, my head tipped against his shoulder.

In the distance, fire truck sirens wailed. Adriel exhaled and held me still.

Chapter Twenty

ADRIEL

"Ade will corrupt all. Ade will corrupt all."

The fire shrieked, but no one seemed to notice except me. Addy's head slumped against my shoulder. She breathed in and out and muttered that this was not how she wanted to end things with her mother. The neighborhood kids clustered around us. They stared at Addy in silence, like they recognized her.

"Ade will corrupt all," the fire hissed. The sound was overpowering, and yet no one looked frightened or fazed.

"Addy," I said. "Do you hear that?"

Turning her head less than a hair, Addy met my gaze. "The fire truck?"

Her cheeks and nose were red, reminding me of the night I'd met her on that lonely road.

"Ade will corrupt all."

I gritted my teeth. That house was bad news. Of all people, I thought Addy would notice.

"Ade will corrupt all."

Addy was still looking at me. "What? Why are you frowning at me?"

"I'm not frowning at you." I stretched my lips into a fake smile.

Why was the fire screaming her name? I wanted to believe the woman in my arms was good, but I just couldn't tell. Not when Michael himself wanted me to hear this message.

†

A firefighter carried Addy's mother out of the house; he had a mask that extended past his mouth, most likely to help him breathe despite the heavy smoke. Addy's mother was slumped in his arms. Red like the fire escaping through the now shattered windows, her hair swayed in the wind. She was a thin woman with soft features much like Addy's. Although I knew she was in her midforties, I could have sworn she was no older than thirty.

Addy pushed out of my arms and ran toward her mother.

"Is she okay?" she asked the firefighter. She followed him across the pale lawn, her eyes on her unconscious mom.

The firefighter assured Addy that Erica would be fine and placed Erica on a stretcher. Medical technicians swarmed around them, forcing Addy out of the way.

With her hand on her forehead, Addy looked distressed. "What's going on?"

No one answered her.

"I thought she was okay. What's wrong?"

I stood next to her, placed my arm over her shoulder, and pulled her in. Her confused eyes met mine. I smiled, and just like that, she relaxed, resting her head against my chest again.

"What if she's dead?" Tears poured down Addy's cheeks. "What will I tell Reed?"

My eyes stayed on the house. "You tell him the truth."

They started lifting the stretcher into the ambulance. Addy moved quickly. She stopped one of the medical technicians before the woman hopped into the ambulance.

"Where are you taking her?"

The technician told Addy they were heading to Latrobe Hospital. Then she disappeared inside the truck and shut the back door.

Addy and I both rushed to the car. Behind us, I heard the fire crackling as the firefighters hosed the house down.

"Ade will corrupt all," it screamed. "You'll see. You'll see!"

I glanced one last time at the house. A second before Addy drove off, I thought I saw a red, veiny figure standing in the doorway. It stared past the oblivious firefighters, its eyes on me.

It opened its mouth. "Ade will corrupt all."

After that, I couldn't see it anymore.

Chapter Twenty-One

ADELAIDE

Erica looked different, but also the same. She'd dyed her hair red and gotten a tattoo of some Chinese letters on her slender wrist. Other than that, she hadn't changed. Still thin and fit as ever, she looked more like my older sister than my mother.

I wanted to know what the tattoo on her wrist meant, but she was sleeping. She'd been like that since they brought her in. They put her in a hospital gown, inserted an IV needle into her arm, and left her to rest, leaving me alone in the room with her.

Adriel waited in the car outside because, as I'd reminded him, the hospital staff probably still remembered his face from when he'd come in five days ago with his burned back. It was crazy that he had healed so fast and with almost no scarring.

While waiting for Erica to wake up, I texted Reed to let him know about the fire and explain that Erica was all right. He responded with questions, wanting to know how it had happened. I told him the truth, that I didn't know.

The heart monitor connected to Erica beeped at a steady pace. Outside, a nurse rolled a cart to the room across the hall; the grinding sound of wheels against tiles felt like a hypnosis trick. I leaned my head against the chair and closed my eyes. With each beep of the heart monitor, I found myself slipping away more and more.

"Ade?" Erica's voice called out.

My eyes snapped open and I found my mother blinking out of her slumber. She wore mascara and the remnants of lipstick.

"Ade, what are you doing here?"

Rising from the chair, I moved to stand beside the bed, keeping a foot between us. "I came to see how you are."

She flashed her sparkly teeth at me.

Growing up with her, she had always set aside a yearly budget to spend on teeth whitening. She'd clearly kept it up.

"You look good," I said and bit my lip.

"I feel like shit, though." She looked at the needle in her hand and winced. When she noticed me staring, she shoved her hand under her blanket and smiled. "You're probably enjoying my pain a little bit, aren't you, Ade?"

"No, not really."

"Are you sure?"

"I've never been the type to gloat at someone's pain. At least, I hope not." I wanted to finish the sentence by saying, "Unlike you, Mom," but I held my tongue.

She closed her eyes.

With a sigh, I looked outside for the nurse with the cart, but the hallway was empty. *Maybe I should just leave.* And yet, I had to ask about the fire. Adriel had seen it in a vision. It couldn't have been an accident.

"Um," I said.

She looked up. "Huh?"

"What do you remember about the fire?"

"Ugh." She rolled her eyes. "I thought you were going to say something else. Like apologize for hanging up on me the other day."

"No. I want to know about the fire."

"How's Reed doing?"

I shoved my hands in my pockets, afraid I'd scratch her face otherwise. "Reed is fine. Don't change the subject."

"I'm not changing the subject. I'm ending it." Pushing herself by the elbows, she tried to sit up. "I feel fifty pounds heavier. What did these nurses do to me?"

"What are *you* trying to do? You should stay down."

"What else? I want to use the bathroom."

Crossing my arms, I said, "I'll help you up if you tell me about the fire."

She glared at me for a long time. Her upper back was awkwardly elevated by the two pillows that had been under her head a moment ago.

"If you don't tell me, I'll leave you here and walk out." I took two steps in the direction of the door.

She dropped her head back, seeming annoyed. "Fine." She kept her eyes on the ceiling as she spoke. "I was in the bathroom doing my hair, and I just remember hearing someone shouting outside the house. I thought it was one of those stupid kids, but then the house was on fire and I was stuck inside."

"Do you remember the voice? What they said?"

"I told you all I know." She tried sitting up again. "Now help me to the bathroom."

I placed my hand behind her back and supported her as she stood up. When she was on two feet, I let her put her weight against me while I pushed the IV pole along.

Taking a few steps forward, she glanced at me. "You know, your brother actually calls me."

"I know."

"You don't call me."

"No, I don't."

We were by the bathroom, so I let go of her arm. She pulled the curtain back, revealing the toilet, and started heading inside. Stabilizing herself, she placed her hand against the wall, her back to me.

"It would make me happy if you'd check up on me more often. Will you do that, Ade?"

With a sigh, I opened my mouth to say yes. But then I noticed something. In between the open gap of Erica's hospital gown, on the upper right corner of her butt cheek, was another tattoo. And it wasn't a normal one.

My mouth dropped. "Is that—"

I lowered my head to get a better look and realized too late that she was staring at me over her shoulder with narrowed eyes. *Is that blackness where white should be around her irises?*

"Never mind. I'm seeing things." I pulled the curtain back in place so she was out of sight and took three steps toward the exit.

"Ade?"

From the edge of the curtain, her hand appeared. Before she could pull the curtain back again, I dashed for the door. Skidding down the hallway, I nearly toppled over the nurse with the cart.

"Sorry," I yelled as I squeezed myself between the wall and the cart and ran.

What I'd just seen couldn't be real. And yet, it made perfect sense. It explained Erica's behavior all those years. All the nights she had come home drunk and angry. The times she had left Reed and me alone in a small apartment and, later, in an empty house. She was a terrible mother, both for neglecting us and for trying to persuade us to be like her. And it had all happened because of that tattoo.

I sprinted across the hospital parking lot to my car. From a few yards away, I could see Adriel's head reclined against the window, his eyes closed. I skidded to a stop and knocked on the glass. His head shot up. As if the boogeyman had emerged, his pupils transformed into big, dark marbles. He unlocked the door and got out.

"What's wrong?" His hands went into my hair, pulling me closer. "What happened?"

I gestured in the direction of the hospital. My mouth hung open. I wanted to explain what I'd seen, but when I spoke, it all came out as an incoherent jumble of words.

"Addy, breathe." He lifted my chin up, forcing me to meet his gaze. "What happened?"

I stared at him for a second while my mind raced. All those years. How had I never noticed that tattoo? My mother had never shied away from dressing in revealing clothes, and yet I'd somehow missed it.

With concern in his eyes, Adriel waited.

I placed my trembling hands against his chest, swallowed, and said, "There's a tattoo of Lucifer's initial on my mother's ass."

Adriel's eyes danced back and forth in front of mine. His expression twisted into rage. If eyes were truly the window to one's soul, I swore I saw Adriel's soul running through a maze and tripping over invisible barriers.

"Say something."

He shook his head.

"Why not?" I removed my hands from his chest and pulled away. "I need you to tell me what you're thinking. I'm freaking out too!"

He rubbed his forehead. "So, you're telling me that your mom sold her soul to the devil, and the devil happens to be your dad."

His eyebrows drew together and he gritted his teeth, making his jaw tense. Revulsion was written all over his face.

Under his angry glare, I started defending myself. "Look, just a few days ago, I had no idea angels and demons were real. You think I want this to be happening? You think I want both my parents to be the shittiest parents on Earth?"

"I just . . ." His chest kept rising and falling.

"You just what?"

Closing his eyes, he let out a harsh breath. "I just don't know whether you're one of them sometimes."

I froze in my spot. "What?"

"Your mother's house . . ."

"What about it?"

"It was shouting."

I raised an eyebrow. "Her house was shouting?"

"No, the fire. The fire kept making a . . . noise."

"Adriel, you're scaring me. What the hell are you talking about?"

"It kept saying, 'Ade will corrupt all,' and I was the only one hearing it."

His words took a second to sink in.

"As in me corrupting people?" My stomach churned, and I felt this morning's breakfast rise. "I think I'm going to be sick." Adriel became a blur in front of me. I planted my hands against the car and bent over, my head hanging low.

"Hey." Adriel stood beside me, rubbing my back.

The demonic fire that my soulless, deplorable mother had just survived claimed that I would corrupt all. I breathed slowly through my mouth while my head spun.

"But I wouldn't," I said. "I wouldn't, right? I mean, not anymore. I got Reed back."

"Come on." Adriel set his hand over mine. "Let's get out of here."

"No, no. What if that's my destiny?"

"Addy, you don't know that. Just because I heard it doesn't make it true. Now, come on."

He held me as we walked toward the driver's side. Once I sat down, he marched around to the passenger side and hopped in.

My legs trembled, but I wasn't cold. Adriel rested his hand on my knee, an act that sent my stomach fluttering even in my current state.

Concern pinched his brows. "Can you drive?"

"No." I'd never been like this, weak and pathetic. Weakness did not suit me.

Adriel stroked his other hand over the dark stubble on his face. "Want to stay here until you feel better?"

"I don't want that, either. I want to leave this disgusting hospital and get away from Erica."

The engine whirred under my seat. Slowly, I drove toward the motel.

†

Drive-throughs were convenient in our chaotic, homeless state. Being on the run didn't allow for proper meals. So, stomachs growling, we stopped at the nearest fast-food restaurant and ordered six cheeseburgers, two large sodas, and four bottles of water to take back with us.

At the motel, I signed paperwork and proved I was of age while Adriel waited in the car. Once everything was settled, Adriel and I found ourselves in a cozy room with one queen-size bed, a nightstand, and a bathroom. The beige floral wallpaper on the walls peeled at the corners. Only one large window with a view of the parking lot came with the room, covered by a thick, brown, and dusty curtain. I left the curtain as is so no one could spy on us.

"What if the demons find us here? They could literally just pop in." I collapsed onto the bed and buried my head in one of the yellow-stained pillows, hoping I wouldn't get some weird disease.

"Michael said he would protect us."

Beside me, the mattress sunk under Adriel's weight.

Lifting my head, I met his dark stare. "The archangel?"

"Yes."

In my pocket, my phone buzzed. I had a feeling Lizzy was the one texting before I checked, and I was right.

"Hey, where are you now?" she wrote from Nate's phone.

It was twelve thirty in the afternoon. The last time we spoke had been a few hours ago. I sent her a text back saying, "At a motel in Latrobe," before setting my phone down on the wooden nightstand with the uneven legs beside Adriel.

As I retreated, Adriel seized my hand and held it for a moment.

"How are you feeling?" He ran his thumb over the back of my hand, his eyes scanning my face. He lingered at my lips before glancing back up.

"Stressed."

The light sensation of his thumb on my skin sent shivers up my spine. I dropped my head against the pillow but kept looking at him.

"It'll be okay, I promise." Letting go of my hand and getting up, he said, "I think we both need to rest."

He opened the duffle bag we shared, dug inside, grabbed Nate's pajama pants and the bag of underwear I bought him that morning, and went inside the bathroom to change. Although it was much too early for sleep, I followed suit, grabbing a white tank top and pajama shorts.

It was cold outside, but I felt warm. Too warm.

With my back to the bathroom, I removed the white T-shirt I wore and dropped it to the floor. Next came the jeans. When I unclasped my bra from the back, the bathroom door creaked open. I stiffened, sensing Adriel's eyes on me.

"I . . . I'm sorry," he said, turning around.

Over my shoulder, I saw he was shirtless again. The ridges of his spine protruded with each movement. I couldn't help but stare at the lightly tanned skin of his back, where the scars were barely visible.

Feeling my face turn a hot red, I slipped my clothes on in two swift moves and coughed, letting him know the coast was clear. I slipped under the covers before he could turn around and lay on my side, my back to him.

After flipping the light switch off, he ambled to bed. "Sorry again."

"It's fine," I mumbled into the dimness.

When he got in, the mattress sagged. His body brushed against my back, cold and refreshing. Thoughts of this morning came back to me, the way he'd pulled me in, his fierce tongue taking control of my mouth. I shut my eyes. Suddenly, the bed felt too small for the two of us.

"Everything all right?" His warm breath caressed my neck.

"Uh huh."

I didn't want to think about him. I knew he didn't approve of me. He worried I was like my parents. He worried I was as wicked as them. The word godforsaken came to mind, and in that moment, I understood its true meaning. It wasn't that I was on my own without any parents; it was that I was on my own in the land of evil. Completely in the dark.

How had I gone from crying over my cheating ex-boyfriend to pining over a former angel in less than a week? How did my life become like this?

Pushing Adriel, Devin, and my parents out of my thoughts, I let exhaustion take over. Not caring how many people had previously slept on these same bedsheets without them being washed, I surrendered to the lumpiness of the mattress.

Not long after, I woke up again. The image of Erica's tattoo had been ingrained in my mind. Peeling the blanket off me, I took a deep breath. Sweat covered my skin and my stomach hurt, a sensation that left me nauseous. With my back to the bed, I stared at the ceiling. *Too close.* Was the wall inching down, ready to crush me?

I burst out of bed. In the bathroom, I banged the door shut in a rush and leaned against the sink as water dripped from the faucet one drop at a time, ticking against the porcelain surface. My breathing was heavy. If Lizzy were here, she would have prepared a cup of peppermint tea for me to drink. She was probably having fun with Nate right now. Maybe they had gone out to lunch, like normal people.

A knock on the door made me flinch.

"Addy, are you okay?"

I moved to sit on the floor with my back against the sink and closed my eyes. "Go back to sleep," I muttered.

"Why did you run out of bed?"

"It's nothing."

"Addy?"

Lucifer's words came back to me. *Do you think I did not make certain a long time ago to create a weapon so powerful that no one would know what it is or how to use it against me?* What could his weapon possibly be? A magical sword that could kill anything but Lucifer? A powerful demon? Perhaps it was all the people whose souls I'd sold to him. Could they be the powerful weapon? And what of my mother? Her soul was long gone.

"Addy?"

My hands trembled. "Go back to bed."

"What's wrong?"

"Nothing. I just want to stay here."

The doorknob turned halfway.

"I'm coming in," he said.

I didn't have time to protest. In a second, he was standing inside with nothing but pajama pants on, looking down at me.

He raked his fingers through his hair. "You are not okay."

Blinking at him, I said, "You shouldn't have come in. What if I was using the toilet?"

"Well, you're not." Crouching down beside me, he leaned in and dug his hand into the spirals of my hair, cupping the nape of my neck as he did. "What's going on?"

I shrugged. "I don't want to talk."

"Can I try to guess, then? It shouldn't be hard, considering." He smirked, his eyes gleaming. "Is it the demons taking over Earth?"

I stared at him without responding.

"Is it your mother?"

No words.

"Is it all of the above?"

It was, but I didn't feel like saying it. He already knew the answer, though he would never understand exactly what I felt.

"Come on, Addy. I told you, we'll figure it out together. We both should rest now."

He grabbed my hands as he stood and helped me to my feet. The minute we reached the bed, my phone vibrated on the nightstand. Reed's image greeted me on the screen. I let go of Adriel's hand and leaped for the phone.

Picking up, I said, "Reed?"

Loud noises came from the other end of the line. A person breathed heavily into the phone but didn't say a word.

I looked at Adriel, my heart beating fast. "Reed, what's going on?"

Adriel came to stand by me, his eyebrows pulled together. He leaned his head close to my ear to listen in.

"Reed? Reed, can you hear me?"

"Addy," Reed finally said. His voice was hushed, and he sounded jittery. "Addy, I'm fine, but others aren't. Someone is shooting at us."

"What do you mean? Where are you?"

Gunshots rattled in the background, shrill and incessant. I screamed Reed's name.

"In the library," Reed whispered. "Please help."

The last gunshot sound exploded through my ear.

"Reed? Reed?"

We'd been disconnected.

I shot Adriel a glance and dashed for my duffle bag. I threw one of Nate's shirts at him, told him to put it on, and grabbed the jeans I was wearing earlier.

With his arms through the shirt, Adriel said, "What's going on?"

"I don't know. He says someone's shooting."

Not caring what Adriel saw, I tossed my pajama shorts on the floor and put on the pants. In a few seconds, I had my keys and phone in hand. Just to be extra safe, I took the Swiss Army knife and hid it in my pocket.

"Come on!" I ran past Adriel toward the door.

"Wait." He took hold of the duffle bag and dug inside. Taking out one of the knives I brought from my apartment, he smiled. "You're not the only one who can carry weapons. Now we can go."

Chapter Twenty-Two

ADRIEL

A dozen police cars tore past us, their sirens blaring and reverberating even after they were out of sight. One after the other, they raced toward the college.

Addy tried to keep up, but every time she stomped on the gas pedal, another police car came ripping through the street. Every few minutes, she had to pull over to the far right of the road and slow down to let the police cars pass.

"You've got to be kidding me!" Her hands gripped the wheel as yet another car came hurrying by. "I should be driving ahead of them."

"They don't know that. Besides, we don't know who is behind this shooting."

She shot me a glare. "You seriously think this is a coincidence? I thought you were smarter than that."

I shrugged. "I'm just saying, we don't know all the facts yet."

Under her breath, I thought I heard her mutter, "Fucking angels."

Saint Vincent Basilica appeared in front of us, tall and imposing. This was the second time I'd seen the church while with Addy.

Addy turned around the corner. "They better not have the entrance blocked."

Three police cars were parked in a line, blockading the driveway. Addy cussed. She pulled the car to the side and stopped the engine.

"We have to go on foot." She grabbed her things and sprang out of the car. She flipped her Swiss Army knife out, exposing the actual blade, and held it tight.

I stumbled out of the car into the cold wind and shivered. Unlike Addy, the freezing temperature that seemed to be constantly dropping didn't suit me. Not when the only source of warmth I had was a thin cotton shirt.

Addy started toward the cops in her equally thin tank top. I followed behind her. In my hand, I had my own knife at the ready.

My eyes skimmed the area. There was one entrance to the school, as far as I could tell, and we couldn't go through there. I wasn't sure what Addy's plans were, but I hoped they were of sound judgment.

"Addy, how are we going to get past the police? There's no way to dodge them."

From where we stood, the school looked busy with cops. There were cops ahead of us, cops near the forest to our left and right, and cops marching in protective gear toward the school.

Addy eyed the cops blocking the road. "I was thinking I would compel them."

"Addy, no." I grabbed her wrist to stop her from going about her plan. Unlike me, her skin felt warm. I wished we could huddle together for warmth, sharing body heat. I shook the idea away. "You can't do that anymore. Besides, you'd be putting yourself at risk too."

"Fine. We'll go 'round back." She drew her hand to her side and ran off the road into the forest. Before I had time to tail her, she was zigzagging between the trees.

She was quick on her feet; sneaky, even. While the ground crunched underneath my feet whenever I stepped on twigs, she was absolutely silent. At some points, she disappeared from my sight, hidden behind the hundreds of trees transforming from orange to brown. I paused to scan the distance.

"Addy?"

She darted out from seven trees to the east of where I stood and gestured for me to hurry up. I chased after her.

The sun burned above us, its rays gliding through the tree branches. Although the wind whistled, the bright forest kept the weather balanced. I was thankful for that. I definitely did not want to freeze.

Once I caught up with Addy, she started moving again. Without looking at me, she said, "Took you long enough."

"You disappeared."

"Just keep up."

211

Two gray squirrels were circling a tree trunk strewn with dead leaves when Addy stormed past them, scaring them to death. They went leaping up the tree, scurrying into the branches.

I was breathless, but I still managed to think straight. "So, what's the plan?"

"Find the shooter and stop him."

"But we don't know anything about the situation. Addy, I don't think this is a good idea. We need to think this through, at least."

She groaned. "There's no time."

Other than the shuffling of the pine leaves, the school seemed calm. Even the cops had disappeared. I wondered if they'd already gone inside and captured the shooter, or shooters.

"I don't hear anything. Do you?" I said.

"No. I don't really know what's happening."

"What if we called Reed back?"

"I'm worried he's hiding; I don't want to blow his cover."

The last of the trees faced us. Behind them, Saint Vincent College looked like a forgotten, lonely land. Addy left the forest and headed in the direction of a small parking lot. Across from us was the basilica. I could see the statue of a man with his hand outstretched in welcome in front of the cathedral's doors, but I couldn't tell if it was Vincent or someone else.

Addy slipped through the few parked cars, ducking behind them. I followed her, mimicking her movements. She glanced back once to make sure I was still with her. Her ponytail swayed like a pendulum.

"Stay with me," she said. "We can't lose each other here."

"You won't lose me."

She ran around the church, hurrying through another parking lot. Buildings surrounded us, creating a dead end. Yet Addy kept going, practically sprinting like a wildcat. She came to a halt in front of a door.

"Through here." She was already inside the building, rushing to the other side.

Before I knew it, we were exiting through another door, which led to a garden. Addy started maneuvering around the trees with the crisp red leaves littered on the ground. She was a better navigator than me.

I sighed and pursued her, trying not to make too much noise.

Finally, we got back on actual ground. To our left were more silent buildings.

Addy walked down the road and pointed at a brick building. "That's the library. Reed's over th—"

A single gunshot cracked in the wind. The sound pulsated through my body, sending the hairs on my arm standing on end.

Addy recoiled and collided with me. "Shit." Her hands trembled.

She grabbed my free hand and ran to the other side of the building. I wasn't sure what she meant to do with her knife—or what I meant to do with mine—but she held hers as though ready to thrust it straight into the shooter's heart.

Right before we reached the entrance, two boys and three girls came running past us. Blood covered their faces and torn clothes. They were panting and crying. Addy pulled me toward the door without seeming to notice them, but I turned my head, watching them go. The boys were helping the girls stay on their feet, their arms wrapped around their backs.

In the distance, cops headed our way. They were equipped with rifles. Addy must've seen them too, because she muttered a bad word, let go of my hand, and slipped inside the library through the door on the side of the curved glass wall.

Past the door, the sound of people shrieking vibrated throughout the building. A large bookshelf lay flat on the floor with books dumped all over, some crumpled and torn.

And blood. Blood stained the tiled floor, making several paths across the library that trailed after their injured donors. A strange metallic smell drifted toward me.

A couple of shots exploded in the room. This time, I heard a large group of people scream.

"Shut up!" a man shouted. "Don't you dare make a move!"

Beside me, Addy stiffened. If Reed hadn't left, he was somewhere in here.

I glanced out the door, wondering why the cops were taking forever to come inside. "Why aren't they taking action?"

Addy didn't say a word. She moved farther inside with the knife as her only weapon.

"Addy, wait," I hissed. "You could get killed."

She didn't listen. With no choice, I went after her. The sound of people sobbing carried from the back. It was a low, clear noise. Taking in a sharp breath, I hoped we weren't rushing to our slaughter.

The library was huge. Aisle after aisle of bookshelves masked the danger that hid somewhere inside. Addy swerved behind the far-right shelf. She hunched low, tiptoeing to the back. My eyes searched the room alongside her, afraid that if she missed something—or someone—she might get hurt.

And honestly, I didn't care much about my life. I was a fallen angel. My only real chance at redemption would be to protect the humans I swore to watch out for from the moment of my creation. Addy being one of those humans.

"No! No!" someone begged a couple of aisles down. A second later, a gun fired and something hit the ground with a thud.

"No!" Addy screamed. She shot up, no longer quiet, and stormed to the back.

I yelled after her, but it was too late. By the time I caught up, she was standing with a dead boy's body at her feet. The boy looked no older than eighteen. His sandy blond hair covered the side of his face. On his forehead, blood trickled out from a single hole.

"How could you?" Addy screamed again. Clutching the knife, she waved her hand in front of her. "You killed him!"

At that moment, I registered the guy across from Addy. His pitch-black eyes rose to my face, noticing me as I noticed him. He frowned, making his crooked nose seem even more crooked.

Devin. The ex-boyfriend whose soul Addy had sold to the devil.

Addy still threatened with her knife. "You killed Sam!"

I wasn't sure who Sam was, but I reached out and placed my hand on her shoulder. "Addy, you should step back."

She spun around to face me. "You think I care that he has a gun? He won't shoot me." She looked over her shoulder at Devin, her next words directed at him. "Will you?"

Devin's hollow eyes did not react. However, a vein in his forehead throbbed. "You did this to me!" He gestured at himself. "Do you understand what you've done? I'm a slave now."

This time, Addy did step back. I moved to stand in front of her. Before I could shield her, she shot me a look that told me to back off and gently pushed me out of the way.

"I'm sorry." She was speaking to Devin, her dark eyes fixed on him. "But you weren't the perfect angel."

He scoffed at her statement. "I cheated. You're the one who destroyed a soul."

Tears welled in her eyes. "You hurt me."

The knife shook in her hand, but she still held it out in front of her like it would keep Devin and the bullets in his pistol at bay. Still, Devin took a step forward. He stared at her face as if she didn't have a weapon in her hand. Then again, he was the one with the gun.

"You think you're so innocent." He shook his head. "Yes, I hurt you, but you did far more than that. When will you get that? You damaged me, and many others."

Addy took another step back. "I'm sorry."

"You're sorry?" He gave a bitter laugh and scrutinized me. "She's sorry."

"I am!"

"Well, thanks for the apology, love, but it's kind of too late."

Tears slid down her cheeks.

"Addy!" someone called out.

I looked to the left. Just behind one of the bookshelves, Reed stuck his head out to see us. He glanced at each one of us before his eyes drifted to the boy—Sam—whose body lay mere inches from our feet.

"Oh my God!" Reed stepped fully into the aisle, gasping for air, his hands on his knees.

Addy hesitated. She looked between Devin and Reed, all while the knife trembled in her hand.

Devin smiled, flashing two dimples.

What happened next felt like a blur. One second Devin stood with his pistol aimed at us, the next he was running down the aisle toward Reed while reloading and chambering a round into his gun.

"No!" Addy and I yelled in unison. We rushed after him.

I didn't know about Addy, but my heart was pounding in my chest.

Devin grabbed Reed by the back of his neck and planted the gun against the side of his head. "It's good to see you again, Reed."

"Devin, please." Addy seemed to forget about the knife. She extended her hands out in surrender, almost handing the knife to Devin.

Reed's whole body shook. "Please," he said, his lips quivering. "I don't want to die."

Devin pouted his lips. "I'm sorry, but I don't control these things. Direct orders and all." His index finger started to pull the trigger.

Not knowing what to do without my wings, I dove for the pistol, hoping to shove the weapon out of Devin's hand in time. Beside me, Addy made a leap for it too. Her knife fell on the floor, the metal thudding against the tiles. Just as my hand met Devin's, Addy pushed her brother out of the way.

And the gun went off.

I managed to force the pistol out of Devin's hand; it went flying and hit the leg of a table in the middle of the room.

Addy gasped. With my heart thumping in my ears, I whirled around to find her on the ground. A red splotch grew and grew and grew in the center of her white tank top. I felt numb. I went down on my knees and hoisted her head into my lap.

Her eyes were wide with fear. And they were on me. I held her, wanting to give her comfort, but finding none for myself amidst the tears pooling in my eyes and the trembling of her body against mine.

Reed crouched beside us, speechless. He brushed Addy's hair out of her face while he cried.

In that moment, we'd all forgotten about Devin; then he suddenly groaned. His hand flew to his forehead. "I'm fucked! He's going to kill me!" His black eyes wavered. For a split second, they flashed blue.

He leaned over once to look at Addy. Then he was gone, leaving his pistol behind.

"Please stay with me." I held Addy tightly, not wanting to let go. I feared if I did, she wouldn't be there anymore.

Her eyes glazed over like she was looking far away, but her chest still rose and fell, just enough to give me hope.

"You said we can't lose each other here. Do you remember? I can't lose you here."

Lifting her tank top above her stomach, I examined the gaping wound. Her liver was clearly hit. The blood oozed out with no sign of stopping. I pressed my hand against the hole, doing anything to stop the injury from getting worse.

Reed managed to collect himself a little. He grabbed his phone and dialed a number. When he spoke, I knew he had called the emergency line. "My sister's been shot. She needs help. She's dying."

My attention traveled to the main door. *Where are the cops?* They had been near the library when we'd walked in, yet there was no sign of them now.

Addy put her hand over mine on the wound and squeezed. "Hey." She drew in a harsh breath. "I think I'm okay."

"What?" I didn't know what she was saying. My hand and both our clothes were bloody, and she was still shivering.

Noting his sister talking, Reed put the phone down and watched her.

Addy lifted her head and looked down. "I'm fine. Look." She pushed my hand away, though I felt reluctant to move. "Adriel, look."

Where the gunshot wound had been a moment ago was bare, smooth flesh. Her stomach had no marks, no sign of an injury other than the blood all over her flesh and clothes.

I rubbed the area to make sure my eyes weren't deceiving me. "Addy, how'd you do that?" My limbs felt like they were melting as relief and shock washed over me.

She pushed herself up into a sitting position and said, "I didn't do anything. I just stopped feeling the pain."

"But how?"

"I don't know."

With tears still in his eyes, Reed smiled. "You're okay?"

"I think so." Addy reached for her brother, drawing him in for a hug. "You almost got shot, Reed!"

He wrapped his arms around her. "Ade, you did get shot . . ."

I sat back, taking the situation in. While I was happy Addy was alive, the whole incident felt like the moment I'd plummeted from heaven to Earth. If it weren't for this miracle, I could have easily lost her today.

A new emotion bubbled up inside me. I couldn't put a finger on it, but as I watched Addy and Reed, I envied their closeness, their familiarity. I wished I could swap places with Reed and have my arms around the young woman whose life I'd recently fallen into. The woman I'd almost lost in the blink of an eye.

Chapter Twenty-Three

ADELAIDE

I recognized Devin's voice the minute it rang out through the library walls, ruthless and shrill. But I did not expect to see him so . . . different. The ocean in his eyes had run dry. Nothing but darkness existed there now. I remembered looking at Adriel a few hours ago, thinking how I could read his soul just by looking at his eyes. That was not the case with Devin. He was completely shut off. The windows to his soul were missing.

"How could you?" I didn't want to look down at the floor. I didn't want to see Sam, Reed's dorm mate, with a bullet in his head. "You killed him!"

Sam's bony hands were still plump and full of color. His sandalwood cologne reeked like incense, seeming to surge from the hole in his head or the fearful energy left behind in his body. It made it hard for me to forget he had been standing here, eyes moving, heart pumping, brain racing before I'd heard that gunshot. If I'd only reached him sooner, just a second sooner, he would be alive right now.

Devin scowled at something behind me. Lucifer's initial, which I'd carved into his wrist four days ago, was still there, just inches from the pistol in his hand. It had scabbed, yet remained bold.

With a shaky hand, I lifted the knife. "You killed Sam!"

I knew I shouldn't have yelled at a man with a gun in his hands, but I did it anyway, my sanity lost. My heart thrummed in my ears, and I could barely hear Devin's next words.

"Do you understand what you've done? I'm a slave now."

He was right to turn the blame on me, because it was all my fault. Yet, the wiser part of my brain had shut off, and I found myself throwing his awful last act as my boyfriend in his face.

He stepped closer. "You think you're so innocent. Yes, I hurt you, but you did far more than that."

I didn't want to show weakness, but I couldn't control the tears. "I'm sorry."

"You're sorry?"

"I am!"

"Well, thanks for the apology, love, but it's kind of too late."

In that wretched moment, Reed came into view from behind one of the bookshelves. Quick on his feet, Devin ran toward Reed, readying his weapon. I dashed after them, begging Devin to stop with what few words I managed to utter. Everything went downhill from there.

I felt my flesh tear from the bullet. My insides felt like a watermelon in a blender, shredding and spewing red juice everywhere until they dissolved. I dropped to the ground.

They say your life flashes before your eyes moments before you die. Mine didn't. In those few seconds, which felt like eternity taking its damn time, I just wanted Reed to be safe. My brother would have no one once I was gone.

As I lay dying, his crying resonated in my ears. He stared at me with pleading eyes while his cold fingers brushed my skin. Everything I'd done up till now had been for him. If I had to go to hell for him again, I would.

Adriel held me in his arms. He pulled me against him in a way I'd never felt. Not even with Devin during our good days. I tried to reach out to him. I wanted to tell him to watch out for Reed, be there for him now that I was leaving. But the blood leaked from the pit right under my rib cage, and I was losing myself.

"You said we can't lose each other here. Do you remember? I can't lose you here," Adriel said.

I did remember. And yet, it made no difference. I had no control over my life anymore. All twenty-two years of my existence I fought to stand out, to be someone people noticed because my mother didn't notice me. I fought, and I'd made it far. This, however, I could not fight. It was beyond my power.

My stomach roiled and everything in my body held on to each ticking moment. It was as if, for the first time, I could identify exactly where my spleen, stomach, heart, lungs, and liver were in my body. The ruptured organ rotted slowly inside me, or at least it felt that way. Lungs working overtime, I drew in a heavy breath.

Sensing my anguish, Adriel pressed down on the wound. He was a blur above my head, and I felt nothing but his touch. Of all the ways to die, I was happy to be doing it in his arms.

The pain eased, and I thought it was time. Time to go. Time to be dragged to hell, where my father reigned. I didn't realize I had been healed, not until Adriel came back into perfect view and I was still there in the library, Devin's bullet hole in my past.

†

After the initial realization that I was alive, it occurred to me that something—or someone—was missing.

"Where's Madadel?" I scanned Reed from head to toe, making sure Devin had not harmed him. "He promised he would protect you."

Reed gave a half shrug. "He disappeared right before the shooting. Said it was important."

My brother was nearly murdered and I had been on the verge of dying because I'd been shot saving his life, yet Madadel had something more important to do?

"I'm going to rip that angel's wings right off when I see him," I hissed.

Wincing, Adriel stood. "The important thing is that we're all alive." His face turned in Sam's direction, but he quickly looked away. "No need to rip anyone's wings off."

I sighed. "If you ask me, Madadel is the worst guardian angel. Simiael died saving me. Where the hell was he just now when Reed needed him to fight off Lucifer's hellhound?"

"You mean your ex," Reed remarked. "The one you turned."

I covered my eyes with my hands and sat still for a while on the floor. "I know I made a mistake, a really bad one, but I can't take it back."

"No," Adriel said. "I guess not."

"Then I'm the reason we all nearly died today. That some people *did* die today. Devin wouldn't have been like that if I hadn't sold his soul."

Adriel grabbed my hands, dragged them from my face, and helped me to my feet. "You made a mistake. Now is the time to fix it. You can't change Devin back, but you can bring Lucifer to an end."

"How?"

He was looking at me in that wild way he sometimes did, though he kept his distance. "Maybe it's time we figure it out."

Reed didn't go near Sam's body, but he beheld him from afar. His eyes were wet. "I can't believe he's gone."

"I'm so sorry." I pulled Reed into an embrace. "I wish I could've saved him."

"There's nothing we can do, is there?"

I shook my head, letting Reed go. "How did this even start?"

"I don't know." Reed scratched his head. His hazel eyes were red from crying, making them look extra fiery. "I was studying with Sam and some classmates—this was after Madadel told me to wait because he had to do something important—and Devin just walked in and sat down with us. He looked bizarre, like those demons in hell. He put his hand over my shoulder and was telling me about you."

"What'd he say?"

"Just that he made a mistake leaving you. Then he walked away. I thought it was weird he was here, but I didn't worry about it. Five minutes later, we heard gunshots. That was when I called you. I didn't know it was him until later."

It was all a nightmare, and I knew I was to blame. "Let's just go find your missing angel."

Reed raised his index finger for me to wait and started walking away. "Before that . . ." He hurried to the back of the library, disappearing behind the aisles and rows of bookshelves. After a minute, he came back with a dozen or more people in tow. "They were hiding," he explained.

Some of the students were obviously hurt, with cuts on their faces and blood dripping from their lips and hands. The rest, however, seemed normal. It was like they had just walked out of a dreadful exam they knew they had failed. While they would be scarred for some time, they didn't look it. I was glad for that.

"Is anyone badly hurt?" I asked.

"Nothing that won't heal in a few days."

One life was lost, but at least no more.

Without saying a word, I led them out. Adriel lingered behind. When we made it outside, he came to stand beside me, Devin's pistol in his hand.

Seeing the weapon, I shrank back. "What are you doing? Your fingerprints are all over that thing now!"

He shrugged. "I wasn't human until a few days ago; there are no records of me."

"Do you even know how to use that thing?"

"I have an idea." He released the magazine from the pistol and unloaded the last bullet. "But I'm not going to start using one today." Walking to the nearest trash can, he dumped the gun and came back with a smile on his face. "No more guns for you."

I had no time to appreciate his reckless gesture when noise stirred among the group of students. They ran off in separate directions with fright contorting their expressions.

Turning around, I discovered where Madadel had been this whole time. Across from us, the angel flapped his huge, white wings in the air. And he was not alone.

"Crap." Reed jumped forward, his eyes never leaving his guardian. "He's going to die."

The herd of cops we had seen earlier was moving in on Madadel. Twenty or so pistols were aimed at the angel, ready to annihilate him.

None of it made sense, but I moved to stand next to Reed. "What are they doing? What's wrong with them?"

The answer became clear when a couple of the officers spotted us. They shifted their bleak, empty eyes onto Adriel, Reed, and me. Madadel shoved them back with his wings. Still, they outnumbered him. Two officers escaped Madadel and hastened in our direction.

"Here." Adriel put a cold, slim object in my palm. "We have to fight them."

I looked down and saw the Swiss Army knife I'd dropped before I was shot. Adriel had retrieved it for me and tucked the knife in for safety. I pulled my favorite stealthy weapon out, knowing what I had to do.

Adriel had apparently also recovered his large knife, one of the few I'd brought in the duffle bag with us. He extracted it from his pocket and dashed across the school's small road to the sidewalk opposite from where we stood.

I went to pursue Adriel but stopped. "Reed, hide!"

"No." Reed stood his ground, his eyes on his angel. "I won't leave until this is over."

"Reed, please . . ."

I wanted to do something about the demented cops, but I couldn't leave Reed unprotected.

Placing his hand on my shoulder, he gave me a reassuring smile. "It's okay. I'm fine. I can take care of myself."

"But, Re—"

"Go!"

He nudged me to the other side. With one last look at him, I ran. I saw Adriel not far down the road, swiveling his knife at an officer in protective gear. Another cop with a thick goatee advanced on him, grinning from ear to ear. The void in their eyes gave me no hope.

Lucifer had warned me about this. He said he had built an army. I just never thought it would include officers of the law.

Taking a deep breath, I charged onward. When I reached Adriel, we snapped into a unified rhythm, working side by side as if we'd done this before. I'd never had any sort of training and never been in a fight as intense as this one, but I somehow knew how to move to avoid the enemies' attacks. As soon as I ducked, Adriel launched an attack, and when his back turned to the enemy, I spotted him. It also helped that Adriel had managed to steal the officers' pistols and unload them somehow. Bullets scattered all over the ground. Now, all they had were their batons and Tasers, both dangerous in their own way.

The fight went like that until all four of us began tiring. The cops slowed down, drawing back. They glanced at each other like they were calculating their next move. We took that time to catch our breath too. When they started attacking again, we struck back twice as hard—or at least, that's what I wanted to believe.

I fell on my behind three times and got Tasered once in the leg. The electric shock passed through my body, moving up my spine and immobilizing me. I lay on the ground for what seemed like forever. All I could think of was that I needed a good, long nap.

Adriel pulled me to my feet, his face lit with rage. In one swift move, he caught an officer by the wrist and, with his other hand, slit his throat. The cop's lifeless body dropped to the ground. Blood trickled from the fountain of his split flesh, leaving a trail around his corpse.

I recoiled. My gut clenched and I swayed back and forth on my feet, wanting to throw up. Though the cop no longer had a soul, I couldn't help but feel terrible. Beside me, Adriel seemed unfazed. His hair stuck to his sweaty temples, and his chest rose and fell with rapid breaths, but it was more from exhaustion than fear.

The vision I had of Lucifer teaching Adriel how to slay demons came to mind. I shuddered.

"Two against one," Adriel said, looking at the second officer with the goatee. "How do you think this will turn out?"

"You're wrong, boy." The officer raised his chin and glanced behind us. "You're the one who's outnumbered."

Adriel didn't look back, probably out of caution, but I did. And I saw nothing.

"What are you talking about?" I stared into the bushes and trees before turning back around. "Are you on drugs?" I asked the cop.

He smirked. "You can't see because they don't want you to, but there are more than you can imagine."

"More what?"

"Demons and angels."

I looked again, still not seeing what he saw. Madadel and the eight other officers were farther down the road, battling behind the officer facing us. I wasn't worried about Madadel; he was defending himself just fine.

"In case you were wondering," the officer said, "there are more of us than there are of you."

Without warning, Adriel leaped forward and stabbed the cop right in the throat. When he pulled the knife out, the officer's pitch-black eyes faltered, turning olive. He wilted over his partner. I watched the blood pool around them, bright red and thick like soggy mud. The smell of metal and sweat filled the air.

My empty hand flew to my mouth. Like a merry-go-round, the earth spun beneath my feet. I took two steps back with my eyes on the floor to avoid Adriel.

"Addy . . ."

I swallowed, attempting to get rid of the vile taste in my mouth. "You made that look easy."

"Because it was easy. They're not humans, Addy. Their souls are gone." Taking three long strides, he closed the distance between us and pulled me against him. He wrapped his free hand behind my back, keeping the bloody knife far from me. "They were going to kill you."

"I know." I just couldn't shake the sense that we had just killed people. Actual living people.

"Hey." To my horror, he slipped the bloodstained knife in his pocket and swept a few loose, runaway strands out of my face. He tucked them behind my ear and looked at me with seriousness. "It had to be done."

"I know."

"We should get out of here."

"But . . ." I glanced around, still seeing nothing. "Didn't you hear him? We're not alone. We have to do something."

Pressing his hand against my cheek, he gazed at me with a scowl on his face. "Not right now. It's too risky."

He started steering me toward the library. I resisted, planting my feet firmly against the ground. From here, I saw Reed where we left him; he held something in his hand.

"This isn't the time to be stubborn," Adriel said as he tugged me forward.

"We can't leave the school like this."

"I promise you they will be fine."

"Except they won't!"

"Addy, that cop was bluffing. There might be a couple of demons more than there are angels, but they don't greatly outnumber them."

"How do you even know?"

"Because of two reasons." He pushed me two steps. "One, Madadel is having an easy time fighting all those cops. He wouldn't still be standing if he couldn't handle it." He pushed me three more steps. "Two, because I can see the rest of them, and they are helping him." He glanced at me. "Besides, you look like you're going to faint."

I crossed my arms. "I am not."

He ignored me and marched on, pulling me with him. "Come on."

Somehow, he managed to drag me down the road to the library. Then again, it wasn't like I weighed much.

Reed didn't notice us until we were within five feet of him.

"You're back," he said, holding a pistol in his hand.

I frowned. "Where'd you get that?"

"Huh?" Reed looked away from Madadel and down at his hand. "Oh, I just fished the gun from the trash and put the bullets back in. Your boyfriend here might not want to use it, but that doesn't mean I can't."

I felt my face turn red at the mention of Adriel being my boyfriend. I glared at Reed, both for using the wrong word and for taking a gun he should've left behind for his own good. Adriel still had his hand behind my back, and out of the corner of my eye, I saw him study me.

Drawing myself away from Adriel, I said, "Reed, you have to come with us. You can't stay here."

Reed's body tensed. "I'm not leaving."

"Reed . . . if you stay, I stay."

"Addy," Adriel interrupted. "You nearly died and then fought demons. It's time for you to rest."

Reed faced me but kept the gun pointed away. "Look, I'll be fine. As soon as this is over, I'll go somewhere and let Madadel do his job as a guardian. But I'm not leaving him."

"What if you get hurt?"

"My best shot is with Madadel."

I sighed. On the one hand, I wanted my baby brother to follow me. On the other hand, I understood where he was coming from. He was an adult now. He had to make his own decisions, no matter how risky they were, and I needed to be a tad less protective over him.

"Will you please call me as soon as you're out of here? Will you tell me when you're safe?" I grabbed his shoulders and squeezed. "Please? I need to know you're safe. I can't lose my brother."

He pulled me in for a hug. "You won't lose me. I promise I'll call."

I kissed him on the forehead and reminded him to point the gun away from himself. "I don't want you dying for a stupid reason."

He grinned. "Yes, ma'am."

As Adriel and I walked away, it occurred to me to tell Reed something. "Hey, Reed," I called out. "Don't talk to Erica anymore."

He raised his eyebrow. "Why is that?"

"Trust me. She's not right."

"Addy?"

I stopped walking and pinched the bridge of my nose. "She sold her soul to Lucifer, Reed. She's been fooling us our whole lives."

No words came from his mouth. He gave a single nod and went back to surveying Madadel and the cops. But I knew the news was hard to grasp.

Letting the subject go, I walked back with Adriel down the path we'd taken on our way in. My thoughts remained with Reed as I hoped and prayed for the first time in a long time for his safety.

Grandma Di would have been proud.

†

Back at the motel, silence overtook us. I kept checking my phone, yet nothing came from Reed. Lizzy, however, had left five text messages asking if we were still alive.

"Yes," I wrote back to her. "Are you?"

She responded with, "I'm peachy. Nate made fajitas." It was as if nothing had happened in the past twenty-four hours.

I threw my phone onto the duffle bag and crashed on the bed. My eyes blinked at the ceiling, counting each piece of peeling paint.

Adriel paced the room for a while without saying anything. I wondered if he was worried about Reed and the others like I was.

Finally, my phone vibrated. I shot to my feet. Adriel stopped pacing and watched me, his hand pulling his hair back. I looked at the screen and saw Reed's name. Taking a deep breath, I read his message.

"It's over. Two angels and ten fallen angels are dead, according to Madadel. The demon cops are mostly dead too. We're safe for now."

"Glad you're good," I wrote back.

"So?" Adriel said.

"It's over."

He gave me a gentle smile. "I told you they'd be fine."

"You did."

Closing the distance between us, he put his hands on my waist, just barely holding on with the tips of his fingers. "Are you sure you're okay?" Seriousness returned to his face.

He had asked me that question ten times during our car ride here. I kept assuring him I was fine, but he continued asking.

"I'm fine," I said again. "I promise."

"You're not secretly in pain?"

I couldn't help it; I smiled even as I rolled my eyes. "No, I'm not secretly in pain."

My joking tone didn't convince him. "You're not feeling faint?"

"Just guilty."

One of his hands went into my hair, cupping the side of my head. "I almost lost you today," he said with a low, soft voice. His gaze lingered on my lips.

I couldn't escape his hard stare. His other hand wrapped around my midsection, pulling me closer against him. I put my hands on him, feeling the tightness in his chest while it rapidly rose and fell.

I swallowed. "But I'm fine."

He leaned his forehead against mine and closed his eyes. "I just found you. I don't know what I'd do if I lost you."

My face flushed red. Everywhere his skin touched felt hot, more so than usual. An electric current charged up my back, dizzying me.

"Adriel?"

He drew my face in the rest of the way, and then his lips were on mine. I closed my eyes, lost in him. He pulled away for two seconds, but only to look at me. Then we crashed together, sharing one breath, arms around each other. His powerful tongue slipped inside my mouth, taking everything it could. I met him halfway in a lightheaded battle.

Lifting me off the ground, he kissed down my neck, trailing his lips against my collarbone. I wrapped my legs around his hips and my arms around his neck, wanting more and more. None of this felt like enough. I wanted him; it was crazy, but I did. I wanted him more than anything else.

I lifted his shirt off and threw it on the floor. He paused for a flicker of a second, his dark eyes studying mine. When he kissed me again, we were moving, me in his arms.

He laid me down on the mattress and hovered above me, hesitant.

"I'm fine," I said and reached to pull him in.

His body relaxed, and his lips fell against mine. His left hand remained under my head, but his right hand descended my body. It swept over the hills and valleys in hunger. My body rose, meeting his bare flesh. I brushed my hands over

234

the grooves at his waistline and curled my fingers into the waistband of his pants, tugging.

I couldn't tell who did what at that point. In the chaos of our kisses, my jeans came off along with his. His hand plunged under my blood-soaked tank top, discovering my body.

With a gasp, I felt him inside me. I opened my eyes and saw that my wide-eyed look mirrored his.

We moved against each other, clinging on for dear life. At some point, my top came off. He let out a groan in my mouth just as my head fell back, and I felt him pulse inside me.

My fingers scraped at the skin on his back, pleasure consuming me. And as the electric wave shot through my body and soul, I knew there was no going back.

Chapter Twenty Four

ADRIEL

Falling for Addy was wrong, but I just didn't care anymore. I didn't care that I once was an angel. I didn't care that I was human now. I just didn't care. Seeing her almost die caused a part of me to feel hollow and lost, like having a pit in my heart, and I hated it.

I'd had hundreds of humans under my care as a guardian angel. Each one died in the end. The only one alive today was Jenna, if they hadn't executed her for killing her son the way humans sometimes did when punishing murder, something that never made sense to me. Why commit murder to bring justice to another murder?

And yet for all the humans I'd lost, the threat of losing Addy brought a sense of finality to my existence. She was everything I had here on Earth, and I didn't want to discover the world on my own.

Addy now stood in our motel room with her phone in hand. The sight of the crimson red on her body pushed me over the edge. Her bloody tank top had nearly dried, but not completely. My hands transformed into fists. I wanted to scream. I wanted to break something. I wanted . . .

I strode toward her. Of their own free will, my hands moved to her waist.

"Are you sure you're okay?" There was a knot in my chest, a worry that she would start bleeding again and disappear from my life. I almost didn't want to know the answer to my question, afraid that she had been lying this whole time, which wasn't unlike her. She was fierce and beautiful in refusing to show weakness, but she was also too stubborn at times.

"I'm fine. I promise," she said.

"You're not secretly in pain?"

She smiled and rolled her eyes. "No, I'm not secretly in pain."

The blood practically coated her white top. I pictured her on the library floor in that moment when she'd gasped. The way her dark-brown eyes had seemed to drift elsewhere, far from here.

"You're not feeling faint?"

"Just guilty."

Her words terrified me. Not because she'd done bad things and collaborated with the devil, but because what she'd gone through was my fault. I'd disappointed God and I didn't make it up by protecting Addy. Because of me, she'd almost died.

Needing to make sure she was truly alive, my hand cupped her head, inching her face a smidge closer. "I almost lost you today."

Her breath caught in her throat, and her smile vanished. I wrapped an arm around her and pulled her in. Blood from her tank top smudged against my white shirt—Nate's shirt. She didn't seem to notice, though, because her eyes never left mine.

Resting her trembling hands against my chest, she repeated her mantra, "But I'm fine." These words seemed to be the one thing that helped carry her through life, what with her psychotic, evil father and her secret-queen-of-the-damned mother.

But I knew the truth behind her façade. I'd seen it in her eyes the first time we met; she carried the weight of the world on her back. Still, even at that first meeting, she'd managed to look me dead on and pull herself together.

Even as she lay dying earlier today, she had been a soldier in battle, pushing all her sorrows and pain away.

I leaned my forehead against hers. Mind against mind. Right before closing my eyes, I saw her rosy cheeks return. The sight broke my heart. "I just found you. I don't know what I'd do if I lost you."

One last time, my conscience reminded me that this was wrong. I knew I should have let Addy go and pulled away, but every part of me burned for her touch.

"Adriel?" she whispered.

I couldn't resist. I drew her face in and kissed her long and hard, my teeth grazing her lips. Blood rushed between my legs, yet I no longer minded the odd human sensation. Her hands pressed against my chest, and I felt her lips react to mine, soft and smooth.

When she moaned, I pulled away and studied her. I didn't want to continue if she didn't want to. But she didn't pull away, and her eyes stayed on me.

Her lips parted and we came together, mouths colliding and hearts hammering against each other. My tongue glided inside her mouth, tasting her, breathing her in. My head spun, drunk on her. It was all I could do not to lose my mind.

My kisses trailed down her body, down the slopes and arches of her neck and collarbone. I searched for the source of madness between us and found only her flesh and beating heart.

I picked her up, hands on the backs of her thighs, and she wrapped her legs around me. Even though every inch of her brushed against me, I wanted more. I couldn't explain the desire and I couldn't think of a way to fix it. Her hands moved around my neck, pulling at the long hairs in the back. She was a small thing in my arms, but she filled all of me with hunger.

Her soft lips danced with mine, passing warm breaths between us. Reaching behind me, she lifted my shirt. When she drew her face away, she helped me out of the shirt and threw it on the floor. Then she leaned in again, her dark eyes serene and her cheeks full of color. She crushed her lips against mine, intoxicating me.

I wanted nothing separating us, not even the thin fabric we wore, so I carried her to the bed and laid her on her back. Not knowing what to do next or what she felt about all of this, I stared at her, my body just inches above hers.

She smiled and said, "I'm fine." She grabbed my shoulders, pulling me toward her.

Our lips linked again in a hungry fight. The blood in my veins surged. Every time I felt her warm breath inside my mouth, I wanted more of her. Her hands were on my back, my chest, the edge of my pants. She lingered there, her slender fingers curling inside the cottony material, digging into my lower abdomen. I groaned on instinct. The bulge between my legs could no longer be tamed.

After that, everything happened fast. Her hands pulled down my pants, and I was struggling to get hers off without knowing my motivation behind it. I knew what humans did. I'd seen it millions of times. But I never understood why. Not until she wrapped her legs around me and pressed my lower body against hers and I pushed inside, wildly, desperately, insanely lost in the moment.

Her eyes mimicked mine, large and full of wonder. And then we surrendered. We shut out the world, shut out this musty room and the people walking and talking outside. It was just me and her.

With our bodies entangled, I pulled her tank top off and threw it into the vast sea that surrounded us and carried us on this tiny island, fit for the two of us and no one else.

Her skin rubbed against mine, warm and soft and all her. We moved in a unified rhythm, heat escalating between us. At first it was slow, then fast, until we lost all our other senses.

When the last thrust came, I felt her shudder in my arms as my soul left, wrapped around her, and came back inside me.

My body sank against hers, my face in the crook of her neck.

I kissed her skin, closed my eyes, and let humanity fill me up. For the first time, I wanted to stay like this, in my human flesh.

†

We woke up what seemed like weeks later, though only an hour had passed. Addy hoisted herself up, slumped her arm across my chest, and leaned in to give me a quick peck on the lips.

"Hey." I reached out and wrapped my arms around her, pulling her on top of me. Feeling ecstatic, I kissed her more.

When she drew away, she had the biggest smile I'd ever seen her don.

"Why'd you, you know, do this?" She rested her head against my shoulder. "I thought you said it was out of line to be with me."

I kissed the top of her head and sighed. "I was wrong before."

"What do you mean?"

"I think . . . I think I was in denial of the fact that I was banished from heaven. I wanted to believe I could be an angel again, but I don't think that's the case anymore." I smiled at the ceiling. "I did this," I said, kissing her forehead, "because I wanted to."

She raised her head and looked down at me, her long curls falling over my chest. Her big brown eyes danced with a question. "You don't regret kissing me this morning?"

Bringing my hand behind her head, I pulled her toward me and sucked on her bottom lip. She tasted sweet, like the first thing I'd savored as a human: honey lemon tea. Invigorating was what she was. Every second our lips touched, a thousand tiny electric currents ran down my body.

Pulling away, I gazed at her almond eyes and the way her hair framed her beautiful face and smiled. "I don't regret being with you. Not at all." The more I stared at her, the more it felt like I'd known her longer than five—soon to be six—days. Like we'd grown up together, or been angel friends. The closeness between us, the pull of our energies from day one; I couldn't explain that. But it felt right. "I only regret not being able to protect you."

"Adriel." She planted her hand on my chest and sighed. "I'm not a child. I don't need protection."

I trailed my fingers up and down each notch of her spine. "I can see that about you, but I still can't help wanting to keep you safe. If it weren't for you, I'd still be in the street right now with a burnt back."

She traced circles over my heart with her index finger. "But your back is fine now. It's completely healed."

I grinned. "My point is, I want to protect you just like you want to protect your brother. I know you're strong at heart; that's not a question. But I just can't grasp the idea of losing you, and I don't want to find out what that's like. I almost did today, but not again. I won't let that happen to you. I'd rather die first than have you go out of this world."

She smiled and slid back down over my chest, resting her head on me. My legs were spread out, and she lay in the center, her chest against mine. For a few moments, we stayed like that. Naked and entangled and happy.

Although I had been a human for five days so far, I felt the most human now. My sensations were heightened, and I tingled all over. I wondered why God created powerful angels only to strip them of the full emotional capacity humans had.

With my skin touching Addy's and our arms desperately clinging on to each other, I felt whole. The world might fall apart and crumble, taking us with it, but Addy and I had this moment. She was real. In this second, I had her. Because of that, I knew I would be fine.

No matter what happened next, I had held the person most dear to me and felt her chest rise and fall against my own beating heart. This was real. No one could take that away.

"Adriel?" Addy murmured.

I hugged her tighter. "Yeah?"

"What's heaven like?"

It was the first time she had ever asked me about my origins. For a second, I wasn't sure how to answer. From a human's perspective, I could see now how overwhelming it was, the grandness and beauty and unmistakable purity of the realm. A floral garden abundant with yellow butterflies or a flowing stream on a sunny day would never compare to the magnitude and awe that was heaven.

Not to say that Earth wasn't beautiful, because it was. I thought of the first time I'd felt the warmth from the sun against my skin. For a human, that sensation was precious, like having God hold your hand. Besides, he was the creator of everything; he wouldn't create an ugly world.

But heaven could not be matched.

"Heaven is complete tranquility," I said. "It is bright and warm, the kind of warm that makes you feel safe and loved."

"What does it look like? Does it look like the sky, like those baroque paintings of angels on clouds?"

"Not exactly. It's a sunny place, you could say, but it's not literally in the sky, nor does it look like the sky."

She giggled. "So, you didn't sleep on clouds?"

I matched her laugh. "No, I never did."

"Then what's it really like?"

"Well, imagine opening a door, and from that door bursts bright light more powerful than the sun's rays. The difference here is that you can look at the light without hurting your eyes. Hills of green and even ponds and gentle waterfalls greet you everywhere. The sounds are subtle, smooth, like hearing the ocean from a distance."

My description didn't come close to the real wonder of heaven, but there was no way to explain it right. A person could only experience that breathtaking realm; heaven was a feeling much more than a sight.

"I can go on; however, I could never do heaven justice. It is beyond description."

"What about hell? Did God create it?"

"Yes. When he decided to kick Lucifer out, he created it and placed demons there, too."

"How come?"

"No one knows. God doesn't exactly explain his reasons to us. Perhaps it's to control or scare the humans who sin beyond saving and become demons upon death, then end up in hell."

She frowned. "Humans are very aware of that, how God doesn't explain his reasons."

I grabbed hold of her hips and flipped her underneath me. She let out a wild shriek and laughed, her belly vibrating with each breath. Her happiness was contagious. I smiled while I stared at her, unable to do anything else. Her coiled strands lay about her like someone had neatly arranged them.

"You're so beautiful," I said.

At my words, her laughter died out. A more serious expression masked her face, and her rosy cheeks made an appearance. Heat swelled in my lower body again. I brought my mouth to hers and consumed her. My fingers learned the dips and curves of her body, molding against the most private parts of her. She quickly relaxed under me, her hands moving to my shoulders and then lower back, urging me closer.

Back in our rhythm, one I would never forget, I found myself. My heart had become entangled with hers. Even though my enemy's blood was a part of her, she was a part of me, and I a part of her. Nothing else mattered.

As I closed my eyes and surrendered to the ferocity pulling us together, I knew it would be impossible to get this feeling out of my system.

And I liked it that way.

Chapter Twenty-Five

ADELAIDE

For a split second, I forgot where I was. Arms wrapped around me, holding me tight. My heart started pounding when my mind jumped to Devin, and not in the good way.

Eyes still closed, I started to plot my way out. I pictured the door in Devin's bedroom and the many steps to the front door. I thought about the way I would grab my things and quietly dress before tiptoeing out. I reminded myself to keep my breathing even and slow as I prepared to lift Devin's hands off me.

But when I opened my eyes, it wasn't Devin holding me. Adriel slept with his lips pursed together. His thick lashes kissed the line of his cheeks. The innocence in his soft and vulnerable expression melted my heart. Relief washed over me. He wasn't Devin. He would never be Devin.

I inched my face closer and pressed my lips against his.

His eyes fluttered open. When he realized what was going on, he kissed me back with force. "Good morning." Smiling, he brushed his thumb against my cheek.

"Good morning," I said.

"I'm glad you woke me up."

I felt tightness in my stomach as it threatened to growl. "I'm glad too, but why?"

"Because I'm starving."

"Me too." I buried my head in his chest. "We should get food, but I'm feeling really lazy right now. I don't want to leave this bed."

He ran his hand through my hair, coiling a strand around his index finger. "But if we leave now, we can get food and come back and do it all over again."

The words coming out of his mouth sounded so casual, as if he were talking about going to work or purchasing a phone. I felt my cheeks redden.

"Come on, Addy." He left the bed and dragged me to my feet. "Today is a good day."

Had we really just spent the night having sex? Not once, not twice, but enough times that I had lost count?

We stood naked in front of each other, and I suddenly felt shy, mostly from the memory of what we'd done in the past twelve hours or so. I didn't care that his eyes ravaged me from head to toe, because I was doing the same to him. But the image of the way we moved, our tongues sliding together, drove me wild. I didn't know where to turn to hide the eager expression on my face.

My eyes searched for my clothes around the dim room. On the floor, I found my blood-soaked tank top. I went to grab it, but Adriel stepped behind me. His hands settled on my hips and he drew me to him, my back touching his chest.

"Throw that shirt out," he said in my ear. "I never want to see that bloody thing again."

I kicked the shirt aside. "I'll wear something else, then."

"Thank you." He kissed my cheek and let go.

Before I could even move, he grabbed one of Nate's shirts and jeans from the duffle bag by our feet. He then pulled on a clean pair of underwear from the package I bought him.

"Your turn." He donned Nate's gray shirt, sat on the edge of the bed, and grinned.

I reached into the duffle bag and dug out a dark-teal button-up shirt, underwear, and a pair of denim jeans. When I started slipping the panties up each leg, he fixed a hard stare on me, no reservation whatsoever.

It wasn't like he hadn't already seen every part of me, but I still felt exposed in front of him.

He smiled, meeting my gaze. "I hope you know, you're the most interesting human I've met, and I've met a lot."

"Have you?"

"Thousands."

I raised an eyebrow at him. "What makes me the most interesting?"

I was still getting dressed when he got up, walked toward me, and placed his hand on my cheek. "You're fearless and beautiful and never let anything stand in your way, not even me."

"You're describing plenty of people."

"None," he said, trailing his lips up my neck to my ear, "so courageous that they'd face the devil and stab a knife through his chest . . . even if that knife couldn't kill him."

My eyes rolled back in my head with pleasure. "You're forgetting those are just the perks of having the devil's blood."

"Maybe, but you're still the most interesting."

Somehow, I managed to button up the rest of my shirt. "If that's the case, then you're the most interesting angel. I don't know many angels, but even so, you're the only one who's now a human. That says something about you."

"Yeah, that God lost hope in me."

"Or"—I gave him a quick kiss—"that he has just enough hope to spare you from being a demon."

Just then, my stomach growled. Adriel smirked and placed his hand against my belly, loudly shushing it. I squeezed my lips shut and fought back a giggle.

"It's official. We need to eat," he said.

We grabbed the essentials: car keys, wallet, phone, my Swiss Army knife, and the sharp kitchen knife that I'd taken from my apartment. Seeing the weapon in his hand reminded me of home, back when Lizzy and I lived normal lives. I missed watching *I Love Lucy* with her. I missed going to Euphoria with her and our friends. And I terribly, terribly missed talking to her about everything.

I unlocked my phone to send her a quick text to Nate's cell phone when I noticed two missed calls from my boss, Melissa.

"Oh, crap."

"What? Is everything okay? Is it Reed?"

"No, it's my boss. I've been absent from work the past few days and I haven't sent in any of the work I was supposed to do."

Dreading the next few minutes, I called Melissa back.

She picked up on the third ring and pretended she had no idea who was calling, even though I was pretty sure she saw my name on her phone screen. "Saronata Signature Designs. Melissa speaking."

"Hi, Melissa. This is Adelaide Shaw."

She was silent for a while. I could hear her tapping her neatly filed fingernails against the mahogany desk in her office. I imagined her stirring sugar into her coffee with her other hand and staring intently at the interior design projects from the interns while having me on speaker.

"Adelaide," she finally said. "I hope for your benefit you've been ill this past week."

"I apologize for not calling. I've had a family emergency. I'm currently in Latrobe."

"When will I receive your designs? The deadline is this Friday."

I mentally cussed. "I'll have them in by then. I promise."

"You better, or you might not have a job here anymore."

After that, she hung up, and I was left making calculations of how long it would take me to finish everything. With everything going on, I just did not have the time to be creative and come up with the amazing new interior design ideas for our clients' homes that I'd dreamed of. But since I had no choice, I would have to make the time and send something in, even if it wasn't my best work.

"This week is becoming the most overwhelming and bizarre week of my life," I told Adriel.

He took my hand and started out the door. "At least we met each other."

As we drove out, we decided to eat at Creed's Diner, the place we had our first discussion. So much had changed; I'd gone from not trusting Adriel at all to trusting him with my life.

"I thought you were some crazy guy who'd escaped jail or something when you ran in front of my car looking the way you did." I flashed him a smile and looked back at the road.

He placed his hand on my knee. "You also tried to kill me that night."

"I'm glad I wasn't successful."

"Trust me, me too."

"How old are you, anyway? You don't look over twenty-five."

People drove to work like on any typical day, unfazed by the fact that a shooting occurred at Saint Vincent College yesterday. Then again, *we* weren't acting any different. We passed by a park. For a split second, I looked to my left out the window, concentrating on the children swinging from the monkey bars. Did they know people had died in their city less than twenty-four hours ago? No one seemed frightened. It was odd, but I brushed it off.

"As an angel, I'm older than this universe," Adriel said. "As a human, I don't really have a physical age."

"Then can I pick an age and birthday for you? A day you can celebrate for years to come?"

He squeezed my knee. "Go ahead."

I didn't need to think about it; the day he landed on Earth made the most sense, so I told him. "That's your birthday. And . . . let's say you turned twenty-three. You look around that age."

"Deal."

Before reaching Creed's, I wanted to fill Lucy's tank. I'd driven from Pittsburgh to Latrobe a lot in the past few days, and my car was running dangerously low. At the nearest gas station, I pulled the car up to a pump.

"I'll be right back," I said. "I'm going to pay with cash inside."

Adriel waited in the car. As I walked, the weight of the Swiss Army knife in the pocket of my pants gave me strength. When more demons, human-turned or hell-based, showed up, I would be ready. Marching inside the store with thirty dollars in my hand, I kept my head high and stayed aware of my surroundings.

I saw four people throughout the store, including the old woman behind the register who chewed gum with her mouth open, making loud popping noises. She smiled when I headed her way with the unmistakable cash in my hand.

Before I reached her, my phone vibrated against my leg. I pulled it from my pocket—the one without the knife—and saw Nate's number.

"Hello?"

"Addy!" Lizzy cried out. "Where are you?"

"In Latrobe still. What's wrong?"

"Are you not seeing the news? It's not safe out there!"

"Out there where, Liz?"

She was panting on the other end of the line. In the background, I heard Nate screaming at her to get away from the window.

"Lizzy? Lizzy, please, what's going on?"

My heart pounded in my chest when she didn't respond right away. I felt certain everyone standing in the store could hear it.

"We're under attack! It's all over the news. Addy, it's not just here. It's the entire country."

I jumped back to look outside through the glass doors. Adriel sat in my Oldsmobile, watching me across the way. "Lizzy, are you sure? I was literally just driving. It's completely quiet out here."

"It's not, Addy. Please find a shelter!"

Before I could ask her what kind of shelter she was talking about, I felt the earth shake. My eyes shot to Adriel, but I couldn't see him. My car's passenger door was wide open, and Adriel was gone. People were filling gas, and he wasn't among them either.

My heart thumped in my ears, and I stepped forward. Outside, the world became bright red. My car came alive, exploding like someone had stuffed it with billions of fireworks. Everyone inside the store yelled, but their voices seemed distant.

Lungs full of screams, I ran to the door and smacked both hands against the glass, dropping my phone and the money somewhere. Fire flared around my car, and the gas pump next to it blasted. One by one, the other pumps blew up until the entire parking lot was aflame.

The glass door and windows where I stood shattered from the blasts. I fell back on the floor, my head missing the ground by an inch. Tiny glass shards cut through my flesh. Crying, I held up my bloody hands and extracted three small glass pieces from my skin.

"Adriel!" I was on my feet in seconds, searching for Adriel through the smoke and fire outside.

I stepped into the chaos that used to be the gas station. Flames surged around me. I somehow dodged them. The scene reminded me of my vision of hell when the gate had exploded and fire raged into my room.

"Adriel?"

Several other cars were on fire. Heavy, burning smoke roiled against the auto glass, trying to escape. There was no sign of the drivers who had been filling gas just a minute ago. My heart sank, knowing they were almost surely dead.

Was Adriel dead, too? I didn't want to think it.

Sweat trickled down my neck. I hurried around the burning station to get a better view of the place. Again, no sign of Adriel. With a tightness in my chest, it finally hit me that he might be gone, that he might have burned in the explosion. The idea of him on fire tore me apart. Just a few minutes before, we'd been in bed together, happy, and now he was dead. He had burned alive, just like that. One second staring at me, the next gone from existence.

I ran back inside the store through the broken glass door. Tears fogged my vision, but I couldn't move my trembling hand to my face to wipe them away. Pain stabbed my throat as my lungs filled with smoke. I wanted to sink to the floor, crash among the broken glass, and cough and wail and die. My chest felt hollow, like the fire had burned a pit in its center.

But I didn't sink to the floor. Adriel's earlier words about me being courageous rang in my ears and kept me up. With shaky hands, I searched for my phone through the mess on the ground. When I found it, I put the screen to my ear.

"Lizzy?" My voice did not sound like it belonged to me. "Lizzy, you still there?" My tone was rigid, hopeless.

"Oh, thank God!" she chirped. "I thought you got hurt!"

"Liz, I can't find Adriel." A cry ripped from my throat. I put my hand to my mouth and let it happen.

"You have to find shelter," she repeated, ignoring my words. "That's what we're going to do."

I shook my head like she could see me. "I can't find him!"

I hung up on her without thinking too much about it and glared at the people on the floor in the back of the store. Like me, they'd survived. The old lady who had been chewing gum was now covered in a layer of dust. I wondered if I looked like her too. Her eyes were wide with fear. Unlike me, she kept low in the corner of her counter, watching everyone without moving.

Leaving the old lady and the others, I walked back outside into the hell storm. How could this happen? And why? I was happy for a good couple of hours, then the world just had to take that away from me, like it always did. This time, though, it was just being cruel.

In the midst of everything, I thought of Reed. Adriel might have been gone, but I still had my brother. I sent him a frantic text with fumbling fingers. Half of what I wrote came out misspelled and incoherent. I just wanted to know he was safe. A few heartbeats later, Reed responded that Madadel was guarding him.

With one less thing to worry about, my thoughts went back to Adriel. My mind raced back and forth between two conflicting thoughts. One, that there was no sign of Adriel and the world outside seemed to have been destroyed, meaning he was dead. Two, that he might have somehow escaped. My car door *was* wide open before it was destroyed. Could he have run? Where was he now? The gas station burned and burned, and I didn't know what to believe.

I hunched over in the middle of the disaster, my hands on my knees, and panted while I cried. Smoke filled my lungs, sending me into a coughing fit. *We shouldn't have left the motel. We shouldn't have, we shouldn't have, we shouldn't have!*

The fire crackled, not in the nice, bonfire kind of way, but in a threatening, aggressive way that sent me shrinking back.

And I slammed into something . . . or someone. Arms snaked around me, holding me still. I smiled, thinking it was Adriel.

"Having a good day, are we?" Lucifer spun me around in his arms and beamed, showcasing his rotten teeth. He had a deranged look in his eyes. "Hello, daughter of mine."

Like someone had poured poison down my throat, the smile washed from my face and the tears vanished, their only remains on my cheeks. Without a second thought, I spit in Lucifer's face. My saliva dribbled down his nose and cheek. He didn't even flinch.

"You have not changed, Adelaide. Just as well. That is how I made you."

"You did not make me!" Putting more force into my upper body, I tried pushing myself free of his embrace. I failed.

"On the contrary, dear. Nonetheless, if the idea that I am not your creator helps you sleep better at night, then perhaps we could arrange something to keep you in restless sleep."

"Fuck you!"

"With pleasure." He smacked his lips against mine. There was no love in the act. He was just displaying how easily he could overpower me.

With bile rising to my throat, I froze. Every part of me was immobilized with disgust. I couldn't move my face, arms, or legs. My stomach roiled at the dirty, bitter taste of his mouth.

When he pulled his face away, he grinned from ear to ear. "Sweet like your mother."

"What is wrong with you? You're sick!"

"I am the devil, child. I do not play by the rules."

"You killed all those people. You killed Adriel!"

He pursed his lips. "No, you killed all those people."

"How? I was minding my own business, filling gas. I'm not to blame for this."

I hated being chest to chest with him. Every tear that fell from my face dropped onto his dark suit of armor.

"My dear." He grabbed me by the back of my head and restrained my face. "The minute you made a few people worship me, you played a role in all of this." When I kept glowering at him, his face softened—despite his scary eyes—and his tone became sweeter, the words sliding off his tongue like syrup. "How do you feel about becoming the president of this country? You know I could make that happen. You just have to say the word."

His eyes searched mine, and when he saw my resolve, his face hardened again.

He shoved me away. For a moment, I felt both relief and confusion. He had let me go, but why? What was his motive? After I rubbed my sore arms, I reached for the Swiss Army knife in my pocket. Even though I couldn't kill him, I didn't want to go down without a fight.

From my right, something moved.

"Grab her!" Lucifer shouted.

Two fallen angels with scarred backs came from either side of me and clasped my arms while my hand was still in my pocket. I recognized Saleos, Lucifer's right hand. Saleos and the other demon shoved my hands behind my back and compelled me forward, pushing me toward the store.

I glowered at Lucifer as I passed by him. "What do you want from me?"

He didn't say anything until we were in the store. The old chewing-gum lady and the other people on the ground rose to their feet and watched me. They all had creepy grins on their faces.

I didn't understand right away. "What . . ." It hit me a second later when I noticed their blank, pitch-black eyes. I wrestled against the demons holding me and shifted my body so I faced Lucifer. "You turned them?"

He lifted his arms into the air. "This is a war, Adelaide."

"You never answered me; what do you want from me? If this is a war, why can't you just leave me out of it?"

"Because." He moved closer, towering a foot over me. "You are still my blood. I want you on my side."

"I won't do that."

He smiled, but it did not reach his eyes. "Perhaps I can change your mind."

I looked him in his two empty holes and did not blink. "Only in your twisted dreams."

"Very well." He turned to the humans and gestured with his head. "You can kill him now."

A strong, broad-shouldered, cleft-chinned man in his thirties marched to the back and opened a door to a storage closet. He went inside. A second later, he came back hauling something over his shoulder. When he came closer, I saw what he was carrying.

He'd draped Adriel's limp body over his shoulder like a big sack of flour. I blinked in disbelief. Adriel—a muscular, lean, and tall man—now looked lifeless. Did they drug him?

"No, stop!" I screamed.

"Have you changed your mind?" Lucifer said. "Perhaps all you have desired this entire time is love. Is that what you want? Do you want the affection of a man? I can make all the men of this world fall at your knees in worship. Choose me, and I will give you that. What will it be, child?"

"Cut the bullshit!"

"Do you want a man to satisfy you? Name anyone, and he will become your sex slave. How about one of the Hemsworth brothers? Or are you more into dark-featured men, like dear old dad? If that is the case, I can certainly bring you one of the Francos or . . . Oh, I know! Women drool over that Somer—what was his name? Somerhot? Somerhold? You get the idea!"

I refused to respond.

The man carrying Adriel dumped his unconscious body on the ground and stepped back, waiting for more instructions.

I couldn't take my eyes off Adriel. He had no obvious scratches on him, but he'd clearly been knocked out, most likely drugged. Turning my anger on Lucifer, I said, "What are you going to do with him, and what the fuck do you want? Stop playing mind games!"

"Shh." He placed his hand on the side of my face. His skin felt hot to the touch, even more so than before. "Child, I told you already. I want you on my side."

"Or you'll kill Adriel?"

"Obviously."

"But what's the point? You've accomplished what you wanted." I pictured the scene behind me. My car was gone, innocent people were dead, and the streets looked like hell. And the angels? They didn't seem to be around. He'd truly achieved his goal. "You destroyed everything. You don't need me anymore."

"That may be the case, but you are still my blood. I would like to keep you on my side."

I jerked my head from his touch, making him drop his hand. "I won't do it. I'll kill myself first."

"No, you will not." He waved his hand at Saleos and pointed to the back corner of the store. "Lock her up."

"Wait, what?" Nothing made sense to me. "I thought you wanted me on your side. Why are you locking me up?"

Saleos and the other demon pushed me along. I wished I were stronger and could fight back, but there were two of them, and I was small. The Swiss Army knife felt heavy in my pocket. If given a single second at freedom, I would take advantage of the moment and pull the weapon out.

In the back, they shoved me inside a small empty office. I stumbled forward and crashed into a wooden desk. When I spun around, it was too late. Saleos slammed the glass door shut and locked it with a key from the outside.

I took a step toward the door and studied the handle. When I saw it had an internal lock, I smiled up at Saleos, feeling proud that I'd outsmarted him. If I twisted the lock, I would be free.

Saleos was two steps ahead of me. He held the door in place as the other demon brought a chair and wedged it underneath the handle. Now, even if I unlocked the door, I could not escape. The handle would not budge.

"Damn it!" I slammed my palm against the glass.

Lucifer strutted over and rested his hand on Saleos's shoulder. His thick, arched eyebrows rose with anticipation. I wanted to think of him as the devil, but his prominent, familiar features reminded me that he was my father. We shared a lot of genes. No matter how hard I tried to forget that, facing him was a slap of reality.

"If you try to kill yourself," Lucifer said, "Adriel will certainly die. If you do not stand by my side, he will also certainly die. What shall your choice be, Daughter?"

"Get me out of here and I'll show you my choice!" I grabbed the Swiss Army knife from my pocket and pulled out the knife. Raising it in front of me, I gave him my silent but obvious answer.

He sighed. "You have chosen the death of your lover. That is what he is, am I right?"

My empty hand fisted. He had been watching us this whole time. I didn't know how, but the idea made my blood heat up. Moving to the back of the office, I picked up a cheap-looking plastic chair, the foldable kind, and lifted it high into the air, ready to throw it at the glass door.

"You do not want to do that." Lucifer looked over his shoulder at the burly man. A second later, the man came, dragging Adriel's body across the floor. "Again, anything you do that is not to my liking will cause Adriel to die."

I dropped the chair; its metal legs banged against the floor. "How much have you seen?"

"Enough. I can mostly sense it in your blood."

"Just let Adriel go, please."

"As soon as you come to my side."

"No, I won't do it. I can't put all the people I love in danger and let go of everything good just for your stupid agenda. I might be your child by blood, but I am not your daughter."

"The world is not fair, you know. Has no one taught you that before?" He turned around, took five steps toward Adriel, leaned down, and pulled him off the ground by the back of his shirt.

The big-shouldered man stood behind Adriel and wound his beefy arms around the fallen angel's torso, allowing Lucifer to let go. Lucifer reached into his dark armor and retrieved a gold dagger.

"Adelaide, Adelaide, Adelaide. What will it take for you to learn? Choosing me is the only way."

He slapped Adriel in the face. A second later, Adriel stirred.

Please fight back.

Adriel blinked, his eyes heavy. "Leave her alone," he said to Lucifer. "She didn't do anything."

Fight back!

Lucifer looked back and forth between Adriel and me, flashing his awful teeth at us. "By the devil, you two are adorable." He turned back to Adriel. "Too bad Adelaide made the wrong choice. Now you must suffer, my old friend."

"Go to hell," Adriel muttered. His head hung forward, and he was having a hard time keeping his eyes open.

I wanted him to fight Saleos and free himself, though it quickly became clear Adriel could not do that in his weak physical condition.

Lucifer gripped Adriel's limp arm, flipped his palm up, and brought the dagger to his forearm. "I will gladly go to hell."

Slamming my hands against the glass again, I yelled, "What are you doing?"

"I told you he would suffer, yet you didn't listen." In one swift motion, Lucifer slit Adriel's forearm, cutting through a major artery. "Let's see how long he'll last before passing out."

A horizontal line of blood seeped out just below Adriel's wrist, trickling down his hand. He raised his head for two seconds and met my eyes before his head sunk back. The blood kept pouring out.

My heart felt wild as it thrashed in my chest. I wanted to scream and cry, but I knew it would get me nowhere. Instead, I grabbed the plastic chair off the ground, ignoring Lucifer's earlier threats, and aimed for the glass door. Saleos saw me coming. He opened his mouth to tell me to stop, realized he had to get out of the way, and dashed away from the door.

The chair came smashing through, shattering the glass all over the place.

Without waiting for Lucifer to react, I propelled myself into the other room despite a few sharp glass pieces still hanging around the frame of the door. A twinge in my shoulder indicated I'd cut myself on the glass. Now my tender, bleeding hands weren't my only battle wounds. They still hadn't healed, unlike the bullet that nearly killed me yesterday. I didn't really care, though; a little pain wasn't news to me.

Saleos jumped in front of me, blocking my path to Lucifer. Although I had my knife in my hand, I decided to kick him in the crotch. When he bent over, groaning, I grinned.

"Lucifer's little bitch," I said. Before he could straighten himself, I jammed my knife into the side of his throat and drew it out. "That's for Simiael."

Blood as thick as black ink covered the knife. Saleos collapsed, his black eyes turning brown. I beamed, knowing that even though I couldn't kill Lucifer, I could destroy his army.

Lucifer regarded me. I didn't have a tactical advantage, and I had to think of something fast. Beside Lucifer, Adriel barely moved.

I raised the knife in front of me. "Let him go."

"Or what?" He waved his own dagger around, bringing it dangerously close to Adriel's face. "You will kill all my servants?"

He wanted me to respond so he could turn my anger into mockery. I kept quiet.

"Silly child of mine." He grabbed Adriel's bleeding forearm again and pressed the tip of the dagger against his flesh, right above the laceration. "Get it through your thick, stubborn head. Either you stand by my side and he gets to live, or you make the wrong choice and he dies."

"Addy," Adriel muttered. He forced his eyes open for a split second. "Don't do it." His skin was pale and his breaths were heavy.

"Done!" Lucifer chirped. He stepped away from Adriel and dropped his arm. He flashed his teeth at me, almost like he had some fatherly joke he needed to share.

I looked where he'd pressed the dagger against Adriel's arm and realized what he'd done. In bold red, Adriel now bled the letter *L*.

Chapter Twenty-Six

ADRIEL

We were tearing through heaven side by side like we always did. Lucifer's wings were white as snow, shimmering in the glow of the light showering us.

"Did you say Father created the first life on Earth?" I stopped upon a hill to let my wings rest.

Acres of green radiated around us. Some angels flew around, others lay in the grass humming, and a few, like Lucifer and I, played in the kingdom of our Father. We loved to race each other in the air and try to outsmart the other in ridiculous ways. Sometimes, I would throw one of the glowing rocks I'd find at him to slow him down; other times, he would shove me with his wings. But it was all out of fun. Our brothers and sisters could hear our laughter from a distance, just as we could hear theirs.

Lucifer landed beside me. He placed his hand on my shoulder and grinned. "You should have seen it, Adriel. Father made a creature that lives underwater!"

My eyes were wide with excitement. "What does it look like?" I grabbed a twig from the grass and handed it to him. "Here, carve it on that tree over there. I want to see."

He moved to the tree and drew a slender, jawless, long creature. "He calls it a fish."

I pulled a leaf from the tree and put it next to the drawing. "The fish looks like a leaf, but longer and thinner. Why does it look so strange? Where are its eyes?"

Lucifer shrugged. "He says it will evolve one day. When he creates humans, this fish will look meatier, scalier, and have a tiny jaw to eat with."

"Why does he not create that evolved fish now?"

"I do not know. Why does Father not let us create things too?" He put his hand on top of my head and ruffled my hair. "One day I shall convince him to let me create my own planet in a universe of my own design."

"How will you manage that?"

"With my charm."

"You are only saying that because you know you are his favorite."

He threw the twig across the hill. It disappeared somewhere in the green. "I am simply the most intelligent and delightful child."

"Clearly the humblest, too."

He ignored my snide remark. "You should have seen that fish in the water."

"One day I will. Now come on!" I slapped him on the back with my wing and soared into the air.

He bolted after me. Even though I'd taken off before him, he flew past me, laughing and chanting that he was the best. It was the kind of fun we always had, and we never suspected it would come to an end.

✝

Addy's voice stirred me awake, and I realized I couldn't move a muscle. Limbs heavy, I tried to get my fingers to twitch, with no luck. My chest rose and fell with rapid breaths, and the back of my head felt like someone had banged it with a brick. Two strong arms wrapped around my midsection.

Through the slits of my heavy eyes, I looked up and saw Addy. She stood a few feet away with her knife aimed in my direction.

"Let him go," she said, not looking at me, but at something to my right.

"Or what?" Lucifer's voice rang out beside me. "You will kill all my servants?"

Glimmering gold flashed in my line of sight. It took me a moment to realize it was a dagger.

"Silly child of mine."

Lucifer gripped my forearm, but I didn't feel the pressure. As if observing from a distance, all I could do was take in the scene. Lucifer brought his dagger's pointy end to my skin. Just below where his weapon touched, my arm bled. I tried moving my fingers again, but I couldn't feel anything below the wrist. My blood dripped down my fingers and onto the floor.

"Get it through your thick, stubborn head," Lucifer continued. "Either you stand by my side and he gets to live, or you make the wrong choice and he dies."

I glanced up at Addy, my heart drumming at the sight of her. Her eyes were wide and full of tears, and she had a minor cut on her left cheek.

Although my mouth felt dry, I managed to say, "Addy, don't do it."

Her lips quivered, and she shook her head at me.

"Done!" Lucifer dropped my arm and stepped toward Addy. "Look at my beautiful masterpiece. Does it melt your soul the way it melts my own dark one?"

Addy gasped. "No!"

Not caring that Lucifer stood so close, she ran to my side. She tucked her knife into her pocket and scratched at the arms holding me hostage.

"Let him go!" She was wild, her curls flying everywhere like a modern-day Medusa.

I didn't understand what had happened, but my heavy breathing let me know it was nothing good. The arms around me let go, and my body swayed. Addy grabbed onto me, her arms underneath my armpits, and helped me fall to the floor with gentleness, her hand moving to steady my head before I hit the porcelain tiles.

"Hey, look at me," she said. "Look at me."

I met her hard stare while my stomach churned. "What . . ." Between the loss of blood and whatever Lucifer had done, I felt lightheaded.

"It's going to be okay." Tears fell down her cheeks. "It's . . ." She leaned in and kissed me, her lips trembling. When she pulled back, her cries became sobs. "I'm so sorry, Adriel."

Lucifer came to stand above us. "Ah, young love."

Addy ignored him and held onto my head. "I'm so sorry."

"I said he would be a dead man if you did not choose my side. However, I did not say he would die with his soul intact." Lucifer crouched down beside Addy and smiled. "If you still want him, you could have him. Choose me, and you will regain your precious Adriel. If you do not, I will let him bleed out at noon. Human time, of course."

Addy kept her eyes on me when she responded to him. "You've already killed him."

"As I said, you can choose me—and him in this state—or he will die."

Lucifer stood, waved his hand at someone, and backed away. A large man with demonic eyes came and hauled me up, ignoring Addy as she yelled and threw punches at him.

"Where are you taking him?" she said.

"To hell, where he belongs. If you change your mind, you know how to find us."

The large man threw me over his shoulder like I weighed nothing and stomped out of the store. Other fallen angels came with us, but a couple waited behind. When Addy tried to rush after me, one of them seized her.

"Stop! Stop!" she yelled.

Everyone ignored her.

Lucifer walked beside the man carrying me and placed his hand over the man's shoulder, his fingers poking into my abdomen. When he touched me, heat coursed through my stomach to the tips of my ears. Although nothing happened externally, I sensed my chest contort as it pushed something out. I groaned from the force and nearly passed out again.

My head spun. Suddenly, I felt content and weightless on the inside. The guilt I'd carried from when Jenna killed her son vanished. I wasn't tied to God. I wasn't tied to useless emotions. I was free to roam and take what I desired. I could do whatever the hell I wanted with nothing stopping me.

With my head hanging so I faced the floor, I smiled and closed my eyes. Addy became a distant memory in a sea of memories I didn't care about.

"By the way, Adelaide," Lucifer said. "The war has just begun. Choose your next move wisely."

Chapter Twenty-Seven

ADELAIDE

I stood in the back of the store after Lucifer and his demons disappeared with Adriel. A vein in my hand pulsed fifty times a second.

Adriel. How could I let him go? My heart clenched in my chest. A lump developed in my throat and would just not go away. The six days I'd spent with Adriel felt more substantial than the two years I'd dated Devin.

But Adriel wasn't himself anymore. I saw it in his eyes when they carried him away. His dark pupils had expanded until they destroyed the brown irises I'd grown attached to.

I grabbed the chair I'd used to break myself out of the small office and smashed it four times into a nearby shelf. Packages of beef jerky fell to the floor.

I barely know him. I paced, trying to pull myself together. *He doesn't mean anything to me. He's just a guy. He's no one.*

I was out of breath, but I kept slamming the chair into things even though it brought me no satisfaction. The chair's metal legs chafed where my hands had been injured, damaging my raw flesh further.

On the other side of the room, I banged the chair against the counter. A loud cracking sound brought me to a stop. In my hand, the plastic backrest of the chair had snapped in half. Letting out a piercing cry, I threw the chair across the room and crashed to the floor, my back against the counter. I didn't know what was going on outside. I didn't know if my friends were safe. All I knew was that I'd lost Adriel forever. But he had become my partner in crime; I couldn't just let him go.

Closing my eyes, I concentrated on the heat in my body. It was my only connection to Lucifer. If I could pinpoint where he was, I could find Adriel.

A hot surge moved down my flesh, prickling my arms. I stared out the broken exit door. Lucifer wasn't far away. In fact, I sensed him here on Earth. His presence was strong, pulling me despite my anger toward him. The feeling made my skin crawl.

I swallowed, pushed myself to my feet, and trudged out the broken door. The hunger I'd felt earlier while in bed with Adriel had become a distant thought. Even my stomach had stopped growling, seeming to realize that I had more urgent matters at hand. Tears kept streaming down my face. Every time I wiped the moisture away, my eyes flooded again.

Outside the store, the smell of burning rubber and gasoline hit me hard. With my hand to my nose, I faced my smoldering Oldsmobile. Lucy's red paint was burned off. Around the bumper, signs of rust had begun to appear. Most of the tires had melted.

Without a car, I had to call Reed. When he answered, I told him what happened and that I needed him to come pick me up. "I know I asked you to stay somewhere safe, but I really need help right now."

"Tell me where you are," he said.

Five minutes later, he pulled up a block from the station, which was where I'd asked him to meet me. His jaw dropped when he saw me. In the middle of the backseat of Reed's old silver sedan sat Madadel, his wings spread out, taking up the entire space and blocking the rear windshield. Unlike my brother, Madadel did not seem distressed when he saw me.

Reed clenched his jaw, waved for me to hop in beside him, and drove off, no questions asked.

"We were driving around trying to figure out where to go," he said. "I thought of going to a hospital or school, but Madadel said demons have taken over those places."

I spun around to look at the angel. "Is that true?"

"Sadly so, sweet Adelaide. Those are the first places to go in a war."

"But . . ." I looked out the window, staring at the sunbeams breaking through the cracks in the gray clouds. "Everything was fine this morning." Unable to help it, I broke into a sob.

Madadel reached forward and patted my back. "There, there, child. It will be—"

"Don't call me child!" I snapped. "I don't want to hear that word again."

He withdrew his hand, crossed his arms, and sat back. "My apologies . . ."

"Addy?" Reed kept glancing at me. "I want to help you, but we kind of have to figure out where to go first."

I nodded. "Okay. How about . . ." I tried to think of some lowkey shelters. "Private properties? Business buildings?"

"Not good enough," Madadel said.

If all the places people typically went to were dangerous, then we had to think of places where people didn't go. "Why not hide in some forest and have Madadel shield us?"

"Sure. I suppose I could do that for the next hour, but even forests will become war zones."

"How do you know all this?"

"This is not the first war between heaven and hell here on Earth."

"And Lucifer didn't die the last time either."

"No, he did not. However, we were able to send him back to hell, which is better than nothing."

My shoulders sagged. "That doesn't make me feel better. Adriel is gone."

Outside the window, the park I'd passed by earlier with Adriel was now deserted. All the kids playing there with their parents were nowhere to be seen. How did they know to run and hide when I didn't? What happened in those few minutes that turned everything around?

"I don't understand what happened. Everything was fine."

"No, Addy," Reed said, "things weren't fine."

Unlike me, Reed liked to drive at the speed limit, mostly because I'd taught him to be safe and not imitate me. In fact, whenever I drove him around, I almost always abided by the law. Even now, in the middle of an apocalypse, he chose to drive with caution.

Along the road, a line of offices, including a post office and a photography studio, all had *"Closed"* signs. Only one diner had its doors open. Driving by, I wondered if the people inside the diner felt as clueless as I did. When I peered through the window, I saw only the owner. Keys in her hand, she shut off the lights and walked out as I watched.

I sighed. "Please tell me what happened."

Reed scratched his head and looked through the rearview mirror at his angel. "Um, so you know how I told you things died down after the shooting at my school? Well, I lied."

"You what?"

He kept his eyes on the road, but I could tell his attention was fully on me. "Just, don't get mad. You needed to rest, and so I told a small lie."

"That's not a small lie, Reed!"

"So, um, after the school shooting, people started ambushing other people on the streets with weapons. Just all kinds of things. Guns, knives, rifles. Heck, even fire. It was all over the news at that point."

"Why didn't I know about this? You should've told me!"

He shrugged and took a left turn. "I wanted you to rest and I kind of . . ." He mumbled something under his breath.

"What was that?"

"I kind of joined the fighting."

I jumped in my seat. The seat belt jammed in place, pulling me back down.

"What the hell, Reed! Why would you ever do that?"

"Because this is a war, and I don't want to sit back and let them win."

Adjusting the seat belt, I sat forward, frowning at my brother. "But there are others fighting. Why would you put yourself in danger?"

"If everyone had that mentality, no one would fight, and we'd all die."

He was right, but I felt a knot in my stomach. My baby brother shouldn't have had to do that. Besides, he had already gone to hell and come back this week. Wasn't that enough?

"I'm fighting for all of us." I leaned my head back against the headrest and closed my eyes. "Don't risk your life."

The car stopped. When I opened my eyes, we were at a red light. The street was empty, just like everywhere else we drove. I could see signs of conflict everywhere. Broken store windows. A few smashed cars on the side of the road. Blood coating an American flag outside a bank. I felt like we were in a zombie movie.

Reed reached over to wipe my tears. "I'm not a little kid anymore, Ade. If you're fighting, I want to fight with you."

After that, we drove in silence for a while. I didn't know where Reed was taking us, but I felt safe knowing Madadel was there. Although I wanted to punch the angel half the time, he'd managed to keep Reed safe since I'd brought him back from hell. So far, I couldn't deny that he was useful.

Ten minutes into not speaking, I said, "If people are fighting in the streets, where are they now?"

"They've been moving all over the place. Once it ends somewhere and the innocent go down, people take their weapons and go to the next block."

"Kids were playing in the park just before the station exploded. Did they not know?"

"It's just like with the cops. A lot of news anchors were turned into demons, providing false news. This morning they said it was safe to go out again. When people don't know any better, they'll trust the media without question."

"Adelaide?" Madadel inched forward in his seat. When he looked at me, his eyes were flickering with awe. "Michael thinks you should return to your childhood home."

Reed peered over his shoulder at the long-haired angel. "Who's Michael?"

"The archangel," I said. "Why would he want me to go back there? It's all burned up."

A smile danced on Madadel's lips. "Or is it?"

†

All three of us stood in front of the beige house with the brown roof and dead lawn. Erica's house. It looked the way it had for years, as if a fire had not burned everything yesterday.

Two houses down, the neighbor's dog kept growling, his voice audible throughout the street. I felt like he was barking at us, or maybe at Erica's house. Either way, I couldn't blame him. I was in the growling mood myself; if only that was an acceptable thing to do for a human.

I chewed on my bottom lip and frowned. "This doesn't make sense. That house was on fire. I swear!" I nudged Reed. "Am I going insane?"

Reed blinked at me several times before making up his mind. "No, but this week is insane. I mean, I spent a month in hell. Now that's insane."

"Should we go in?"

Madadel clasped his hands behind his back, his wings tucked on either side of him. "Michael wants us to go in."

"Is Michael still with us?"

Madadel squared his shoulders. "As a human, the courteous name to call him is 'Archangel Michael.' And yes, he is here."

I rolled my eyes and muttered under my breath, "You angels are so petty."

Taking a deep breath, I headed to the door. Reed followed beside me. When we reached the front steps, I stopped and evaluated my decision to come here. Was it wise, returning to the scene of the crime? To the place where Erica had neglected us and where she had been a demon this entire time? Was it the safest choice we could make? No, it certainly was not.

But we needed to find out why the house looked undamaged. If Michael—Archangel Michael—wanted us here, then there were probably answers inside.

"Okay." I tried the handle and, surprisingly, the door creaked open.

Taking Reed's hand, I stepped in. Reed appeared calm and comfortable, reminding me that he didn't mind coming back here as much as I did. He had chosen to remain in contact with Erica, after all. I'd never understood his ability to forgive her, especially not now.

"Please don't let go of my hand," I said. "I'm honestly scared."

He squeezed my hand. "I won't."

The living room hadn't changed a bit. On our right was the suede chaise lounge Reed and I had colored on with crayons as kids, and that Erica made us clean for an hour afterward. The champagne curtains on the front window hung in place, no sign of any burns.

"I swear I saw the house burn." I pointed at the curtains. "Those things were the first to go. When I opened the door, I nearly died from how strong the fire was."

"I believe you."

"Perhaps," said Madadel, "you should not worry so much about the fire, and instead concentrate on the house."

Staring down the hall, I eyed my old bedroom door. "What do you mean?"

"Does nothing stand out to you?"

Same furniture. Quiet house. Nothing out of place. Seeing the ceiling fan spin at a slow speed was strange, but it wasn't that unusual.

Reed, seeming to have the same thought process, said, "What's supposed to stand out? Nothing's changed in years."

Madadel made himself comfortable on the chaise lounge. He propped his legs up and wrapped his wings around him. "I was told not to interfere with Adelaide's journey." Slouching lower, he closed his eyes. "She must figure this out on her own. However, I will say this: What you are looking for is under the surface and cannot be seen with the human eye."

I rubbed my forehead. "What?"

Madadel didn't respond. I eyed him for a second, wanting to strangle him. He didn't move, and I wondered if angels slept.

Shrugging it off, I nudged Reed again. "Let's keep going."

We walked down the hall. I caught my breath when we stopped in front of my room. Reed looked at me, hesitating. When I didn't say anything, he opened the door. Seeing the twin-size bed I left four years ago, I tensed. My old posters were gone, along with the childhood toys I'd left behind.

"She threw everything out," I said. I wasn't mad, but a sense of loss hit me. "I know it's stupid to feel sad over little things like this, especially when I have bigger problems to worry about, but I just can't help it. She's taken so much from me, and now this."

"Let's not think about that now. You said this is war, right? In war, we've got to put our fears and problems aside."

"You're right." I let go of his hand and strode into my old room. "It's just so crazy being back here."

Above my bed, the window was shut and the blinds were drawn, making the room look somewhat dim. I walked over and pulled the blinds aside. Bright light shone in.

That was when I saw it. In the corner of the wooden headboard, about the size of my fist, lurked a burn mark.

"Look." I pointed at the blackened wood, my hand shaking. "It was charred in the fire, Reed. That wasn't there before. I knew I saw this house burn."

Reed examined the mark. He put his fingers on it and immediately jumped back, yelping in pain.

"Are you okay? What happened?"

He puffed at his hand. "It's hot!"

I followed in his steps and touched the burn mark. Rather than feeling heat, a chill traveled down my body. The hairs on the nape of my neck stood on end. I gasped and squeezed my eyes shut.

"Addy?" Reed put his hand on my shoulder. "Addy, let go! What are you doing? Let go!"

"I can't."

"You're going to burn your hand."

"No, I won't. It feels cold to me."

Behind my closed eyelids, a spark of light appeared. It wasn't vibrant, but it let me see movement, reminding me of the vision I had when Lucifer gave me his blood water.

"I'm seeing something."

"What?"

My eyes narrowed in on the movement. I saw a round-bellied woman walking into a room with her hands resting on her lower back. Short of breath, she sat down on a couch, raised her feet, and closed her eyes. She rubbed and rubbed her big belly. When I focused on her face, I recognized her immediately.

"It's Erica . . . Pregnant Erica."

She looked so young. She could've passed as my sister with only a year's difference between us. For the longest time, I stared at her face and belly, mesmerized. Was I the one she carried, or was it Reed? Although Reed was born after me, I couldn't remember Erica pregnant with him. I'd seen a few pictures showing me hugging her stomach while Reed was a fetus, but being two years old at the time made it hard to cling to those memories.

Reed was still next to me, his hand where it had been this whole time, on my shoulder. He nudged me now. "What else do you see?"

Once he said that, I noticed Erica moving her lips. My vision's lens moved around until I discovered to whom she was speaking. Not far from her feet stood a man with long black hair and solid-black eyes. His face bore no expression.

"Lucifer," I said, gritting my teeth.

"What is he doing there?"

"I don't know."

Lucifer offered something to Erica. While she admired the item, Lucifer pierced his thumb with what looked like a needle.

Realization hit me. "I think he's doing the same thing he did to me."

"What do you mean?"

281

"I think he's making Erica drink his blood."

My eyes homed in on the item in Erica's hand. Sure enough, it was the wooden chalice with the snake engraving spiraled around the circumference.

Erica brought the cup to her lips and drank deeply. Cringing, I shifted my vision's lens to her belly. I felt certain she was carrying me inside her. Lucifer would not be in the picture otherwise.

She handed the chalice back to Lucifer and threw her head back. A second later, her stomach shoved this way and that, the baby kicking violently. Erica rubbed her hand against her belly, but the fetus would not rest.

A twinge of pain in my chest made me cry out. I reached for Reed and gripped his hand.

"What's going on?" he said. "Addy, you're scaring me!"

"It's poisoning the baby!" Moisture descended my cheeks, and I screamed. Every time the baby kicked, my chest burned. "It's poisoning me." My body shuddered.

"Addy, let go! Get out of there."

"I can't. I need to see everything."

"But it's hurting you."

Ignoring Reed, I tried to control the pain and dim it down. I looked back at Erica and found her screaming, too. Although I couldn't hear her, her wide mouth and red, agonized face told me what I needed to know. "Oh, God, I think she's giving birth."

"Addy, please . . ."

"I'm fine." I wasn't, but I didn't want him to worry.

I pushed through the pain and tried my hardest to see what this vision was trying to tell me.

Looking around, I noticed Lucifer was gone. He had done his part as a father. That left Erica screaming alone as the baby kicked. I couldn't help it; in that moment, I felt sorry for her. Her worth had been tied to Lucifer's agenda of creating me this whole time.

Through a blur of pain, the baby finally came. Erica stopped crying and closed her eyes. Her entire body surrendered to unconsciousness.

Pain left me. The baby, covered in blood, lay on her face at the end of the couch with the umbilical cord still tied to Erica. For a few seconds, she didn't cry.

Someone appeared in the vision, taking in the scene with obvious rage and immediately snatching the baby up. It took me a moment to realize the figure was Grandma Di with her bob haircut. Seeing her made me relax.

Somehow, my grandma managed to cut the umbilical cord like an expert and wrap the baby in a towel. In return, the baby opened her eyes and blinked at her before letting out a wail. I still couldn't hear the sound, but it vibrated inside my head like a distant memory.

Erica did not look at the baby. She glanced to the side, her eyes moving past Grandma Di.

I watched until there was no more to see. Then I withdrew my fingers from the burned headboard. Just before my physical contact ended, the baby in the vision doubled. Somehow, there were two babies, side by side, in Grandma Di's arms.

The second baby looked unusual, though. It had a veiny red body, practically skeletal. Its unblinking eyes looked pitch-black, just like Lucifer's.

Grandma Di didn't seem to notice the second infant. It took me a second to realize, but the baby wasn't physically there. Unlike the original baby, I could see right through it, like a ghost.

And this wasn't the first time I'd seen this monster.

My fingers came off the headboard.

Reed tilted his head to see me better. "What happened?"

I sat down on the edge of the bed and stared at my brother. "I have a twin."

Reed's eyes grew wide. "What?"

"It's not human. It's some kind of demonic double."

Had it been yesterday or two days ago when I'd seen that veiny demonic thing? I couldn't tell the days apart anymore. They jumbled together. But I knew I'd seen this monster, this twin. It had grown, like me, except it had become something out of a nightmare. Just as Lucifer had obviously intended when he gave Erica his blood.

Chapter Twenty-Eight

ADRIEL

Castilla, another fallen angel, landed a punch on my stomach, making me groan. I remembered her from long ago, before she joined Lucifer's army.

"I've missed you, brother," she said and punched me again.

I gritted my teeth. "Can't say I've missed you."

Lucifer had had my hands shackled to the ceiling while I stood on two feet, my head slumped. At some point, someone must have wrapped a cloth around my bleeding forearm to slow down the blood.

I'd woken up ten minutes ago to Castilla smacking me across the jaw. She'd been singing an old lullaby the angels loved to sing. "Up the hill we go, into the light we go, until our old wings can fly no more."

When she saw my eyes flutter open, she landed her first out of many punches, hitting me in the ribs. "Good morning, sweet angel—or should I say, demon."

In the midst of a groan, I managed to ask where we were, but she didn't answer. Either way, it didn't matter. I had a hard time keeping my eyes open; pain and exhaustion weighed them down, and the white fluorescent light in the room felt far too bright. Still, before my eyes surrendered again, I glimpsed a ripped punching bag hanging from the wall ten feet behind Castilla, and a boxing ring in my peripheral vision.

"I told you once to please, come play with me, but you had to leave, leave me and go," she continued singing. "Now you sit still with your human by your side, and both of us know, you will return once more." She gripped my cheeks. "I love that song!"

Her blows went on for what seemed like an eternity while she sang. I didn't know whether to fall asleep or cry out in pain.

"Oh, sweet, pretty angel," she said, slowing down her attacks. "You have strayed so far from home, haven't you?"

I opened my soulless eyes to stare at her. "I like where I am."

She grinned. "I am sure you do." She patted my cheek. "You are going to be such a help to us."

I saw Lucifer before Castilla did. He approached her from behind, his arms folded. The door he came through closed slowly, letting in a little sunlight.

A line etched between his brows. "Why have you wrapped his arm, Castilla? I told you to let him bleed out."

Castilla cowered and dove back, almost hiding behind me. Unlike the other fallen angels, I realized, she wore a worn-out shirt to cover her scars.

"Step forward," Lucifer snarled at her.

"My lord." Her eyes stayed on the ground. "I only thought it might be more fun to torture him. Isn't that what you wanted? To hurt him and get back at Adelaide?"

"Shut up, Castilla! I ordered you to tie him to the ceiling and leave. I never said to rescue him or beat him up. Now he is awake. Do you see what you have done?"

"I . . . I am sorry, my lord. I will fix it." She reached up to unwrap the cloth around my forearm.

"No," Lucifer said. "Just go. You have done enough."

Castilla dashed around Lucifer, muttered, "Yes, my lord," and ran out the exit.

She had once been a good angel, as all angels were. I liked her better this way. If I weren't tied and bleeding, I would've laughed at her.

Lucifer pinned me with his eyes. "Old friend, you keep fighting."

My mouth twitched, but I couldn't get myself to smile. Every inch of my body felt bruised. "Because I want to live," I said.

"Of course, friend. Although, just think of all the wonderful things you will do if you die. For one, Adelaide will be heartbroken, and maybe then she will see that God cannot help her, just as he cannot help the world. That should wake her and make her see that I am the answer."

He moved closer. The dagger that had slit my forearm was back in his hand. Seeming to read my mind, he smirked and tucked the dagger into a sheath. Then he reached above my head and untied the cloth. Though rather than throwing the bloody rag away, he held it for me to see.

With the cloth an inch from his nose, he said, "Smells like revenge."

"No doubt."

"Tell me, Adriel. How does it feel to finally view the world from my perspective?"

I stared at his black, empty eyes, which could not reflect my own black ones. "It's not so special."

"So, you do not like this new you?"

I managed to lift my head just a sliver. "I never said that."

"Then, how do you feel?" He threw the blood-soaked cloth over his shoulder and crossed his arms. "I remember you refusing to join my army, even though you were the first I asked. Do you remember, old friend?"

"I remember, but that was long ago."

"Have you changed your mind, then?"

"I'm here, aren't I?"

He smiled and reached for his dagger again. "Not of your own free will."

My head spun, and I fought hard to stay awake. Words were my only weapon out of these tight shackles. "That doesn't change the fact that I'm here, and I want to join your war."

"Is that so?"

I forced my eyes open for as long as I could and kept them steady on Lucifer. "If you'll let me live, you won't regret it. Killing me might serve one purpose, but I know keeping me alive will help you convince Addy to join our war."

While he watched me, he ran his thumb over the sharp edge of his dagger gently enough that he didn't slice it open. "How is that?"

"I think she has fallen in love with me." Despite the pain in my jaw, my lips curved upward. "And as you know, humans attach themselves to others. For them, a broken heart is always best avoided. And so, I have no doubt she'll join our side just to be with me."

"Is it that easy?"

"She's human. She wouldn't have it any other way."

"It is their flaw, is it not?" He tucked the dagger back into the sheath and smiled. "Fine! You have convinced me. However, before I let you down, I have an important question to ask." He held his hand to his chin. "Do you care for Adelaide?"

I scoffed and felt pain in my chest. "Do I look like I do?"

His blank eyes looked at me, empty of expression. "Very well."

Rather than releasing the shackles himself, he gestured with his head. A second later, a fallen angel stepped from behind me and unlocked the shackles. I fell to the ground and stayed there, not caring to move. I wondered how long the fallen angel had been in the room and if others had been watching the show this whole time.

Lucifer hovered above my head. "How are you feeling, old friend?"

"Like a newborn with a mind of his own," I said, shutting my eyes. "Leave me be for a while. I want to sleep."

His footsteps moved farther and farther away. "Already giving orders, that one," he said from a distance.

I heard the door close. Afterward, the room was silent. I didn't know if I was alone, and I didn't give a damn.

†

I dreamed of Simiael's ringlets. They'd always been the color of blood. However, the night she'd died, they'd radiated crimson.

In the dream, I walked up to Simiael's corpse and lingered beside it. Addy was somewhere in the room, too, and she would not quiet down. Her cries deafened me. I yelled at her to shut up because I wanted to rest. But she was not a bright girl and continued crying.

I grabbed Simiael's curls in my fist and yanked her head up. "Look," I screamed at Addy, "she's a pathetic, dead thing."

Addy's eyes welled up, like a stupid child looking for attention. "She protected me."

"Who cares?"

With Simiael's hair still in my grasp, I took out my knife, the one from Addy's kitchen, and cut the hair nearly to its roots.

"What are you doing?" Addy leaped for the knife in my hand.

Quick on my feet, I raised my hand high, holding the knife out of her reach.

"You cut her hair!"

She jumped for my arm, but being taller than her, I won this mediocre fight. I pushed her. She stumbled against the couch and sat there, looking up at me with a horrified expression on her senseless face.

"Will you seal your loud mouth, or should I seal it for you?"

That shut her up.

I slipped Simiael's hair inside my pocket and contemplated whether or not Castilla knew how to knit. I had a vivid image of Castilla making a fine red sweater using this angel hair.

"Wake up," Addy said after a moment. "War is waiting for you."

"Didn't I tell you to keep quiet?"

She didn't move.

I felt tugging on my arms. Without warning, I was no longer in Addy's apartment.

"Wake up," someone growled at me.

I woke on the floor with my head resting on my bloody forearm, though now the blood had dried. The fallen angel who freed me from the shackles earlier crouched next to me. His name was Kaisek, I recalled. He was gawking at me like it was his job. Which it probably was.

"Will you chill?" I said. "It's not the end of the world. I was just taking a little nap, you dimwit."

He scoffed. "You have been asleep for almost two hours in Earth time. It is almost noon."

"What's it to me?"

"Lucifer wants you ready for war."

I shut my eyes again. "I am ready. Now go away."

To my annoyance, he grabbed my arm with his gnarled fingers and tied something around my wrist.

I pulled away and nearly slapped his fat nose with the back of my hand. "What the hell do you think you're doing?"

His solid-black eyes challenged me. "I was wrapping your filthy wound. But . . . if you prefer to keep bleeding, I could leave it."

Kaisek had clearly mastered reverse psychology.

"Oh." I gave him back my arm. "In that case, get back to it."

After doing his thing, Kaisek hurried away, grumbling something under his breath.

"I heard that!" I yelled after him, even though I hadn't heard anything coherent.

I got up, still feeling groggy and beat down. The back of my head, in particular, sent a twinge down my spine when I moved.

Lucifer's war didn't seem as important as my sleep, but I shrugged off the laziness anyway and began moving, one leg in front of the other. The room was empty. I took the exit door and headed toward the big building on fire down the street. All the demons were heading that way, including Kaisek, who walked a couple yards ahead of me.

Screams and cries rang everywhere. People ran past me, some doing a double take when they saw my face—my eyes. I flashed them my teeth until they ran in the opposite direction, tripping over their own feet.

Although I scared the living hell out of these wretched humans, dizziness slowed me down every couple of feet. Halfway to the building, an old man stumbled into me, a gun in his hand. I realized I had no weapon.

"Damn you, Lucifer," I cursed, remembering that Lucifer took my knife when he kidnapped me.

A gun fired, but my instincts told me to duck. When I stood, the old man was inserting more bullets into his gun. I stepped forward and shoved the weapon out of his hand. His eyes reminded me of helpless deer the moment they realize they are about to be trampled by a car.

My hand wrapped around his throat, squeezing the life out of him.

Chapter Twenty-Nine

ADELAIDE

Using a pen and paper I found lying around my old room, I drew a quick sketch of my double. Red, juicy veins. Fire for eyes. Hairless. Nothing about the skeletal figure resembled me. But I knew what I knew, what I saw in that vision. It was a part of me just as I was a part of it.

Reed looked over my shoulder at the drawing. When I finished the sketch, I tapped the sheet of paper and handed it to him. "That's what I saw."

While he examined the double, I stepped outside the room to call Lizzy. She answered Nate's cell phone right away, which I hoped was a good sign. In the background, I heard yelling and banging.

"Liz, where are you? What is that noise?"

She said they were driving around with no clue where to go. People were trying to get inside their car by hitting the windows with their hands. "We're going to die, Addy." Her voice trembled.

Her fear hit me through the phone. My hand went to my forehead, pulling down at my hair. I didn't see how any of us could make things right. I didn't even know if we'd survive the day.

Adriel . . . I'd already lost him. A few tears escaped my eyes, though I held my voice steady and pushed back the pain.

I still felt his body against all the places he'd touched me. My lips were still swollen from his kisses. His fingers still wound in my hair, down my neck, and caressed the low spot of my back. I felt him holding me, pulling me against him in my sleep.

I hoped he was dead. Better dead than a demon.

With the back of my hand, I wiped the tears away. I couldn't let Lizzy lose hope just because I had. "Lizzy, I need you to take a deep breath and tell me what you see."

"There's fire all over the place. People's cars and houses . . . they're gone, Addy. It's all gone."

I wondered if our apartment was gone too, if the demons had started there.

"Liz, tell Nate to drive to Latrobe. I'm at my mother's house with Reed and his guardian. I need you to meet me here. Can you do that?"

She sounded far for a few seconds as I heard her give Nate directions. Then she said, "Yes, yes, we'll be there! We'll try to get on the highway."

I hung up, my heart miles away with her and my lost angel.

In the living room, Madadel was—or pretended to be—sleeping. I watched him for a second, not understanding how he could be so calm at a time like this.

"You're so lazy," I said loudly, wanting him to hear me and wake up.

His eyes shot open and landed on me. "Did you say something?"

"I said you're lazy."

"Why do you say that, sweet Adelaide?"

"Because." I gestured in his direction, indicating his current state. "Look at you. The world is burning, and you're taking a nap."

He sat up, his wings launching in separate directions. His right wing struck my mother's table lamp in the corner of the room. The lamp plummeted to the floor and shattered.

He didn't even blink or look at the mess he'd just made. "For your information, I was communicating with Michael," he said.

I placed my hands on my hips. "Tell the damn angel to show himself. I'm tired of all of you playing games with me. 'Adelaide, does nothing stand out to you?' 'Adelaide, Michael wants you to do this.' 'Adelaide—'"

"Whoa, whoa, whoa! Calm down." He jumped to his feet. "No need for hostility." He came to stand before me, his long locks sashaying with each movement. "Angels have their own matters to discuss, you know. Not everything revolves around you."

"No?" My eyebrows scrunched together so tightly my forehead hurt. "Then, answer me this: Why is my father going after the people I love? Why is my father trying to kill all the angels? And why is my father your worst nightmare? If this isn't about me, then how come my blood is the problem?"

For a pinch of a second, Madadel's jaw dropped. "You know nothing, chi—" Looking down, he detected my fisted hands and his expression hardened. "We have work to do."

Rather than discussing the matter further, he disappeared into the hallway behind me.

Subject closed. For now . . .

I stayed behind and stared at the now-empty chaise lounge. "I know you can hear me, archangel," I said. "Where the fuck are you?"

Of course, no response came. I expected as much.

"You were supposed to protect us! At least that's what Adriel was led to believe. Is that not what you do?"

I paced around the room, my eyes darting at the walls like a ghost would emerge from within them. When I reached the broken table lamp, I picked up a few of the shattered pieces and flung them, one by one, around the room. I wanted to hit the smug angel for hiding, for letting them take Adriel.

"Did you know my grandmother used to pray to you?"

One of the broken pieces I threw stuck like a dart in the wall on the opposite side of the room.

"I still remember a few lines from what she taught me. 'Prince of the heavenly hosts, by the power of God, thrust into hell Satan and all the evil spirits who prowl about the world seeking the ruin of souls.'"

I bent down to grab more broken pieces, choosing the sharpest ones.

"You know, I haven't thought of that prayer in forever. Is that why you let them take him? Is that why you didn't protect him? Was that a punishment?"

I threw a piece into the air without a specific aim. Before it landed, my arm lifted, ready to throw another. Madness consumed me.

"Where the hell are you?"

Giant golden wings flapped into the room and a beaming yellow light shimmered all around an immense figure. A face surrounded by short blond coils and wearing a pure smile came into view. I'd never seen him in my life, but I knew who it was.

Archangel Michael.

The broken shard I'd thrown a second ago flew in his direction, directly toward his eye. Not wanting to see the gruesome sight of blood gushing out of his eyeball, I squeezed my eyes shut.

"I hear you desperately want to see me." His voice washed over me like a hummed classical melody.

Upon opening my eyes, I realized two things. One, this angel was like no other I'd seen; his wings didn't have a speck of white in them, and he wore gold-plated armor around his powerfully built torso. Two, he had a strange calming effect on me. Because of him, a genuine smile stretched across my face.

His right hand was two inches away from his face. In it, he held the shard I'd thrown. "Here I am."

"Finally!" I let out a harsh breath. With my hands at my sides, I released the broken lamp pieces to the floor.

"Hello, Adelaide."

Here stood one of the highest-ranking angels. I could have talked to him about anything; I could have even blamed him for everything that had happened. Instead, my mouth hung open as I took him in.

"You are hurt," he said, dropping the shard to the floor. He advanced toward me and held his strong hands out for me to take. "Let me see your wounds."

I looked down at my hands. Stress and exhaustion had made me forget about them. But now, seeing the torn skin, the stinging started again. I placed my hands in his soft palms like a frail animal wanting to lessen her pain. His thumbs brushed over the deep cuts, making me whimper. When he let go, the pain was gone and the wounds had healed.

Unable to help it, I gaped at him, dumbfounded by his ability. Did Adriel have the power to heal when he was a guardian angel?

Michael bent his knees to be at my eye level, his blue-green eyes piercing me. "And let me see those cuts on your face and shoulder," he said, putting a hand on my cheek and another on my shoulder. A second later, he pulled away, leaving me painless. Except in my heart; but that kind of pain was different. It could not be healed. It sucked me down like gravity, tugging at my chest and deepening wounds none could see.

"Thank you." I stared at him with total awe before remembering why I'd called him here. "I have to ask, why didn't you protect Adriel?"

A gentle smile played at his lips. "I did as much as I could, but certain things play out the way they were meant to."

"What do you mean?"

"Humanity has free will, and the angels cannot always interfere. We can guide and urge humans in the right direction. We can warn them of certain dangers. However, we cannot protect them from their own decisions. Once they have made a decision and acted upon it, everything falls in their own hands. We can only sit back and watch."

"Did you warn Adriel? Did he know Lucifer would turn him?" I felt strangely peaceful as I asked my questions, despite the anxiety and hurt roiling inside me. Even my exhausted body no longer felt weak.

Michael waved his hands around the house while planting his eyes on me. "I showed him this place and warned him of the dangers ahead. He did not understand. And yes, I did warn him, in my own way, to watch out for Lucifer."

"How?"

"This morning, I told him to get out of your car and run far from the station. He chose to go after you. It was the wrong choice; nevertheless, it was his. I could not interfere once he made it."

From the hallway, Madadel stuck his head into the room. When he saw his fellow angel, he beamed. "Brother, I see you have come to explain the rules to Adelaide."

Michael did not respond. Although he shifted his head a smidge toward Madadel, he kept his focus on me.

Madadel folded his arms and looked at me, his face thoughtful. "I just came to let you know that Reed is calling some of his friends and asking them to join our side in battle. It would greatly help us."

In my head, I pictured thousands of kids barely out of their teens falling to the same fate as Sam. Bullet in the head. Bullet in the chest. "No," I said and charged toward my room, squeezing myself past Madadel.

When I entered the room, Reed had his phone to his ear. "Yes, meet us at that address. Bring as many people as you can."

"Reed, what are you doing?" I wanted to grab the phone out of his hand. Instead, I tugged at his arm. "Reed, don't bring more people into this."

His hazel eyes narrowed as he lowered the phone. "Hiding isn't the solution."

Without giving me time to respond, he left the room. My mouth hung open in complete disbelief. I heard him open his bedroom door down the hall and shut it after him. Taking a deep breath, I fell against the bed and stared at the ceiling, wondering when my baby brother became this tough.

Michael and Madadel came in a few moments later. While both had to duck to get inside, Michael was clearly the larger angel. He crammed his wings through the door.

"Adelaide." Michael's tall frame hovered above me. "We do need more people on our side."

I closed my eyes. "They're going to get hurt, and this is all my fault. I can't stand the idea of bringing innocent people into this."

"They will get hurt for certain if they do not protect themselves. At this moment, there is more evil than good on earth. People must defend themselves. It is not enough for us to defend them."

My fingernails dug into the skin of my palms. "Is that why you didn't fight Lucifer this morning when he hurt Adriel? Because Adriel had to defend himself?" I looked up at the angel, hoping he noticed my defiance.

"No, not at all." He leaned down and touched my fisted hands, forcing me to relax them. "Like I said, Adriel made his choice. Furthermore, I was not about to enter a demon den on my own. I might be an archangel, but I am not reckless."

"And for that, Adriel is gone."

"If I may interrupt." Madadel stood in the back of the room, examining the few books I'd left behind on the bookshelf years ago. In his hand, he held *Brave New World*.

"May I ask why you called your friend when you do not want to bring innocent lives into this battle?"

He meant Lizzy, of course. Sitting up, I took a moment to think everything through, then said, "I let a few people in because they're already part of the mess that is my life. I can't tell them to sit back now."

Michael shuffled from one foot to the other, his hand reaching to his side. Without a word, he pulled out an enormous sword I hadn't seen before. I shrieked as he thrust it into the air.

"What are you doing?" My heart hammered in my chest in response to the proximity of the five-foot-long weapon to my body.

He tore out of the door, his footsteps nearly silent.

"What the fuck?"

Madadel placed my book back on the sparse bookshelf and shrugged. "A demon is outside."

"You've got to be kidding me!" I jumped to my feet and ran after Michael.

Pulling my Swiss Army knife out of my pocket felt natural at this point. My week of training had prepared me for this. I ran out the front door, Reed shouting behind me, and liberated the knife. Black stains covered my weapon; Saleos's blood. I'd killed the bastard and would kill more of his kind.

Michael soared into the air, traveling so fast that tree leaves ruffled on both sides of the road. On the ground, not far from where Michael flew, a woman had a young boy in her grasp.

Michael plummeted to the ground and thrust his sword straight into the woman's head. Blood sprayed the boy, who screamed and cried. I reached them just in time to see the woman fall to the ground, taking the boy down with her.

"Mommy!" The kid's face filled with tears. "Mommy!"

I grabbed the kid out of the dead woman's hold and hugged him against me. He didn't look older than eight; that alone scared me.

"What did you do?" I glowered at the angel. "You killed his mom!"

Michael tucked his sword away. "That is not his mother."

"What?"

"This demon was kidnapping him."

At a closer look, I realized he was right. The woman didn't resemble the child one bit. Besides, her black eyes, now transforming back to brown, made her unfit to be a parent.

"Where's his mom, then?"

Michael pointed at a front porch five houses down. "She is dead."

On the grass lay a woman with her guts spilled out. The kid shuddered in my arms. When I felt his tears soak my shirt, I held him tighter.

"Oh, sweetie," I said. "It's okay." It wasn't, but I didn't know what else to say. I pulled back to look at him. "What's your name?"

"Johnny," he muttered in between sniffles, his small, round eyes gawking at the angel.

"Do you know where your dad is?"

He nodded, his attention still captured by the archangel. "He's with my little sister."

"He's home?"

"Yeah."

I picked him up and headed to his house. "Hey, I need you to close your eyes. Can you do that, Johnny?"

He did as I asked. Moments later, I managed to get him past his dead mother and to his front door. His father met us there, clearly hysterical. He seized Johnny from me, and his worried eyes inspected the road.

Just as he said, "Where's Gina?" his gaze fell on her body not far from where we stood.

"Did you do this?" he yelled. "Did you kill her?"

I shook my head. "I'm so sorry."

Michael came up beside me and rested his hand on the man's shoulder. "Take care of your family and forget the rest."

His wing enfolded me, pulling me away from these unfortunate people.

"That's it?" I said. "We're just going to walk away?"

"Go back to your home." Calmness overtook me once more as his blue-green eyes focused on me. "I am going to revive her."

And he did. Over my shoulder, I saw him bring the woman back to life. She stood on two feet without a scratch on her body. I put my hand over my own stomach, right where the bullet had pierced, and wondered, my eyes on the archangel, if he was what had kept me from dying.

†

When Nate and Lizzy arrived at my mother's house, Lizzy threw her arms around me and told me she was sorry about Adriel and that we would fix things somehow. Then they opened their car's trunk to reveal an assortment of weapons.

My eyes lingered on the one weapon that did not belong with the rest. "Why do you have an axe? Where'd all these weapons come from, actually?"

Nate picked up the axe from the jungle of knives, pistols, rifles, hammers, and baseball bats. "I sometimes go camping with friends. Somebody has to cut wood for fire. The rifles and fancy knives are for when we go hunting."

My Swiss Army knife felt like a lump of rock in my pocket compared to the killing machine Nate was holding, but I didn't want him to know that. "Cool," I said and looked away, trying to hide my jealousy.

Inside, Reed had gathered some of his friends. When Lizzy, Nate, and I entered the house, Michael and Madadel were standing among them. Although all of us stared from time to time, Reed's friends Valerie and Greg couldn't take their eyes off the angels.

"I feel like I'm in a dream, but I keep pinching myself, and I'm still here," Valerie said, earning a smile from me.

Six days ago, I was one of the few people on this planet who knew about angels and demons. That wasn't the case anymore.

I gave Reed a knowing look. "We need to head out. It's about to hit noon, and I have a feeling Lucifer is going to do his worst when it does."

Adriel would die in a few minutes, as Lucifer had declared. I stared out the window, away from everyone in the room, and tried to push back the lump in my throat. He had truly died hours ago, when his soul left his body, though thinking that way didn't stifle the tears.

We headed out not long after. Everyone grabbed their choice of weapons. Most of them went for guns. Lizzy couldn't decide which weapon she could handle, so she grabbed both a baseball bat and a pistol for emergencies. Although I would have loved to have the axe, I wasn't confident in my ability to use it, so I grabbed a baseball bat, since it was light and gave me some reach. When I thought about grabbing the pistol, a knot formed in the pit of my stomach, and all I could think about was Devin shooting Sam and then me. Nope, no guns for me.

Reed split us up in four different cars. He told Valerie and Greg to ride with him and gave me orders to drive Mom's Chrysler, which had been parked in the garage. With me came Michael and another one of Reed's friends, whose name I couldn't remember. He was a scrawny little guy. I worried about him the most. He hopped in beside me with a gun clutched in his hand. I told him to keep it pointed at the floor.

Madadel sat in the back of Reed's car, crammed now that Valerie shared the seat with him. Reed's other friends drove their own cars. And off we went.

Since I could sense Lucifer's presence, I led the group. The closer I drove in his direction, the more my blood boiled in my veins. He wasn't far. In fact, it almost felt like he was also heading toward me.

"Before we get there," I said, shooting Michael a glance in my rearview mirror. He blocked the back windshield, preventing me from seeing anything on the road behind us. "I need to ask you about Lucifer's weapon. What do you know about it?"

Michael looked grim. "I know everything." His mouth set in a hard line.

"Can you tell me what it is? Lucifer made it clear I can't kill him so long as I don't know anything about it."

He watched me in the mirror but didn't answer.

"What? You said you know everything about it. What aren't you telling me?"

"I cannot tell you about the weapon." In the mirror, his eyes burned right through me, leading me to think he wanted me to know something he couldn't say out loud. "Telling you what the weapon is would interfere with a choice you have to make on your own. And I do not have permission to guide you with this issue."

That left me quiet for a while. I zipped down the road, avoiding a few cars trying to get out of the city, drivers who misguidedly thought there would be peace elsewhere. Behind me, I sensed my brother and friends trying to match my speed. If we had time, I would have slowed down.

Closer still. Lucifer's blood thumped in my ears. I pressed down on the gas, not caring if the rest caught up. We were almost there. In a few minutes, I'd face my father.

"Did you heal me yesterday?" I looked at Michael. "When I was shot?" The question came out of nowhere, but I suddenly needed to know.

Reed's skinny friend's head snapped in my direction. "You were shot?"

Both Michael and I ignored him.

"No, Adelaide." Michael sighed. "That was not an angel's work."

"Then what was it?"

"You will figure it out."

As we neared the main battle zone where Lucifer waited, we saw more people in the streets. They ran in the opposite direction of where we were heading. When I slowed down, some brave souls banged against the car's windows, shouting for us to let them in. I weaved around them. The sound of my honk carried throughout the streets like a siren announcing my arrival. I wanted Lucifer to know I was here. I wanted all his demons to know.

"What are you doing?" Reed's friend looked frantic. He reached over and grabbed my hand, trying to remove it from the horn. "Are you trying to get us killed?"

"Shut it." I slapped his hand away. "You shouldn't have come. I told Reed bringing people into this wasn't a good idea."

His fingers dug into his seat. "I can handle myself. It's you that scares me."

I shot him an angry look. "What's your name?"

"Shen." He let out a sharp breath. "You've met me four times already."

"Great. Shut up, Shen."

He didn't. Shen turned to Michael, blabbering his troubles away.

I kept my eyes on the road and soon saw a fallen angel appear in the distance, crouching next to a body on the sidewalk by a grocery store. I recognized the fallen angel by his scarred back. He seemed to sense me too. His blank eyes shifted in my direction, and he grinned, welcoming me to the battle.

I slowed the car to a standstill. Shen yelled out, twisting in his seat so that he faced the road, and let out one last screech that sounded a lot like a cuss word.

"We're here." I put the car into park and jumped out.

Michael's long strides ensured he stayed beside me with every step. Shen, on the other hand, had gotten lost, probably still stuck in the car. I glanced over my shoulder and saw Reed and the others running after us.

"You sure you can't tell me about the weapon?" I asked Michael one last time.

Michael's long sword glistened in my peripheral vision. He ran ahead of me, leaving my question unanswered.

The fallen angel ahead of us sprinted toward Michael, a sword of his own in his hand. It was smaller than Michael's but still impressive.

Pulling my Swiss Army knife out of my pocket so that I held the knife and the bat in each hand, I hurried after them. I didn't have time to do much, though. Before I'd even caught up, Michael's sword had ripped through the fallen angel's body, slicing him in half. I came to a halt, vomit rising to my throat. The demon's two halves crashed to the ground, his organs leaking out in the middle.

"Gross." I looked away, trying not to smell the urine-like odor coming from the dead demon.

Michael grabbed my wrist and pulled me away from the scene. "We must continue." He pointed at the sky. "We need to follow them."

Dozens of angels poured from the sky. They plunged around the corner of an abandoned car wash. I knew they were heading in the right direction; my blood burned the closer I got. Michael ran ahead of me and around the empty shop. When I caught up, we were on another street lined with buildings . . . and facing a herd of demons eager for battle.

In the center of the fight, surrounded by his monsters, Lucifer's tall figure loomed. Michael might have seen him, but I was the one who went after him. Lucifer swung left and right, and angels dropped at his feet like flies.

I slowed down when his sword—engraved with what looked like six coiled snakes—flashed a bright silver. He pointed its curved blade at me. For a sliver of a second, Lucifer's solid-black eyes met mine. When he looked away, his weapon came down, cutting through another angel.

My weapons paled in comparison. The cold feel of the knife against my palm did not reassure me. I stopped moving and stared at the mayhem. I couldn't sense my feet. A mixture of demon and angel blood saturated the asphalt and got on my shoes.

"Did you come for me?" A familiar voice spoke behind me.

I spun around, coming face to face with Adriel. The corners of his lips curved upward, but his jet-black eyes seemed angry.

My breath caught in my throat.

"You don't look happy to see me," he said.

A metallic taste clung to my tongue, followed by the reeking smell of decay.

Chapter Thirty

ADRIEL

A part of me felt a pinch of desire for the girl. Her loose curls falling across her face reminded me of the way they'd spilled over me in the middle of the night. I'd done everything to her body, and I would do more.

Another part of me just wanted to cut her wrists and make her feel the nauseating pain I had endured this morning because of her.

For a second, she just looked at me. "You're alive?" When reality kicked in, she pointed her delicate knife in my direction in warning. She held a baseball bat in her other hand, but it was limp at her side, as if she'd forgotten all about it.

I had my own sword now. Although I held it tightly in preparation, I kept it low and away from her. She needed to trust me so I could lure her in.

Behind her, demons and angels fought to the death. Mixed blood—red and black—coated the asphalt. Lucifer stood not too far off, with some of his demons circling us from a distance. They struck anyone who came our way. It was all part of Lucifer's plan. He didn't want anyone to hurt his daughter, but he wouldn't say why.

Taking a step toward her, I opened my empty hand as a sign of peace, showing her I would not attack. Humans loved their body language, and they loved believing in lies they hoped were true.

"I'm okay." Despite the knot deepening in between her eyebrows, I inched forward until just a foot separated us. "Lucifer spared me. See, I'm fine."

She went to take a step back, her foot sliding away from me. I gripped her forearm to stop her, but that only made her stiffen. Eyes full of fear, she stared at me.

"I thought you'd be happy to see me."

She yanked her arm free but didn't move. "What do you want?"

"You."

I brought my free hand to her cheek and brushed my fingers along the flush of her skin. I wished I could scrape that first layer of flesh off with my sword and see what was underneath. But Lucifer had cautioned me to behave.

"The real Adriel is dead." She took a step back. "I don't want anything to do with a demon."

For a small girl, she was quick. She thrust her knife at my midsection, attempting to stab me. I sprang back, my sword smashing into her knife and knocking it to the blood-soaked ground.

She jerked away, her chest rising and falling. I took her momentary halt as an opportunity to snatch her other weapon and toss it out of reach. Her eyes flickered between the knife and my sword, calculating her next move. A second later, she dashed for the blade, just as I'd expected.

Dropping my sword, I rushed forward and slammed her to the ground before she could reach the knife. "Your knife is useless." My body pressed against hers, making her immobile. "Don't be naïve." I brushed my lips against her ear and whispered, "It won't do you any good."

"Get off me!" She struggled underneath me and scratched her fingernails against my skin. Her eyes were wild and angry.

"I don't want to."

The Swiss Army knife was only inches out of her reach. Extending her arm, she tried to grab the weapon, but I restrained her and seized it. Her legs wrestled against me, trying to push me off now that her arms were in my grasp.

"You want to play rough, huh?" I touched the knife's pointy end to her throat. "Then let's play a game."

A squeal escaped her lips when I scraped the first thin layer of her neck with the knife. Her eyes interlocked with mine for a moment before she shut them and froze. A line of blood oozed out. It wasn't enough to kill her, though it was enough for me to enjoy.

"How does it feel," I said, "to be sliced while someone sits idly by?"

"Please, don't do this."

"Open your eyes and look at me."

Dark-brown irises stared at me, begging for mercy. Her hands, resting over her rib cage in my tight hold, stirred until her fingers clung onto my shirt, brushing against the hard surface of my chest. "You don't want to do this. Please let me go."

I flashed my teeth. "But I want to see you covered in red."

She shouted cuss words at me, too many to keep track of. "Go to hell!"

Her legs kicked, and one of her hands escaped my grip. She planted her palm on my face and pushed me away.

"What? You think you're going to fly away now?" I bit her hand. The minute she retracted it, I slashed her arm several times. "You are weak."

Six bloody lines appeared on her skin. She looked down to see the injuries I made, each one proof of what I was capable of. I could tell reality was finally setting in.

Tears welled in her eyes. "Please let me go," she said again, this time without strength in her voice.

"I will if you'll join me. Turn yourself."

She shook her head.

"I'll have to kill you if you don't."

"Or you can just let me go."

"You know . . ." I pressed the knife to her forearm over the radial artery, the same artery that nearly killed me earlier that day. "Lucifer really wants you alive. I have no idea why, and honestly, I don't care. He has his agenda; I have mine."

Though she kept her arm still where I dug in the knife, the rest of her thrashed against me. "You don't want to do this."

Letting out a sigh, I pushed the knife deeper into her skin. She screamed and dug her fingers into my chest, trying once more to push me off. Battling on the sideline, a few angels noticed us. Among them was Michael. Their fierce eyes focused on me for a moment. But rather than coming to Addy's rescue, they jumped back into their respective battles. I didn't understand why they were ignoring me, though I wasn't opposed to it.

Addy's head lolled to the side, looking away from me at the archangel. More blood spilled out of her flesh and flowed down her wrist to the ground, intermingling with the blood of the humans, angels, and demons battling around us. A quiet, shuddering cry escaped from her parted lips. Michael kept watching her as he fought, his blue-green eyes shimmering in the distance. He didn't seem fazed.

"Looks like our friend wants you dead," I said.

When she didn't say anything, I cut her other arm. Starting from her artery, I moved up, slicing zigzags all over her flesh. This time around, she was quiet. She stared at the archangel, but he had shifted his attention back to the battle.

I tore at her, dragging the knife all over her arm and up to her shoulder, then across to her chest. I paused there, digging the tip of the blade into her skin through the shirt.

I pinched her cheeks between my fingers like a claw and turned her face toward me. "Would you like to give me a few memorable last words to remember you by after you're dead?"

No words came, but her tear-soaked lashes said enough.

"No worries. I'll remember you anyway."

Clutching my shirt with her fists, she shut her eyes again and took raspy breaths. Her heart's heavy beats vibrated through the steel knife into my hand. Each beat jolted my senses like electric shock waves traveling up my arm and into my spine.

Something about her face, the way it froze in fear, blocking out the world, prevented me from doing what I wanted to do. I wavered, lifting the knife away from her skin.

Her wet eyes flashed open and stared at me. Without moving, she glanced down at her bleeding arms. She still had her fingers wound around the collar of my shirt.

"How?" she muttered.

I looked and saw what had caught her interest. While the minor cuts on her arm remained, the deep wounds I'd made over her arteries no longer bled. The torn flesh came together, healing back into place.

Addy placed her hand on top of mine, pushing the knife away. "You can't kill me. Or . . . you don't want to."

Dropping the knife to the ground, I threw my hands around her throat and squeezed just enough to scare her. "You don't know anything!"

She grinned. "Then kill me."

My hands shook around her fragile neck, wanting to break it and prove her wrong. Moments ago, I had been slicing the life out of her. What was stopping me now?

I intensified my grip until her black pupils dilated. In them, I saw my face. Angry, bitter, lost. And for the second time, I couldn't kill her.

I pushed myself off her and lay on my back. "You're right. I can't kill you."

She sat up and coughed to let the air back into her lungs. Once she recovered, she focused on me. "The real Adriel is still in there, whether you like it or not."

"I don't like it." I watched the gray clouds move by above us, threatening to spill rain.

"The real Adriel doesn't like you either, so it's okay."

She picked her knife up off the ground, stood, and reached for my hand. I gave it to her, unsure if she was going to kill me. She pulled me up. Face to face, I was surprised when she smiled and pulled me away from the fight happening around us. She led me to a small alley in between two buildings. The scent of old, wet trash and mold from the garbage disposal bins hit me in the face. It was a sour smell, and not a pleasant one.

Addy pushed me against the wall and kissed me.

"I want you," she said in between kisses.

"Right now?"

She kissed me harder, and I forgot all about my agenda. My desire to have her again burned inside. I yanked her by the hips, closing the distance between us. When she moaned, she grabbed onto the back of my head and tugged at the long hairs.

"I knew you were in there," she said.

I opened my mouth to object to her insinuation, but her lips sucked on mine before I could say a word. So, I told myself to enjoy her body and take advantage of the situation. All I had to do was pretend to be her Adriel and let her think she was in control. Then, once I'd had my fun, I would kill her.

She drew her face away, and I saw her nose wrinkle in disgust. She spat her next words out at me. "Your eyes are freaking me out!"

Relocating her hands to my temples, she drew my head toward hers, said a quick apology, and thrust my head back against the wall.

Chapter Thirty-One

ADELAIDE

I stared at Adriel's limp body on the ground for the longest time, wondering if he was unconscious or just fooling me like I'd fooled him by kissing him seconds ago. It was the only thing I could think of to get him to not strike back when I attacked. His eyelids now hid his demonic appearance, and so I let myself pretend he was just sleeping. Placing two fingers against his neck, I felt his pulse. It was steady, calm.

Not far away—just around the corner, really—the sounds of battle shook the earth. People were falling to their untimely deaths at the hands of demons and demonic humans. And while the angels were doing their best, no one knew how to end a war when the one big beast could not be destroyed.

I examined my arms. A few minutes ago, I was sure my injuries were deep and deadly. Now, most of them were gone, except for a few scratches on my skin. I ran my fingers all over. Sure enough, no major pain, just what felt like slight bruising. What was going on? Yesterday, it was a bullet hole in my chest. Today, it was my torn veins.

Adriel stirred but didn't wake up. If I was going to get myself out of this mess with Lucifer, protect the people I love, and somehow still live to see tomorrow, I needed to do something fast. But I didn't have a plan.

Leaving Adriel, I started walking back toward the battle.

"You're becoming more like me with every passing day, dollface," a raspy voice spoke from the shadows to my right, silencing all other noise.

My head turned before the rest of me did. In the darkness, a figure about my height leaned against the wall. A little sunlight struck a small portion of its body, revealing a veiny, disfigured hand planted on a red stomach made of just muscle tissue and no flesh. When the hand moved, a gray rat fell out and landed at the feet of the creature, dead.

"Do you recognize yourself?" my double said.

The Swiss Army knife slipped from my clammy hand. It clanged against the asphalt, shaking the earth and my heart.

I stepped back a few feet. "What are you talking about?"

The veiny figure chuckled. "You're always playing dumb, huh?"

"I'm not playing anything. Who are you?"

Its eyes flashed red like two balls of fire. "You already know."

Recollecting this morning's vision of the two babies, one real and one demonic, I said, "You're my demon twin."

Shrill laughter erupted out of my double's mouth. "You're close, yet so wrong."

Straightening up, my double walked toward the light and flashed yellow-stained teeth at me out of its veiny, burned gums. Its fiery eyes didn't die out, but out of the darkness, they didn't look as vibrant. From head to toe, there was no hair, no flesh, and no color other than red. Only the two mammary glands protruding from its chest indicated it was female.

"You know who I am, Ade."

I had the spine-chilling feeling that something wasn't right. I looked around the alley. No one else was there, and Adriel didn't count because he was comatose. Although I couldn't put my finger on it, my gut twisted in warning. This wasn't going to end well.

I swallowed back my fears. "Why don't you tell me who you are?"

My double took a step closer. "But where's the fun in that? I really thought you would try to guess."

"I did guess. Now the guessing is over."

My feet refused to budge as my double moved in on me. The better part of me wanted to run, yet my racing heart paralyzed me. Hundreds of scenarios popped into my head, some where I somehow managed to kill this monster, others where my heart just stopped. But I knew if I stood still, I died. So, when my double was two yards away, I reached down and snatched the knife.

"How about I show you who I am?" My double closed the distance, reached over, and clenched my wrists, squeezing until my fingers were numb.

I yanked my arms back but couldn't free myself. My double disappeared into thin air, saying "Shush" as it went. For a split second, its hold remained on my wrists. Then something entered my body. My insides felt like they were being squished to make room.

My double's voice rang close, too close, almost as if it were standing beside me. "Do you recognize me, or are you still in denial?"

I spun, searching for the source of the voice, even though I knew in my heart where it was coming from. My eyes glanced left and right, looking at every crack in the ground, every dust particle in the air, every subtle shift in the alley. But there was nothing except my paranoia.

"You look outside of you," my double whispered inside my head, "yet you should be looking within. Has it never occurred to you that I *am* you?"

I stopped moving and stared down at my hands. "What do you mean?"

"You keep asking stupid questions. Close your eyes and look."

"I don't understand."

"Close your eyes, I said!"

Shutting my eyes, I waited for more commands, but my double didn't speak again, and nothing stirred.

"What's going on?"

Rather than getting an answer, my insides pinched and shifted. The air felt thick around me. Stomach roiling, I opened my eyes and bent over with my hands on my knees and drew in heavy breaths.

"What the fuck are you?"

I looked up from my spot and realized I wasn't in the alley anymore. Adriel was gone and so were the moldy garbage bins and the two buildings that had concealed us. I stood in the middle of an intersection, and each side of the intersection went on and on without a visible end. On top of that, dark clouds shielded the sun above, threatening a rainstorm. Luckily, I still held my knife in my hand.

"Where am I?"

"Where do you think?" my double said while out of sight.

"Look, I'm tired of playing games. Tell me what's going on. Is this another vision?"

"You are seeing your mind. In case it still hasn't dawned on you yet, I reside here because you and I are one being."

"You're lying."

My insides shifted around again. A second later, I felt lighter. My double emerged out of me like a ghost passing through and spun around to face me.

"I have no intention of lying to myself." My double's eyes burned bright. "From birth I was connected to you, and till our death I will stay. We are one."

"*We* . . ." I waved my hand between the two of us. ". . . Are not one."

"But we are. I am not your double; I am a part of you."

"You look nothing like me!"

"That's because I'm the superior part of you, the one Lucifer created before you were born."

"You are not me."

It bared its teeth, the corners of its raw mouth curving up. "Keep telling yourself that, darling."

My double circled around me at a slow pace, studying me from head to toe. Its eyes lingered on the long waves of my hair.

Sweat trickled down my back from the dampness in the air. Keeping my guard, I swirled around every time my double moved behind me. I needed an advantage, anything to get me out of here and away from this beast. I clenched and unclenched my fists, took a deep breath, and dug into my mind for a plan.

"What exactly do you want?" I said, stalling.

It paused midstride, the veiny tissue on its forehead crinkling upward. "Want?"

"You brought me here." I gazed at the never-ending horizon. "Why?"

Its burning eyes gaped at me for the longest minute before it shrugged. "You needed to know who I am."

"But why in the middle of a war?" Despite the pummeling of my heart against my chest, I took a step closer to my double, channeling my brave side. "You had years to do it. Why now?"

My double crossed its arms. Without any eyebrows, the only indication of a frown was its wrinkled, red forehead. From three feet away, I heard a guttural sound escape its mouth.

And that was how I knew I'd hit the nail on the head.

"What? Did I say something wrong?" I pulled my hair back, feigning confusion. "I just want to learn more about you . . . about us."

"No, you don't. You still think I'm some freaky double."

"I'm just trying to understand. Please, help me understand who you are. Why did you bring me here now, when you could have done it when we were young?"

My double threw its hands into the air. "Because you weren't ready then!"

Finally, I was getting somewhere.

"What do you mean? Ready how? For what?"

Shaking its head, it backed away. "No . . . no, I can't tell you."

I took another step to close the distance. "But aren't you a part of me? You can tell me anything."

"I can't."

"Why not? Do you not trust yourself?" Using my double's logic seemed to be the most effective way of getting answers.

"I was told not to say anything."

"But you brought me here. You clearly wanted to tell me what's on your mind. Otherwise you would have kept to yourself."

My double kept silent and looked up at the dark, fast-moving clouds. It was acting timid for a beast, but just to be safe, I kept a strong grip on the knife.

"Hey," I said, "don't you trust yourself?"

It set its eyes on me. "Trust has nothing to do with it."

Sighing, I moved away. When Reed and I were little, he used to have stubborn fits every now and then. One time, when he was in third grade, he had come home crying and wouldn't say why. After an hour of trying to get it out of him, I'd decided on a new tactic. I walked away. Eventually, he had come and told me about the bully in his class. I never made the same mistake again.

People sometimes needed a little space before they got the courage to say what they needed to say. My double wasn't a person, but I hoped the same rules applied.

So, I walked in the other direction, toward one of the four roads. I didn't explain myself. I just walked. My double hurried after me.

"Hey!" it called out with its raspy voice. "Where are you going?"

"I don't know."

"Then stop."

"You clearly don't want me here. I should find my way back. It was nice meeting you, though."

It caught up to me and grabbed my arm, pulling me back. "I said stop!"

I turned and stared into its burning eyes. While the other demons had a blank, empty stare that seemed to suck the life out of everything nearby, this demon's eyes had the opposite effect. They shook a person from the core. If I didn't know about angels and demons, I would have fallen to my knees and wept after staring into the eyes of my double.

"You should stay here." It let go of my hand and looked down at the asphalt, the flames in its eyes fading. "I mean, stay with me."

A lightning bolt illuminated the skyline, followed by the shuddering sound of thunder. The clouds surged, one by one, as if in a race. I had a feeling the lightning would strike me in a few minutes if I stayed around.

Wanting to get away from the inevitable storm, I kept on walking. "This isn't a real place, is it?"

My double's feet thumped against the ground with every big step it took to catch up with me. "No. This is only your mind. The more anxious you are, the more that happens." It hurried to my side and pointed toward another lightning bolt. This time, the bolt was closer than the first one.

"You think I'm anxious?"

"I know you are."

"Well, that's probably because I don't have the answers I need. Like why I'm here now."

The tips of its fingers touched my arm, but a second later, it pulled away, tucking its hands underneath its red and raw armpits. "Sorry."

"What is it?"

Though my double kept up with me, its gaze stayed on the ground. "It's dangerous for you to stay anxious while here."

"You mean the lightning could hit me?"

"Yes, but it's more than that. It can physically end your life."

I paused to look back at the moving storm. "But I thought this was my mind. How can my mind kill me?"

"Dark emotions can hurt the mind, and a weak, overwhelmed mind can hurt the body."

"But this isn't a real place. It's all in my head."

"People who dream they are falling from a height sometimes die when they hit the ground in the dream. Their heart stops, tricked by the dream into thinking the fall was real."

"Are you saying my mind could trick my body into dying?"

Another lightning bolt struck in the distance behind us, bringing an explosion of thunder with it. I shrieked and covered my ears with my hands. When I looked to my left, my double was doing the same. Heart thudding, I started to run.

"Fear can kill," my double yelled out while it ran after me. "You need to calm down. That's the only way it'll stop. Otherwise, we're both dead, and I don't want to die."

I glanced at my double. The fire in its eyes was fading; what had been the size of an apricot was now the size of a peanut. Did that mean it was scared?

I stopped running and tried to catch my breath.

My double came to a halt a few feet later. "Why did you stop?"

Pinching the bridge of my nose, I said, "If I can't get the answers I need, then I might as well die. I don't really give a shit anymore."

Of course, that wasn't true. I did give a shit. In fact, I gave many shits. I was probably the last person on Earth who wanted to die. After coming close to death yesterday, I wanted nothing more than to have more time with the people I loved. Reed needed me, but I needed him more. And Lizzy . . . she was battling demons right now. How could I leave her with a problem I'd created?

But a lie seemed necessary in that moment. If my double feared death as much as I feared death, that meant it would do anything to survive, including telling me what it was hesitant to let me know.

I let out a scream. My double froze, its mouth hanging open. Knife still in hand, I began cutting myself. At first, I only lacerated the first layer of skin on my arm. When that caused the thunder to bellow nearer and the ground to tremor, I knew it was working. I started making deeper cuts that filled my eyes with tears.

"What are you doing?" my double shouted, hands on its bald, skinless head. "You're going to kill us!"

"It's better than living without answers."

I tore through my forearm, right over the artery that Adriel had cut into earlier.

A dozen or so yards away, lightning flashed. Its brightness blinded me for a few seconds. I looked away until I finally regained my sight.

My double grabbed my shoulders and pulled me from my spot. "Please stop!"

"Why should I? I don't know anything. Adriel's gone, and we're all going to die anyway. There's no reason for me to live."

Blood poured from my arms like a fountain onto the ground, my sneakers, and my double's bare, deformed feet.

Another lightning bolt hit the ground, this time a few feet away. If I'd extended my arm, I would have felt its lethal touch.

"Please," my double whimpered. "I don't want to die!"

"Then why did you bring me here, and what are you keeping from me?"

The muscle tissue on my double's forehead creased, but it kept its mouth shut. It pulled me harder, but I planted my feet on the ground, moving my body backward every time it tried to drag me forward.

Staring my double in the eyes, I placed the knife on my other wrist and dug its tip into my skin.

A lightning bolt clashed against the ground close enough that my double and I fell back from its intensity. My head hit the ground and a ringing sound echoed in my ears. I sat up, putting my hands on either side of my head.

It was now or never, I realized. I would either get answers or I would die a terrible death. I closed my eyes.

"Stop! Stop!" my double screamed. "You're the weapon!"

Everything stilled for a moment. The thunder buzzed in the distance, sounding even lower with the ringing in my ears.

I opened my eyes and stared at my double. "What?"

"You weren't ready to know! That's what he said." It sat hunched over, its hands covering its eyes. "Father didn't want you to know yet."

"I'm the weapon?"

"If we die, Father would be weak."

"Is that why my body kept healing these past two days? Because he made me into a weapon?"

My double lifted its head and looked at me. It had tears in its eyes . . . real eyes. The fire had died out. In its place, eyeballs with brown irises stared back at me. "You've been healing all your life, you just didn't know it."

"But I've injured myself before. I've always taken time to heal, just like everybody else."

"Minor injuries don't count."

I planted my palms against the ground and pushed myself into a standing position. Even though my arms kept bleeding, the thunder stilled and my heartbeat slowed down to its normal pace.

"You said I could die here. Were you lying?"

"No, you can die here." My double sat up but remained on the ground. "If your mind thinks you're dead, you die. There will be nothing to fix you anymore."

"But what makes me the weapon, and why can't I be killed in the real world?"

"Your connection to me makes you a weapon. Father made sure to tie us together until death do us part. Meaning you stay alive if no one can get to me. With you alive, he stays invincible because I'm protected."

"So, essentially, you're his weapon—his shield, really—and he hid you inside me."

I couldn't believe it. This whole time I had the power to end Lucifer's life and didn't know it.

More tears welled in my double's eyes as it looked up at me. "Don't go out there. I don't want to be alone."

I shook my head in disbelief. "Do you realize what you've done?"

My double looked at me with glazed, wet eyes.

"You've allowed the entire world to be terrorized, and I was your tool! You're so pathetic! You don't want to be alone? Really? You've literally helped a biblical apocalypse come to fruition, and you're worried about being lonely? How dare you make me the Antichrist!"

My body shook as a powerful realization dawned on me. For a second, I froze, a pit in my chest.

When the last lightning bolt struck, the knife had fallen out of my hand. I gathered myself now and searched around, discovering it a few yards away.

Looking down at my empty hands, I let out a small cry. I wasn't ready to do what I was about to do, but I was also not ready to let my friends get hurt because of me.

"I'm not staying," I told my double. With a trembling hand, I grabbed the knife and pointed it at my heart. "But neither are you."

Wild flames flashed in my double's eyes. "No!"

One breath. Two breaths. Three breaths. I dug the knife into my chest and fell, blood gushing everywhere. I knew this was my end, and even though I didn't want it to be, it needed to happen. My death severed my tie to Lucifer. I hoped that meant someone would kill him soon.

My double rushed over, pulled the knife out, and pushed its hand over the wound. "What have you done?"

"What needed . . . to be done."

I felt—or imagined—blood filling my lungs, rising to my throat. I was drowning in a sea of red. There was a strange metallic taste in my mouth. A deep ache branched out from the center of my body while the world twirled around me. Blinking several times, I had a hard time keeping my eyes open. My entire body began to shake violently.

The gray sky flashed white, smelling of static electricity. I shut my eyes as a spark of lightning crashed down.

Chapter Thirty-Two

ADRIEL

I woke up in total darkness. I had nothing to feel, nothing to hold on to, except the mental image of Addy. When I tried to move my body, I found nothing there. Hollowness encapsulated me.

With nothing to see, taste, touch, or hear, I didn't know what to do. My thoughts raced. Was this place—this void—purgatory? Having already known hell, I knew this wasn't it. Had God put me away in my own personal prison? Or perhaps it was just a dream, one I was having a hard time waking from.

I wished I could grab onto something just to have some sort of clue, anything really, about where I was. When that didn't happen, I hoped for an end to both my life and my burning thoughts.

A flicker of light danced in the distance.

Thump. Thump. Thump. My heart whacked against my chest, the first sign of life within me.

The light kept moving. The closer it got, the more I could tell it was small. I could also see a pair of wings maneuvering within the light.

"Son," a powerful voice spoke all around me. "This is not the end of your battle."

I recognized the voice immediately, but I couldn't quite believe my ears.

"You have strayed, but you are not lost."

The dot of light reached me, though it wasn't light at all. It was a firefly. My old, winged friend tapped my nose with its leg, greeting me.

"You must wake up, Adriel," God said.

The firefly glimmered one last time. When its light died down, my eyes fluttered open, and I found myself back in the real world. I was slumped against a wall without a clue as to how I got there. I had a vague memory of holding Addy down and slicing deep cuts into her skin, and the feeling of her thrashing against me lingered. Did I bring her here to kill her? My stomach churned.

Voices yelled nearby, yet I didn't see anyone around; then I looked a few yards away. Addy lay flat on the ground with her arm twisted underneath her in an odd position. Her body shook back and forth.

I pushed myself up to my feet despite the pounding in my head. "Addy?" I stumbled and fell on my knees beside her, my heart beating wildly in my chest.

She was having a seizure, it seemed. Her head shuddered with the rest of her. I went to turn her on her side, but she stopped moving. She was paler than Reed when we'd brought him back from hell.

"Addy!"

Her sweaty hair clung to her temples. I swept the strands back and waited for her to move or flinch or do something. I wished she would open her eyes, but she didn't. Her chest wasn't rising or falling. I put my fingers over her wrist and checked for a pulse. My heart thudded in my head, but hers was silent.

"No . . ."

I turned her over to face me. She was strangely stiff.

"No, no, no, no, no!" I lifted her off the ground and cradled her, the first tears flooding out. Several of them landed on her cheeks. "Don't die on me!"

My fingers vibrated against her cheeks as I held her close. I felt the earth spin underneath me. My lips found her forehead, and I let out a sob. I did this to her. I killed her. My memory wasn't the best, but I knew it had to be me. The last thing I remembered was her dark-brown eyes looking away from me as I went to plunge the knife into her chest.

The knife now lay not far from her hand, bloodied by all the cuts I'd made.

"I'm so sorry. I'm so sorry."

Her arms had a few grazes. Somehow, the deeper wounds I'd made were gone, leaving me without proof of my horrible actions.

"Addy."

I picked her up and stood.

Michael would know what to do. He would bring her back. He had to!

I tripped on my way out of the alley, nearly falling with Addy in my arms when I passed by the garbage disposal bins. My arms and legs trembled. I also couldn't see straight, not when my eyes blurred with tears.

The carnage outside the alley was still happening. The crackle of shattered ribs rang in the wind. Hundreds, if not more, of angels, demons, and people swarmed the street. Each side sought to kill the other, and both made sure blood was spilled. Decorating the battlefield were torn-off wings, fallen feathers, and bloodied, broken teeth.

Of all the beings present, no one looked my way twice or noticed the dead woman in my arms. The daughter of Lucifer was gone, and no one cared.

I passed by the corpse of a young human woman. Someone had killed her and tossed her body aside, away from the fighting crowd. The pale color of her skin almost matched Addy's. I looked away.

My heart sporadically skipping beats, I hurried around the crowd. The demons that saw me shrugged me off, probably thinking I was with them. The humans didn't even look scared to see me; rather than killing me on sight, they left me alone to carry my girl.

I couldn't see Michael from where I stood on the edge of the battle. Who knew how far the archangel had gotten into the swarm?

I looked at Addy. "It's going to be okay! I promise!"

A dozen yards down, I glimpsed Reed in battle. He had an angel's sword in his hand. Aside from a few minor wounds, he seemed fine on his own. In fact, the rigidity in his jaw made him a little daunting.

How am I going to tell him his sister is dead?

An angel fought near Reed. I started toward him, hoping he would know where Michael was. But I didn't get far. A man with short, light brown hair thrust a knife into another human's chest in front of me. When he turned, both of us froze.

It was Devin, Addy's ex who'd shot her in the chest.

"Your eyes." He leaned his head closer and stared at me with his two black holes. "How are they changing color? Didn't you turn?"

My heart burst inside my chest. Unlike Devin, I was not feeling chatty. I set Addy down, keeping her on the sideline and away from the fighting, and glared at the human-turned-demon. It wasn't his fault Addy made him like this, but I didn't care. Not now.

Snatching a sword from a dead angel, I moved in on him. "You hurt her!"

Devin glanced at Addy. "But I didn't kill her."

"Shut up!"

I lunged at him with the sword. At the last second, he skipped back and came out unscratched. He raised his hand and aimed the blade my way.

"How could you do that to her?" I spat at him. "How could you shoot her?"

"We both know she was alive this morning." He raised an eyebrow and frowned. "You better hope Lucifer doesn't find out."

At the mention of Lucifer, I dropped the sword and dashed forward, shoving Devin to the ground. I missed his knife by an inch and fell with him. Before I knew what I was doing, my hands became fists and I was landing punches across his face and chest. Every time he tried to push himself up, I hit him again and again until his teeth became bloodstained. He raised his arms over his head, but I did not let him surrender. I spat at him and rose.

"This is for Addy!"

My foot struck his skull like a soccer ball. He groaned once, his head lolling to the side. I kicked again, this time against the back of his head. His eyes submitted and he fell asleep.

"You. Shot. Her!"

I knelt beside him and grabbed his head, ready to bang it against the ground while he was unconscious.

"No!" A weak, husky voice called out behind me. "Don't kill him!"

Looking over my shoulder, I saw *her* sitting up. She blinked slowly, as if she had just woken from a deep slumber. Seeing me take her in, the corners of her mouth quirked up.

I drew in a deep breath.

"Addy?" I let Devin go and rushed over. My fingers tangled with her hair, pulling her close. My thumbs stroked her cheeks, each painted with a glorious pink. "You died in front of me. I saw you die! How are you . . . how did you . . ."

The intensity of my beating heart outmatched my earlier anger. She felt warm even in the chill of the afternoon. I pulled her in and crashed our lips together, needing to taste her. When I let go, I held onto her, not sure if my eyes deceived me.

She leaned into one of my hands and closed her eyes. "I did die. I killed myself. But . . . but something brought me back."

"You killed yourself?"

335

She opened her eyes and smiled again. "It's a long story. Probably just as long as your story." Her eyes danced between mine. "You'll have to tell me how you became human again, but not right now." Grabbing my hands, she stood. "We don't have much time. We have to find Lucifer."

"Addy . . ." I stood too and pulled her against me. "You can't go."

My hands trembled on her hips; I didn't want to let go.

"Listen." She rested her hand to my chest and gazed into my eyes. "It's going to be okay."

"How do you know that? A minute ago, you were dead."

"I know because when I died, I saw a green hill over acres of stunning land, and billions of fireflies flew around me. And you know what I felt? I felt light, like every pain I've ever gone through disappeared. That was when I knew I'd be okay, and I woke up."

Fireflies. Yet again, God did not let me down.

"We have to find Lucifer," she repeated. "Adriel, I was the weapon—or actually, I was more a shield than a weapon, and Lucifer didn't want anyone to realize that. But when I killed myself, I disconnected our tie."

I stared at her, trying to sort everything out in my head.

She pulled away from me long enough to grab the angel's sword I'd thrown on the ground. "Don't you see? We can actually kill him now!"

Chapter Thirty-Three

ADELAIDE

The green, immaculate hills upon which the glimmering fireflies had danced never left my mind, not even as I searched for Lucifer. I thought of how the sun's intoxicating warmth had wrapped around my body, and my skin tingled. Unlike hell, where I'd felt suffocated by the heat, this warmth had enveloped my being and made me feel whole. If the Garden of Eden was real, the place I had visited was it.

Colors, some I had never known existed, caressed my senses in the form of flowers and butterflies. Winged angels had sung in the distance, their voices pure. Light had carried me.

Then Grandma Di's face appeared before me. She looked younger than I remembered. Her curls were long and bouncy, and not a wrinkle marked the corners of her smiling lips. She took my hand, and we drifted over the hills together. Sometime later, I heard her voice inside my head, saying, "You have more to live for, sweetheart. God is sending you back."

That was the last thing I remembered of heaven.

Coming back from that place, I didn't feel like I'd died and come back; reborn was a truer word. I felt tears—happy tears—in my eyes and hope rising in my chest.

Without my demonic double, I couldn't sense Lucifer anymore, which meant he also couldn't sense me.

I sucked the cold air in and let it fill my lungs. For the first time ever, my body shivered, truly shivered.

Adriel marched beside me. His eyes didn't wander from me for more than a second. Every chance he got, he leaned in and put his hand on my back, steering me through the bloodbath around us.

"You're cold," he said, looking at the goosebumps on my arms.

I grinned. "I know. It's great." It wasn't the most appropriate thing to say in such a setting, yet I couldn't help myself. The happiness that filled me helped me stomach the dead bodies around us. I saw them, but they didn't make me lose hope.

Just as Adriel kept glancing at me, I kept glancing at him, examining the way the blackness in his eyes was diminishing. Every few seconds, the color faded more until his eyes were entirely human. I didn't know how he had done it, but then again, I didn't know how I was alive either.

Too many angels—good and fallen—demons, and humans packed the street, making it impossible to walk in a straight line.

I lifted myself on my toes and scanned the nearby faces. "Do you see him anywhere?"

"Not yet."

Reed wasn't far. He knocked a fallen angel to the ground and stabbed him in the chest. When he straightened up, he spotted me and smiled, but the smile only lasted a second. He turned on another fallen angel, strong as ever.

When I looked back at Adriel, he was kneeling by a fallen angel's corpse. I was surprised to see she was a girl with long hair. Unlike most of the fallen angels I'd met, she wore a worn-out shirt. Three knife wounds marred her body, as did a bullet hole in her shoulder. Her honey eyes stared at the sky, unflinching. The only sign she wasn't human was her thick, black blood.

Adriel touched the fallen angel's wounds, applying blood to his fingers.

I tapped his shoulder. "What are you doing?"

He rubbed his bloody fingers over his eyelids and above his cheeks. "Making sure no one can see my human eyes. If I keep my eyes down, the black blood might conceal the white around my irises and fool some demons."

Other than Devin and me, no one knew he had turned back into a human.

I moved through the crowd, realizing a bit too late that I couldn't see Reed anymore. Pushing people and demons aside, I searched for him. Every time a demon came toward me, I lashed out at them with the sword I'd taken earlier and kept moving, not waiting to see if I'd killed them or not.

Reed hadn't been more than ten feet away. He couldn't have gone far. Unless . . . unless he was hurt. I lost the feeling in my hands and began looking for his face through the many corpses on the ground. I kicked through the bodies. Some were missing limbs and others were missing heads. One decapitated head lay facedown. From the back, it looked like the shape of Reed's head.

My heart stopped, and my breath caught in my throat. *No*, I thought. *Not like this. He can't die!*

Not wanting to touch the head, I used the sword in my hand to turn the face around. When green, frozen eyes gazed back at me from the pasty face, I let out a heavy breath. It wasn't Reed.

Circling, I found myself far from Adriel. He caught sight of me, his eyes going wide, just as someone called my name from behind.

I turned around and saw Lucifer five yards away. He wasn't alone.

"How in the world did you break the tie?" he said, holding Reed against him and moving his snake-engraved sword with the curved blade to my brother's throat. In his other hand, by his side, dangled a pale head. But it wasn't just any head; he clutched Madadel's long locks in a fist, giving me a clear view of the last grim face the angel wore.

Words choked in my throat. I watched Reed be still while his eyes fixed on me, pleading.

"Must I repeat myself?" Lucifer's eyes looked darker than ever before, if that were even possible. His hand moved a sliver. If I hadn't been holding my breath, I wouldn't have noticed the sharp edge of his sword inch closer to Reed's flesh. "How did you break the tie?"

"I died," I muttered.

All the muscles in my body became numb and helpless. I was acutely aware of the sword in my grip and knew I needed to act, but in that crucial moment, I lost my senses. I froze.

"Do not lie, child. You damn well know that is not possible."

"It . . . it's true. I killed myself."

"But you cannot get hurt; you heal. Tell me the truth, or your brother loses his head like his angel!" He pushed the sword into Reed's skin.

A pit formed in my chest as I watched a red, bloody line form on my brother's neck and heard him squeal.

"No! Please, please, stop! I'll tell you everything. Just, please, don't hurt him!"

Everyone seemed far away. All the angels were too busy to notice us.

Lucifer didn't flinch. His empty eyes stared at me, waiting.

"I swear I'm telling the truth. I did kill myself. I saw my twin—the demon thing you put inside me or whatever you call it. I got it to confess everything, and it told me that if I think I'm dead, I really die. You probably didn't think of that when you put that thing inside me."

"You are still lying. How else would you be here right now if you truly died?"

"I swear I'm telling the truth. I did die. Then something happened that brought me back. God wanted it. I don't exactly know why, I just know that he did."

Lucifer's nose creased when I mentioned God, but he didn't budge.

"You have been such a disappointment." He put his mouth to Reed's ear and whispered something. When he looked up at me, he chuckled. "I just told your brother how he is going to die in a minute. If you care to stop his death, you will end your life this instant."

"Let him go first."

"I do not trust you, daughter. If I let him go, I would be letting both of you go."

"And I don't trust that you'll let him live."

He smirked. "We think alike, do we not?" He pressed the sword harder against Reed's neck, causing more blood to trickle out.

Tears escaped my eyes. "Please . . ."

"I want you dead, child of mine. You could have chosen to be by my side, and I would have given you everything. I would have handed you the world and made you its queen. Instead, you chose to cut our tie, and I cannot have others know I can be killed." He said the last part in a low voice.

"Then you'll have to kill me yourself."

Lucifer lowered his sword. "Very well."

He drew back, letting my brother go while still holding on to Madadel's head. Reed started running toward me when Lucifer raised his weapon and plunged it forward. Reed let out a sharp breath and froze. It took me a second to see why.

"I would rather kill you both." Lucifer pulled the sword out of my brother.

Reed fell on his back, blood oozing from his chest, and turned his face toward me. He took heavy, short breaths, his eyes wide.

I rushed forward, tears in my eyes and a never-ending scream in my throat. *This isn't happening. This isn't real.* Before I could reach my brother, someone pulled me back by the collar of my shirt.

"Let go! Let go!" My brother needed me, and I was ready to kick and claw my way to him. "Let me fucking go!" I felt the blood drain from my face as I realized what had just occurred.

The person stopping me moved in front of me, and I saw it was Adriel. The black blood covered most of his eyes. Without hesitation, he pointed a dagger at my chest. There was a hardness to his jaw, one that made me take a step back.

"Kill her," Lucifer said, "and then let's get on with this new world."

Chapter Thirty Four

ADRIEL

Reed gasped for air, reminding me with every ticking second that he had little time. The more he tried to breathe, the heavier each breath sounded.

I maintained eye contact with Addy. Though her face had paled and she had tears streaming down her cheeks, I looked to her for guidance. She didn't know it, but she was the only thing keeping me collected. I studied the arches of her brows, the flickering of each almond eye between mine, and I considered what Addy would do if she were me.

Lucifer's eyes bored into my back. I felt them without needing to look over my shoulder. "Kill her, and then let's get on with this new world," he said.

What would you do, Addy?

Reed was dying. If we didn't get him to a hospital or Michael in the next few minutes, he would be gone. And I was the only one left who could make a move. Besides, if I didn't do anything, we were all dead for sure.

"What are you waiting for?" Lucifer's steps were heavy as he moved closer. "Must I do everything myself, you incompetent bastard?"

Addy looked behind me, her mouth hanging open.

Another step closer.

I spun around—dagger still pointed ahead of me—saw Lucifer a couple of feet away, and made a mental calculation. What would Addy do? I knew the answer. She would fight with her last bit of fading strength. That was why she was alive right now. God made no mistakes. He brought her back for a reason. He saw goodness in her and the will to keep fighting for everybody who couldn't.

Now, it was my turn. I had let Jenna kill Matt without so much as trying to guide her in the right direction. I wouldn't make the same mistake now. Fighting for a life—that was what mattered.

Another step. Lucifer glanced at my face and did a double take when he noticed my eyes. "What the—"

A harrowing scream shook the earth. Through my peripheral vision, I saw Addy dash forward. She raised her sword, which she wasn't holding properly, high into the air. Her hands shook. I envisioned the weapon slipping from her loose grip and feared Lucifer hurting her like he had Reed.

"Addy, no!"

Lucifer grinned. He held his sword steady in his hand.

Addy thrust her weapon forward. As expected, Lucifer intercepted the hit. Steel clashed against steel. Addy's sword flew from her hand and landed with a loud thud several feet out of reach. She staggered back.

Without missing a beat, Lucifer lifted his sword. "I made you; now I end you. I am pleased to see you go."

Addy looked to her brother, and I knew she was giving up, something she never did.

I felt my arm move, but it took me a second to realize what I'd done. My dagger flew from my hand. I watched it soar in the air for what seemed like many minutes, although it was only a second. I didn't dare look away. A blink of an eye, I feared, would disrupt the weapon's trajectory.

Lucifer brought his sword down, leveling it with Addy's neck.

Reed struggled with another heavy breath. *Thump thump, thump thump.* My heart drummed in my ears.

"Addy, duck!" I screamed.

The dagger I'd thrown at Lucifer somersaulted halfway before finally landing. Right. In. His. Heart.

Addy fell on her back, Lucifer's sword missing her head by a second.

"What . . ." Lucifer looked down at his bleeding chest, the corners of his lips twitching upward. "You cannot kill me!" Madadel's head slipped from his hand and rolled like a ball for several seconds before coming to a complete stop. With his hand free now, Lucifer pulled the dagger out and released a hysterical laugh. "An eye for an eye; I killeth thy brother, and you kill I." His eyes shot to Addy's face as he collapsed.

Addy didn't wait to make sure he was dead. She jumped to her feet and ran to her brother with a fierce look in her eyes.

Taken aback by what I'd done, I moved toward the devil and lingered above his body.

"You have killed your friend," Lucifer muttered, looking at me.

"You are not my friend."

"Go to hell."

"No, thank you."

He reached out to grab my foot, but his arm sank to the ground. The black in his eyes reverted to its old brown, pronouncing him dead. In another lifetime, had he not been what he was, he could have passed as Addy's brother.

I rushed to Addy's side. She was struggling to keep pressure on Reed's wound and mumbling words like "Don't die."

"Come on. We've got to get him to a hospital. They'll hopefully be functioning normally again now that humans have their souls back." I lifted Reed and carried him in my arms.

"We're not going to make it!" Addy said, a cry vibrating in her throat.

"Don't say that!"

We hurried past the demons, angels, and humans, all of whom had stopped fighting at some point. They stared at us and at Lucifer's body, all of them confused.

"Get out of the way!" Addy screamed.

Fallen angels started disappearing into thin air. Going back to hell, I hoped. Even the angels reacted to Lucifer's death. They clapped their wings together in a cheer and twirled in the sky.

"Move!" Addy pushed people aside. "Go away!"

She bumped into Devin but didn't notice.

"Addy?" he said.

For a fleeting second, she looked at him. Then she kept moving, not stopping to take in the fact that his eyes had returned to blue. That all the humans who had been turned into demons had changed back to their true selves.

"Move!"

Reed's gasping was getting rougher.

Ignoring the chaos around us, I scanned the parked cars on the street ahead. "Addy, where's your car?"

"It's gone. I'm driving the Chrysler now." She pointed at a shiny black car and ran in its direction.

"Hold on," I told Reed as I followed her. "We're getting you help."

Reed's only response was another gasp. I felt his body quiver in my hands.

"Do not take him to a hospital. He will not make it," a calm voice spoke.

Both Addy and I turned at the same time. Michael stood with his arms crossed over his gold-plated armor. He neither smiled nor frowned. He moved toward me and planted his hand on Reed's chest. "It is his time to go."

"No." Addy shook her head and grabbed hold of Reed's hand, almost pushing Michael away. "Heal him!"

Michael looked between her and Reed. "I cannot. It is his time. God has a different plan for him now."

Addy forced Reed out of my arms and slumped on the ground, cradling him. She stared up at the archangel, more tears flooding her now-red eyes. "You healed that woman. Why can't you heal him too?"

Reed's gasps were growing fainter.

"Are you punishing me? Is this because I sold people's souls?"

I put my hand on her shoulder, but she shrugged me off.

"Don't take him away from me. He's all I have!" she cried.

"You should say your goodbyes," Michael said.

Addy shook her head again. "No!"

The color in Reed's face was fading, and he was getting quieter.

"Addy, please," I begged. "Reed needs you now."

As if coming to her senses, her eyes shot to her brother. "I'm so sorry, Reed. I'm so sorry." She pulled his face toward hers. Saliva dripped from the corner of her mouth and landed on his neck. "I love you."

Reed blinked once, seeming to pass a silent message to his sister, then closed his eyes.

Addy hugged Reed to her chest and let out a piercing, inhuman sound. It came from deep within her throat. I felt my heart break for the fourth time since a week ago, when Jenna had killed Matt. Tears flooded my eyes, reminding me of my humanity.

I wasn't sure how much time passed with Addy sobbing before her body finally surrendered and she sat still, tears trailing down her face and raining over Reed. I wasn't sure about anything, except that there was nothing calm about Addy's stillness. Though she was suddenly quiet, I felt her internal scream threatening to explode.

I couldn't move either. My heart shook inside my chest. There should have been a kinder ending to Reed's fate. Addy must have thought the same. She must have imagined a whole future where her brother grew older, made a man out of himself, had a family of his own, and stayed by her side. Reed's fate, we now knew, was twisted, and certainly not kind.

She stared into the distance, her eyes blank and wet, and her mind seemed to go elsewhere. Her arms held on to Reed's body as though worried that if she let him go, everything would become real.

"Addy." I touched her cheek, though she didn't respond.

Michael tore one of his golden feathers from his right wing and handed it to me. "Father is proud, I am certain." Then he shot into the air, his golden wings flapping.

Epilogue

ADELAIDE

My new—used—car's tires shuffled, and I reminded Adriel he needed to shift the car into drive first. "You're doing it all wrong!"

"Am I?" He grinned at me and leaned in for a kiss.

I'd been teaching him how to drive for the past three weeks, now that the weather was starting to warm up. While he was getting the hang of it, sometimes he reverted to the ways of the caveman. Either that, or he was just messing with me. I had a suspicious feeling that might have been it.

I smacked his arm and laughed. "It's going to take forever before you actually get to drive me somewhere, but that's okay. I like driving."

After another half hour of the driving lesson, we headed back to the apartment. We'd tidied everything up since the near apocalypse almost six months ago. But the furniture wasn't the only change around here. Since killing my double and Lucifer, I'd stopped feeling restless and managed to get my home design ideas organized, and had even worked on several projects—more than I'd ever been able to before—with Melissa, who had overlooked my behavior when all hell literally broke loose. Among the many changes I'd made, a magnet now held a photo of Reed on the fridge door. His face stared back at me, and that was all it took to bring the pain back.

I slipped past Adriel and made my way to our room. The disheveled bed with the new mattress called out to me. I dove into it, wrapping the comforter around me, and shut my eyes. There were days when I thought of Reed incessantly with hollowness in my chest, and there were days when I pretended he was still at Saint Vincent College. It was easy to believe he'd walk right into my apartment one day with arms wide open.

"Addy," Reed's voice called out.

I sat up and looked around. The gate to hell stood in place of my door, which meant I was dreaming.

"Addy."

I heard him so clearly that even the air seemed to carry the warmth of his breath toward me.

"Reed?" I called back.

And then he came into view. He stood to my right, a smile stretching across his lips. The hazel in his eyes twinkled, full of joy.

"Hi," he said, reaching to touch my face.

On his back were two large wings, their feathers white. At first, I thought this was all in my imagination, but the warm touch of his hand on my cheek told me otherwise.

"You're an angel."

He nodded. "I'm your guardian angel."

I jumped off the bed and threw my arms around him. "I've missed you so much! I'm so sorry you died."

My weight lifted from the ground, and I realized Reed had picked me up in his famous bear hug.

"I've been here by your side this whole time, Addy, and I'm staying here. Except when you need a little privacy." He let out a chuckle and set me back down. "I'm happy where I am. I have a purpose."

I stroked the beautiful feathers of his wings and sighed. For the past few months, I'd known he was in heaven. The fact that I had gone there myself helped me come to terms with his death. Still, seeing him made a world of a difference.

"I didn't know humans could become angels."

"They can't." He tore a feather from his wing and closed my hand around it. "I was an exception."

With a kiss on my cheek, Reed disappeared. I woke up, finding myself still in bed. To my surprise, a single white feather lay in my palm. After studying it for the longest time, I took it to the kitchen and put it beside Reed's photo on the fridge.

"Hey." Adriel embraced me from behind, his cheek against mine. "I didn't want to wake you up. Are you feeling better?"

"I just needed to fight my inner demons." I tapped the feather. "But I'm feeling much better."

He planted a kiss on the side of my head and steered me into the living room. "I'll slay your demons any day, love."

I wrapped my arms around his neck and buried my face in his chest. Memories from my childhood popped into my head. Grandma Di reading me a story before bed. Reed and I making blanket forts in our rooms. Erica coming home in the dead of night and bumping into things, the smell of booze on her breath when she'd snatch Reed and me from bed and order us to make her food. I couldn't forget those things, neither the good nor the bad, but I could learn to live with them.

"Hey." Adriel swept my hair back while his other hand rubbed my shoulders. "Nate and Lizzy invited us over for dinner."

"Oh?"

"They want to celebrate moving in together, but only if you're down."

"Of course I'm down. I'm happy for them." I'd said those words a thousand times over the past few weeks, but this time I truly meant them. Even my smile came naturally.

It took me a minute to freshen up and change clothes. Before Adriel and I stepped out of the apartment, I had to ask him one question, since Reed's appearance got me thinking about everything that had happened. "What if someone else comes along and tries to mess with the world like Lucifer did?"

He tilted my head toward his, the corners of his lips stretching upward. "Then people will have to choose whether they'll stand with the good or with the bad."

For the rest of the evening, Adriel's words haunted me. I kept thinking about my own choices. When faced with a choice, I'd stood by my brother against the world. Choices weren't always fair, and angels couldn't always heal people from death.

"Is everything okay?" Lizzy asked at the dinner table, her eyes on me.

Adriel squeezed my knee.

I smiled and raised my glass. My champagne was full of bubbles and a promise that the next hour would be great. It would be joyful and mark the start of a new life.

"To Lizzy and Nate," I said. In my head, I added, *And to a world of fair choices and people courageous enough to do what's right.* I sensed Reed smiling my way.

Acknowledgements

Where would this novel be without the help of the amazing people backing me up? There is one specific person who I wouldn't have been able to complete this story without, and that is my boyfriend, Michael. Not only was he my thesaurus whenever I suffered from "the tip of my tongue" syndrome, he also went above and beyond in keeping me sane, helping me plot this novel, and staying up with me into the wee hours of the night just so I could figure out how to torture my characters some more. There is no one as amazing as you, my love. Thank you!

Of course, I cannot go on without thanking my family. Thank you, Mom and Dad, for giving me life and then letting me soar as a writer despite how rocky the road appeared at first. Thank you to my cousins Karin, Aboud, and Haya for being some of my first supporters in my writing endeavors. Your excitement during my writing process means the world to me. I'm so lucky to have you all on my team.

A huge thank-you to my editor Courtney Rae Andersson for taking my masterpiece and making it dazzle. You treated my baby like your baby, and for that, you deserve endless orders of free yummy pizzas.

Crystal Watanabe, a big thanks for being my go-to proofreader. You and your editorial team deserve an enormous cake.

I want to shout a big thank-you to Claire and Chris Lucas over at Eight Little Pages for designing my gorgeous cover and doing the lovely interior formatting. This book is mesmerizing at first sight because of you. I cannot thank you enough!

A very special thank-you to Lable for taking the time to read my novel and guiding me in the development of characters for many hours on the phone. You have been a wonderful mentor and friend, and I'm very lucky to have your support.

To my friends, Andy and Caitlin, for reading my novel, giving me the nicest, funniest, and most authentic feedback, and encouraging me to get published. You guys rock!

To my best friend Christina for always encouraging me to be true to myself despite hardships. I so appreciate our long conversations and friendship.

This book would also not be complete without Isa's amazing creative support. She is such a brilliant artist. I'm so thankful for her help, whether in designing character art for my book, creating posters for me, or encouraging me throughout the publishing process. You are an amazing friend, Isa!

Last but certainly not least, a big, fat shout-out to all my readers. I would not be here without you. You are all very dear to me, and I'm so thankful for your support!

About the Author

Nour Zikra graduated summa cum laude from the University of Central Florida with a B.A. in creative writing. She is a YouTube host of a writing advice and humor series. Born and raised for the first decade of her life in Aleppo, Syria, she moved to America in 2004 and currently resides in Orlando, Florida. When Nour is not writing or reading, she makes kissy faces at her turtle, binge-watches shows on Netflix, and endlessly decorates her writing space.

NourZikra.com
Twitter: @nourzikra
Instagram: @nourzikra
Facebook: Facebook.com/AuthorNourZikra
YouTube: YouTube.com/NourZikraAuthor